He thought to lean with it. The exhaustion for Christine, the co madness coupled with the one woman who made him feel alive, was unbearable punishment.

“I never believed in Your sincerity of bringing Anna to me. Shocked are we? Surprised for a brief moment I believed?” Erik rolled his head toward the side and pressed his cheek to the stone. His accusatory eyes could have shattered the pinpricks of light across the heavens. “Congratulations, Oh Merciful God, You failed again. Anna can have You and Your Son.” He yanked himself upright, his body going rigid with his anger. “I am pleased Philippe is dead!”

Spittle flew from sob soaked lips. His mouth spread upward. He may be alone for now, but not forever. There was to be an heir to his kingdom, a child with his mind and his madness. Erik spoke to the shattered stone below with an unblinking stare.

“I will have my child, in all his hideous imperfections. I will need no one but him and my music. I will need only his love. As for Christine?” Erik leapt to his feet. The wind flapped his cloak behind him. He leaned into the gust and taunted the streets below like a great yellow-eyed bird ready to swoop on unsuspecting prey. “Our character becomes our destiny. Music, like life, is inexpressible silence without its instrument. Am I not its master? I hold the baton. I will conduct what I want. I will have what I want. What is Erik without Christine?" Leaping back to the roof he retrieved his mask and turned to the opera house, his boots drumming a cadence so the ferryman could dutifully follow. A haunting whisper carried his sadness forward on the wind.

"What is Erik without the Phantom?"

Abendlied

Jennifer Linforth

Abendlied

An Original Publication of
Highland Press Publishing - 2009

Cover Concept – Hannah Phillips

For information, please contact
Highland Press Publishing,
PO Box 2292, High Springs, FL 32655.
www.highlandpress.org

ISBN - 978-0-9842499-0-9

HIGHLAND PRESS PUBLISHING

Excalibur Imprint

DEDICATION

For Liebling,
who believed enough to ask me my thoughts,
and that has made all the difference.
Croyez.

ACKNOWLEDGEMENT

Writing a series is a daunting task. With endless details to follow, it is frightfully easy to stumble through the process not knowing if you are coming or going. If it is hard for the author, it is equally challenging for the support network that keeps the ink flowing.

Nina Pierce, a brilliant author, has my thanks again for being a consummate critique partner. I cannot express my ardent appreciation to her for holding my hand and jumping in joy with me during the course of this series. Ronna Hochbein, another wonderfully creative mind, is my rock. Without her, I would have given up many times on many books. Her patience with me this year I can never repay.

Thanks to my editors Patty Howell and Amber Wentworth for their time once again in working with me on The Madrigals.

Hannah Phillips and her cover concepts truly capture the heartbeat of this series. I am lucky to have someone like her to be able to place the story in pictures, but more so I am blessed to call her friend. Ken Altobello has crafted another amazing cover for this book. He has made this series shine with his eye for detail.

Diana, Ami and Alix . . . pie! Thanks for the weekend, and for the years of your steadfast friendship. Lisa would be proud . . .

And, lastly, to those who have shaped this series the most:

To Lisa Schmidt, a dear friend taken from me far too soon, whose memory will live on in my books until the day I lay down my quill. A true heroine to me, I will never forget the blessing she placed in my life, or her belief in me. She is a significant reason as to why I am an author. Though God took her from me far too early, He did not take her completely, for each memory is now an infinite treasure.

To Abigail, who has influenced my imagination more than anyone in the world . . . you are my happy thought.

To Liebling, my comte, and the ultimate best friend a girl could ever have, you have more than I am able to articulate. The journey in life is not just an amble on a path, but a true destination. One which, through laughs and tears, lives have been enriched in ways no word but one can express. There is no way to repay such a gift except to say thanks for hearing me. I am indebted to God for citrus.

Finally to my husband, Tony, whose words to me and whose emotion during Madrigal's launch I will never forget. His ability to see the world through my intimate and personal art is my inspiration. He was there from the moment I wrote my first book when I was twelve. He has my eternal thanks for believing in me and my career, through the highs and lows, but more so for supporting and encouraging the deepest and most ardent friendships brought into my life because of this series. May I continue to make him proud, one book, one story, one vibrant imagination at a time . . .

What if a demon were to creep after you one night, in your loneliest loneliness and say,
'This life which you live must be lived
by you once again and innumerable times more;
and every pain and joy and thought and sigh must come again to you,
all in the same sequence. The eternal hourglass will again and again
be turned and you with it dust of the dust!' Would you throw yourself
down and gnash your teeth and curse that demon? Or would you answer
'Never have I heard anything more divine'?

—Friedrich Nietzsche

Prologue

Paris outskirts, 1885

"Leave the camp. Leave the camp!"

Her shout pierced the tranquility of dawn, shattering it as a rock does a mirror. Erik whirled in time to see a small explosion of arms and legs erupt from the tree line. Anna charged forward. A stray branch tangled her skirts, sending her tumbling into their makeshift hideaway.

"How many?" he demanded.

"Ten . . . fifteen . . ." Anna grabbed her side and drew a ragged breath. Her boots frantically doused what embers were left of the fire. "Take the horse. I'll make it on foot."

"You are not staying here!"

"Don't argue, go—now," she shouted.

As she twirled around the camp in an untamed state of panic, he knew better than to challenge her. He mounted the stallion in one swift motion, wincing when searing pain raced through the gunshot wound in his upper arm.

"Head east then south," she commanded breathlessly. In the distance, horses' hooves pummeling the ground forced the urgency he heard in her voice. "Go!"

Erik turned the stallion in a tight circling that matched the supreme, writhing hatred in his gut. Loath to leave her behind, he made several attempts to lift her onto the horse. He would not see her sacrifice herself for his transgressions again.

Anna's small but powerful fist slammed into the horse's flank. She threw her hands over her head and stumbled to the side. The stallion jolted forward.

"You find me," he shouted over his shoulder. "Are you listening to me? They have no right to hunt us. You find me."

The stallion thundered through the tree line and up the ridge with long, purposeful strides. A loud snort burst out its mouth when Erik yanked on the reins. The orange glow of torches joined the graying light of dawn. Angry shouts and beating hooves rose from the ransacked camp below. His heart pounded against his ribcage, fury swelling like a boil to the surface. Searching the mayhem below, he squinted to make out Anna's form, but he couldn't see if she'd made it into hiding or not. His eyes tapered on one man dismounting in the center of the fray.

Erik's face heated beneath his mask as he surveyed the camp. With remorse filling his body and the weight of his sins on his shoulders, he reluctantly turned the horse east. Looking over his shoulder, his eyes drilled into the back of that man's head. Once again he could kill him, but chose not to.

He'd made a promise never to lift a hand to another man and he'd already broken it once. He would not break it again.

Raoul, the Vicomte de Chagny, should consider himself a very lucky man.

One

Countryside of France, 1886

Falling in love carried a primitive allure and a majestic dignity that should have been the start of wondrous things.

The manhunt was a minor stumbling block to his well-laid plans.

Although not the life he expected once he fell in love, the life Erik led now was of great importance. For years he'd existed in the haunting silence of a world he'd built several stories beneath the Paris streets. An underground sanctuary, part womb part tomb, sheltering him from judging eyes of man and the follies his fate denied him. With a haunting voice not bested outside of heaven, he was an odd combination of the splendor of genius and the monstrosity of sin.

The unjust ugliness of his face made him certain no woman would ever turn to him with longing in her eyes.

Currently, her eyes churned anger like a storm does the sea.

"Absolutely not, Anna." Unmasked, he took full advantage of the fact she could see his ugly displeasure. Though they'd weathered many things in their brief time together, he couldn't endure his companion's pint-sized stubbornness. He glared at her in the moonlight.

The little woman at his side ignored his suffering and stared toward the center of camp. Dozens of wayward misfits danced happily from partner to partner. Ordinarily her pout would have him bowing before her in worshipful supplication, but this time he would not back down.

"You need to get used to these camps," Anna insisted. "Fugitives do not have the luxury of Parisian gentlemen." She grabbed his hand and leaned all her weight away from him in an attempt to coax him into the crowd.

He pulled back. "I will not, you insolent shrew." He pointed toward the mob. "These camps are nothing short of slums and that type of dancing is absolutely barbaric."

"They're not slums. Everyone here looks out for their neighbor without judgment. The contredance is a way of meeting and greeting."

He blocked those words with folded arms.

"Fine, suit yourself," she dismissed. "I'm spending tonight enjoying what fun I can while the authorities are not nipping at my heels."

Anna stomped toward the center of the camp, her long, auburn braid swaying against the top of her rump. Staring at her though the darkness, he cursed the direction of his life. Love should be comfortable, not complex. He spun toward their fire and slammed another log on the flames. Orange sparks twisted their way to the stars as he sank to the ground.

How many campfires passed since their transgressions at the Opera Garnier? Grumbling under his breath, he pulled a worn horse blanket around him. He rolled his left shoulder, working out the stiffness the cold caused his old wound. The fire beckoned him to shift closer to it.

Stretched beside it, propped up on one arm, he ignored the revelry of the other travelers. The music sheets before him crumpled as he scratched at them. A fine gray layer of ash coated the pages. The notes usually flew from his mind at night, but now they were locked in his head.

Rolling to his back, he studied the stars trimming the sky. If life were like those stars, each one would represent a drastic change. He used to be a wealthy Maestro burrowed like a mole in the cellars of an opera house. Now what was he? Nothing more than a fugitive composing by a campfire, wrapping himself in a vulgar horse blanket. He couldn't possibly be missing that theater?

Depressive vaults.

Rubbing his unmasked face, he moved to his side. The heat from the flames licked at his cheeks, warming the bare ridges of his cruelly faceless visage to an uncomfortable level. This must be what it felt like to burn in hell.

Laughter swirled around him. He seethed in response. Anna skipped from man to man and woman to woman, seemingly completely comfortable in the life he found degrading. His heart fell to his stomach. Why couldn't he place the world at her feet?

She stood at the end of the line smiling with the rest of the vagabonds. Tiny hands beat in tune to the music with her unending optimism that had restored his faith in man. Their eyes locked and she tilted her head in a last attempt to coax him into her world.

Erik frowned and turned back to the fire. Staring intently through the flames, he bitterly reflected on Christine Daaé, the Vicomtess de Chagny. Was she comfortable in her grand chateau? Wining and dining on all the things he longed to give his Anna?

From beside him, he lifted the black mask that usually concealed his face, save his thin lips. His unusually long fingers fondled it with sickly erotic loathing. Christine was now a nobleman's prize and his burden. What would life be like had he never crossed paths with her again? Would he be here now, the elusive Phantom of the Opera, wanted by half of France for murders and a kidnapping—this time—he did not commit?

A cautious look found its way to Anna. Some murders he did not commit . . .

He never should have risen from his blissfully faked death. Those years were a salve that lessened the slap of ugly shouts, that numbed pain of stones stinging his flesh, and dulled images of men spitting in his path as he walked by. Living in darkness held more allure than enjoying light when it meant facing the life his face had created. The mask landed in the dirt beside him.

Contemptuous jailer.

Like a log bursting under too much heat, his anger cracked. Damn this manhunt! Curses slammed into the ground, his fists sent sparks skidding toward the mask. How dare Christine intrude! That love must be forgotten . . .

Jubilant sounds whooped into the air as another dance began. Anna wove in and out of her partners, not giving a care to anything but the moment.

He replaced the mask on his face with one fluid motion. It molded to his skull like a second skin. He strode toward the noise—for he refused to call such racket music—grabbed Anna's hand and hauled her from her revelry. She sputtered her protest as he dragged her to their distant campfire. One powerful yank of her hand she was free. Erik bucked backward as she shoved a small fist in his face. No easy task given her size and his height. The gold band around her ring finger caught the firelight and flared almost as bright as the bolts of lightning shooting from her eyes. Swallowing a smile, he studied her pout. He did find that bottom lip alluring.

"Erik, your possessiveness has got to change. I have been to hell and back over the last year. The least you can permit me is a moment to forget I am unjustly wanted by half of France because of you. I will not stay at your side if you are not willing to—"

One abrupt assault on her waist silenced her flapping tongue. He hauled her so tightly against him a small puff of shock broke through her lips. Once in his arms, he held her like fragile silk and waltzed around their campfire. Any breath she held released in her sigh.

"We dance," he whispered. "No opera houses, no masquerades, no leering strangers." He nodded toward the center of camp.

Lifted in melody, Erik's voice filled their section of camp with an unearthly beauty. They danced eloquently. Were that they had an audience of a thousand eyes on a stage lit by limelight or a simple campfire, nothing in his imagination spared for his Anna.

"Why do you do such things?" she mused, a dreaminess to her voice.

His long legs made easy work of whirling her around the fire. He might have been dancing with a feather—she weighed nothing in his arms.

"Why?" he asked curiously. Was the answer not so simple to her?

She looked up at him, her smile lit orange from the flames. The country charm to her face would never turn the head of any ordinary gentleman. The copper highlights in her hair blazed in the light. He stopped and traced her lips with his thumb. To him, she outshone Aphrodite.

"I can love," he answered simply, kissing an old burn upon her temple. It widened her smile. "I love," he stressed again, his voice fading to a whisper as he first kissed one cheek and then the other. "I love." He pecked the tip of her nose and collected her face in both his hands. Erik slowly slanted his lips over hers. "I love."

He breathed her name against her lips moving them in a slow, circular motion. Erik threaded his hand around her braid and held the base of her head against his passion. The weight of her body slipped to the crook of his arm. Not daring to break their kiss, he pressed one leg between hers and lowered them to the bedroll. With his tongue, he parted her mouth and probed her with delirious need. Hesitantly, he pulled away to study if she desired more. The blush running from her cheeks down her neck gave him all the answer he needed. Her hands lifted to his face. Erik's breath hitched. The mask dropped to the ground.

How she could look on his monstrous face with such love in her eyes, he never knew.

"Anna." With the husky sound of that word, she surrendered completely to him. He paused in his worship only long enough to press his desire against her and say,

"We dance."

* * * *

Human behavior fascinated him. Erik inspected the contents of the abandoned sack, wondering what sort of fool would discard it. Various sundries hit the ground around him. He flipped them aside, baffled to the senselessness of most of them. Perplexed by it all, he surveyed the area.

The blackness of the countryside befriended a life on the run. Only he and one other traveler—an annoying old man who constantly whistled—picked through the remains of the camp. A rusty cup and a useless key hit the ground. It disgusted Erik that he had to resort to picking through trash to find things that might be of use. The more his past caught up to him, the further it progressed from the comforts his genius and wealth afforded him.

That blasted opera house he had lived beneath notwithstanding . . .

The leftover loaf was a foolish thing to leave. That he would take. A pain raced up his jaw as he clenched his teeth. What he would not give to take Anna to a fine restaurant, end a meal with the best Tokay, and lay a fresh platter of pastry before her.

What he would not give to rip the lips off of that old man . . .

The satchel upended. Erik shook the contents to his feet. The leftover sack of coffee would go with the loaf. A flash of color caught his eye. Picking up the ribbon, he ran it nimbly over and under his fingers in one long undulating wave of color.

His heart dropped to his boots. Someday he would buy his Anna the finest dress with the best bustle in all of Paris. He would walk arm in arm with her through the Bois. No one would shout at him in fear of his mask and all would think her finer than the most beautiful empress. After their stroll, he would find a milliner and purchase her a fashionable hat to match the dress.

For now, a discarded hair silk would have to do.

The old man eyed him with one shaggy brow raised. When Erik shot him a look of pure venom, he whistled even louder. The muddy ribbon safe in his pocket, he tucked the loaf and coffee under his arm, and headed to Anna's side.

A shout cracked through the camp. The old man swallowed his whistle. An arrow of tension shot up Erik's spine.

"That pack is ours," Anna yelled.

"I'm not interested in the contents of any bag, little lady."

A sharp cry and then a dull thud made Erik's heart seize.

"Pig," she cried.

"Struggle any harder and I will strike you again."

"Bloody pig!"

The loaf and coffee hit the ground. Erik propelled himself across the camp, his eyes narrowed to hateful slits the instant he saw the vagabond atop her. Murderous rage filled his veins.

The man attempted to pin her, and Anna's legs flailed wildly as she fought, sending mud flying through the air. A vicious growl emanating from behind Erik's teeth punctuated his anger as he savagely tore the man off her. The scum tried to gargle out a cry of shock, but Erik's hand encased his throat, halting the sound. He caged him against his chest with a grip tighter than steel. Beneath his hands, the flesh of his windpipe collapsed as the man struggled for control.

"I swore, Monsieur, that my days of murder were over. However, if I cross paths with you again, I will rip your throat out and feed it to the next pathetic creature I come across. Understand?"

The man tried to nod. Poised to shove the trembling mess on his way, Erik stopped when Anna struggled to her feet.

"Wait," she spat.

Pushing the hair out of her face, she tugged angrily on her rumpled dress and stormed toward his captive. A hand shot forward like a tiny bullet. Erik watched Anna's face twist violently as her hand wrenched into the sensitive—and still exposed—organ between the man's legs. A great cry of agony tore from his lips.

Beneath his mask Erik's face contorted, too.

"Now you can let him go." With one final squeeze and a yank that made the man lurch his last meal at Erik's feet, Anna jumped out of the way and watched her attacker stagger toward the trees. "I hope you can't piss for a year!"

"Anna?" She turned to him, her shoulders still heaving from her heavy breaths. Her scowl faded to a bottom lip that shook like a leaf in a breeze. Guiding her into him, he held her close until she stopped trembling and wiped the blood on her lip. "Did he—" She shook her head. The relief did little to keep his heart from pounding. "Come," he said gently. "We need to move. He was not one of the usual wanderers. We cannot stay here."

With her hand locked firmly in his, he whistled for the stallion to follow. Dutifully, the stolen beast obeyed. The fear for her had turned to outright rage. If not for this manhunt, he would have the world at her feet by now. They passed the old man, the loaf stuck neatly under one arm, coffee under the other. His brow lifted higher in question as soon as the stallion ambled by. Erik followed his gaze to the bridle and the coat of arms of its former master still emblazed upon it. He schooled his anger. Having to put up with being tailed by the old man drove him mad enough. Couldn't they just be left in peace? It was bad enough his past followed him around. Strangers were not a welcomed attribute to life—his trust only went so far and wasting his extraordinary temper on an old man was not worth the self-loathing it caused.

Fury this profound was best spent directed at the Vicomte de Chagny. Holding Anna's hand tighter in an attempt to govern himself, he hastened out of the camp.

The old man's whistling abraded his senses like desert wind.

* * * *

In her short twenty-three years, Anna had seen it all and participated in most of it. Not a hardened criminal, she was merely a product of her upbringing. One does what one must in order to survive, especially the child of one of Europe's most infamous con-artists. She had run from that life years ago, preferring to spend her days repenting by ministering to the less fortunate. Had she known doing so would have dropped her in the lap of a man as notorious as the Phantom of the Opera, she would have thought twice about a lot of things.

"Let me kill him," he begged.

"No."

"Let me kill him?"

"No."

"Please, this once, let me kill him?"

"This once? What sort of comment is that?"

"Let me kill him?"

"No," Anna's voice slammed into the grass.

She kept her belly down, her focus on her target. The grass beneath tickled her nose, the damp ground soaked her dress, and the man beside her tried her patience. This was not a good day. She should have stayed behind in their last camp.

Erik, lying next to her in the same prone position, focused on a larger, less adorable target than a rabbit. Anna remained perfectly calm under the annoying out of tune song that made him squirm. She fought the temptation to thrust a dagger into his ear and put him out of his misery. The steady clip of the old mare's hooves became louder as did the infuriating whistling of his desired prey. Finally he snapped and scrambled to his feet. His patience, Anna noted, was at least getting better.

"I am going to kill him."

"If you do not get back down here, I'm going to kill *you*." She yanked Erik back to the ground, her eyes never having left her target.

A seductive groan rumbled out his lips. "Is it terribly odd of a man to be aroused by that comment?"

She gave him a seething glare meant for him to dodge the knives flying from her eyes. "Erik, the only thing you are arousing in me right now is my temper."

Anna ignored his expression, knowing what it indicated. She could not see the eyebrow he raised—being hidden beneath the depths of his mask—but he had done so. Every nuance of Erik's body read like an open book to her. She understood the odd tilts of his head, the tremble of a finger, and the particular ways his lips would move with his mood. She turned her attention toward the task at hand. As much as she wanted to blame him for their situation, she could not. The roles she played were just as animate and if she had to choose again, she would do so.

While his thoughts ran along the lines of murder and carnal pleasure, Anna's focused completely on another part of her anatomy. A thin length of silk coiled artfully around her wrist. Mud ground into her dress, turning faded blue to sludgy brown. Arms and legs moved with military precision. Not a sound rustled from her clothing. Her eyes narrowed, her mouth twisted into a cruel grin.

"I beg you. Let me kill him."

Frustrated, she screamed, sending the rabbit scurrying into the underbrush.

"That was my dinner!" She twirled, reaching up with one hand and pulling his face to hers. "Erik, I am testy. I have not slept. I have not eaten. I have not bathed in days. You are not helping. You are one throw of my Punjab away from meeting your maker."

"Wonderful," he sarcastically bit, waving his thin hand over the black leather concealing his face. "There is a small matter I have been meaning to discuss with Him."

Anna jerked forward to flounce him when additional hooves blended in with the approach of the old mare. They hared into the underbrush.

"Anna, where is the horse?"

"Out of sight." She surveyed the oncoming men.

"How many are there?"

"Three."

"Can you tell?"

She squinted. Her head barely lifted before she ducked. "Two Paris authorities, one from Chagny."

Erik reached for her, drawing her in closer against him. She snuggled into his iron grip and prayed her pounding heart would not betray them. Bile inched into her throat as a burning, physical manifestation of fear and anger. She inched her head to where she could just see through dense brush without exposing herself.

The horses stopped in a small circle around a graying man and his mare. The old man pulled on his reins and stopped his whistling to stare down the gendarmes. His face, grubby and riddled with wrinkles, puckered comically when he scowled. The old coot shifted on his horse, his shocking mass of gray hair tumbling every which way on his head.

He sniffed loudly. “Can’t continue on my way if you’re blocking the damn road.”

“May we have a moment of your time, good Monsieur? We are looking for some undesirables who may be heading in this direction. Perhaps you’ve seen them?”

The old man spat something distasteful at their feet. “Undesirables? That depends on what you classify as an undesirable.”

The gendarmes curled their lips. “We are looking for two people, a petite woman and a tall man. The man should be easy to recognize he is—eccentric. He claims to be a genius and a Maestro. His voice is incredibly unusual, but you should take care not to listen too closely. He is dangerously insane. A mask covers his face. He is known across Paris as The Phantom, and was last seen in this area after a failed attempt at killing a traveler.”

Erik’s lip twitched again—not a good sign. It only twitched when his anger reached murderous levels.

“You don’t say . . .” The old man rubbed his wrinkles and scratched his stubble. “I’ve seen them.”

Anna’s lungs filled. She heard Erik’s intake of breath, too. “You should have killed him,” she whispered.

Erik’s lips tightened to a thin line.

“Can you tell us which direction they went?”

The old man passed his hand through his untamed hair. “Yup,” he pointed toward a distant road. “I saw them two days back heading north.”

Erik and Anna shared a confused look. Leather cracked as the horsemen shifted anxiously.

“Are you certain?” One of them asked.

“What? A crazy man in a mask and a little woman. Yes, I’m certain. I may be old, but I’m not blind.” He leaned over in his saddle and gestured for the men to come closer. “Spunky little vixen that woman. Vim and vigor. I would love to get me a bit of her. Wouldn’t call her undesirable if you know what I mean.” He laughed. “The man is a hummer, keeps moving his head about like the damn thing is screwed on wrong. Can’t carry a tune for his life.”

The geezer wagged his head in a lame impersonation, causing Anna to bite her tongue. Erik seemed inches away from taking perverse pleasure in killing the old goat. A marksman reached into his vest and extended a small pouch.

"Merci, Monsieur. Something for your assistance courtesy of the estate de Chagny." He called to his men, and they thundered down the road and out of sight.

The old man waved them away. Gnarled fingers eagerly rippled through the coins. He stuffed them in his pocked and removed a chewed-up pipe. "You can haul your sorry asses out of the underbrush now. They're gone."

Erik froze, as did his lip. They remained rooted to their spots before cautiously approaching the roadside. The old man slouched in his saddle.

"Still want to kill me?" he drawled.

"Who are you, old man?" Erik insisted, looking at him out of the corner of his eye.

"Just that. An old man. Who are you?"

Erik replied with another question. "Why are you following us?"

"Not following you. I'm going in the same direction."

Anna approached with their horse, equally curious as to the mindset of the old timer. "Why did you do that?"

A grin spread from ear to ear, making his loose flesh pile into mountains of comical wrinkles. "Because you're entertaining and I don't have much in life to entertain me." He clicked to his mare and started down the road. "Now, I have money jingling in my pocket, and there's a village nearby where I am sure there's food with no fur still on it. You look like you could use a good meal and I need a smoke. Either you follow or you lead, but no matter what, I'm whistling."

Erik and Anna stared incredulously at the mare as it plodded down the road. Artfully, he swung her up onto the stallion's back before mounting the spot behind. He followed for a while before letting the horse fall into step next to the mare. The old man stared directly into Erik's mask and Erik stared at the wrinkled old man.

"I hum in tune," Erik snapped, making the coot laugh so heartedly Anna rocked back against Erik's chest.

That knotted finger wagged between them again. "See, that's entertainment. You two obviously have trouble following you around and Maestro over here is concerned about me insulting his humming."

"Men have died for less, old man," Erik threatened.

He flicked a finger. "Pappy. Not old man. If you're going to kill me, I'd like to know your name."

Anna snickered. Erik's arms constricted her waist.

"Erik, just Erik."

"Well, just Erik, if you don't mind, I'm going to whistle now."

* * * *

Any conversation Erik and Anna may have had ceased as they roamed the dusty roads, trying to make sense of the curmudgeon who had desperately latched onto them. The idea of marksmen following them around obviously didn't concern him.

Anna chuckled as Pappy launched into another tune. She couldn't see Erik's face, but she felt certain it turned purple with fury. Tramps were a unique sort, and she had met quite a few in her years roaming the countryside as a runaway. Consequently, none of Pappy's random tales, strange observations, or lively off-tune songs bothered her.

They wandered aimlessly down the main thoroughfare of a country village, stopping when Pappy dismounted outside a small pub. Raucous laughter and even worse music spilled into the streets. Erik dismounted and tied the stallion in line with the other horses. He looked at the entrance and warily pulled Anna off the horse.

"We should leave. I do not trust this place or him." He jerked his head toward the old man.

Granted the pub was crowded, but the churning of her stomach was proof enough she was starved. "Erik, please? I'm hungry."

Pappy yanked a worn woolen cloak from his saddlebag. "I know what you're thinking, so here." The cloak soared through the air, smacking against Erik's chest. "That hood is broad enough to keep your face hidden from whatever it is you are already hiding it from. I have seen some weird things in my life, but living beneath a mask? Seems cowardly to me."

Erik swung the cloak on and drew up the hood. Pappy's face warped like a tree bending in the wind. For a minute the old goat finally seemed unnerved. A yellow gaze of warning had leveled on the old man as soon as darkness shrouded Erik's face. His eyes, so deeply set they were nearly unseen, had an inhuman hue and a way of pinning people to their spot.

"You should know I do not trust you, old man."

"Pardon me while I quake in fear," Pappy grumbled sarcastically. He entered the pub, giving them no choice but to follow or leave.

He pointed them to a distant table in a darkened corner and turned to the bar. Once concealed in shadow, they surveyed the room. Backs to the wall, Erik and Anna relaxed, confident they were not drawing attention. Pappy returned, placing a tray with bowls of stew and a few ales on the table.

"*Merci, Monsieur,*" Anna said, her mouth watering.

"*Bitte sehr, Fräulein,*" Pappy replied.

She knew it! From the first moment they'd passed the old man on the road she suspected him of being German, but did not want to even approach the subject lest she ignite Erik's already aggravated temper.

"*Prosit?*" She raised her glass in cheers.

Pappy winked in obvious flirtation. "*Prosit.*"

Anna turned to Erik, beaming with glee. The glower she met smoldered behind golden eyes.

"Pardon?"

"*Nein, entschuldigen, Sie,*" Anna corrected.

She had been making attempts for weeks to break through his distaste for Germans and get him to learn her native tongue. It was no easy task for an Austrian to win over a Frenchman, given politic. Erik would need to learn the language if they intended to make it out of France, across Germany, and safely to the Austrian border.

"You are going to have to learn sometime." Anna gestured to her right. "Pappy here is German."

"Prussian," he corrected.

Erik grabbed the edge of the table. His already pallid knuckles turned even whiter. "Wonderful," he grumbled.

"*Wunderbar,*" Anna said between mouthfuls of saucy stew.

Pappy lit his pipe and took a long, contented puff. "See . . . there's that entertainment again." He took a good look at both of them. "You're an odd sort. The yarns I could spin about the pair of you could be endless entertainment at the next communal campfire. So, are you going to fill me in on the details as to why you apparently have half of France breathing down your necks?"

Erik pushed his stew away. Anna greedily slid it toward her bowl.

"No," he replied.

"Come on, you've told me enough to whet my curiosity. When first we met, you said you were a murderer, Maestro, magician, and mastermind. Who did you kill?"

Anna kept her mouth shut and poked anxiously at a potato. Erik leaned across the table. She thought about calming his foul mood, but what good would it do? He clearly wanted to intimidate. She had a strange feeling it couldn't be done. She popped the potato in her mouth.

"That depends, old man. Which one are we talking about?"

Anna looked to Pappy. The buzzard didn't flinch. She fished for a carrot to cover her grin.

"Let's simply keep it focused on the one that irritated France."

Erik laughed sadistically. He drew the back of his cold hand down the length of Anna's stew stuffed cheek before slinging his arm over the back of his chair.

"Then that would be her father. Or perhaps you speak of the alleged kidnapping of a nobleman's wife; the so-called murders of the pompous cheats behind the scheme . . . pick your poison. Of these crimes I am mostly innocent."

Stew flew from her mouth as she choked. Pappy leaned back and scrutinized her.

"You're traveling with your father's murderer?"

Anna flicked her eye to Erik. Only she could register the droop to his shoulder that betrayed his remorse. Such events they did not speak of often. It always launched Erik into a pit of self-despair. He'd spent years fighting the side of his persona that labeled him a madman.

He did not like being forced to kill.

"What does it matter to you whom she travels with?" Erik warned. "*She* is not your concern."

"But the man who abducted and killed my only kin was." He jerked his head toward Anna, his voice a raspy whisper. "So when I see a seemingly innocent little lady traveling with a man like you—"

"A man like me?" Erik interrupted menacingly. "You assume because I live behind a mask I have killed for the pleasure of killing?"

Anna spoke softly to a piece of celery. "My father was not a very nice man. What Erik did, he did to protect me and the Vicomtess de Chagny." Erik stiffened. She could not fault him his possessiveness of her. He fiercely protected her honor like a wolf does his pack. She chased a boiled onion around her bowl. "The crimes we are accused of were committed by my father, not us. However, seeing as the past is the only way in which a man is judged, our voices will not be heard. We are the victims in a game of lies. Not that it is your business."

Anna followed Pappy's glimpse to the gold band on her ring finger. She covered it with her thumb.

"I still think it is strange you would travel with a murderer. Don't you?"

Anna almost searched for the invisible hook Pappy baited. Erik's posture wound tighter than a spring the longer they sat there. His history didn't matter to her. She judged people by their character. She wiped her mouth on the back of her hand and leaned toward the old man.

"Would you believe he's a thoroughly fulfilling, highly skilled, completely sensual, and well-versed lover?" Anna could not hold her flirtatious stance. Her forehead hit the table as she burst out laughing. She yanked her head up in time to duck the glasses and bowls that flew across the table. Erik had cleared it with one swipe of his arm. The patrons turned. Pappy waved the crowded room off and the din returned to its usual timbre. She rose.

"You had better be damn happy I have a sense of humor over all this. Because despite the circumstance it still does not sit well with me." She wiped her dress free of ale and plunked back in her chair.

"Maestro apparently has a temper?"

"Hold your tongue, old man."

"Carries a grudge, too?"

"I said hold your tongue." Erik's voice switched to an all too familiar tone.

Anna rose. She sighed in dismay. "My thanks, *Herr*. However, I find it best if we were to continue on our way. You've been most kind."

Erik stood as well. He took Anna's arm and made a few steps toward the door before turning. "A wise man would not to follow us."

Pappy did not seem alarmed by the authority behind Erik's angelic voice. He studied the manner in which he held her arm. Could he be concerned that she may not be a willing partner to the travels with him? She laid her hand over Erik's and lightly rubbed a thumb across his grip in an obvious loving manner. Pappy nodded. Anna knew she had driven her point home. She was no stranger to wandering. With the old man's confession of the loss of his kin, she could not fault him his concern. However, she could care for herself. She hid a smile as Pappy stared at Erik.

He raised a bushy eyebrow and slowly drew out his heavy German accent. "Not following. I'm going in the same damn direction."

Two

Life on the run meant keeping shadows close and his eyes never off the road behind him. The thought of one day finding a place where he could live unmasked and free from unjust persecution, kept Erik pushing forward. He spent years in chilling solitude, trying to put to rest his past transgressions. The dream of creating a castle for Anna prevented him from slipping into the ever-beckoning memories of a darker time.

The unfairness of this manhunt boiled his blood. "This is getting ridiculous." Irritable, he surveyed the livery. "I did not spend years crafting my own asylum and hording my wealth only to be prostituted back to the life of repugnant freaks."

Anna flicked him an annoyed look. "Don't criticize my life. You had an unusual arrangement at the Garnier despite your indiscretions. I, on the other hand, grew up like this. The way of the wanderer has its positives as well. We can't exactly invade a salon or dine on turtle." Sarcasm pooled at her feet. "We're wanted criminals."

"I find it vexing that you continue to call us that."

"Oh joy, it's the humming wonder."

That gruff, masculine voice snapped Erik's spine ramrod straight. "Is this one of your positives?" he rumbled to Anna.

She snuck around him. "Pappy, *Guten abend*."

"*Abend,* yourself little lady. I never did have the pleasure of your name."

"Anna."

Erik turned to see the old goat smile smugly.

"Bundle up some hay and have a seat," Pappy invited, patting a bed of straw.

Hay fluttered aside as Anna flopped. Her smile reached across her face. She gestured to Erik, signaling for sparks to fly.

He governed his temper. "Why are you—?"

"I didn't follow. I got here first. Took the good hay for

myself. Old bones you know."

A girlish squeak slipped out her lips as Erik reached down and plucked her into his arms. He did so with such passion her feet left the ground. "If you do not mind, old man, I would much prefer my woman sleep by me." He tugged her along with him to a spot across the livery, and sat, hauling her into his lap. Arms came around her in a vise tight grip. He buried his lips in the top of her hair

"So," Pappy proclaimed, lighting a pipe, "are you going to tell me about the mask?"

"No."

"Fine, I'll just assume you're uglier than my horse's ass. Go back to that murder then."

"No."

If he held Anna any tighter he would crack her rib, but grasping her kept him in check. On as heavy a sigh as she could manage, Anna settled into the crook of his arm and amused herself with the only thing in reach, a discarded copy of last month's Époque.

"No," Erik replied to yet another inquiry. He turned from the annoying old goat and focused on the paper. Eyes met the cover story and shock jolted through him like lightning to a rod. He leapt to his feet, tumbling Anna to the floor so abruptly her braid flipped over her head, arms splayed before her.

She blew hay out of her mouth. "Erik!"

He snatched the paper from her hands, crushing a fist to his mouth. His body hunched as his strides pounded against the earthen floor. The unbelievable magnitude of what he read pumped blood into his ears.

"Erik?" she asked. "What's going on?"

He returned to the floor beside her. His gaze never left the front story.

"Philippe Georges Marie, the Comte de Chagny—is dead." He crumpled the paper to his chest.

"*Philippe* de Chagny?" Anna huffed. "Is he any acquaintance of Raoul de Chagny?" The pressure in Erik's chest rose when she turned to Pappy. "Noblemen. I have little respect for the lot of them. Especially Raoul de Chagny. Save the life of his wife and this is the kind of respect we get." She stabbed the air with her finger, gesturing to no one in particular. "This entire manhunt is her fault. If she had a spine to stand up for what she knew was right and if everyone was not so focused on the dead and buried, we wouldn't be in this mess. Who was Philippe?" she asked indignantly. "Or do I not want to know?"

Erik looked at Anna, his heart slowing in his chest. The profound degree of his grief lay hidden beneath his mask. "Who was he?" he recalled brokenly. "He was not his brother . . ."

Lowering his lids summoned forth the memories and gave birth to the unsettled noise in his mind—the familiar allure of madness. He rolled to his side and pulled his knees to his chest, refusing to meet her eyes.

* * * *

The Phantom's labyrinth, cellars of the Opera Garnier 1881

Blood—it tasted metallic. He didn't know where it came from, nor did he care.

His shout pierced the silence as he rolled down the stone steps in his drawing room. It spun like an out of control kaleidoscope. One by one the candles around him were burning out. He thought he could still hear the shouts of the men, but they were only in his mind. The labyrinth was silent as a tomb.

At least they overcame him quickly. He was able to unleash his fury on a few before they left him for dead.

He had nothing remaining in his life now. Nothing since Christine Daaé ran off with her vicomte lover, Raoul de Chagny. It was fitting that his return from confessing his sins to an old Persian friend should end this way. Mugged and beaten as soon as his feet left the cab.

Arm over arm, like an injured reptile, he dragged himself to his bedchambers where he could die surrounded by his memories of her.

Erik shuddered violently, his body swelling where the fists collided. Not able to make it, he balled into the fetal position, half in half out of his doorway and willed death to be soon. He closed his eyes. The shouts in his mind faded away and were replaced with the metronome of his labyrinth: the rhythmic lap of the water as it beat out what time he had left. It would be a welcome change to slip into darkness. He had always been one with the shadows . . .

Christine had been his only ray of light.

The sounds faded. Born alone . . . die alone . . . die unloved.

Succumbing to the pain, Erik laid his face against the cold stone floor. He had no idea where his mask was. It didn't matter anymore.

His lips trembled his lonely requiem.

"Dies irae, dies illa, solvet saeclum in favilla: teste David cum Sibylla . . ."

* * * *

He cracked opened his eyes: rock, candle, organ. He closed them. He had no concept of how long he lay there, but the pain grew exquisite. Erik's body blazed with fever, his mind danced a duet with Mephistopheles.

He lifted a lid: rock, candle . . . His unfocused eyes tried to make sense of the black shape blocking his sideways view of his organ.

"Stay still, you are terribly hurt."

A man gingerly reached for him sending panic ripping across his body. "No," he roared. "Do not touch me."

"Stop! You should not move. You will injure yourself further."

"No!" Erik screamed in a fever driven insanity as the man grabbed for him. "I will not die like this."

Kicking and scratching like a cornered animal, he fought to make contact with any bit of available flesh on his assailant. Let him die with some vestige of human dignity, not like a beaten mongrel.

The man fought back, grabbing at Erik's wild hands, matching him scream for scream. "Calm yourself, I am here to help."

Erik continued to flail, using craze to the fullest.

The man was not deterred. "I do not want to do this, Monsieur, but seeing as you are being most uncooperative—and I must admit I have been dying to do this for some time now—you give me no other choice."

The fist landed against his face like a catapulted rock, knocking him into submission. The floor bit into his back and legs as he was dragged across his home. Next he knew, his head lifted with the utmost care and he sank against his divan. Erik stared across the room in confusion at his usual bed. Why was he not in his coffin? Had he yet to die?

"Relax," he heard, "you are hurt."

An unfocused eye bobbed away from the macabre box to

look at the man above him. Impeccably clothed, aside from the worn cloak and threadbare felt hat he wore, his blue eyes shown with compassion yet oozed repressed anger. How could that be? Erik surrendered to blackness while his mind poised the question that would haunt his dreams.

Why do you look familiar?

Three

Christine slid the library doors shut behind her until they softly clicked together. A sad smile inched across her lips as she studied her husband. He sat almost as stoic as the ancient halls around him that had stood through centuries of births and deaths. Chagny rose like an awesome presence in the region it commanded, its flags displaying the family colors always snapping proudly in the breeze. The ivy covering the walls outside sheltered secrets as ardently as it embraced the love, compassion, and outreach of its namesake. Nevertheless, now it stood cocooned in grief, the ivy the only fingers catching the tears of France as a noble son was mourned. Though Chagny was Raoul's childhood home, he seemed out of place filling the shoes of his brother. Philippe left no heir to the massive estate, leaving Raoul head of one of the most powerful families in France.

A brief regard of the room explained the weight on Raoul's shoulders. The library screamed Philippe's name, further adding to the contrast of seeing him behind the desk. The colors of the coat of arms were scattered throughout, reflecting Philippe's pride, power, and masculinity. Cases holding service medals mingled with other noteworthy accomplishments. His sword shone proudly above the dark mahogany of the fireplace mantel. A nicked and dented model of a frigate, an ancient childhood toy, perched on the corner of the desk. It reflected the playful inner child Philippe had been. A countenance only revealed to his closest loved ones.

Raoul mindlessly rocked the ship on its stand. The unfathomable grief Christine read in his eyes could diminish the sun. In his other hand, Raoul nursed a hot cup of tea. Philippe never touched a drop of alcohol, no small feat for a man of his power. Christine knew it was in tribute that Raoul sipped. She suspected he could use something stronger.

"There you are," she said. "You've been hiding."

Raoul looked up. A dark cloud moved across his face. "Do you blame me?"

The week had been long. Well-wishers and mourners still streamed across the grounds. If Christine closed her eyes, she could picture Philippe's coffin and see Raoul's white-knuckled grip upon his sword as he stared at the box containing his brother. Now, with barely any time to mourn, he faced mountains of technical and legal affairs.

A weak smile lifted his lips. "You should not be moving about."

Christine laid a hand on the swell of her belly. The death of Philippe had overshadowed the joy of this child. "You fret too much. I'll not be held prisoner by you again with this baby."

"Fret I may. I will not have my little lady jeopardized by your need to constantly be on your feet." He sternly pointed for her to sit.

"It could be another boy," she teased. André continued to be their bright spot in the long year since the affairs at the Opera Garnier.

"Where is my heir?"

"He is content with the wet-nurse. I'm fine, Raoul," she insisted gently. "Your sisters have returned home. They felt it was time. They asked I shower you with kisses as they did not want to disturb you."

He was stronger than she expected. Raoul handled the condolences with grace and accepted the title of Comte de Chagny with pride, honor, and what she registered as a bit of fear. What she saw now as his hand rested against a toy ship, was a man missing the brother he adored.

She indicated the file spread before him. "What's all this?"

He laid his teacup down, gathered the papers into a neat stack, then cleared his throat. "Jules secured the police report. I was reviewing it."

"Philippe's drowning was accidental." Christine cocked her head.

"On the surface it looks that way."

"The surface? You don't think anyone intended to harm Philippe?" An unfamiliar air dressed his posture that went deeper than grief. "Raoul, what's going on?"

The awkward silence that settled between them knotted

Christine's stomach. It clenched tighter than wet leather when the door opened. Turning, she frowned as Jules Legard entered. He peeled off his riding gloves and formally greeted her before hastening to her husband's side.

"Was he there?" Raoul asked eagerly.

"No one was at the flat."

"Has he left Paris?"

"No. I pressed the landlord. The Daroga still lives on the Rue de Rivoli, but has been staying for a spell in Lyon."

"The Daroga?" Christine stammered. "That Persian fellow who was with us in the cellars when Erik first abducted me? Why . . . it's been years since your contact with him. What on earth are you bothering that old man for?" She pressed her husband when he did not reply. "Raoul?"

The mantel clock ticked like a telltale heart for a few long seconds before he shifted his eyes from Legard to her.

"Do you know where Philippe was found?" he asked quietly.

Christine settled her stomach with her hand and looked upon his quiet despair. "By the shores of a lake. There is nothing to fret. You know Philippe often went for long walks. He enjoyed nature as much as he did the pageantry of your nobility."

"Christine," Raoul tapped the folder. "He was found on the shores of *his* lake."

"His lake?"

"The Phantom's. His lake under the opera house."

The notion pushed her backward. "You speak lies. Why . . . how . . ." Her look of disbelief shot to Legard. "*Again*?" Christine lifted a hand to her mouth. "Raoul, this is impossible. You cannot possibly think Erik had anything to do with this? We don't even know where he is."

"Exactly, Christine. What am I supposed to think? That monster attempted to drown my brother on those banks once already. It would be just like him to find his way to my heart through Philippe again. I sent Legard to Paris. I had to know if perhaps the Persian knew anything."

She moved to the desk and gripped his hands. "Raoul, think nothing of it. Dredging up the past will not help us move forward. This was an accident. One we will never know the reasons behind. You cannot believe Erik would be so brazen as to seek revenge on you for this manhunt by killing your brother?"

"Your words, not mine."

"Jules, what do you believe? You are chief of our estates now, what say you?"

Legard kept his lips tight and moved toward the window.

Raoul answered for him. "He thinks like you. Evidence speaks loudly to him. Years ago when the Persian alerted Judge Faure of Philippe's suspected death, the authorities dismissed it as the ramblings of madmen. No one investigated. No one looked for my brother. He lay in that dank, awful spot for days before he dragged himself out. It was a miracle he survived." Raoul rubbed his brow as if trying to erase the memory. "I have yet to forgive myself for fleeing Paris with you as I did and not checking on my family first." Raoul pressed his fist to his lips. "I never even knew he was down there."

"No evidence proved Erik responsible for that incident, Raoul."

"History is an endless circle in our lives, Christine. I know his culpability back then, and I know he is responsible now. Like an hourglass this nightmare turns on me again." He gestured toward the file. "There apparently is nothing to suggest anything this time other than Philippe took a stroll along the darkest tributary of the Seine, and the why will never be known. Why would he return to that abysmal place knowing what horrors it held for us? For him?"

Christine didn't like the tone of Raoul's voice. "What do you intend to do?"

Her eyes flicked to a stray paper. She watched him twirl his signet around his finger. Christine stared at the ring, her head bowed in acknowledgement of the awesome power it represented. The ring was far too new in its creation and too premature to be sitting upon his finger. They knew one day he would wear the official Chagny signet. Both assumed it would be the same one that adorned Philippe's hand. But Philippe's signet disappeared years ago during an unfortunate mugging on the streets of Paris.

Raoul's posture possessed an undaunted determination. He didn't take kindly to being known as a man who bore the burden of tracking the Phantom. Christine cocked her head to read the words on the page. Foreboding filled her veins. Legard offered no comfort. He kept his hands locked tightly behind his back and his contemplation out the window. Her husband was equally as stoic.

The decree Raoul was about to send out would make certain the past met Erik wherever he went. He intended to flush her Angel of Music out by the hands of noblemen and farmers alike. Christine's heart slowed when Raoul lifted the paper. He spoke more to unseen ghosts than to her.

"I will not have his death at the shores of the Phantom's lake go ignored."

"Raoul, you must let this go," she urged. "We have so much uncertainly in our lives surrounding Erik. It is too much to believe he would come back here to harm us in this way."

"Is it, Christine? I know how deeply you once cared for Erik, despite your fear of him. You teeter between a man you admire and abhor. It's maddening to watch. But what am I to believe? All Erik ever wanted in life was you. Standing in his way is me. My brother is dead! I love you far too much to allow even the idea that you, André, or even my unborn child, may be next on his list in his need to see me harmed. Time and again that man has sought to destroy my family. There is no other explanation as to why Philippe was found dead in such a despicable place as the Phantom's lair." He nodded cautiously to Legard. "If it means a trip to Lyon to find out, then so be it."

Christine wrestled with a Titan of confusion as Raoul's passionate words filled the room. They had charged back and forth on this battleground for months. Erik's presence lived in her to the core of her being. Ever since the moment she discovered his death was faked and laid eyes on him again, his power and his awesome command over her filled her soul. The hours spent alone in the church begged the Lord to silence her heart, for she was mindlessly enslaved by a man who was more specter than flesh. As much as she loved Raoul, part of her longed to once more be the passionate obsession of the man she called her Angel of Music.

She traced her fingers around her swollen belly. Hundreds of thoughts circled in her mind. Raoul would never understand what it was like to be chosen by Erik.

She shook her head clear of such misplaced feelings. Perhaps once he had been her Angel and the music tutor that made her the darling of the Paris stage, but he was a madman, a monster. She could not be compelled to dwell on him.

Chagny grieved the loss of its son—Raoul the loss of his brother. Her eyes filled as she reached out to her husband. He had not wept once since Philippe's passing. She cried the tears she wished he would shed.

His profound sadness rode on a current of swift and terrible hatred and she feared the Siren that would drown them.

Four

Finally, the rain relented. They fled the abandoned livery when the horizon met the blue hint of twilight. Anna filled her lungs and breathed deeply the scent of fresh rain. The cloudless night lifted her spirits, but did nothing for Erik's distant and solemn mood. His eyes held an unfocused intensity, while his body twisted occasionally like he rotated puzzle pieces in his mind. Anna slipped her hand in his. She briefly studied the contrast of her small fingers intertwined with his extraordinarily long, skeletal ones. The stallion ambled dutifully beside them.

"Erik, tell me about the Comte de Chagny."

"I do not want to discuss it. It would be wise to let it go."

Anna bit the side of her cheek. She knew her ability to defy him would only amplify his already darkened humor. At times, prudence called to leave him to his thoughts.

"Maestro. Anna," came a distant voice.

A smile crept across her mouth. She stole a fleeting peek at Erik's twitching lip and turned in the direction of that voice. Pappy plodded up the road behind them.

"What did I tell you, old man?" Erik rumbled.

A leather rock soared through the air. It bounced off Erik's chest. Coins rained from the pouch. "*Now*, I'm following you. I find it disagreeable to wake with pompous rich folk staring down at me asking questions about your ugly mug. Nevertheless, it does pay off." He gestured toward the coins. "Courtesy of the newly ennobled Comte de Chagny."

Erik's back became rigid.

"Gendarmes arrived?" Anna asked cautiously.

"A couple of hours after you left," Pappy grumped as he dismounted. "I don't take a liking to being tracked because I'm heading in the same direction as you two."

More air met her lungs as she gasped. The trees flew by as

Erik grabbed her abruptly and swung her onto the horse. He snatched the reins and sent the old man a seething glare.

"Calm down, Maestro. I'm not stupid. I told them you were going to Belgium and headed them north. The only reason I protected you was to keep unjust harm from coming to that little lady." He jabbed a finger toward Anna. "What do you say to us finding another village to plunder? You're stuck with me and I could use some coffee." Pappy headed for the stallion, dragging his mare along. He rifled through the satchel. "Unless you have some in here . . ."

Erik yanked out his hand. "Do you have a death wish, old man?"

Pappy jerked his wrist free to resume his meddling. He replied by holding up a grubby hair ribbon and conducting the air with it. "Yup, sing me a requiem. Your voice sure is pretty."

Anna sucked her lips between her teeth in an effort not to crack. It was to no avail. She burst out laughing. Pappy was the relief she needed. His lighthearted words were of no comfort to her companion, however. Those thin lips, pulled into a deep frown, poured out more sadness than if she saw his entire face. Snatching the ribbon from Pappy's hands, he shoved off the horse and headed down the path alone.

"Erik?" Her plea was met with a harsh wave of the back of his hand.

"What is it with that one?" Pappy scowled. "Why on earth would a gentle creature like yourself be married to him?"

Anna stared at Erik's distancing cloak, then briefly to the question on the old man's face. Her thumb absently rolled the gold band around her finger. "We are not wed in the eyes of God." The wrinkles at the corner of Pappy's eyes deepened. "There is much you don't understand. You'll get used to him, then you'll see the repressed, but ardent gentleman I do. Leave him be until you know who he is. Whatever he dwells upon, it's not our right to know. It's best we don't complicate things." She regretted the words as soon as she said them. A major complication was on its way, but putting it aside for a while longer would be fine.

She hoped.

* * * *

The campfire crackled and remnants of the beast they stopped to eat still smoldered on the coals. The old man had faded off to a content slumber, bringing Erik the break he needed from Pappy's unrelenting questions to compose his music.

The notes and stanzas finally pouring out his fingers calmed a rising storm in his mind. The noise had cracked open like Pandora's Box upon knowing of the death of Philippe de Chagny. Music dampened the sound like a drug did for a desperate addict.

"What are you writing?" Anna asked softly.

Erik looked up. So focused had he been, he was surprised to find her beside him. He searched beyond her to study the night. Scanning the darkness had become habitual. They would not stay in the area long.

"The Madrigals," he replied.

"I thought Madrigal was a song you wrote for Christine—to explain why you rose from your faked death." Bitterness cracked into her voice. "Is that why you've been sullen since that Philippe person died? Because the death of one Chagny reminds you of another? So much so you have to write her another Madrigal?"

Anna folded her arms, protecting her breast like a bird that had impaled itself on the sword of jealousy. Rising, Erik stepped toward her.

"I told you, Anna. I do not want to discuss Comte Philippe." Notes exploded in his mind. Merely an arm dragged across her shoulder could ignite the most exquisite sound. It took nothing for one long arm to encircle her waist. He drew her back against his chest remembering he would not have her if not for Philippe . . .

"My Madrigal Operas have several movements," he explained. "This one has nothing to do with any messages for Christine." Erik hesitated before sheepishly entwining their fingers. Being this close to a woman could still fill him with such a welcomed, yet foreign sensation. He gestured to the score scattered beneath the tree. "This is the *Abendlied.*"

"A what?"

"An *Abendlied.* A song that is contemplative and quiet in its theme." He turned his head to the stars. "Their sound is mournful, like a soul weeping its sins toward heaven in hope of finding something deeper and better than itself. They tell of the reflections of human life as well as the natural beauties found within simple things."

"I know what they are, Erik. My mother sang them to calm me at night. I thought they were lullabies."

"They can be—as oft they were used." His fingers found their way up her neck. He caressed her like a sculptor does fine marble. "This *Abendlied* is solely for you, Anna. I am putting in this opera all I cannot give you right now."

"Would . . . would you write it as a lullaby?"

"No. I would never desire to write such."

He was not prepared for what stammered past her lips. Erik's hands clasped air as she broke away. It took a few moments before his thoughts cleared. When they did, he found her stroking the mane of their sleepy stallion. He came up behind her. An invisible hand slammed into his gut. He could hear her swallow tears.

"Can you repeat that?" He laid his hands across hers to stop her rippling fingers.

"You heard me the first time. Go away."

Shock rocked him back like a blow from a man five times his size. Erik turned, his head spinning, his heart pounding out of control. He walked like an automaton back to the cheerful glow of the campfire. Sickness churned his stomach. His selfish needs to feel love; his desires as a man for a woman were going to be made flesh? How could it be that possibility had never crossed his mind? Anna had never been with child. She told him she thought she could not carry. When he heard that, like a man deprived of water, he greedily drank. Many times without a worry in the world he poured his passion into that woman.

Panic coiled around his body, constricting his chest. It was a blessing she was barren. How could he subject her to bearing a child such as him? Erik had been born a demon, a cruel mix of monster and man that turned his mother into a hateful shadow of a woman. His knees slammed into the ground. He grasped desperately at his mask. What pitiful creature would she bear? Anna would nurture and carry his child safe from the world until it was born and the world saw it for what it was . . . *his* child.

Anguish curled his body forward. He did nothing in his life that warranted such a noble title as father. His mother had wanted him until the moment he was born and then there were no arms to hold him. No one to love him. Not a single parental kiss ever touched his flesh. Masked the instant he entered the world he grew up a living corpse—an unwanted, unloved, reject . . .

Fear and confusion coursed through him. Erik crushed himself against his knees. He squeezed his eyes tight and tried to force aside the image of Anna's horror when the time came for that child to be born. For that child to be rejected . . .

Erik snapped his head up.

Anna would reject that child and him!

His eyes locked with hers before she swung her head back into the stallion's mane. Even now she couldn't look at him. Struggling to his feet, his confusion turned to outright anger. If there was one aspect of life he would not tolerate, it was rejection. He studied the camp. Their lives were complicated enough; he now had this to face?

A frustrated shout burst out his lips as he kicked the nearest rock. He hated not being in control. He calculated each move in his life as carefully as the music he composed. Displace anything, change anything, and the tune would shift. Randomness did not enter his life until Anna, an unwanted Samaritan turned unlikely friend, left him those infernal packages of paper, ink, and figs. Her compassion coaxed him out of his prison to rejoin the world, and now this was the result? He tried to control the trembling in his hands. He did not ask for this and there was nothing he could do about it.

His face blazed beneath the mask.

Damn you, Philippe de Chagny. Why did I let you meddle with my life?

Erik paced in small circles, a dull ache of tension winding from his jaw to the back of his neck. Anna refused to meet his eyes. If she could not even look at him now, how would she treat that child? He would not be the one to blame for that infant's misery and he sure as hell would not be rejected by anyone ever again.

It would be best not to stay in the camp. Erik pushed beyond the stallion and into the trees. He did not bother a second glace backward.

"Erik?" Anna whimpered.

"Not now."

His fury could have lit the forest ablaze.

* * * *

The camp faded into silence as snapping twigs and branches died with his footfalls. Anna sank in front of the fire. She added a log and watched unblinking as the sparks floated away.

Her chin sagged to her chest. She was used to being cast aside when she wore out her welcome. In her past, she only stayed in one area long enough to work off her father's debts. Then she was dismissed, either running from the law, or some other mistake her father had made. It was only a matter of time until Erik's needs were met and she no longer warranted his attention. How foolish to think the friendship she established with him was any different than the rest of her life. It didn't surprise her, but the rejection hurt.

He loved Christine—ardently. Anna didn't know music, or have the stature and beauty of his former musical protégé. She absently rubbed the fading scar on her temple, testimony to all she'd done to free Erik from the injustice of the Opera Garnier. Christine had a deeply rooted connection to him. What did she have? Their friendship developed slowly, but love? The idea was thrust upon them suddenly, and then Erik's past hit him right between the eyes. It launched them into whirlwind decisions and the throes of a manhunt. They never had a chance to figure anything out, let alone this.

Anna stared into space. He still thought of Christine. The whisper of her name would be on his lips those rare nights when he needed rest, and at that he tossed and turned. Anna was the second and least complicated choice for love, that's why he kept her around. She didn't mind, she was used to such, but now . . .

The thumbs she pressed against her temples did nothing to force away the throb in her head. Where was the joy she should be feeling? She was pregnant! Fear wrapped its fingers around her and choked out any glimmer of happiness. A wanted woman, how was she to run while expecting? What life would this child lead with an unjust bounty on her head? A sob massed in her throat.

"Anna?" Pappy called groggily. "Where's Maestro?"

"Walking."

"What has you upset?"

Pappy's face warped as she looked at him through eyes brimming with tears. "You really like me don't you? You barely know me, but you want me around."

"Of course. You're honest, spirited . . ." his voice dipped. "Much like my little girl was."

"He hates me, Pappy. I can't be like her and now I've ruined everything for him."

"Can't be like whom? That Christine you told me about? I thought he didn't love her."

"He does Pappy, deeply. I was a huge diversion for him. I should have left the opera house when he told me to. I'm not useful to him anymore, and I've only been in his way. Now, I've prevented him from being with his true love. I only wanted him to be happy."

"Anna, what on earth happened?" Pappy scanned the camp.

"I'm in the family way." When the old man jerked back with huge eyes, Anna stuttered. "I can't do this, Pappy. We're on the run!"

His slack-jaw inched toward a grin. "Don't expect me to be a nursemaid or anything. I have my limits. That can be Maestro's job."

"Erik was so angry with me he left."

The old man's gaze went cold. "That dog! I knew something was wrong with him the day I met him. I never did understand why you two were together and now I know. Just his filthy needs. His selfish manipulative thoughts. That rotten dog! You listen to me," Pappy looked her directly in the eyes. "You are too good to be mixed up with him. He's not in his right mind. I've seen it in those strange eyes of his. This whole manhunt, *mein Gott,* you don't deserve this. Maestro is too old for you anyway and, well, so am I, but at least I will take care of you and your baby. Do you hear me?" Pappy's head whipped back and forth. "Which way did he go? I'll find him and I'll—"

"Pappy?"

"What, little lady?"

Anna fought back tears. It was not in her nature to cry herself to sleep. "Promise you won't leave me?"

Pappy leaned away, his shaggy brows inching upward. He nodded. Anna scanned the camp. The tears she shed she forced deep in her gut to drown with her weakness. She wanted Erik to see the hurt in her eyes when he had the gall to show his face again.

Five

The night had deepened to ebony when Erik burst through the trees. Curses rained around his unsuspecting companions. Leaves and branches flew everywhere.

"Anna, on the horse!" He kicked the embers of the fire. A coal and bit of charred polecat flew over her shoulder.

Pappy looked. "I don't see any anyone. We're fine."

"Check the ridge." Erik pointed. "Up, Anna, on the horse. Now!"

She froze and stared at his hands. "You're covered in blood."

"It is canine." He grabbed her and swung her onto the stallion's back.

Anna pivoted to stare at the hillside. Barking dogs mingled with distant, angry shouts. "How did they locate us? This pursuit had been dormant for weeks!"

Erik leapt onto the spot behind her. "They are not gendarmes. They are farmers and are armed. Obviously word has spread." He reeled the stallion in the opposite direction of the oncoming mob. Pappy and his mare already made time out of the camp.

"Erik, wait!" Anna gestured toward the tree where he had left his papers. "My lullaby. Your Madrigals!"

She moved to dismount, but Erik, his concern more on protecting her than an opera, caged her in a steely grip. He gave a final look at the horses thundering down the hillside and dug his heels into the stallion. The adrenaline that pounded them out of the camp was numbed by the crunching leaves and breaking branches as the horse pushed forward. The stallion slowed even more upon being reunited with Pappy's mare.

"You're not going to be happy about this," Pappy said, holding out a paper. "Found it tacked to a tree."

The light from the match Pappy flared made them all

squint. Erik and Anna read in silence. The decree was written in multiple languages and provided detailed descriptions of Erik masked and unmasked, listing their crimes and the bounty for his and Anna's capture.

The single line accusing him of the murder of Philippe de Chagny made the note crush under the intensity of his anger. "Safe to say whatever dignity I had left is now gone."

Pappy snuffed the miniscule torch. "That information has probably been sent to regions you can't even begin to imagine." He spoke more to Anna than Erik. "That bounty explains why farmers are taking to the hunt."

Anna smeared the blood on Erik's hands. "What dog did you kill?" she said uneasily.

"What does it matter? It was a mongrel bird dog."

She lurched. Her stomach emptied over the side of the horse, spilling her last meal to the ground.

A rumble of frustration rolled out Erik's throat. He furiously rubbed his hands to remove the blood, lest it sicken her more. "You are in no condition to worry over a dog. There is nothing we can do about farmers taking interest. France is large. We move where the marksmen are not. Chagny will not be able to keep pace with me."

"Perhaps not with you, but this is going to become complicated." She scrubbed her lips with her hand and scanned the trees. "I don't like dogs."

"About that complication, Maestro."

Erik ignored the disapproving tone to Pappy's voice. "That matter is of no concern to you, old man."

"It is when I spend the night comforting an innocent little lady. Where did you go? This woman is doing enough already to stay by your despicable side. You find out you're going to be a father and run off?"

"Hold your tongue lest you want me to make you mute."

"She deserves more respect than what you gave her. She knows she's not your precious Christine, whoever she is."

Erik's jaw clenched so tightly he swore his teeth would shatter. "Leave that name out of this."

"I would if I didn't think she had a lot to do with why you ran off."

"You have no idea why I needed the time I took," Erik said, voice rising.

Pappy's rose as well. "My suspicions? You're clinging to something much tighter than Anna. I suggest you consider the consequences of your actions before you ever raise that baton of yours again. You'll need a Samaritan in all this and I'm the best you got. If you can't face this like a man then I will, for Anna's sake. I don't have any divas in *my* way."

"Christine is not in my way," Erik snapped. The noise in his mind climaxed with the memory. He winced and drove the horse deeper into the sanctuary of the trees.

* * * *

The Phantom's Labyrinth

Erik moaned. Every bone in his body ached.

"Ah . . . you are awake!"

He jolted upright, sending the room into a spin. A violent wave of nausea emptied his stomach over the side of the divan. The convulsions sent stabbing pains up and down his chest. Spitting out the remains of bitter acid, Erik slid a shaking hand up to his face. His palm drenched instantly with sweat. Groping unsteadily, he pawed his naked face and bare torso. Something bound his chest.

"That had to hurt," a man groaned. "Your fever is gone. One of the only good things to have broken I think."

Erik cocked an eye; the vomiting at least helped to clear his dizziness. He focused enough to realize he was still in his house by the lake. Inch by inch he turned his head toward that voice. He stiffened. "Who are you?"

"I would not move too suddenly. I suspect your ribs are broken. I bound them the best I could. Not much you can do about broken ribs. Had a few myself back in the day."

Pain knotted him into a ball. Erik looked at the bandage that hugged his chest. That explained why breathing hurt and why he was half naked. A hand flew to his face while his other scrambled to cover his deformed body.

"I figured you would want me to locate this," the stranger said. He extended Erik's mask and nodded toward a blanket. "Every man needs his dignity in one form or another."

Erik squinted and accepted his mask, being comforted by the familiar weight of it on his face. He pulled the blanket around his shoulders and hugged it close against him.

"Who are you?" he asked again, hesitantly.

"No one of concern. Lay back, you should not be sitting

up."

Erik groaned and fell against the divan. "What happened?"

"Looks like you were beaten rather profoundly. You should be thankful there are not many mirrors here. You are not a pleasant sight."

Erik grabbed his head. There were huge blank spaces in his mind.

"I thought to yell for the authorities when I witnessed your mugging, but realized given my circumstance that would not be a good idea." The man continued. "I passed the thugs as they ran off. I thought it best not to chase after them. They did not look friendly. Due to recent events of The Phantom of the Opera everyone undesirable is suspect to abuse it seems."

Mugged on the streets by vermin? Erik's head throbbed. He lost Christine, his dignity, and came inches away from losing life and the secrets of his labyrinth to common thugs? He eyed the stranger suspiciously. The trousers he wore were finely pressed, his vest and jacket immaculately tailored. The diamond stick in his cravat seemed too formal for roaming sewers and catacombs. Perfection dressed him, save for that felt hat upon his head and the tattered cloak draped across his shoulders. Caution sliced across Erik.

Yes . . . he had seen that cloak and hat before . . .

"How did you get down here if they ran off and you did not follow?" he demanded.

The stranger pursed his lips. "Inconsequential. What matters is I found you. Lucky me, I get to be your Samaritan."

"How long since I was insulted?"

"Does time matter?"

Somehow it did not. Not when he would have died at the hands of common thieves defending his inner sanctum from the morbidly curious. His life had come full circle. He was yet again an oddity, a fascinating sideshow freak. A spectacle to be sought out then plundered and abused. His legacy would not be the greatness of the Opera Garnier and the empire he had built. It would not be the career of a young woman bound for glory of the stage. No, his legacy would be the mask and the deformed monster that lay beneath. What dignity did he have left now? What life?

"Rest," the stranger commanded. "I will find you some food. You will need your strength."

Erik did not want strength. He wanted to be left alone to wallow in his self-inflicted pity, to agree with the world he was an unworthy mongrel destined to be shamed into the darkest parts of hell. The man rose. He ignored Erik's angry cries.

"Stay away from me! Who are you, damn it?"

Six

Raoul tapped his crop against a gloved hand as he waited in his library for Legard. He knew he would have to convince him of his decision to head to Lyon to interrogate the Persian and what better way to do so than on the trails. Confidence and power exuded from him the most when astride one of his stallions. The crop wrung in his hands when he thought of Erik traipsing across France on his finest mount.

"Good Morning, Jules," Raoul said as cheerfully as he could when the door opened. He slapped his crop against the top of his leather boot. "You are not dressed. Have you declined the invitation for a ride?"

"There is no time for riding." The door slammed.

Raoul's attention shot beyond Legard to the oddest fellow he had ever seen. "I beg your pardon. Who are you?"

"Perhaps, if you were paying attention to who lurked on your estate instead of shagging your pregnant wife, you would have known I was here. You really should keep those balcony doors closed."

Anger propelled Raoul forward, but Legard intercepted him before he could reach their guest. "Hold your temper, Raoul."

"Hold my temper?" He pointed the crop toward the intruder. "No one disgraces my wife. Who is he? It is your job to keep people *off* my estate."

The man walked the perimeter of the library, knocking books off the shelves with quick flicks of his finger.

"I don't know who he is," Legard said under his breath. "I found him prowling in your private gardens. He claims he has business with you and refused to leave the grounds. I thought to force him off, but he's wearing a signet."

"I can hear you, gentlemen," the uninvited guest said loudly. Stopping at the desk, he pulled a brief from his pocket and tossed it on the blotter. "Tell me about this man." He gestured to the decree and lowered himself onto the chair.

"It seems you are well aware of who I am," Raoul began cautiously. "Would you be so kind as to provide me with your full title?" He indicated the elaborate ring decorating the man's left hand.

"A bauble from my employer." He wagged his fingers in the air. "Tell me of this Phantom, Comte de Chagny."

"The Phantom?" Looking to Legard only added to the confusion. His arms spread indicating he knew nothing. "Everything you need to know is in that decree. He is wanted for multiple crimes committed against France and the Chagny bloodline."

"Do you know where he is?"

"Not presently."

The man stood. He carried an odd air about him, his appearance a living contradiction. His costume bespoke wealth, but the wild glaze to his eyes and unkempt hair was not to be trusted. He lifted a small sculpture of a naked muse and fondled it lewdly. He held it close to his eyes, too close, as if scrutinizing it for any tiny flaw. "What of the girl it mentions, Comte de Chagny? Where is she?"

"Mademoiselle Barret?"

The man dryly repeated her name. "Mademoiselle Barret. Yes." With a loud crack, he snapped the neck of the maiden and tossed the pieces on the sideboard.

Raoul jerked back. The man had cracked solid marble! "Her whereabouts are unknown."

"How long have you been tracking her?"

"Going on a year," Raoul replied irritably, throwing his crop to a nearby chair. "I will answer no more of your questions until you tell me who you are."

The man's lips opened to expose pearly teeth. Crisp and white, they contrasted his dark beady eyes. "They call me Loup. The wolf. I am employed by Duke de Molyneux of Belgium." He leaned against the sideboard and folded his arms across his chest. "Anna belongs to me."

The air in the room turned thick. "I beg your pardon," Raoul said.

"She was sixteen at the time, and destined to be the mistress to Duke de Molyneux's son before she killed him. I have been employed by His Grace to track her and have been doing so for eight years." He shrugged. "Some men hunt foxes. I hunt Anna. Cunning little wench, *mon Alouette*. Very elusive. My prize trophy, actually. Her hunt has kept me a rich man, but nothing will compare to mounting her." His eyes gleamed, wolf-like. "Anna has been a thorn in my side for far too long. This Phantom, she is connected to him somehow?"

Disbelief scratched its way out Raoul's voice. "At one point she seemed to be. It could be likely he still commands her."

"You paint an intriguing picture of this man. Is he really dangerous?"

"More than you will ever know."

"You truly desire to find him?"

"I do."

"Excellent." Loup pointed, indicating the courtyard.

Raoul strode toward the window and shoved aside the drapes. His jaw clenched making his nostrils flare the instant he stared into his courtyard. It seemed Chagny had additional guests. A small battalion of men on horseback trotted up the road. Raoul swore he looked at living, breathing Centaurs. Fine rifles were strapped to the saddles and a dozen lean hounds wove in and out of the horses.

"They're the finest around, Comte de Chagny, experts in their field," Loup explained. "They know nothing other than hunting men. When I saw this decree of yours, I took to the chase. The hounds are well trained to Anna's scent. When we hit this region some of my men branched east while I came here to visit your quaint little house." He laughed loudly. "The dogs would not have started tracking if Anna was not afoot. My men might have already found her. Now, if she is connected to your Phantom we have a bit of a problem." Loup strolled to the server. "I am a hunter and am paid handsomely for my services. Molyneux has kept me a happy man primarily because he knows I am not one to cross." Snifters were shoved aside. "He wants Anna brought in alive so he can have some fun with her before her execution. Your Phantom fellow might get in my way." He nonchalantly painted the air with a hand. "If I kill him, I will provide you with some sort of relic of proof. Either way, I don't touch this Phantom without a substantial sum of money from you." He inspected a decanter of cognac and slammed it down. "Not the right color."

"Shit." Legard ground through his teeth. He turned his back

to Loup and leaned in toward Raoul's ear. "Piece it together. His eyes, the intonation of his speech, his weird twitches. He's a damned absinthe addict!"

"I can hear you," Loup said in a singsong voice. "There are terms to discuss. Mademoiselle Barret is mine as mentioned before, should she be found."

Raoul's jaw began to hurt from clamping down on it. "I am not fond of Mademoiselle Barret, but was raised to view women with a modicum of dignity and respect. I will not have her spoken of as if property."

Loup snorted. "The hunted is always a hunter's property, Monsieur. You have spent far too much time between the legs of one woman. Very virtuous, but utterly pathetic. When I find Anna I will let you have her for a night. She is a delightful, if not combative, shag."

"You will leave the grounds immediately," Legard insisted. "My men will consider the accusations you brought to light regarding Mademoiselle Barret. If they are true, I will see to it once she and the Phantom are found that she is investigated for the murder of this nobleman in addition to any other crimes she may have committed at the Opera Garnier. You are through here."

"You deny me my toy?" Before Legard could utter a word, Loup lunged, decanter in hand. "You derisive son-of-a-bitch! You will not counter me! No-one takes my toys!"

The decanter rammed into Legard's ribs. A sharp cry filled the library when he doubled into the pain. Raoul took two strides forward only to stop dead as the wolf pivoted on him. His deep set eyes held an unfocused malice that ran Raoul's blood cold. Decanter still in hand, Loup shoved Legard aside and backed Raoul several paces away, hunching over him like a hungry dog. Raoul turned his head to the side. Loup's lips twitched in rage, his unusually white teeth contradicting the rancid stench that passed them.

"Perhaps I did not make myself clear," he annunciated, spittle coating Raoul's cheek. "I want Anna Reneé Barret and I will deal with any bastard who gets in my way. If this estate is involved with *her* then you are involved with *me*. Do you or do you not want this Phantom as well, Comte de Chagny? My methods can be a bit unorthodox, but effective."

Just how unorthodox became quickly apparent . . .

The library door slammed inward. A marksman entered followed by the flummoxed footman who tried to keep him away. Reverently, the man laid the body of a dog on the floor. As soon as he settled the hound, he scurried away as if a boy in fear of a whip. Loup jerked a finger to the heap, his words cut into choppy sentences.

"My dog? Dead?"

Loup's displeasure soared into the fireside. Legard stumbled out of the way, clutching his bruised ribs as the decanter shattered, spraying glass and cognac across the library. The marksman stammered his reply, fumbling about the masked man who killed the hound. His hand shook as he extended a stack of papers. Loup snatched them and growled a string of expletives.

"You had her?" One swift backhand cracked the nose of the marksman, sending blood splattering across his face. Loup turned toward Raoul and slammed the papers on the desk. The pages fluttered in every direction and slid across the polished mahogany, littering the blotter and floor.

"I am not exactly even tempered when people mess with my dogs, Comte de Chagny," he shouted. "Proof that your beloved Phantom is in my way. Lesson one: the hunted will never stray far from civilization if they can help it. It keeps them connected to their former life. Lesson two: when hunting, never underestimate the greedy palms of the simple man. They will tell what they know for a handful of coin. He is somewhere in the region. If the rumors I have heard are true and this Phantom is a musical genius, there can be no doubt that music is his. The question remains, is Anna with him? If the dogs picked up her scent, I can only assume she is."

Raoul lifted the papers. "The Madrigals." Those words shot like bullets to his heart. He paced circles around his desk. "Get that damn hound out of my library!"

The marksman didn't move until Loup jerked his head toward the door. "The longer I stand here watching you twirl like a top, Monsieur le Comte, the farther she runs." He picked up the broken muse and lifted it before his eyes, stroking the marred surface. His thumbs focused on the marbled breasts. "I will have my trophy buck. Anna is my toy . . . my candy . . . my whore. Rule number three: the hunted tend to linger near those they know." His penetrating eyes leveled on Raoul. "It seems to me there is someone in this house the Phantom knows. Since you are connected to Anna and this Phantom to your family, I will hound you night and day until I find her." He nodded to Legard. "Any information your pathetic investigator uncovers belongs to me. I will make your life a living nightmare in order to get what is mine. Unless, of course, you work with me and the price is right."

Raoul's nostrils flared in anger. His hands shot forward in an attempt to snatch the muse from Loup's grip. The wolf refused to relinquish his prize. Jerking forward, their arms locked, bringing them chest-to-chest and eye-to-eye. A black and violent cloud of warning flashed across Loup's face, but Raoul would not be deterred.

"Get your men and those hounds out of my courtyard. Leave me to my morning affairs, do not insult my investigator, and then perhaps we will discuss things civ—"

"There is nothing to discuss," Legard interrupted, one hand still upon his side.

Loup wrenched the muse free. He snapped his teeth in Raoul's face, nipping the air inches from his nose. Raoul recoiled. Sliding Legard a contemptuous look, Loup cooed endearments at the broken muse.

"He is blackmailing you for your purse." Legard pointed to the papers in Raoul's hand. "He has no proof those are Erik's. Anyone can take a sheet of music and scribble Madrigal atop it—"

"Madrigal?"

All present swung toward the door. Christine stood in the entryway, her delicate hand touching the chain around her neck. Her lips pursed as a bloodied marksman passed with the limp hound.

"What's going on?" She inched her way toward her husband. "Who are these gentlemen?"

"Ah. The alluring Comtess de Chagny." Loup bowed, any sign of instability vanishing. The man was a well-trained circus animal. "I can see why your husband enjoys filling you with his seed." He circled her like a lion smelling the heat of his lioness. "One can also see why the Phantom is so compelled to claim you as his own."

"The Phantom? Raoul?" She clutched at her unborn child and leaned away.

"Enough," Raoul snapped. He nodded toward the door, not entirely certain the man would obey. "Leave. Get rid of the dog and wait for me in my carrel. We will discuss conditions further. You are never to disrespect my wife again. Do I make myself clear?"

A slow smile spread across Loup's face. His tongue bounced lewdly on his teeth when he savored his words. "I only disrespect Anna."

With a laugh, he tossed the broken muse to the sideboard. His perfect aim shattered a bottle of Raoul's finest cognac.

The tension in the room dropped a notch as soon as he was gone. All struck silent; the only sound the waterfall of amber liquid pooling on the carpet. Raoul looked at the score he held before turning to Christine. "Are you at ease?" She nodded. He eyed Legard and addressed him. "Are you as well?" It pained him to see how Legard still clutched his side. Clearly embarrassed at being overcome, Legard waved him off with an annoyed flick of his wrist. "Christine, that man is an associate. You need not know anything more than that."

"But the Phantom?"

"Erik could be in the area and possibly Mademoiselle Barret."

"This close?"

"I am afraid so. Fear not. He will not come near you or André. He will be behind bars soon. I have a means to make that happen quickly now."

Legard cleared his throat. "Monsieur le Comte, may I speak as your friend?" Raoul nodded. Legard indicated Christine. "Privately."

"There is nothing you can say to me that you cannot say before the lady of this house, Legard."

Christine straightened as if expecting unwelcome news. With a deep breath of frustration, Raoul nodded for her to sit. If this accursed pursuit dared to harm her or his unborn child, he would never forgive himself. Before she sat, Christine retrieved the stray leaf of music at her feet.

"I will not stand for this," Legard said. "I have seen looks upon your face only ever etched on the most hardened individuals. I know what you are thinking, and hiring some bounty hunter is not going to solve anything. It is not Chagny's position to be involved with the affairs of a Belgian duke."

Raoul watched Christine's delicate fingers stroke the notes and stanzas on the page. They moved across the music like hands across a long lost lover.

"Bounty hunter?" she quavered.

Raoul caught the title of the Madrigal as she pressed it to her breast. He resisted the urge to rip the *Abendlied* out of her hand and tear it to shreds.

"I appreciate your concern, Legard," Raoul stressed. "I am handling Philippe's murder—"

"What? Murder?" Legard jerked back. "Is that what this stems from? Raoul, it was an accident. You are a nobleman not an investigator. I will not have an absinthe addict on the grounds of the estate I promised to protect because you think Erik had something to do with Philippe's death."

Raoul's brows knitted. He slowly pushed himself toward the window and indicated the distant Chagny crypt. "I have been up to that vault every day since Philippe's passing. I stand before the doors separating me from my brother, and beg my grief to come. But no matter how hard I try, my tears will not fall. There is a crater in my life, and I feel as if my inability to respect my brother's death with grief is a betrayal of the most formidable kind."

Christine hastened to his side, the music still tightly against her bosom. She took his hand. "Raoul you are angry over his loss and under tremendous stress. You must give yourself time."

Legard attempted to lay a hand on his shoulder. Raoul turned from both of them and headed back to his desk. "She's right," Legard said. "Revenge is a wild justice."

"I am angry over his murder. I will not rest until the man responsible is out of our life forever. If it means associating with a man such as Loup to find Anna Barret—and with her the Phantom—then so be it." Staring out the window at the distant stone house, he nodded in silent affirmation of his decision. "We will leave in a fortnight. Shall we see firsthand what is so alluring for the Persian in Lyon?"

"Raoul, you are being ridiculous," Christine said sternly. "Erik had nothing to do with Philippe's death."

His fist hit the desk. The sharp crack of his signet made his wife and aide jump. "Why must you constantly defend that man? I need your support in this. In the year since Erik mysteriously rose from the dead you have gone from fearing him to being his advocate."

Legard shifted uncomfortably while Christine approached the desk. The music in her hand wrinkled against her breast. "How dare you say I am an advocate to that madman."

"How dare I? These last months I have poured my heart and soul into finding this man in order to keep you and my son safe. One moment you support it, the next I find you weeping into your pillow over it."

"I weep for the loss of my art. I weep for the man I knew as the Angel of Music, not the monster—"

"The Angel of Music was a fable invented by your father and changed by Erik to build your trust! He *never* existed." Raoul's shout reverberated across the library. Christine's ruby lips thrust forward in the deep frown of a wounded child. "I am tired of your indecisiveness, Christine." Her injury deepened. "I am trying to change the direction of our lives so we are not haunted by that man anymore. He tried to kill me once, he has killed my brother, and you still despise a Phantom but love an Angel. Half the time I wonder if you know whose bed you share."

Regret knifed Raoul in the stomach the instant Christine's expression hardened and her eyes pinched.

"Change yourself Raoul, then you can worry about changing the course of destiny."

Glancing at the music his wife cradled as she quit the room, his soul filled with profound foreboding.

* * * *

Massive trees lined the back lanes between the Chagny estate and the village proper. A blanket of fine snow shone against the ground. As the day lengthened, so did the shadows leading to and from the noble estate. The colossal stone Chateau stood proud and omniscient against the world of white innocence.

The tears that were dry on her cheeks made Christine's face especially cold. Using the back of a gloved hand, she wiped the stone bench free of crusty leaves and sat beneath the ancient oak. She pulled her other hand free from her muffler, and with it the small velvet box. Opening the lid, Christine caressed the recently blessed St. Nicholas medallion. She said a silent prayer Raoul's gift would help him heal from his brother's death.

She squeezed her eyes shut, the tears still lingering in the corner instantly growing cold. The look upon Raoul's face when he spoke of this pursuit was one she never wished to see again. Stroking her fingers between arched brows, she looked toward Chagny. Every day the stressors of this manhunt seeped deeper into her soul, spreading an unbidden confusion through her veins.

The shadows lengthened and the breeze picked up, tapping the branches toward her like bony fingers of shame. No amount of prayer would convince her she still did not feel for Erik. Horrible guilt flooded her for her words toward her husband and for feeling anything for the man he swore killed his brother.

She gripped the medallion tightly in her hands. The throb in her fingertips mocked of the state of her heart. She felt the pulse once, twice before her hand sprung open. A small army of snorting and sniffing hounds raced in her direction. Their snouts were pressed into the snow, their tales wagging wildly in thrill of the hunt. Leaping to her feet, Christine stiffened. One small drift of the breeze sent them rushing toward her.

Her shriek echoed around Loup's laugh.

"Call them off! What do they want?" Snapping dogs nipped at her ankles.

"They are merely running though their drill, Comtess de Chagny." He indicated her from head to toe. "You are far too refined and elegant compared to my Anna, but a woman is a woman."

Christine kicked at a snapping dog, but succeeded in only injuring air. "How dare you. How dare you train these dogs to my scent!"

"Not your scent, pretty lady, the Phantom's."

She froze. He whistled and commanded his dogs to rest. Instantly, the hounds flattened themselves against the ground. Their eyes never left their target.

"What are you talking about?" Christine bit out. Loup meandered over and circled her. He sniffed loudly. She flinched at the disgusting, watery sound.

"They are practicing. You are looking forward to Lyon, no?"

"I'm not going to Lyon."

Loup pulled a letter out of his pocket and handed it to her. Her name flashed in front of her eyes seconds before he snatched it away.

Christine gasped indignantly. "You opened my personal correspondence? When my husband finds out about this—"

"Your husband is the one who gave it to me," Loup said, sweetly. "It was addressed to him." He handed her the note.

Her heart turned over when she read: "The Opera National would be honored to have the famous diva perform." She hugged the letter to her chest in utter disbelief. Christine had longed to sing one last time before becoming a mother and before her role as a noblewoman took over her soul. She begged Raoul time and again for one last chance to sing when pregnant with André. But heated discussions every time she had broached the subject would ensue. He argued about roles and responsibilities and reminded her that her place was no longer on the stage. More ardent than that, he expressed his fear of sending her into the jaws of a lion. What if Erik were to find out, he had pleaded? How could he live if anything happened to her? How would he explain to their son?

She unfolded a smaller piece of paper scrawled with Raoul's handwriting. Christine's sigh left on a smoky puff of white.

You know why I leave for Lyon and I know you do not agree with my quest for information. I promised you the world when I gave you my heart and title. Forgive me my words, Little Lotte. If singing one last time forgives me for what I do to your 'Angel of Music,' then take my blessings and do what you must. Be by my side in this, Christine. My brother is already gone. I cannot lose the woman who stole my heart.

She folded the note and thrust it into her muffler to make haste to her husband's arms.

Loup's hand shot out. He grabbed her sleeve. "Not so fast, my dear Comtess. We must get to know each other."

Christine instantly recoiled at his touch, yanking out of his reach. The sleeve tore; leaving a gaping hole in what was an elegant lace cuff. Loup held the bit of lace before his eyes. His lips puckered as he kissed it and shoved it in his waistcoat pocket. She stared at him wide-eyed. Loup shrugged.

"I like tokens of my toys. Your husband insists I accompany you on your jaunt to the Opera National. He mentioned something about fearing for your pretty head and his darling little daughter." Christine backed away when he reached for her belly. He sniffed again. "You must have seen the Phantom many times for his scent to linger so strongly around you."

"I don't know what you mean. I have not seen him since this manhunt started."

Loup clicked his tongue. It twisted his face in such a way Christine shrunk. "Come now, even a stranger barely on your estate for any amount of time can see you shying away from the Comte." He nodded down the path where the spire of the church jutted toward the clouds. "You head to the forgiving arms of the church. You purchase charms to convince yourself of your affections for your husband." Her lips slipped open as she clutched the medallion. "You spread you legs to keep him content. You try to act all demure and innocent, but I know."

"You know what?"

"I won't get in your way. I promise," Loup assured. "The stories I have heard of him are fascinating. Is it an alluring fantasy? His bony body pressed against your soft flesh? Perhaps I will participate. Do you think he will like three?"

"I don't know what you are talking about."

"I speak of the Phantom, Comtess." Stopping behind her, he reached around with his arm, giving a broad gesture though the air. "Perhaps you wonder what elegantly appointed room in your humble chateau you will have your next rendezvous? Perhaps Monsieur le Comte will watch? I like to watch."

"You disgusting man! Finding him is why my husband hired you. I want the Phantom locked away."

Loup cooed into her ear. "Rumors have lingered through the years of your obsession with him—your secret love for another man. You must still be obsessed with him. Why else would you be covered in his scent?"

She stared at the cloak, pulling it tightly around her. "This was never near him. What do you want of me?"

Loup's hands snaked around her waist. She took an intake of breath as he pulled her back to his chest.

"I want *mon Alouette*," he said sharply. "Tell me, what do you know of Mademoiselle Barret? Do you think for one minute I want to protect you from the Phantom? I only do so because the price was right. Being your personal guard is a waste of my time if it will not lead me to her."

"Unhand me! She would not be with him."

"It's your job to find out," he intimidated. "I suggest you cooperate with me. If you don't, I will make you. Perhaps you can find out where she is when you lay with him? That is your deepest desire, no?"

"You speak lies. I love my husband. I lay only with him. I know nothing of Mademoiselle Barret and the Phantom." She squirmed in Loup's grip. His excitement pressed against her hip like an iron rod.

A piercing whistle nearly shattered her eardrum. The dogs immediately began their tracking stance. Fur lifted, and teeth were bared as they moved closer.

"Now, now, Comtess, dogs and wolves don't lie. I know what you crave. The dogs know you still desire him. The question is if the other wolf knows."

A cold sweat beaded her brow. The breeze sent shivers down her spine. "What other wolf?"

"Answer my question, then you can retreat to your little hovel and Loup will leave you alone. Now, would the Phantom know of *mon Alouette*?" Fear clogged her throat as Loup dragged his hand across her bodice. "Do you think they are together? Perhaps instead of moaning out your name as he thrusts . . ." Loup slammed her backward against his erection. "He moans out hers?"

"He will be with her," she blurted. "They left the opera house together. I saw them in Paris. I begged him not to go with her. I need him. He dares not be in love with her . . . he dare not! He is supposed to love me. The Angel of Music chose me!"

Her stomach clenched, forcing acid into her throat. A trembling hand fluttered at the base of her throat. What had she admitted?

Loup shoved her toward Chagny. "Thank you. It's much easier to know I will indeed kill two birds with one stone." He bowed politely. "Fear not, your secret is safe with Loup. I won't tell of your earthly desires for another man. I'm not the wolf you need to fear."

The cold air dried her eyes as she pulled them wide. "What other wolf?"

"What is in a name, Madame? Your husband and I are one in the same, same hunters, different prey. Loup . . . Raoul . . . both mean the wolf."

Christine stiffened when he approached her. He thrust his hand into the cloak and pulled out a worn piece of wool. She watched in dumbstruck horror as he lifted the faded scrap and allowed the breeze to take it. The dogs chased after it, snouts to the ground.

"Like I said, a woman is a woman. The dogs don't care who they track." He tipped his nose to her neck and breathed deeply. "So long as it smells like Anna" Christine jerked her head away as soon as his tongue swirled round her ear. "I wouldn't tell your husband of this Comtess de Chagny, if you know what is good for you. Whatever will he do if I told him of your confession? I wish I had trained the dogs to the Phantom's scent after all. Either way, what I uncovered is enlightening."

Seven

Soft gauze served as a divide between fear and loneliness. Traveling the countryside of Belgium and France in her youth, Anna never had a need to touch that veil. It fell where it fell and her ability to see through it was never obscured. Loneliness didn't touch her as a child when nights brought vagabonds together in communal camps. Fear was something she pushed aside like an unwanted dog, prompted by the life of crime she had been forced to live. Oddly, as the roads wore on, Anna finally found fear and loneliness creeping under the protective shroud.

She sat on the outskirts of the latest communal camp away from the camaraderie of the other travelers. Her thoughts were scattered as she scanned the area for dogs. The rabbit blood on her hands vividly reminded her of the hound Erik killed. It sparked a long history of memories she dared not voice.

There had barely been any discussion regarding the night the decree showed up and the child she carried. Anna tried to convince herself Erik's distance had nothing to do with Christine, though mention of her name would launch him into a distant melancholy. The thoughts hung over her head like a thundercloud threatening to break open and drown her at any moment.

Her stomach clenched as she watched a stray hound jog from camp to camp, nose to ground in search of food. If that dog came near her, she swore she would snap in two. She used her dress to clear her bloody hands before she wiped her brow. Word had spread far and wide, forcing the unlikely trio to move at a fevered pace. The countryside was not gentle to pregnancy and the stress began to take its toll. When Anna lowered her hand, she caught the seething look behind Erik's eyes.

"We are staying in the next village," he said.

"We are not," she replied pointedly to the rabbit she skinned.

"You cannot keep going at this pace. You are not healthy. You are tiring and entirely too thin."

"I'm fine," she mumbled, using her dress again to wipe her hands clear of fur and blood. She threaded the rabbit onto a makeshift spit and handed it to Pappy.

"You are not fine," Erik declared with an insane wag of his head.

Anna recoiled. Pappy gestured at him with the naked rabbit. "Watch it, Maestro, calm down." He pointed to her. "He's right."

"I'm fine," she lied. "Besides, explain to me why you care about my state?"

"You are with child. You need pause to get healthy." The ice behind Erik's words nearly doused the fire.

Tossing the pelt aside, she stood. Skinning and gutting rabbits did not exactly do a service to a stomach already unsettled by pregnancy. The stray hound padded around. Anna hastened out of camp, Erik nipping at her heels.

* * * *

He loomed over her as she plunked down beneath a distant tree. Standing in front of her, he watched as she tore blades of grass up by the roots. First the injustice to an innocent rabbit, now she abused perfectly good grass instead of acknowledging his glares. The blades she dug at turned her fingers green. She kept her attention on the ground and refused to meet his eyes.

"There are things you do not understand, Anna."

She yanked a clump and threw it in a pile. "How do you expect us to settle in some village?"

"I have moved freely all my life. I am not a man to be held at bay by any other. I will find a room for us to let."

"A room to let? With what money?" Anna shot him such a look of contempt he knew better than to suggest the money he stripped from her dead father's pocket before crushing his windpipe.

"You forget, I returned to the opera house while the carriage house burned so I could see to your needs. I took what coin I had before I left."

"Then forgive me for forcing you to waste your wealth on me and for demeaning you to live like a peasant. I truly apologize for being a wanted criminal and altering your rich and illustrious future."

Her testy sarcasm heated the back of his neck. “I care not for my future, but that of my child. Frankly woman, you have no say in the matter. Do not challenge me, you will lose.”

Her head jerked up. She looked him squarely in the face. “Your child?”

The intensity of her stare forced him to seek composure in the night around them. The thoughts that churned in his head for weeks tumbled unorganized in his mind. All he wanted as a child was to be loved. He would be damned if another infant came into this world rejected and unwanted by his mother.

“Anna.” Erik came to his knees before her. He gestured for her with a ripple of his fingers. She hesitantly slid closer. Unable to meet her eyes, he splayed his hand across her belly. The first indication of the life she carried came visible beneath her skirts. His voice carried a gentle, yet deep threat. “Do not reject this child when it is born.”

“What?”

Erik somberly removed his mask. “Look at my face and tell me you will not be frightened when this is what you bear.”

“Erik, I’m terrified.”

His hand jerked off her womb as if it were a fiery rock. One well practiced motion had his face caged beneath his mask again. He jumped to his feet.

“You always professed I did not frighten you! You claimed you could look upon this horrific skull and not cringe in disgust. That your perfect lips could press against the pitiful excuse for mine and not care of the deformity that lay beyond them!” He gestured to her abdomen with a voice low as a whisper, but cutting through the air with the magnitude of hundreds. “But now we know. You would lie to me as Christine did when she so professed to be able to look beyond this face and tremble only from the splendor in my soul. You lie and reject me, and you will deny and reject my child and there will be hell to pay if anyone does that. I may not be a man worthy of love and I am certainly not a man worthy of loving a child, but mark my words: my kin will not be rejected!”

“I’m not Christine!” Anna strangled the fabric of her dress. “You stupid ass! We are in the middle of nowhere. Our only possessions are a horse, a violin, and a crusty old man. Half of France is on our backs; there is not a friendly face wherever we go. You have been accused of murdering a nobleman. Do you even know what that implies?"

"It is nothing of concern—"

"It's everything of concern! Dogs are tracking us. I hate dogs. Now I'm pregnant and . . . I can't . . . we can't . . . why now? That's what frightens me!"

Shock washed over him like a flash flood. In the blink of an eye Erik yanked her up and twirled her against him. "*Mon dieu ! Merci! Merci, merci!*

Dumbfounded, Anna bolted out of his grip. "Erik, this can't happen."

"It can, and it will. For the first time in my life love does not confuse me. I have been trying to determine how and when you would reject me and the child I was secretly falling in love with. I have only known for a matter of seconds you would not, and I have never in my life been more in love with anything." He gathered her again, rubbing at his child, laughing through his surprise. "He will be perfect. My little piece of you. He will be all we need. He is mine. Mine! I gave him life. He is ours . . ."

Anna's mouth opened and closed as she struggled for words. Erik silenced her with a fierce hug, his joy coming late but coming sincere. He took his time leading her back to the camp. If he thought her precious to him before, now she was infinitely so. He nodded in the direction of the nearest major city.

"I will see what I can come across for a place to stay." Erik gently lowered her to the bedroll and sat beside her. "In the meantime, I want you to sleep as much as you can and when you can."

"Erik, you don't understand. If you're accused of murdering—"

He pressed his hand to her lips and held her until she burrowed in his lap. Erik stroked her hair and laid her head into the crook of his arm. "You will not carry the weight of my child alone, Anna. I will not have him suffer your ill health."

It took a while and several rocks launched toward a mongrel dog before she fell asleep. Pappy's displeasure interrupted the peace he found in watching her rest.

"I suggest you fill her in on whatever you have been mulling over," he rumbled. Erik lifted his eyes and looked at him with all the seriousness of a jungle predator. "One noble act of keeping her safe through winter is not enough." He jerked a crooked finger at him. "You have been acting queer ever since you read about that Comte's death. I'm old, not stupid. Don't use Anna's baby as a reason to convince yourself that you're not still pining for that diva."

Pappy shoved the rabbit into the fire and headed off to the company of his mare.

Erik held Anna close, keeping an intense stare on Pappy's back. He wrestled the pain his words had jammed into his chest. No man would tell him what secrets he should share. Erik's secrets concerned no one but Erik. He lowered his gaze and lost himself in the sensation of holding Anna in his arms. His temper was lulled into submission by the rhythmic rise and fall of her chest. No matter how far he had to reach or what demons he had to battle, his arms would always hold her.

Erik swore she would never know the piercing sounds of utter loneliness.

He kept that promise close to his breast as the night fell darker and wore on. The notes of the melancholy fiddler on the opposite side of camp rose and fell in tandem with a far off nightingale. With Anna nestled neatly in the crook of his arm, her warm body against him, Erik fought sleep with everything he could.

The music possessed him. How long had it been since he played? Absently, he reached across Anna to touch his shoulder. Fingers probed the flesh where the bullet had entered. Did Raoul not take enough from him? Did he have to mar his skills with a bow as well?

Slow, steady breaths abated his anger. He dared not pick up his violin. Music was his salvation, his hope, his one power . . . and one element that would make them more of a target.

Nonetheless, Erik longed to mold his voice with those notes in that sweet intoxication of years ago. Music soothed all things new and unfamiliar to him. The notes shifted as he rearranged them in his mind, filling his head with an unmatched symphony.

Erik abandoned himself to the sounds. With such an uncertain future looming on the horizon, he lost himself in the music. Sleep tugged at him, but he resisted. He dare not dream again. Too many memories of his years in the labyrinth plagued him at night, summoning forth that blanket of madness he tried hard to fray.

His body swayed in tune to what he heard. The cold leather of his mask touched to the top of Anna's head. She was inviting. Warm. He buried his lips in her hair. When she softly moaned, heat shot down his spine and settled in his core. She was always entranced by his music. She filled so many of his dreams. Even now, she filled so many dreams . . .

Erik turned Anna slightly. His lips came down around hers. In the distance, the nightingale mingled with the violin. "Sing, for me?"

Anna cooed sleepily in reply. Heavy lidded, Erik watched a smile creep across her lips. Tilting her head backward, he took that smile as his own, commanding her lips as the music in his mind rose. The noise grew. "Christine . . ." he cooed.

Anna jerked her head, breaking apart the kiss. Erik caught her chin and turned her to him again, the whisper of Christine still perched on his lips.

"Holy Mother-of-God!" Anna smacked him on the side of his head, first with one hand then the other. It bolted Erik back into his right mind. "Unhand me!"

Anna swung again; full fisted this time. Her small hand glanced off his jaw line with a loud pop. She rolled from his lap and pushed herself to her feet, pregnancy and lack of sleep not doing her well. She retched into a nearby bush.

The fiddler continued his melody and the nightingale warbled on. Erik staggered to his feet. He grabbed the back of his head and rubbed his jaw. Was he entranced? The camp slowly came into focus. Aghast, he pounded the heel of his palms against his eyes.

Christine was not in his head! Sweat moistened the flesh beneath his mask to an uncomfortable level. More and more since reading of Comte Philippe's death, he was being pulled back into the memories of those years in the labyrinth. Would they possess him at their will now? His chest seized.

"I strongly suggest you rectify that, Maestro."

Erik swung toward Pappy. The old coot cocked one eye open and shot him a look capable of leveling a mountain. Pappy rolled over and propped himself up on his elbows.

"I have had it." He was as pleasant as an old bear with nasty temperament. He pointed with a hooked finger and spoke angrily through clenched teeth. "Anna is willing to be out here with you, and you've been keeping something from her ever since you read that paper. I have had many more women in my life than you, and one thing I have learned is women don't like secrets being kept from them. Nor do they like what you just managed to do."

Erik slammed his palms harder against his eyes. How had he done that?

"You need to get your ugly mug across this camp and let that woman into your deranged mind or trust me, you'll regret it. You stand warned. As far as I'm concerned, you are not entitled to her love or that life she is carrying." He spat at Erik's feet. "I don't care if you are the father."

Such words flared Erik's anger but he fought it down. He turned to the bush Anna knelt before. She ran a finger across her lips and she refused to look at him.

"Leave off," she warned.

"Anna—"

"Erik, leave me be."

"Anna, there are reasons—"

She grabbed fistfuls of her hair. "There is no reason for you to confuse me with Christine!"

Erik sank to his knees and recoiled at how she lashed out when he touched her. "Anna, I cannot think clearly. So much has settled in my mind since I read the Époque. There is noise." He tapped his temples.

Her face contorted. "I figured as much, but you seem reluctant to let me in to share whatever it is the announcement of that Comte's death caused you to remember."

"I am sorry. Please—"

"How many more times is she going to be driven into my mind? I accept I'm second best, but how many times am I going to be told without word how much you loved her? This is not the first time since we left the Garnier that you have whispered for her in your dreams. You've reached for me before while asleep—"

"You are not second best. Damn it, woman. Listen to me—"

"Just tell me what's going on." She jammed a finger against the center of his forehead. Erik jerked away. "Madness or no madness, you need to let me in that head of yours. It is the only way I know how to understand you."

"Can you truly handle what is in this mind?" Barely governable, his frustration threatened to explode.

"I handled the time you broke this wrist." A hand shoved in his face. "I managed watching you kill my father. I handled burning down a carriage house and committing horse theft for you. I think I can handle your reasons for trying to make me into Christine!"

"You could never be Christine!"

Anna angrily pushed her hands against his chest and shoved him backward. Instinctively, his hands flew before him, blocking her second attempt. He grabbed both her wrists so passionately she lost her footing and splayed before him. As quickly as delusion descended upon him, it whisked away like a trail of smoke.

"My God, forgive me. Did I hurt you? Did I hurt my baby?" Erik crushed her tightly in his embrace. "I love you. Please know I love you."

She didn't reply. He couldn't blame her. He gathered her close despite the obvious tension between them. Emotion clamped his throat. There was no denying he would have none of this if not for Philippe.

"When did you arrive at my Opera House?" he muttered, hunching deeply to bury his lips against the nape of her neck

"Fall of' '82."

"You started leaving packages . . ."

She tore her neck away from him. "After the series on Händel, winter, of '84."

"Our first contact?"

"Spring of '85. What is your point, Erik?"

"My point is, until our contact in '85, you know nothing. My existence beneath that Opera House was like burning in the eternal fires of hell. The year was 1881. Shortly after I became involved with Mademoiselle Daaé and the vicomte, I had the unfortunate pleasure of meeting Philippe Georges Marie, the Comte de Chagny."

He curled an arm around Anna's belly, spreading a possessive hand across his child. From across the camp he pinned Pappy to his spot with his gaze. The old man should stand warned.

Erik *was* entitled.

* * * *

The Phantom's Labyrinth

He yanked the final bandage off and took a satisfying

breath. He cringed. The purple bruises up and down his side had faded to a sickening shade of yellow-green. His ribs throbbed, but not nearly as bad as they once did. Shirt on after much effort, he settled back on the divan. The piercing pain in his stomach cried for food. He should eat something, but it didn't matter. Nothing mattered except the memory of Christine.

"I did not purchase all this food to feed the rats."

Erik threw an arm over his eyes, hoping that voice would not come from the person he suspected. He rose and staggered out of his chambers. The stranger casually peeled off his gloves, removed his hat and cloak, and relit a few candles.

"How do you keep getting down here?" Erik stared contemptuously at the man's costuming.

The reply was bright. "I have my ways."

"I really should kill you. But I am afraid there is only one thing I want to kill at present. If you will excuse me?" Erik gave him a mock bow and turned to head back into his chambers.

"Speaking of killing, now that you seem to be up and about, I have a small request."

"So do I—go to hell."

"Stay away from the Vicomte de Chagny."

Erik moved too quickly and lurched. His ribs throbbed in protest.

His uninvited guest folded his arms. "I only assume you have a desire to kill him."

"What makes you so sure of that?"

The stranger casually lifted one shoulder. "You killed the vicomte's brother; the Comte de Chagny recently, did you not?"

Erik tapered his eyes as he scanned the room. He vaguely recalled the incident. "An unfortunate accident, my good Monsieur. When the Comte dashed into these infernal vaults after his brother, he merely fell into the lake." Erik gestured beyond his house in an attempt to cover his lie. "That corpse was already on the shores when I arrived. I had nothing to do with its rather untimely demise."

His stranger jutted his bottom jaw and scratched a fine moustache. "Tell me, how well did you know the Comte?"

Erik waved his hand over his mask, wishing he had the

strength to strangle his interloper with his questions. "I do not wish to speak about Comte Philippe." The man lifted a brow. With a gesture of impatience, Erik sneered. "He was no more than a face among thousands in my opera house. One rat among many sneaking about the shores of my lake. You can say I would not know his body if I fell over it."

"Ah. I see. It makes no matter whom you kill so long as it is in an effort to protect your humble abode." The stranger lifted his arms in defeat and let them slap back to his sides. "Well then, if he is dead he is dead. That is all that matters to you, correct?"

"You know nothing of what matters to me!" Erik thrust violently with his arms, grunting from the pain it caused. "Go already! Leave me!"

The stranger laughed. "I know what I can piece together. I cannot imagine you enjoy being here like a rat in a maze." He picked up an untouched basket of food, removed what was perishing, and carried the rest closer to Erik. "If I were you, my desires would lie in the arms of Christine Daaé, and I would have a taste to wring the noble neck of that vicomte she chose over you. Loneliness and betrayal is a piercing pain you know." He tapped his chest. "Like an arrow into a man's heart."

"Really?" Erik's voice dripped with sarcasm. "I was unaware."

"Keep away from the vicomte. He is not responsible for your loneliness. You orchestrate your destiny."

"What do you care for the Vicomte de Chagny?"

"I care for all men. Just leave him be. He is young, headstrong, and overly zealous at times. You gave him his life once. Allow him to keep it. Let him build upon it by staying away from him and his intended."

"A bold request, Monsieur. One I fear I cannot honor so long as I live."

"Then I will make you a proposition. You honor my request of leaving them in peace, and I will see to it you are left undisturbed and any preposterous investigations into your whereabouts dropped."

"How will you see to that?"

"First by turning the attention away from the regretful death of Comte Philippe."

Erik rolled his eyes and pinched the bridge of the false nose on his mask. "You are obsessed. Tell me, are you his lover? Because I am curious as to how that works . . ."

A low sound rumbled out of the man's throat. "Furthermore," he snapped, "I will prove that Christine Daaé's heart lies not with you. You asked her to return here and bury you upon your death, did you not?"

Erik's heart raced to his stomach. "How do you know that?"

"Let us say I came as a recent shock to an old Persian friend of yours."

Anger rose like a plume of smoke. No one knew of his connection to the Persian. He eyed the man's current state of dress. He again donned fine clothes, but covered them with the dress of a pauper. No one knew of him and the Persian except for one meddling man constantly underfoot in his labyrinth...

"Who are you?" Erik demanded hotly. "Why do you come here and question me about Comte Philippe? How do you know my Persian acquaintance?"

The man did not address the question. "Prior to your unfortunate mugging, you visited The Persian, no? He grilled you over the Comte—accused you of his death—which you denied. You told him he would need to pay for a line in L'Epoque announcing your death?" His stranger laughed. "Do you actually expect the Vicomte de Chagny will allow her to bury you should you actually die? You'd be rotting down here, never knowing if she ever returned. Is that what you want?"

Erik turned away. His face rippled beneath his mask. The stranger had a point.

"Are you such a genius you can predict your death, or are you a coward and intending to kill yourself? Think you will die of a broken heart perhaps?"

Erik's fist lifted to his lips. The agony of the man's words was too much to bear.

"If you want to see her one last time," the stranger continued, "then I will help, under the condition you do not set foot near them again. You never lift a hand to another person and you never murder another man—whether justifiable or not. You live in blissful oblivion. Allow me to assist in faking your death and I will see to it Christine arrives here as you wished."

Erik's lipped twitched. Fake his death? Absurd! Why would he want to live? Still . . . "How?"

"I am quite close to the family. She will listen to me. I am giving you the opportunity to slip out of their lives forever, perhaps even putting you on a path of more noble intentions. You are a genius, Monsieur. It would be a shame to see the greatness you could do, if offered the chance, go to waste. There is an entire world of forgiving men beyond these vaults. I dare say I am living proof. I suggest you take this offer, Monsieur. It comes at great cost to me."

"What is that cost?" Erik eyed him suspiciously.

The man's lips tightened. "I do not do all this merely for you. I do it so the Vicomte de Chagny can overcome this stigma you have pressed upon his good name. If you continue to press me, I will refuse to help, and you will never see Mademoiselle Daaé again."

Those words wrung his spleen. The idea of anonymity had been seeping down his spine for years. The thought of having joy in his life died the moment his mother masked him. He had been riding a false euphoria ever since, hoping to find a glimmer of happiness in his life. If this stranger could assure him, he would see Christine one final time—reach for hope one last time—then so be it. It might be worth the chance of living . . .

"I accept your proposal, stranger. However, you would be a wise man to leave my labyrinth before the person I kill one final time is you."

Eight

Erik's past had long been shrouded in the chill silence of the grave. For years, living in a self-inflicted tomb, the only roads he traveled were the ones built out of necessity—the paths that lead away from the optimism of men and into the dark sanctuary of silence. Years ago he gave up on glad tidings until a glimmer of light, like a small finger of hope breaking though his bitter destiny, bid him accept life could change.

There was no point in dwelling on his music, the Garnier, or his lost Madrigals. His life had become the road in front of him. He was not the curious pilgrim of his past, but forced forward by deeds that soiled his stomach with regret.

The hood of his cloak served to hide his mask from anyone they encountered. A freakish manipulation of his vocal chords had the boy at the livery obeying his every word without question. Erik took care to scrape free the coat of arms on the bridle sometime ago. He had no worries the stallion would arouse suspicion. It would have been preferable to keep the horses close, but where they were heading it would make for cramped quarters.

He could not afford the extortionate fees asked of him for a room, yet was determined to find a spot where Anna could rest without worry or question. He had the means to merely take what he wanted, but that blasted conscience Philippe birthed in him forced his feet forward.

He looked at the woman to his side. This was not how he envisioned life would be if he ever left the sanctuary of the Phantom. Somewhere along the line, Erik created the idea love was simple. When had it become complex?

Calling another woman's name while initiating par amore certainly had something to do with it . . .

Finding a place to settle proved a challenge. They wandered for weeks in search of a region that didn't know of the decree. He found it cruelly ironic a large city like Lyon would still be blissfully ignorant. Hastening west through the old sectors and up the hill rising from the river Saône, Erik didn't pause until his eyes stared pointedly on a forlorn building.

"This is it," he said somberly.

"Since when are you a man of God," Pappy grumbled, his breath huffing like a medieval dragon.

"I will take what is afforded me, old man. Do not get in my way." Tearing his eyes away from the church, he pressed forward. "I am in no mood."

Erik headed up the path, cloak billowing behind him.

* * * *

If the tunnels saved the Catholics from having their blood spilt by Roman persecution, they would do for the time being to shelter his Anna. An ear-numbing silence cloaked them and punctuated the maddening darkness. The makeshift torch of burning cloth wrapped around an old board added an acrid stench to the air. Erik wound them deeper into the catacombs beneath the Church of St. Irénée. He noted a small well still flowed. With the amount of underground springs ruining Lyon's streets, it did not surprise him. He stooped and dipped his fingers into the pool. A quick taste confirmed the water was not putrid. He leaned the torch against the wall and sent the old man in search of rags and some oil. Anna would need a fire for warmth and more light. His eyes were sharp as a cat. Darkness never bothered him. The tunnels were better than a communal camp where no one could be trusted, but still not the palace he longed to give her.

The thought of such failure made his chest tighten.

"Anna, it may be depressive, but networks like this will keep you safe and warm. I speak from experience. I will do what I can to find more suitable arrangements. It might take time, but you have my word."

He drew her into his embrace. Intimacy had been denied him all his life. It still amazed him he had a woman willing to have his arms folded around her. Forlorn and resigned, Anna didn't peer up at him. Her forehead remained pressed against his chest bringing warmth to what he always thought of as a barren housing for his heart. His hand trailed over stiff muscles as he followed the length of her braid to rub the small of her back.

"This will do well for us. The region appears to know

nothing about us, but if you must venture out, be mindful to whom you speak. I need you to rest. There will be no telling when we may have to leave. It seems to take a while for the decrees to spread, but if we are separated—"

"Head to Dieppe," she responded. Erik nodded in satisfaction. If Chagny forced them to move in separate ways, they would meet again by the small town by the sea. "Erik, I don't want to stay in one spot."

"Winter is fast upon us. You are with child. I gave you my word. I will find us a home one day." His lithe hand gestured around him in disgust. "Until then I will do what I can with this accursed life to see to it you are comfortable. For now . . . this is what we have. We cannot wander—manhunt or no manhunt."

"Manhunts," she shouted, shoving from his embrace. "Always the hunted, never the hunter! All my life I have been chased by circumstances not my fault, and now I outrun Christine's memory as well."

"What are you talking about?"

She waved around her new home. "Look at this place. Doesn't it seem familiar to you?" Erik followed her frantic pantomime. "You accepted the help of Philippe de Chagny and faked your death in underground tunnels just like this merely to have the opportunity to catch a glimpse of the woman you loved again. How am I to compete against such intense affection?" She wove dizzying circles around him. "I don't understand music. I'm not beautiful. I'm not graceful. I can't blame you for calling her name—"

"Anna—"

"You obviously belong with her. Why else would the death of such a man affect you so profoundly? Why would you run here? You don't have to keep it a secret from me that you love her. I discovered that in Paris. I'm sorry I got in your way. But I promise I can be useful; even if that's all I am, just don't leave me down here."

"Leave? Useful? Anna?"

"You don't have to love me. I'll understand. I don't want to be rejected anymore."

"What do you mean rejected?" Erik reached for her, having had enough of her twirling. "I do not *have* to love you?"

"I was in the right place when we met. You needed a woman. I was there. You said I could stay as long as I continued to entertain you in that curious way I did." Tiny hands pawed at the fabric of her skirt. "I know I'm a burden and you must want to return to her, but please don't."

Heat rose along the back of his neck. "What?" he roared, hands flying to the side of his head. "Have you gone mad?"

"Have you? All the people I dare come close to end up setting me aside because I've completed the job or the debts have been paid, or the dogs show up. Or I've finished shoeing the horses or mending the clothes or sheering the sheep, but I don't have anyplace else to go this time! So you bring me to a place like this, not to keep me safe but to find her."

"Is that what you have been brooding about? That you think I am through with you? That I set out from the beginning to use you to my advantage, because I could not have Christine?"

Anna nodded curtly.

The heat on his neck grew and burned like fire down his chest. "You think your job was to stay until I no longer needed your services? That I put my ring on your finger to claim you as my property until I figured out what I wanted? That is wonderful, Anna. Thank you for clarifying." Erik perched his hands on his hips. He did not bother with his usual efforts to control the resonance of his voice. "That damn ring has been on my finger for so many years I lost count. For you to think I would give it to any woman willing to bed me because I needed a woman . . . to think I am leaving because I am through with you . . . is it so strange to think that I am with you?"

"I'm not with you. I belong to you. We are not wed in the eyes of God, in faith before—"

"Do not drag your God into this. I gave you my ring for a reason. Look beyond your past. Do you think you are the only woman ever available to me?"

Anna shrank.

"What has crawled into that head of yours?" He gestured behind him down the tunnel and walked toward her. "That old man and his accusations? His stupid charges that I still desire a life with Christine? Do you think I would seed your womb and disappear?"

"You can't possibly love me. I have never been worthy."

Erik gestured at her, the fire behind his eyes blazing hotter than the heat on his neck. "Where is this coming from? I know your history. There were isolated instances in your payments to your father's debts that went beyond appropriate trades." The moments he knew about were not many, but clearly in the life of a woman, more than enough. "Are you telling me you think you are a whore in my eyes? Like those other men in your life?" Her downcast gaze said it all. "I am a murderer, Anna. I admit to doing what I had to protect my life and my dignity. I will even admit to not being stable all the time." He angrily tapped his temple. "Yes, it was simple to fantasize about becoming a common rapist for one brief taste of the life I was denied, but I would never use a woman to my advantage like that. I never did, and I certainly would never do that to you." Erik's voice dropped an octave. "When I bed you, it is because I love you. I ardently love you."

"Then why call her name? You lie with me, but still whisper her name. The stories you tell—"

"Did you hear anything I said?" Anger lit the catacomb like a flame to a powder keg. He rolled his hands into fists. No matter how hard he tried not to think of her, Christine seeped into his mind day and night. The memory served as a poison burning its way through his sanity, leaving the one relationship he thought he could grasp smoldering in its wake. "You do not want me to love you?" He searched her face for some sort of reaction, but she gave none. "Would you prefer I used you?"

"You don't love me like you love her."

The volatile keg exploded. "I have put up with watching the ruins of my life tumble around me, but this I will not put up with." He snatched her hand. "I strongly suggest you figure out what it is you wish of me, because I want the woman who wears my ring . . ."—he yanked it from her finger—". . . never to reject the Phantom's gifts, because frankly *Fräulein*, I will not stand here and be rejected in the way you are rejecting me. Trust me, when it comes to that I am an expert."

He paced circles around her, hunching into his words. "I allowed you into my life because you awakened a man in me I long forgot existed. I have lived my life like an unwanted rat in tunnels like these for longer than I want to admit. Philippe de Chagny faked my death to allow me the opportunity to start my wretched life over. He attempted to point me toward an existence beyond Christine—not allow me one last chance to start anew with her. If anything, retreating here is to remind me of him. Or did that never cross your mind? I had my reasons for sharing my life with you, and I will not have those reasons altered and manipulated by anyone. I will not be told I do not know what I feel or I do not know how to feel. I do not need people in my life, Anna. I want them in it. That I learned from the man whose death you so arrogantly claim is forcing me to Christine. It took me far longer than I care to admit to realize I was not destined to be alone. However, since it is clear you do not desire to have *me*, I will make that departure you fear quick and painless. I have been alone before."

Anna lunged, grabbing his arm. "Don't leave me. Erik, please—don't leave." She instinctually reached for his mask and lifted it free.

Erik snapped. A nonsensical cry clawed the air. His hand flew to protect his face. He stomped his feet in cadence with his anger.

"You insolent little child! Do you think looking me in the eye will make me stay? Do you? Then do it! Do it I say! Look Erik in the eye and tell Erik that you are different from all the others who came and went in his life. Look Erik in the eye and tell him his damnable ugliness is not to blame for your blithering self-pity." His face was inches from hers. She blinked rapidly, her lips moving in senseless sputters. "Look Erik in the eye and tell him you want this to stay."

He watched her try to form words. All she succeeded in doing was gasping for breath through a tear-clogged throat. Erik snatched his mask from her hands, the force of his pain rocking her forward at his feet. He stared at her bowed stance, momentarily struck silent by her seeming supplication. *So like Christine . . .*

"I have dealt with a lifetime of rejection because of my abhorred curse. I have lived with the guilt of my sins branded on my soul. I thought having my dignity raped in the face of Christine's rejection was painful, but your rejection of me . . ." Erik had to clamp his jaw shut to keep his vulnerability hidden. He pushed the words from his mouth ". . . is sheer agony."

He thundered through the winding tunnels. Warmth surrounded his cold flesh the instant he covered his face with his mask. Erik slipped the ring back on his finger. To have his love discarded by the woman he considered his soul, by the mother of his child, was too much to bear. To have her think she a mere whore—unfathomable. He thought she understood the way he loved. Erik refused to address perhaps he didn't understand it himself. Possession, control, what other ways did he know? Anger set course through him. He could barely contain it when he came across Pappy.

"What's got your knickers in a twitch?" the old man asked.

Erik reeled. His long arm cut the expanse between them. The instant Pappy's back rammed against the wall, air burst from his chest. "Stay out of her mind," Erik snarled. "Keep your mouth shut and your opinions to yourself, and begin to count your blessings once again that you have not met my rope."

In a matter of minutes, Erik merged with the darkness as vines of grief wove around him. He clutched at the void in his heart. How could she think his embraces were those of a contemptible beast, lusting to spear a woman with his need? He could never want a woman merely for the sake of pleasure, never, least of all Anna. The thought made him want to die. But he knew he could not.

Death was a luxury denied him.

He blamed Philippe de Chagny—his conscience and his only friend.

He swiped angrily at his face and tore off the mask, allowing the night air to cool his heated flesh. He didn't bother replacing it for a long while.

Tears flowed easier with it off.

* * * *

The Phantom's Labyrinth

Erik was on his feet, for what that was worth. The room swayed with each step, but at least he walked. He cautiously looked around for any signs he may not be alone, but the place remained deathly silent.

He made his way over to his organ, steadying himself against furniture or candelabras. He hissed in pain with every step until he collapsed onto the bench.

Hands upon his knees, he fought for a deep breath. An unfamiliar basket sat near the pedals. A sharp pang of hunger stabbed him in the stomach the instant he spied the loaf. Bread, cheese, boiled eggs, some random fruit . . . A note was attached written in his scarlet ink.

Maestro,

I sincerely hope it is appropriate for me to refer to you as that. It is too personal for me to use your Christian name, and I find it unnerving to call you Opera Ghost or Phantom.

I have gathered enough provisions to last you a while. I strongly urge you remain in bed. Last I checked you were still a broken man, and, if you are reading this now, hopefully you are well on the mend. However, you are in no shape to be wandering about. I will return to check on you in a fortnight. I have an affair to attend to in Norway. While this ceremony is being held in the utmost secrecy, I feel you might as well know it is for the wedding of the Vicomte de Chagny to Mademoiselle Daaé. I thought it appropriate you were made aware. Seeing as you are a man like the rest of the world, far be it for me to deny your affections for the girl, though I truly suggest you learn other means to display it. Kidnapping and attempted murder are not the ways to a woman's heart and being possessive and controlling not the best avenues for love.

Enclosed you will see the results of our bargain. Have patience and in due time I will see to it Christine returns to these catacombs to bury you. That Persian fellow will deliver news of your demise to them. He has followed through on paying for your obituary. I took it upon myself to pen the words. Put the past to rest, Maestro. See through the eyes of forgiving men (and believe me, they do exist). Have faith that someone will be willing to love you one day. We are all entitled. I expect you to adhere to your half of this agreement and leave the vicomte and Mademoiselle Daaé in peace.

Amicalement,

Your Obedient Servant . . . (My apologies. I could not resist).

Erik pulled out the clipping and stared at it. Slowly crumpling the page in his fist, he closed his burning eyes. Christine had married the boy. When she returned to him, it would be as a married woman.

He stood, his spirit more broken than his bones. He was not a man; he was nothing to anyone, nothing to the world, and nothing to her. The obituary fell from his grip; the sound it made upon hitting the stone, the loudest he had ever heard. Erik slunk back to his chambers not even conscious of the pain it involved. There, the small platform that held the macabre box which had been his bed for many years beaconed to him.

Inside the coffin, he wrapped his arms around himself as tightly as he could and curled into a ball. They would be the only arms to ever hold him.

Listening to the silence of his sanctuary, three words changed him forever:

Erik is dead.

Nine

Erik lingered in the shadows of the alleyways for hours, wandering from dark corner to dark corner without aim. Around him, Lyon throbbed with life. Hood up and face down, he could have been just another gentleman making his way through bitterly cold streets. Though unlike most he passed, his belly was empty and he was not drunk on fine wine. He avoided looking at the young couples huddled close together as they walked.

What right did he, a funereal beast in a mask, have to demand love from any woman?

He thought to return to Anna like a dog with his tail between his legs, but the buzzing in his mind made him stay away. She would only reject him again. What woman would take back a man with such an inexcusable temper? The rising noise in his mind grew unbearable and harder to think rationally around.

Stopping before a glowing store window, he stared beyond his black reflection to the trimmings on display. Ribbons and hair silks of every kind displayed the milliner's taste for the finer things. The ugly emotions he dwelled upon faded upon the idea of seeing her hair woven with such silk.

Insufferable fool! Was he condemned to destroy all that was good in his life? Erik pulled the hood tighter around his mask and entered the small shop, determined to do what he could to seek normalcy.

The bell jangled.

"*Bonsoir, Monsieur*," the shopkeeper said drolly, only lifting his eyes from the woman he doted upon for a curt survey of the room. Erik briefly regarded him then focused his attention on the dizzying display of ribbons. "Can I help you?"

Colors swirled before Erik's eyes. The bold emerald one would look shocking against her hair. "I want the finest ribbon you have," he said. "The green one—wrap it in your best casket and tell me where I might find a gift for an infant."

"Why might you need those?"

The tone to the man's voice lifted Erik's eyes. He slid them menacingly in the owner's direction and looked on him with a great deal of annoyance. "For the woman I love and the child she bears."

The shopkeeper never turned from his patron, who, back to Erik, stood like a statue as the owner fussed with the bonnet on her head. "The silk in Lyon is the finest, Monsieur. My price is firm and will not be haggled with."

"What makes you think I cannot afford your fee?" The pile of coin he poured on the counter clinked like high-pitched chimes.

The owner huffed and adjusted the hat. He looked coolly at the coin dumped on his counter. "You cannot afford to keep mud off your cloak, your boots are not polished and you wear wool—not cashmere."

"You would reject me solely because of the way I look? My coin is as good as the next man's."

The shopkeeper grunted.

Unthinkable resentment spread through Erik. His eyes darted everywhere until they landed on a paper behind the counter. Instantly anger molded to him like hot wax. Not even here—in a store to purchase a ribbon for the woman he loved—was he dismissed of the past. Noise mushroomed in his mind until the sounds became insufferable. He would never be permitted a normal life. The mere chance to apologize to Anna with a fancy gift evaporated with the words on that page. His destiny lay not in being a normal man . . .

With the reflexes of a cat and the skill of a pickpocket, Erik's hand shot out from his cloak. He stuffed the decree into his pocket. Having already dismissed him, the shopkeeper and his patron continued to study their reflections in the mirror. Erik watched them with utter distaste. The woman's eyes, however, were not on the latest fashion atop her head.

They were locked on Erik's blackened face.

Coins scattered across the floor as if Judas tossed them at the feet of priests in his rush to leave. Returning to the catacombs now would only jeopardize Anna and what sanity he thought he had left.

Only one place was worthy of him.

He had been battling the memory of Christine for a year and with one glimpse of the shock behind her sapphire eyes, he was convinced he should be hung from the highest fly in the Opéra National.

* * * *

The bell on the door rattled behind her, matching the way her hands shook against her throat. Looking left to right, Christine scanned the crowded streets. Erik had evaporated like a puff of smoke. Dazed and feeling she had a rock in her belly instead of her child, she turned to her reflection in the store window. Beyond the hollow eyes that stared back at her, the green ribbon was indeed the finest of the bunch. She touched her hair.

Emerald was her favorite color. Raoul always gifted her with blue.

She searched around her for her lost senses. Erik wanted a hair ribbon for the woman he loved and a gift for the child she carried . . .

"Christine?"

Her breath hitched when Raoul made haste from their carriage.

"Are you well? You look as if you have seen a ghost."

A coy flutter of her eyes and timid tap of her fingers added to her well-performed lie. "I'm fine, Raoul. Shopping has simply left me a bit winded." Her eyes roved over their carriage across the street to Legard and that devilish bounty hunter. If Erik was around, they hadn't spotted him.

"Come," Raoul encouraged. "Enough shopping this evening. My man will take you back to the hotel."

"No," she exclaimed, gathering her cloak close around her and pushing toward the carriage. "Your intent is to continue to the Persian tonight?"

"Yes, but—"

She stared at the evil gleam behind the dark beads of Loup's eyes. "But nothing. This involved me from the beginning. It will involve me until the end. I too have a Persian to see."

* * * *

"Knock again. Harder."

Christine looked down the hall toward the shadowy figure of Loup. Perched on the windowsill, his head moved in a constant scan of the streets below. To her right, Legard balled his hand into a fist and did as Raoul asked. The Persian's door rattled in its jamb.

"You seem uncomfortable, Christine," Raoul observed. "Why the sudden investment in seeing the Persian? You were against this before."

Christine lowered the hood of her cloak and discreetly cleared her throat. "Is it wrong of a wife to stand by her husband's side in matters such as this?"

The look of appreciation that heightened the blue of his eyes tore into her like brambles. She quickly looked away and stiffened upon hearing a deeply accented voice calling with annoyance from behind the door.

"It's ten o'clock at night. Who knocks at ten o'clock at night?"

A servant opened the door to reveal an older man scowling at them with displeasure. His color drained as if a cork was undone in his heart.

"Daroga of Mazanderan. Might we have a word?" Legard greeted the Persian as he removed his hat and gloves.

"No you may not. Go away." The Persian responded shortly. Legard shoved a boot between the door and jamb before his servant could slam it shut.

"Forgive our intrusion, Daroga. It is not our intent to disrupt your evening," Raoul said cordially.

The Daroga's jade eyes widened as they shot beyond Legard to lock on Raoul's face. Christine noticed a faint twitch to her husband's cheek that made his fine moustache jump. Raoul didn't often display any form of nerves. A curt mumble in a foreign tongue sent the manservant away. The Daroga invited their small party in. Christine stood behind her husband and watched the Persian's face twist as Loup entered last.

"I know it has been some years, but there is no point in wasting words, Daroga." Raoul said. "I trust you are aware that a year ago Erik mysteriously rose from the dead, causing my family great distress."

Christine shifted under the intense scrutiny of the older man. His gaze left her face for a moment to rest on the swell of her child.

"One hears rumors," he replied.

"Rumors cannot murder," Raoul said with little preamble. "My brother was recently found dead on the banks of the Phantom's lake. Are you to tell me that Erik is a rumor?"

The Daroga moved around the room toward a table and his decanter. Christine studied him with the same critical eye he did their small party, recalling a Daroga to be a member of the royal Persian police. Once a police investigator—no matter the country—always an investigator it seemed. He poured a small glass of amber liquid, carried it to the window and didn't turn around.

"What do you want of me?" he asked softly.

Christine jumped as Loup's sharp laugh broke the tension in the room. "Such formality. Tell me; are you two always this cordial?"

The Daroga turned, his green eyes narrowing at Loup's arrogant saunter through his small apartment. "Who are you?"

Christine licked her lips in an attempt to moisten her dry tongue. She wanted to shove everyone out of the room for a moment alone with Erik's former confidant, but she dare not act improper or betray the true reason she came. She moved closer to her husband as he replied.

"Loup is my bounty hunter and is working with Inspector Legard. He has been hired to track Erik."

"And Anna," Loup said coolly.

The Daroga set his glass down and lifted a graying brow.

"The Phantom's other lover," Loup explained. When he stopped uncomfortably close to her, Christine stepped away.

"Gentlemen, I severed ties with everything associated with the Phantom five years ago. It's late. You're no longer welcome here." He headed for his door and yanked it open.

"Are you telling us you know nothing about Erik's whereabouts?" Raoul asked.

One swift twitch of the Daroga's wrist slammed the door shut. Arms akimbo, he expressed his anger freely. "I'm telling you, I refuse to get involved. I know nothing of his apparent resurrection. The situation that occurred a year ago involved you and your family. Not me. If you are hunting Erik, that is your problem. He is no longer on my conscience."

"Do you have any idea where he may travel? What he may do? Where he might go?"

"Monsieur le Comte," the Daroga urged, "if I were to look for Erik I would not start by disturbing innocent people's holidays."

Christine looked in his direction in time to meet the Daroga's eyes.

"Please, Daroga," Raoul pleaded. "For the sake of my brother's good name. You always admired him . . ."

Those words bowed the Persian's head. Silent for a time, he studied the floor as though seeking an answer in the intricate pattern of the rug. When he looked at Raoul, it was with the intensity of a man carefully weighing his words. "I regret the recent passing of your brother, Monsieur, no one deserves the scandal or treatment that befell him. But I will have no part in any vendettas against what is history."

"You can't hinder an investigation, Daroga," Legard added. "In Persia, you were an officer of the law just as I am here."

The Persian folded his arms. "Is that so, Monsieur? Then tell me what evidence you have against Erik that should make me help you?"

"The mere fact he is alive should be evidence enough of his desire to see my family harmed," Raoul replied. "You know of what he is capable."

The Persian studied each person in the room before he addressed Christine. "You are with child."

It took a few seconds to unknot her tongue. "My second already, Daroga. André Thaddeus Marie, the Vicomte de Chagny was born almost a year ago."

His breath left on a heavy sigh and he hesitated. "Children are always the ones harmed by the sins of the parents," he said somberly. "For the sake of his innocence, if I were to look for Erik I would start where I left off. Paris, after all, is not the only place with an opera house." He scowled at the greedy smile that flashed across Loup's face. "But I would eliminate him traveling with any women. As much as he might have desired such in the time I knew him, he only had one true love."

Raoul's tongue clicked as he extended his hand to Christine. She avoided Loup's wink as her husband took her into his arms.

"Thank you for your time, Daroga," Raoul said, opening the door. He was about to pull it shut behind them when the Persian called out.

"I never want to see you again, Comte de Chagny. Erik is your concern. Not mine. But you must know one other thing. " The crowd turned. " No matter how calculated you think Erik is in his vengeance, deep within he is a repressed gentleman. He would never harm a child."

Raoul tipped his head in a polite nod and shut the door behind them. Once reconvened in the hall, Christine grabbed his arm. "I forgot a glove. I'll only be a minute." She quickened away before he could see the evidence of her fib still dressing her hands.

Palm on the door, she waited until Raoul and the rest of the party slipped around the corner before rapping once. She did not wait for an invitation to enter. Making haste to where the Daroga frowned at her from the window, she took his dark and wrinkled hand in hers. She pressed her calling card into his palm with a strength she never knew she had.

"If you ever hear from him, contact me privately." She said the words before she could control them and by the time her back hit the door the Persian's shock was imbedded in her mind. "He would not be with that woman. He does not love her. He does *not* . . ."

Ten

Anna puffed heavily as she hastened through the tunnels. The morning walks she began taking were doing little to clear her head. Pregnancy was a thief robbing her body of its usual lithe form. Everything seemed to be an effort now. The next few months were going to be long.

She frowned and stared at the bump barely evident through her skirts. How far along was this child?—she had no idea. Biting into an apple swiped from a pushcart, she made her way forward into darkness. How quickly she had come to know these tunnels.

Though wonderful to wander in daylight and feel weak winter sun on her skin, the walks became more of a secret patrol for dogs than anything for her health. She didn't mind the cramped tunnels of Lyon, they were far better than the rue Saint Antoine in Paris and the Cour de Miracles she used to call home. Filthy, sewage ridden streets, debauchery around every corner . . .

She tossed the apple core aside and tried not to think of the real reason she kept risking exposure. Erik was still nowhere to be found.

Unsuccessful in drowning her thoughts, she headed toward the dead end of a tunnel and her current home. Pappy puffed on his pipe. The usual wrinkles in his brow had turned into permanent furrows of disapproval since they had burrowed deep underground like giant moles. The weathered piece of paper she carried in her opposite hand crumpled when she shoved it into the folds of her dress.

"I fail to see why you keep looking for him," he grumped.

"Pardon?"

The pipe jabbed in her direction. "Your morning walks. You're thinking of him and you shouldn't. He's a perverse, selfish, and violent man. You should be counting your blessings he's gone. Good riddance, I say."

Anna folded her lips into her mouth. "He is none of those things. I just hope he doesn't hate me."

Pappy snorted. "I find it hard to believe that anyone could hate you, Anna."

Palms forward, she warmed her hands before the fire. The paper she protected floated free from its hiding spot. Her reflexes were not quick enough, and she watched painfully as it landed at Pappy's feet.

"The decree," he said in a strangled voice. "Where did you find this?"

"Tacked to a hitching post." Anna cleared her throat. "It's of no matter. They won't find us."

"Us!" Pappy tossed the decree into the flames, his nostrils flaring as the paper burned. "I'm getting a bit tired of the 'us' part. I've remained partly because you've endeared yourself to me, and I didn't do enough to protect my daughter."

Anna folded her arms. While she sympathized with Pappy's guilt, she didn't need to be protected.

"For another matter, I—for one—am a gentleman who will not race off and abandon a pregnant lady. But I demand to know why my blood runs cold every time you see a decree. If you expect me to stay at your side, then I demand to know the entire story. There's more to this, isn't there?"

"You know all you need to."

"I don't think I do. If Maestro is such a saint having saved Christine Daaé from danger and this whole manhunt one huge misunderstanding, then why do you walk clear across a road merely to avoid a dog?"

The fire was plenty warm, but Anna's cheeks chilled as blood drained from them. How could she avoid that question? Faced with having no idea whether or not Erik would even return, she made a snap decision. She had to think of the baby. As strong as she was, she was also a wanted woman. All she could do was hope the unlikely curmudgeon glaring at her would have a big enough heart to understand the transgressions of the two people he got irreversibly involved with.

"Erik is a great man. He is a misunderstood genius and, yes, he has murdered. But if his hands murdered, then all our hands have, because man made him into what he is. And if he did not sin, then I would be dead right now and my baby . . ."—Anna choked—"would never have had the chance at life."

Over the long hour it took to first confess what she knew of Erik's past and all that transpired at the Opera Garnier, Anna had never experienced such stares. Through it all, she saw the sympathy in Pappy's eyes and knew she'd convinced him of their plight. But now, after confessing her past, which had complicated matters even more, Pappy sat like an unemotional rock before the dying fire.

"Swear to me, Pappy, you swear," she pleaded. "Never tell him. Do you understand? Erik can know nothing of Brussels, nothing of Duke de Molyneux, nothing of my past."

Pappy rubbed his stubble and swiped the sweat on his brow. "Why? Why did you keep this from me? After all I have done to stay with you? Why shouldn't I tell Maestro? You're birds of a feather!"

"I didn't want you to hate me."

He blocked such words with a shove of his hands and got to his feet.

"Pappy, Erik can't know I'm a murderer. Now I'm running from two noble families. I'm certain the dog Erik killed belonged to Duke de Molyneux's head huntsman, Loup. Erik will do horrible things if he finds out about my past. You have seen how protective he is of my honor. If he discovers my father gambled me away in a card game when I was barely fifteen to be a whore to Molyneux's heir, I can't fathom what he will do. It's best our lives remain separate. I don't expect you to stay with me. I'm not exactly the right person for Erik, but I love him. I don't want him to know that I'm capable of murder."

"Anna, how do you expect me to accept all this?"

"How do I expect you to accept this?" she shrieked. "That is just it. I don't expect you to accept this. I'm asking you to. How does one accept murder? Tell me, how? I've been trying to find that answer for the better part of my life. It becomes the spot that won't wash away. It's the imperfection you cannot overcome. Christine is perfect, Pappy. Why would he have fallen so in love with her if not looking for his counterpoint—someone that did not match his imperfections? That's why he can't know, because it only makes me more imperfect. I'm already competing against so much."

The passion behind Pappy's gesture momentarily caused

Anna to jam her teeth into her tongue. A battle of wills was not on her agenda.

"What is this power she has over you? For that matter, what is this power he has over you?" He indicated the dark tunnel around them. "Do you see him here? No! I don't like him. I don't trust him. I still don't believe you should be with him. I certainly don't trust him and this Christine together. But all that isn't my choice. It's yours . . . or his . . . or hers . . . Bah! I don't understand this whole damn thing." He grabbed a broken board and shoved it into the fire.

Anna dodged bullets of sparks. "I'm not asking you to understand it. I'm asking for you to understand *me*." She nearly bruised her chest when she banged her heart. "I'm the product of the world I grew into. I've fought my entire existence to overcome my transgressions and this hunt is bringing it all back to life. I made peace with what I did. I spent years ministering to the poor wherever I went to make up for the life I took." Her finger dug into the swell of her child. "I'm now actually giving life. Can you ever understand what that means to someone who has murdered?" The expression on his face had gone hard, erasing the weathered lines Anna had grown fond of.

"I choose to be with you, Anna, but I never dreamed you would have been capable of such horror."

Her words ground out through clenched teeth. "That boy and his father would rape me—together—every night. They tied my hands so I could not fight. They struck me. I was scared! My innocence could only take so much—"

"I know, but murderers are murderers. Like the bastard that killed my—"

"That bastard was not like me! Pappy, please! My life has been one big con. Not a day goes by that I don't dwell on killing a boy my age." She shook her hands. "I still feel the jar of the knife passing though his back. I can still smell his blood in my nose, and every time I sleep I can still feel the weight of them on me. Every time Erik reaches to love me, I can't help but remember . . ." She shoved the feeling aside. "Despite all that, I feel guilty for taking a life. Molyneux and his wolves have shadowed me for years. I swear to you I thought they'd given up looking for me." When Pappy shook his head curtly, she cupped his cheek. "Pappy, you are the father I always dreamed of having. I won't stand in your way if you prefer to leave knowing how crime has destroyed your life—but it has destroyed mine too. You made a choice to associate yourself with this manhunt by covering for us. Chagny must know of you, and you can be sure Loup does as well. He'll mercilessly seek you out. I'm sorry. I truly am. But I can't change the past." She rubbed her child. "I can only look to the future. I've never had that. Let me live for you the life your daughter cannot. Let this be her child too."

Pappy folded his hands together in his lap and leveled his eyes with hers. The air in her lungs burned as she tried to read between the wrinkled lines twitching on his face. She tried her bravest to keep the tears in her eyes as his shone with emotion of his own.

"Swear to me Pappy, never tell Erik of Brussels."

With a whisper of her name and a nod of his head he made his promise and his choice.

Anna never knew it could feel so good to weep.

* * * *

Far opposite an underground tunnel, high above the streets, the wind caught Erik's cloak and whipped it around his ankles. Arms folded, he looked down on Lyon like a massive creature of the night. The opera house was a web, and he was drawn to it like a spider in need of a meal.

Frozen blades of air jabbed his lungs. He didn't even feel the biting wind. He had wandered without thought or aim through the opera house, higher and higher until he stood on the rooftop, staring across Lyon with contempt swimming through his veins. The wind howled across the roof. He needed no one. Wanted no one. Wanted nothing to do with the life he once tried to lead. Bitterness floated around him like his misty breath.

His life would be here, full circle and alone.

Erik laughed, making no effort to control the supreme power of his voice. Who would hear him anyway? He glared at the stars. The Lord? What a pitiful puppeteer He was. Did He think He could tempt him by yanking the string of one woman before his face while dangling the memories of another?

Pitiful fool.

Erik leaned far over the edge of the rooftop, the wind stinging his skin. A stone dislodged and tumbled toward the street. Anna was like stone. She was solid and tough, yet easy to break once he knew how.

The moon rose to its apex, making the stone rail shimmer with its imperfections. Like stone, she was ordinary on the surface until studied closely. Then, she was as intricate of a creation as he'd ever seen. Rugged enough to cause pain, yet able to build fantastic foundations that made him never want to stop exploring its limits.

Erik stroked his palms against the rail. The stone in one light looked one way, yet in another it was entirely different. All the hidden pieces shone in moonlight and blinded him with its beauty. Erik's eyes tapered. He dug out a piece of masonry.

Like stone, Anna was easy to dismiss as plain and simple. He flicked the piece off the edge of the roof and waited for it to shatter on the ground below. Easy to dismiss, until it multiplies into more than one piece . . .

"Why!" He spit at the heavens. "You wretched excuse for a Savior! What ridiculous cheat are you forcing upon the world by allowing me to multiply? Were you not thinking of your Angel of Death?"

The moonlight played across the rooftop, filling it with silver shadows. Erik pounced upon the railing and walked, heel to toe, perfectly balanced between life and certain death.

"Yet another cruel and distorted game You play is it not? Rear me in a life of no love and then dangle Christine in front of me by one hand, Anna by the other." Erik arrogantly spread his arms. He arched backward. "Are You taunting me to make the choice now, like I forced Christine? Is this some lesson?" He rapped his temples with both hands and squinted like a child whose point was not coming across. "Did You merely think bringing Anna into my life would change anything? You are more of a laughable Ghost than I."

Noise wailed like hungry babes in his mind. Erik deliriously allowed it to come. The only reason he was here was because of Anna's rejection and the alarming reality that seeing Christine again made it so he dare not return to her. Would he even want to now, thinking himself more imperfect than before? If there were a God, would he have allowed Christine to waltz into his path? Her belly swollen with what would certainly be a perfect child reared in a privileged life . . .

He closed his eyes as guilt glutted in his veins. "Create what You want in Anna's womb. You have already practiced on me, perfect it in that child. Perhaps You can get it right this time." He tore off his mask and savagely thrust it aside. He delighted in the cold blast of air that slapped across his skull. "Give the world another walking, talking corpse. Yet another signature of Your mistakes and Your imperfections. Breathe all the music and genius You want into it. Do what You want with it, but be forewarned." Erik's finger shot toward the heavens, pointing at a faceless God. "You will not destroy me, and You will not destroy my child. All the love You swing before me like a pendulum only to sever in my heart, is his now. I will not be rejected again. Not by Anna. Not by Christine. Not by Your damn world." Erik slammed a fist into his chest. "I do not need anyone."

The words chased around him like the wind. He followed the echo until they were nothing more than a memory of an awesome confession. Kneeling, he stared at the stone beneath him until his vision blurred. Perched precariously on the edge of the railing, on the fringes of sanity and madness, he clawed at the stone's perfections and imperfections until the tips of his fingers were red with blood. He didn't know how to stop wanting. He didn't know how to stop needing.

He wanted and needed his child.

Sobs racked his body, forcing his forehead forward until it met the unfeeling stone. Was this the weight of God pushing him to submit? Forcing him to bow before His throne? Erik's body bucked with the force of his cries. Alone on the rooftop he wept out years of frustration.

He thought to lean to one side and be done with it. The exhaustion over fighting his desires for Christine, the constant tug of war with madness coupled with fearing he would destroy the one woman who made him feel alive, was unbearable punishment.

"I never believed in Your sincerity of bringing Anna to me. Shocked are we? Surprised for a brief moment I believed?" Erik rolled his head toward the side and pressed his cheek to the stone. His accusatory eyes could have shattered the pinpricks of light across the heavens. "Congratulations, Oh Merciful God, You failed again. Anna can have You and Your Son." He yanked himself upright, his body going rigid with his anger. "I am pleased Philippe is dead!"

Spittle flew from sob soaked lips. His mouth spread upward. He may be alone for now, but not forever. There was to be an heir to his kingdom, a child with his mind and his madness. Erik spoke to the shattered stone below with an unblinking stare.

"I will have my child, in all his hideous imperfections. I will need no one but him and my music. I will need only his love. As for Christine?" Erik leapt to his feet. The wind flapped his cloak behind him. He leaned into the gust and taunted the streets below like a great yellow-eyed bird ready to swoop on unsuspecting prey. "Our character becomes our destiny. Music, like life, is inexpressible silence without its instrument. Am I not its master? I hold the baton. I will conduct what I want. I will have what I want. What is Erik without Christine?" Leaping back to the roof he retrieved his mask and turned to the opera house, his boots drumming a cadence so the ferryman could dutifully follow. A haunting whisper carried his sadness forward on the wind.

"What is Erik without the Phantom?"

Eleven

People were mindless sheep herded forward by their aimless belief in a Shepherd.

Hauling himself up ropes and across flies, Erik nestled unseen high above the stage. He closed his eyes as the instruments warmed up and listened to the familiar hum of patrons.

Idiots. Had they no idea of the wolf in their midst?

His shoulders knotted upon the thought of Raoul living high and mighty in his chateau. Perhaps, while he sipped his wine and dined on quail, he occasionally read a report of a Phantom sighting. Glowering at a box, Erik watched a young man escort a lady into the seat beside him. She cradled a boy of about five. The child might as well have been a moth around a flame he fluttered so much.

Erik's heart was just as unsettled.

His child solely kept total insanity at bay. He filled his mind by counting down the time until his birth. When the time came he would return to Anna, given that she didn't move on without him. He thought hard to hunt her down if she did, but would only remain long enough to claim what was his. Such would spare her the horror of raising a child like him. He would slip away to live out his life in peaceful oblivion. She was better off without him and the baby anyway.

Erik filled his lungs and allowed his discontent to dissipate. Slowly breathing out, he stared at the box that would be the equivalent of the Chagny's had this been the Garnier. If Chagny only knew he could be found exactly where they left off. He wondered, with Lyon being so close, if the boy ever thought to take in a show here? Wouldn't that be a delight!

Below him violins buzzed. The desire he felt when Christine would take the stage made his skin tingle. He pushed down his longing for Anna and shoved aside the image of Christine in that shop. The idea of taking Anna out on Sundays, swinging a child gleefully between their arms, yielded to a surge of jealousy. It squeezed his gut the instant he saw Christine's swollen womb. *That* child would have everything.

Erik rattled such thoughts from his brain and focused on the concert. Tonight belonged to him. He would think only of the music, nothing else. The patrons hushed and the lights dimmed. He would not think of—

Christine?

* * * *

"Again, thank you, you are kind."

Christine politely pushed her way though the throngs of people that crowded around her dressing room. She squeezed through the door, sighing in relief as Raoul made certain to lock it behind her. The resultant click was music to her ears. She took a seat at the dressing table and looked at him though eyes weighted with misgivings.

"You were magnificent," he encouraged. "Nothing outside of heaven could have bested you."

"You really think so?"

"The management would like to extend your performances."

Tight-lipped, she studied the forced smile on his face. Raoul never hid his disapproval well. "I am the Comtess de Chagny, Raoul." She took his hand. "My duty is to be by your side, not on the stage. Thank you for permitting this last performance."

"Come," he said gently. "I will take you to an early supper."

"No, Raoul. Please? If I am to give all this up . . . permit me a moment? Alone?"

His head dipped in acknowledgment of her words. "I will see to it the hall is cleared and the managers make sure you are left in peace. Take your time. I will return later." She turned her head to give his lips both her cheeks. "You were truly magnificent."

Christine kept a broad smile on her face until he shut the door behind him. The mirror mocking her did not hide the rings beneath her eyes.

"That, Christine, was horrible," she mumbled.

Pregnancy clearly took its toll on her. The surge of hormones changed her range and her abdominal muscles were shot, affecting her control. The audience seemed not to notice, thank heavens, and Raoul remained ignorant. She did have a reputation to uphold.

Christine tossed her head back and groaned. What was she even doing here? She never should have accepted Raoul's suggestion to sing again no matter how much she desired it. Singing came with conditions. Her skin pebbled at the idea of Loup lurking about. Raoul insisted the huntsman stay close for her protection. The sight of him made spiders march down her spine. He hid in shadows, drilled unsuspecting people with questions about Anna Barret, and had the hounds, those awful sniffing hounds!

More dreadful than the hunter himself was the vivid reminder of the confession to Loup that shook her core. Not to mention the fact that Erik was close—very close.

"Damn you," she whispered, sheepishly glancing to see if anyone heard her cuss, though she knew she was alone.

Five years ago she knew what she wanted. She had all the pieces of her life carefully arranged. But time is a caravan that tends to sway and shift as it wanders down the road. What caused hers to sway so drastically in the opposite direction of all she knew as safe and secure? She lightly touched the cold mirror momentarily searching the image for a missing piece of her life.

"Damn you. Damn, damn, damn."

Raoul had what he needed from the Persian. They only stayed in Lyon so she could sing. Selfish woman! She should cancel her appearances and return to Chagny. Lock herself away behind the security of its walls before she went completely mad. Hands flat on the dressing table, she steadied herself with a deep breath. She had no right being here dwelling on her lost connection to Erik.

Christine's head fell into her hands. Bit by bit she lost herself and was too weak to gather the pieces. The glimpse of Erik at the milliner brought it all back to her like a flash flood. "That was simply horrible."

"I would say abysmal, an abomination, an atrocity and—for good measure—an absolute outrage."

Christine leapt to her feet. The chair toppled. Her arm sent hairbrushes and various sundries careening across the floor. A brush skidded into shadow. Picking it up, Erik emerged.

Blood rushed from her face to her stomach. Erik returned the brush to its table and uprighted the chair. "You act as if you have seen a ghost, Christine. It is not becoming on you."

She backed away. "You."

Erik took a seat beside her dressing table. "You looked well, a bit tired perhaps, but life is obviously treating you with kind regard." He nodded toward the door. "Seeing as you locked that, I am assuming you fancy privacy. Your marksman is a bit daft. Really, did your husband not provide an accurate description of me? I am quite distinguished."

Christine returned to her chair. "It *was* you I saw at the milliner."

"Yes. With so many black masked men shopping for ribbons I can see how you might question that."

She sat stiffly, a sharp contrast to the casual way he reclined. "What . . . what are you doing here?"

"Last I checked I was fleeing from marksmen. Which would be why I am here, because they are not. Where I am, and what I am doing is of no concern to you."

"My husband has been searching the wilds of France for you. I knew all along you would be found where there would be music."

"Congratulations are in order then. You found me. Are you going to scamper off and tell the boy?" He leaned toward her. "Because if you are, I would appreciate you telling him I freed you from Richard Barret and Anna risked her neck to save yours. Perhaps if you do, I can get rid of the annoying kink I am getting from watching my back."

Christine clamped her teeth and took a moment to compose herself. "You act as if I can stop this whole thing."

"Have you even tried?" Erik's voice bounced from wall to wall.

"Why should I? You're a murderer." She said the words like ridding herself from a bite of a poisoned apple.

Erik sat forward in his chair, the legs scraping loudly against the polished wood floor. "That was in the distant past."

"Distant past? How dare you! You just killed my brother-in-law!"

A majestic silence leveled upon him. She swallowed a heated lump and watched him press his fingertips together in an attitude of prayer. His lip twitched as if he fought the words that wanted to burst from his mouth.

"I will not address that other than saying I did not come here to speak of Comte Philippe. I had nothing to do with his death. I suggest you recall what I did a year ago, Christine." He dropped his hands from their previous position and tilted his head. He crossed his legs and made a casual gesture that, for her, seemed far too—human. "You grow white. Do I frighten you still? I am merely sitting here. I would never harm you. But forgive me my temper. You see it has not been a comfortable year."

"Where have you been?" Christine studied her lap.

"Wherever the wandering takes me. I left everything behind—music, wealth, a roof. It has not been ideal. I would very much like those comforts returned to me for more pressing reasons. So, tell me, will you say nothing?"

"If you're asking if I am going to tell my husband you're here—no." She met his eyes. "I cannot see you locked away."

Erik rose. "You insult me. I will never be locked away. Nevertheless, in light of your arrival, I will not be here much longer. I tend not to stay in one place for very long. I have obligations to tend." He headed for the door.

"Are you here alone?" A yoke seemed to wrap around his shoulders, making them stiff as a board. "They're looking for both of you."

"If you think you are some sort of drug for me, do not flatter yourself. My affairs are my business." Without warning, he lunged across the dressing table, caging her in the chair. "You tell your beloved Comte, no matter what they want, or what they think because of the lies you are so adept at weaving, they are to leave her out of this. Anna's involvement in this charade is because of you. If I ever hear that so much as one of your Chagny guards has come near her, Raoul will learn just how unpredictable I can be." The chair tipped onto its back legs as he shoved away.

Christine grabbed the edge of the table to contain the tremble to her hands and steady the chair. He paced, his livid strides making his cloak writhe behind him.

"Not that I neither know, nor care where she is," he added, his laughter derisive. "If Erik is alone it is by choice." Christine cringed. He referred to himself in that bizarre manner again.

Madness made him do that. "It was merely coincidence you and I ended up in the same place."

Her jaw unhinged. "Coincidence you ended up hiding in shadows in my dressing room?"

"That . . . was intentional." He laid a hand on the doorknob. "I could not leave Lyon without giving you my review of your performance. Adieu, Christine."

"It's gone! I have lost the music." She panicked. "My voice, it is ruined. It's over!" She squeezed her eyes shut. What was she doing?

"So I noticed." Erik's head fell forward. It knocked lightly against the door. "What happened?"

She said the first thing that came to mind. "I fell ill."

"Ill? How ill?"

The genuine concern in his voice made a puff of air break through her lips. "I'm fine, but it took me away from the music for quite some time. My entire respiratory system was affected. I lost control of my voice, my diaphragm—"

"I know. Your pitch. Your range. Your stamina. Your breathing was hoarse. Your voice muffled. You had no control over your sound; your top range has all but disappeared . . . You have become a female baritone! Did your husband ever think of getting you the appropriate medical attention? You have destroyed my instrument!"

"I assure you he provided the appropriate medical attention. It has been hard to train again. I don't know what to do."

Erik jerked a finger toward her womb. "Think twice before lying with your husband."

Christine indignantly straightened as if poked from behind. So—he did acknowledge her condition. "Who should I have lain with, you? Jealousy is unbecoming of you, Erik" A perverse anger seemed to roll off him as he turned the doorknob. She instantly regretted her sharp tone and scrambled to her feet. "Please don't leave! If you are in Lyon and I am as well, then please help. I know I'm the enemy, but I'm not going to tell them where you are." When she took his hand, Erik pulled it from her grasp. "I need my tutor again. Am I not your music? If you still look on me as your instrument, then I know you cannot turn your back on me."

He threw his hood up and flung open the door, causing Christine to stumble backward.

"Watch me."

Twelve

His departure had been short lived. Like a man deprived of water, he had to satiate his thirst. Erik didn't want to drink from this pool even though he was led right to it. An undertow pulled him toward the currents of the world he knew and understood, and for once he couldn't swim. The monster of jealousy perched on one shoulder poked unrelentingly at the guilt that stood opposite. He didn't want to be jealous of Raoul with a child of his own on the way, but the power of such emotion was overbearing.

He found Christine, as suspected, still sitting pensively in her dressing room. A wise man would have fled Lyon by now. He resisted the urge to drown in Christine's allure and fought the blame that made him want to plunge himself off the National's roof.

She was a Siren and Orpheus unattainable.

One by one he laid his fingers upon her shoulder. Christine jumped.

"Somehow I never tire of that reaction."

"How did you get in here?" She looked in wonderment at the door.

Erik lowered his hood and made no effort to conceal his smugness. "Do you think a Phantom is only a Phantom when at the Garnier? The Comte's marksman is far too easy to entertain with a throw of the voice. That dog nipping his heel does enjoy rotting meat. Honestly, do you think marksmen and hounds could track me so easily? You really should educate your husband on all that I am capable."

"I thought you left Lyon."

"I will when I desire. While I am here, I might as well assist you—briefly." As soon as her eyes pulled wide he added his restriction. "On the condition you end this hunt."

"I told you, no one will believe my story. I don't think you realize how determined they are to find you. The past is the way a man is judged. Murder is murder."

"Murder is a necessary evil often forced upon a man. You cannot speak for what people will or will not believe. You believed in angels. Forgive me, but my halo is being polished." He flexed his hands. They tingled with the anticipation of conducting her voice once more. "F major and do my standard warm ups. Then we begin with *Lord of Our Being*. Seeing as you are singing Händel for this pathetic excuse of a concert series, perhaps you can bring him the respect he deserves."

As the lesson wove on, Erik almost completely forgot Christine sang, immersing himself in the music that had been separated from his soul for entirely too long. Eyes closed, he encouraged her voice. His hand undulated through the air like an elegant bird coursing its way across the heavens. Erik pulled the final note from her lips. It lingered until he closed his fist and ended her song. He held that note in his hand, like a man holding a blown kiss. He opened his eyes and breathed deeply.

"That was . . ."—he admired the beam on Christine's face—". . . mediocre." Taking a seat on the settee, he glowered. "I expected more out of you."

Christine studied the ceiling. "I have been keeping up with my music, I assure you. I just have a lot of other things which to which I must attend."

"Nothing should come between you and music. I thought I made that perfectly clear through the years."

"Time changes things."

Impressive, she'd found a backbone. Finding that he stared, he turned to look beyond her.

"Being back on stage is harder than I thought," she admitted. "I'm emotional over visiting the life I gave up. I'm not a Prima Donna anymore."

"Those are foolish words." He rose and stepped behind her. "Stand tall." She obeyed without hesitation. His arms carved the air around her waist, as if he were molding the idea of her against him. "Keep your shoulders perfectly straight and slightly back, elbows bent so your hands are able to rest on the junction between thigh and hip. If you do all of this, you should feel your chest cavity expand. It will relieve the pressure the baby has placed on your diaphragm."

The instant he came back into her view she fidgeted. Her delicate white hands, clasped before her like a dutiful student, were the picture of perfection—ideal for a woman of her beauty. He indicated for her to sit. Her hands stroked the fine fabric of her dress as she lowered herself down. He found himself regarding the elegant ruby ring upon her left hand. The scratched gold band around his pinky suddenly weighed more than a millstone.

"Tell me, does he treat you well?"

She discreetly cleared her throat. "He gives me the world and more."

"More than I could have?"

Christine pivoted. Ridges of shock cracked her porcelain skin seconds before her rapid fire queries bubbled out. "What sort of question is that? What is it about you I don't understand? Why do I want to resist you, but obey your every command over me? I cannot stop thinking about you. I'm lured to you and I don't know why. You insisted when you left the Garnier that I forget you, and yet you dare ask such questions of me? Tell me I'm not alone in such infidelity, for I betray Raoul over and over in my mind because of you. You are . . . you are—"

"Dangerous?" The room split with that single word. Erik's emotion was thick and suffocating. "I inspire you with horror, yet you cannot hate?" He lifted his hands in front of her face and caressed the air on either side of her cheeks. Though he wanted to, he dared not touch her. "I am that mysterious man in the palace underground? A man with a kind of love that gives you a thrill when you think of it?" He shook his head sadly. "I am poor Erik. The same poor Erik who has been subject to your lies. The lies your words described as hideous as the monster that inspired them. The same poor Erik who is subject to the lies you told a year ago that now chain him to a manhunt."

"You are not the same, and neither am I. There is a force luring us together. Can't you see that? You have no concept what that is like for me. You never have. You have no idea what it is like to have you suddenly reappear in my life. You flit in and out of it whenever you see fit."

"You resurfaced in mine," Erik said expressionlessly. "You did in Paris. You do so here."

"So be it, but when I do I speak the *truth*. You, however, claim to so ardently love *her* and yet where is she? I meant what I told you at the Garnier a year ago, Erik. If given the chance I can see you achieve greatness—as you did for me. I have tried desperately over this past year to give my heart completely to my husband. But I can't. Not when my soul belongs to another. I should spend my life in prayer for such feelings toward the man who killed my dear brother-in-law."

"Do not accuse me of crimes against Comte Philippe. I did not kill him! I gave you a choice years ago, Christine. Choice is dead, as I am." He stared into the surface of the dressing table. The reflection of his mask blended perfectly with the black polish. He was truly faceless now.

"Then why are you here? Because you take pity on the condition of my voice, or are you looking for something you lost? I'm not Anna." Erik's head snapped up. "You obviously lost your love for her somewhere along the way. You criticized me for loving Raoul, but perhaps you realize the complexity of true love. How easy it is to make mistakes and misguided choices when pushed into them."

Was it fear, desire, or dread in her voice?

The way she looked at him didn't hold a hint of rejection. What was this new confidence in her stance? Without warning, he called her name. It brought her toward him with slavish obedience. How long had it been since he had such control? The unexpected power made him swing around to face the mirror. His back to hers, he watched their joined reflections.

"You call my name and then remain silent?" she said boldly. Erik turned to look over his shoulder at her. "I could never express in words what it is like to hear you call for me. The Angel of Music chooses me, yet I am unworthy of having my name pass his lips. To this day I feel rewarded when it does. Tell me I am alone in feeling this unearthly connection between us."

Erik reprimanded her into a clenched fist. "You know nothing of being alone."

"You didn't answer my question."

Braving the agony mirrors signified, he stared intensely at their reflections, recalling all she had said to him in his labyrinth after his Madrigal and recalling all Anna had said to him in the tunnels. Like sand in a fist, he slipped through tiny cracks, unable to contain his confusion over Anna and caving to the look of empathy in Christine's eyes. He crept toward the door, wrestling with his mind and trying to decipher where his true emotions lay.

"Erik, don't leave."

The simple request threatened to consume him. Nothing outdid the unique bond of Maestro and student. No matter how he tried through the years, the chain connecting them remained linked. So many nights since Philippe's death and the memories of his more dramatic death, had he heard her whisper his name in his loneliest moments. A sarcastic laugh struggled to burst from him, but he fought it down.

See Philippe, she did return to love me. Late, but to love me . . .

Christine stepped closer and cocked her head to look into his downtrodden gaze. "Erik?"

The sweet sound of his name on her lips he couldn't resist. Erik fell into her lips before the warning in his mind had a chance to surface. His fingers looped the golden strands of her hair, and plunged deeply into the tresses. Holding her close against their kiss, he savored her delicately sweet taste. Any control he had disappeared, fueled by the desire for her that had never left his heart.

The noise in his mind rose to a painful level, pounding a savage rhythm matching his blind need. On the tip of his madness was Anna's name. Erik pushed it aside as Christine's hands slid around his cloak to find his back. He crushed his lips solidly against hers in reply, the hand entwined in her hair pulling her head backward so he could tower above her.

Erik stiffened when she traced the bony mountains of his spine through his shirt. She explored hesitantly, a signal that flared the warning in his mind. He was used to being touched without apprehension . . .

The noise in his mind threatened to split his skull. Erik ignored it. He trailed his lips down the delicate arch of her neck. He found her pulse and tickled it with his tongue. Her breath came rapidly. One arm supported her against his chest while his other slid freely over her throat, to the nape of her collarbone, down to hover above her bodice. A sound escaped her lips.

The warmth of a woman and the feeling of soft skin spurred him forward. He kissed her deeply, slipping his fingers down the cool beading on her gown. He molded her tightly against him as he left her lips to explore her flushed cheeks. Christine turned her face away from his mask and softly panted. Her eyes stayed tightly shut while her fingers dug against his spine. She arched her belly against him.

A throaty moan carved its way through his throat. That warning in his mind got louder.

Holding her closer, he found her lips again. How easy it would be to have her.

That warning pulsed in tandem with want for her.

Christine's breath swirled hotly against his mask. His body beat with something besides the natural need in his loin. The music he usually heard in his mind at the cusp of such congress was off, the rhythm and tempo wrong.

How many times had he dreamt of this moment? How many lonely nights had he spent with her on his mind and never in his arms? How many times had he thought to be with her like this?

Erik had experienced the joys of love; he understood how to please; yet this woman did not move with him. She did not know how he conducted; she did not move and sway against his lips when he did. This woman desired his embrace, but did not understand the music in his mind.

Roving fingers moved beyond her ribcage . . . lower . . .

Music and body were one with him. The two were as inseparable as man and madman. The noise rose higher and higher in his mind and mingled with that unrelenting warning.

His sensitive fingertips explored the sensual curves of a woman with child.

There were choices to be made. He heard the sounds of his name float from Christine's lips, heard the caution in his mind and chose between the two.

Thirteen

Christine Daaé.

Anna flexed her fingers as her muscles knotted in the cold. She looked around and pulled the newly lined cloak closer about her shoulders, thankful she kept the pelts from endless nights skinning rabbits. Biting her inner cheek, she inched her eyes up the massive marquee again and prayed the cold played tricks on her.

Christine Daaé.

It was no trick. The marquee displayed the diva's name as clearly as the sky did the moon. A suffocating sensation rose in her chest that could not be solely contributed to her extended walk. She glimpsed behind her. Surely the old man would string her up when he found her gone for so long, but the last thing she needed was two overprotective men vying for her wellbeing.

Days had passed since Erik left, and the more Anna thought about it, the more logical it seemed he would be at the National. Anna knew intimately the side that labeled him a Phantom. Now, there was no doubt in her mind he was here.

The doors to the Opera National were the only barriers preventing her from finding the truth. After spending years serving the Opera Garnier—mopping floors, polishing brass, cleaning boxes—she knew where servants could leave and enter a theater on their own accord. Staff hustled in and out around her. She pondered her choices. Enter and if this mysterious bond still existed between student and teacher, leave. Or, abandon this manhunt and abandon Erik.

She shifted, her breath coloring the air white. Her eyes cooled as they misted. Since he left, the life inside of her started to rustle for the first time. It made her not care who he was—her child needed a father. Hers might have been there in body—but never emotionally. Whatever Erik may have been in his life, he was still a gentleman with a heart capable of holding an empire.

But still . . . if he'd fled to Christine Daaé, everything would change. If he wanted his former life and love that badly, Anna would not stand in the wings and endure it. She hadn't become a woman wanted by France, so Christine Daaé could have the Angel of Music again.

Laying a hand on the life greeting her from inside, Anna scowled, took a deep breath, and plowed through the doors of the Opera National.

* * * *

Erik sat in a shadowy corner watching Christine doze. A few whispers of her name, a certain pitch to his voice, and she had fainted in his arms in mere seconds. His forehead tipped to his hands. The world crushed against his shoulders as that warning in his mind pounded like a hammer to an anvil. He clutched his temple with such force he could have crushed his skull. The woman he watched was not the Maestro that had taught him how to please, not the pacifier of his madness...

Not my life. Not my heart. Not my love. Not my Anna.

Reality slapped him harshly across his face. The last woman he had kissed in such manner filled his mind with music. Here there was only noise.

God's blood, what was I thinking? "Wake up!"

The sudden explosion shocked Christine upright.

He leaned out of his shadow, perching his forearms on his knees hoping the position would shove the blade he conjured deeper into his heart. "Forgive me," he whispered.

She fumbled in her spot as if waking from a sudden dream. "Did I . . . was I sleeping?"

"You needed rest. Neither of us was thinking clearly."

"What's the matter?"

A sarcastic laugh rolled out of his mouth. Such a question! There was so much wrong with this moment, he was drowning in his attempt to figure out which part was the lesser of evils: him, or the mistake he'd just made.

"Go back to your husband, Christine. A prison like this is no place for you. Tell him about this nightmare. Let this manhunt continue if you must, but recognize one thing." He stood. "This was a mistake. A weakness on the part of an old fool. I am a part of your past. Not the present, not the future—your past."

Christine's eyes fluttered. "Erik, this is not a nightmare."

"It is." He staggered from the shock, crying more to the voices in his mind than to her. "God's Blood, I am a stupid man. This is what she meant. She has been thinking I meant to reject her. That all along she was a substitute for *you*. I betrayed her." If he could, he would scrub his lips clear from his face to erase the memory of where they had been. *I betrayed them. She is with child.* "I have made my choice a thousand times over now."

"You said you were alone. You're still with her?"

Erik hastened toward the door.

"You can't leave. You need to accept that there are feelings here."

"I have accepted it." He gestured to the disaster he created. "I realize I am indeed blindly and passionately in love with a woman and I cannot keep trying to make her into you." A finger jammed in her direction. "This manhunt and my damn inability to let go of the past. It has prevented me from moving on. Kept me from being willing to accept my life as it is. Kept me clinging to you. No more, Christine. No more memories of my hell, no more thoughts of madness, and no more memories of you. I do not want them. I want to be free. I want her." He watched Christine's face pale and her eyes well up. It softened his anger. "Tell Raoul about this. I do not care what he will do to me, but you cannot hide behind this. It will destroy you. I strongly suggest you do, because this is the last time you will ever see my face. For both our sakes."

"Tell him?" Christine gasped. "I can't do that. This will add one more reason to his list to hunt you down. He will kill you, Erik."

His hand rested upon the knob.

"Don't leave me again. You can't kiss a woman with such passion and simply dismiss her."

Erik rounded. Responsibility for the deed they'd committed would not land solely on him. "That took two people, Christine, and you freely partook. But it only takes one to end it. You do not need me; you need your Angel of Music. Is that not what you sought first before it came to this?"

"My affections were to show you I love you. Am I to believe you no longer need or want that?"

"I do want love, Christine. But you do not love me. Infatuation is different from love. I know because I found love and finally recognize the difference."

His words dropped her jaw. "You have no idea what you want. You cannot treat me like this. This is not over."

"It never should have begun. I should have known better." He calmed himself by closing his eyes and seeking the darkness he found. "I am not the man on that pedestal you have built, and you are not the woman I have placed there either. I do not represent the love you need or want."

"What love do I need and want? Don't try to change what I feel."

"You need what is safe and certain. I cannot give you that. Your husband can."

"You're so sure that is what I desire?"

What is it she desired? Erik studied her. Her indignant stance was straight and elegant, her hands rested protectively on the noble blood in her womb. He reached out and caressed her cheek. "Tell me then," he asked softly, "would you spend your life in shadows never knowing where you will rest? Would you not complain about being judged because of the masked man at your side? Would you endure cold nights, an empty belly and an uncertain future until I could give you all the riches of the world?" As he stroked her cheek, he reached into the pocket of his cloak and wound his fingers around a muddy ribbon. "Would you run from my sins day in and day out and rear a child with me, never knowing if it would be mad, merely because you love me?"

With the ribbon a lifeline to Anna, he stepped away from Christine. She would look anywhere but at him. Forlornly, he turned toward the door.

"You may walk out that door, Erik, but you can't escape history. When will you wake and realize that?"

Erik slammed his palms against the door, rattling it in its jamb. "I did wake. The moment you removed my mask and ran from me, I did wake. I woke the moment a stranger entered my labyrinth and challenged me to make a choice. I woke years later the instant a second woman removed my mask and stepped toward me, weeping as I kissed her because she saw beauty in me. I did wake, Christine." He looked at her. "The moment that same woman laid with me, bringing to this withered corpse the splendor of flesh and for the first time made me a man. I have someone who loves me unconditionally and for the last year, I have been systematically pushing that aside, out of disbelief something like that could finally happen to me."

He yanked open the door to stare straight into the eyes of Satan.

The hound leapt. His front paws slammed into Erik's chest. Dog and man fell backward in a loud wrestling match of snarls and curses. A scream tore from Christine's lips. In a matter of seconds a pistol pressed against Erik's face.

"I waited until you were done with your lover's quarrel," the man said. "I haven't had the liberty of bedding a whore of late. Listening to you two made me stiffer than I have been in a long time." Turning to Christine, the man's tongue darted across his lips.

"Your name, Monsieur?" Erik held his sovereign anger at bay.

"Loup, the wolf. Do you think me a fool? One must think like a cobra in this game, Monsieur. Coil quietly while the world goes by and wait for the moment to strike." Loup knelt on one knee. "While your voice tricks are amusing, I don't appreciate you distracting my dog by feeding her vile meat."

"Does Chagny think one man is enough to control me?"

"Clearly it is." The pistol cocked.

Erik's attention volleyed away from the pistol and across the room. Christine's face rapidly drained of color. A short nod of his head toward a chair and she obediently sat. He moved his eyes to the barrel, inches from his temple. "A gentleman would put such a weapon away in the presence of a lady in the family way."

"I'm not a gentleman, and the way your lover over here whores her lips out, she is not a lady." Loup winked at Christine. "Next time you should learn to lock your doors. You never know who might be peering through a crack. Now . . . tell me Phantom . . . do you have any other lovers I might need to know about?"

"What makes you think a creature like me would have multiple lovers?"

Loup dug the pistol deep into Erik's temple. Beneath his mask, he tasted blood as his teeth jammed into his tongue.

"Where is she, Monsieur? Chagny will be pleased that one stone killed two birds. Where is—"

"Mademoiselle Barret," Christine cried, leaping to her feet.

Loup jolted off Erik and moved with the speed of Mercury. Anna stood like a frozen deer until his arm swung around and the bullet shot from his pistol.

"Anna!" Erik screamed. "Mon Anna! You nefarious—"

He rolled toward the dog. One savage kick knocked the beast into blackness and clear across the room. A raw and savage urge to protect rounded him with a great cry back toward Loup. A thin length of silk whipped through the air neatly finding the flesh of his neck. Like sheet lightning, Erik's fury lit the room.

Christine screamed again.

Killing was a natural and commonplace instinct tattooed on his soul, but the primal need to protect the woman he worshiped was free-flowing in his veins. With split second reflexes, Erik jerked the length of the rope, yanking Loup toward him. One violent crack of his elbow against his face landed him into bloody submission. Loup collapsed in a heap by his dog.

Christine stood in open-mouthed horror as Erik bent and removed the lasso from Loup's neck. "Tell your husband should I meet this man again, I will not be so generous with my talents. The only reason he is not dead is because I have promises to keep."

The sound of that pistol echoing in his ears drowned out the first honest prayer he said in his life. His shoulder brushed the shattered wood of the doorframe as he bolted through it. Never had such profound and foreboding fear raced through him. He didn't even know how his lips formed her name.

"Over here," Anna replied hoarsely.

The enormous relief that threatened to slit his chest disappeared the instant he found her huddled against a wall. Scarlet seeped through her dress. Within two strides, Erik scooped her into his embrace and rushed for the shadows.

* * * *

The awesome rage behind Erik's gold eyes resonated in her steps as Christine tentatively inched from the corner. Like a child approaching a wounded bird, she reached down to touch the huntsman.

He ensnared her wrist. "Where did she go?" He angrily wiped his forearm across his nose. His shirtsleeve smeared with blood.

"Unhand me," Christine said, twisting her arm free.

"What in blazes is happening here?" Raoul's voice sliced through the room. He entered, Legard equally perplexed at his side.

Christine propelled herself into his arms. Speech became a terrible burden that had rendered her mute. Ice filled her as she watched Inspector Legard dig a spent ball out of the freshly shattered doorframe. He held it in front of his eyes, a sickly green hue coloring his face.

"What were you firing on?" Raoul shouted. "Are you mad? You could have killed someone."

The flare to Loup's bloody nostrils made him appear deranged. "That was my intent. So long as you are standing in that doorway you are keeping me from pursuing her."

"Her?" Legard asked.

"Mademoiselle Barret," Christine stammered.

"She was here?" Raoul said incredulously. "I leave and all hell breaks loose. How did you let her get away?"

"I didn't let her." Loup plunked down on a chair. "Anna is more cunning than you think. Besides, I was more concerned with protecting your wife. After all, that is why you posted me here, now isn't it? You would not have wanted *him* to get too close?"

Christine swallowed hard as her heart began to beat far too fast.

"Him? Erik? Erik was here?" Raoul held his arm in front of Christine as if holding her back from an unseen presence.

Loup sniffed and snapped his neck from side to side. "I can't say for certain. All I saw was Anna." His eyes bobbed unnaturally to Christine. She kept her shock well hidden behind the kerchief she dabbed to her lips.

"How did you get bloodied?" Raoul asked.

He spread his arms and lifted his shoulders. His waistcoat moved away from his body "An earlier disagreement over cards . . ."

Legard stormed over and yanked the flask and spoon from Loup's vest pocket. He unscrewed the lid. "Empty."

Raoul stepped away from Christine's side. "I will not have

this manhunt and the safety of my family jeopardized by your absinthism. You are to stay by my wife's side—at all times. Not leave to indulge in your filthy habits." Christine pressed the kerchief harder against her mouth as the lines around Loup's eyes deepened with his sarcastic smile. "Your liberty over this manhunt ends here. I find you with that flask again or near any drop of alcohol, no matter what the color, your business with this affair ends. Do I make myself clear?"

"You can't control me, or what anyone wraps their lips around." Loup slung an arm over the back of the chair. He rolled his head toward Christine.

"You should be lucky your face is already disarranged," Raoul snapped. "If I was not a titled man, I would add to the decoration. Duke de Molyneux will not be happy to find out the real reason his pursuit for Anna has fallen lax over the years is because you would prefer to chase enlightenment on more than the wings of green fairies. Dare I assume your tastes include laudanum as well? Has that perhaps slowed you in more ways than one?"

Raoul's moustache twitched betraying his nerves. He made a risky move with such a bluff, but it worked. Loup stiffened.

"If you so much as touch your lips to anything again, I will see you on a one-way ride to the mad house," Raoul said.

"It is no place I haven't seen before." Loup got to his feet and straightened his waistcoat.

The resolve dressing her husband made her hands tremble, but didn't faze the wolf one bit. He clearly appeared to her to have the upper hand.

"*Mon Alouette* is cunning." Loup leered at his incapacitated dog. "I will need the balance of my hounds kenneled at Chagny. When we return, I will leave immediately to see for myself if Anna Barret is still a part of your Phantom. Instead of pondering mad houses, perhaps you should consider checking in with your Persian fellow again. Remember, the hunted linger around those they know." Loup regarded Christine. "You should be sure he is not—lingering."

The smile Loup gave her as he pushed into the hall made Christine nearly crumble like old stone.

Wherever Loup's well-planned plot led her, she was bound to follow it to its end.

Fourteen

Erik burst in on the nearest establishment. Kicking in the alleyway door of the hotel, Anna cradled in his arms, he cornered the first person he stumbled upon. The dumbfounded maid backed against a wall.

Erik poured all the menace he could into his voice. "A room. Now."

The girl stammered nonsensically, stumbling backward up the servants' stairs as Erik came toward her. With a trembling hand and two mousy eyes that never left his black face, she pointed toward a door at the top and leaned far out of his way as he pushed past her.

"You will follow," he commanded. Erik bounded the steps two at a time. Once upon it, he kicked the door open and rushed Anna to the bed. His head snapped toward the maid. "Find me hot water and what clean towels you can. If you do this without breathing a word as to why, I will pay you handsomely."

The girl whirled out of the room.

"Erik, I'm fine," Anna said breathlessly.

"You are bleeding."

"It's nothing . . ."

Erik tore off her cloak and frantically rolled her sleeve. The breath he'd held escaped his lungs as soon as he saw her arm. Aside from jagged bits of wood impaled in her arm and some badly torn flesh, the damage Loup did was mostly to the door. The only thing saving his knees from buckling in relief was the door opening. The white-faced maid trembled with such ferocity the bowl and pitcher of steaming water rattled in her arms.

Striding across the room, he spoke as softly as he could. "Speak of this to no one. You are in no trouble." He relieved her of her wares and pressed two coins into her palm. He nodded her toward the hall. “Go.” Obediently, as if she had known and adhered to his whims for years, she left and closed the door behind her.

Erik’s thoughts sloshed in his head like the water did in the basin he carried. He tended Anna’s arm, wincing when she did. He couldn’t help but notice something beyond pain in her eyes.

For all his years on the earth, he never suspected he would bear the mark of infidelity. Murderer, madman, those were both badges well tarnished on his chest, but lover? Even the simple joy of having a woman merely look on him in love was an unfathomable thought when it occurred. For the most part, his life had been lived in vain, until Anna arrived. The task of setting right the wrong he’d committed terrified more than that gunshot.

Erik never bothered to right a wrong.

“Chagny’s new marksman had no right to bring you into this,” he muttered remorsefully, pulling at a sliver of wood. “He is fortunate I did not kill him.”

“His name?”

“Loup.”

He eased up on tending her arm when ugly emotion flashed across her face. A combination of utter revulsion and fear unlike anything he had ever seen. He dabbed lightly at her swollen flesh. “He is an inconsequential human, Anna. Pay him no mind. He is merely an annoying bump to navigate around.” She was silent for a long while. Erik wrung the towel out in the water partly to have some noise in the room. “You were a fool to leave those catacombs,” he scolded.

“It seems there are many fools in this room then.”

The look in her eyes he could not comprehend. He tore a second towel into strips, bandaged her arm, and slowly rose. Only a small oil lamp lit his path toward the window. He stared down at the bustling streets of Lyon then lifted his eyes in the direction of the opera house. There was no telling how long they would be safe. No telling if, when he left, she would follow.

“Anna, promise me after what I tell you, that you will still love me.”

Silence.

His tongue felt thick in his mouth. “The theater . . . it was a comforting sanctuary . . . something familiar in so much change. With the noise . . .” He struggled to find room for words. "I taught again, or rather the Angel of Music taught."

Silence lingered longer than death.

"The Angel of Music?" she echoed. Erik curtly nodded. The small hand that caressed her brow seemed to try to erase the image from her mind. "You didn't merely cross paths with Christine then."

"She was performing. I assure you I did not seek her out. It was a coincidence. But I did call on her after she finished. I had to see if she would end this madness."

"Will she?"

Erik held his hand up in command for her to keep her tongue. "She still believes she has no control over anything, but she assured me she has no intent of telling Raoul where I was. Her voice was completely ruined. She apparently fell ill, if you call bedding that confounding boy ill. She asked for my help in retraining her."

Anna caressed her bandaged arm. "She is with child as well?"

Erik slowed his pacing. From what he could tell, Christine thrived in the throes of motherhood. Anna was terribly small and pale. His heart pinched so tightly he thought worry would bleed through his shirt. "Apparently."

Anna spoke to the ceiling. "You were her Maestro. You spent years working with her. I suppose you couldn't reject her request."

"Reject her? Wonderful choice of words!"

"What's do you mean by that?"

"I did not." His disgust flooded the room. "I did not reject her and she finally did not reject me. But *you* did. When I left it was clear you did not want me, clear how you perceived me. When I arrived at that theater I was wanted. My music *and* me. I thought only of me. When I would think of you, I thought only of my child, and it felt good to blindly think of someone who did not know rejection."

"What are you telling me?"

Erik folded his arms, daring her to challenge his next words. "I was intimate with her."

The sting of his words reflected in her eyes. Her hands clenched the edge of the bed so severely her knuckles went white. She breathed in and out, and for a wrenching moment Erik feared she would faint. Her lids shut as she laid a hand against her stomach. He turned his back, knowing he had sickened her.

"You . . . laid with her?"

He spun, his eyes pulling wide in shock. "God in heaven woman—no!"

"Then what?"

"Merely a kiss. That is all."

"Merely a kiss? *Merely* a kiss? I never meant to reject you, Erik. I felt I was being rejected because of how much you are connected to her. How much you seem to rely on the memory of Philippe de Chagny instead of me. She's been in your life so much longer than I have. I didn't want to be her substitute—or his. That's. . . we're not. . . we're not married, not in the eyes of the church. You. . . you left. . . you can be with whatever woman you want."

Erik swept the room with his eyes. He couldn't bear to see the tears welling in hers. "I can be with whatever woman I want? You act as if amorous rites would have been a lesser offense."

"It would have!"

"You are unbelievable. So that is it to you? I just have the right to mate? Like any common beast? Are you going to sit there and profess you understood this so simply?"

Anna shook her head, sending her braid whipping side to side. "No, Erik. I don't understand this. I don't understand any of this. Except what I feared is true. I became hunted for no reason. I am second in your eyes to Christine. I was from the start and will be from now on, so just go." She leapt to her feet. "Leave me alone, but tell me one thing first." A finger appeared in his face. He knocked it away. "As you were kissing her was that thing on or off?"

"What?"

"That mask, on or off?"

Erik's hands convulsed open and closed. His teeth ground together so he heard it in his ears. Fury bubbled from deep in his spleen. That moment with Christine hadn't been without barriers. "On."

"Before you leave, you remember one thing," she bit, pressing the back of her hand against her mouth and nose. "My body has been the vessel for many men. The one thing they would never do as they abused my honor was to kiss me with any sense of longing or affection. They only took what they needed to get their filthy relief. So, yes, if you had lain with her, it would have been less of an offense." The tears in her voice caused her tongue to tangle. "Because the most intimate moment in my life, is and was, when you gave me my first kiss—a real, loving, desired kiss. Now that is gone." When she grabbed her arm and bent her body, Erik had the sense the pain was from more than her wound. "When I would reach for you, the first thing I always took off was that mask because I made love to the man, not the Angel of Music, not the Phantom—the man." She raced for the door.

Erik lunged, snaring her hand. "It did not feel right."

"That doesn't make it any better. Not after the choice I made for you, not after carrying a part of you inside me."

"I did not want this to happen, Anna."

"But did you want her? After all she has caused, did you want her?"

Erik could easily lie, but Anna would see right through that. "Yes, but it did not feel right."

"Your lips touched hers. You wanted her. You could have fulfilled her. I don't care what it felt like." She leaned all her weight away.

"When I kissed her, there was something between us."

"Good for you. Glad to know of your passions!"

"There was *something* between us!" He twirled Anna into him, his fingers grabbing at his child. "I could have kept this from you and you would have been none the wiser, but I cannot lie to you. I betrayed you as the world betrayed me, and you need to understand one thing." He pressed his lips close to her ear so she would feel the fervor of his words. "I am not a normal man. I spent my life creating ways to keep the world, man, out of my existence, because mankind did nothing but shun me. I am not comfortable walking among men and dealing with emotions that belong to normal men. I will deal with deciphering them in my ways. Does that give me permission to do what I did to you? No. But in many ways this face gives me liberty to do as I please and curses me with the consequences." He lessened his grip. "What I realized when I did not have my infant before me, was the Opera Ghost finally played himself the fool." He pushed himself away and turned to look at her.

"Anna, you gave voice to a future I never had. I do not

expect you to forgive me, and do not expect me to apologize. This had to happen. I want to move on. I cannot escape this manhunt, so to hell with it! I will run as long and as far as I have to, because I am in love with you and I am hopelessly in love with my baby. If it took Christine to make me realize that, then I finally did something right."

Anna's tears fell like a steady rain. Erik looked around the room before reaching to stroke her cheeks dry. She yanked her head away.

"I don't have a mask to serve as the cross I bear, Erik. I only have the burden of my past. When are you going to understand me? Do you think a young girl like me will dwell on the rare, good moment in her life, or do you think she will focus on the bad?" Erik crossed his arms, attempting to block her words. "I dwell on the moments when forced to return to Barret and the managers of the Garnier. I can't get them out of my head. But I got beyond them by thinking with you I would never be shoved aside again when I was through being useful. I never had an opera house or two people to love me. You did." Erik unfolded his arms. They hung at his side as he watched Anna wither like a violet plucked too soon. "You have both Christine and me, and even though I hate saying this I don't want you to have us both. Not when one of us is responsible for so much injustice in the other's life." She pointed to the door. "I'm used to life on the run. This hunt for both of us ends now. We go our separate ways. Leave."

"No."

"Leave, now."

Erik dug his nails into his palms until veins surfaced on the back of his hands. "No."

"You don't love me. You love her. Now leave."

Without warning his arm arched out, releasing his anger on the wall. The mirror flew off its hook shattering as it hit the floor "I do love her, damn you! There was to be our wedding at the Madeleine. I wrote the Kyrie and composed our nuptial mass! Our wedding," Erik shouted, "was to be the end to my miserable life and that end never came." He collapsed to the floor at her feet. Glass bit into his knees. "Why did I even start The Madrigals, Anna? Why?" When she shook her head, Erik slammed his fists in frustration against the plank floor. "My life is consumed by music, Opera is my soul. I see music in everything. I hear music in every passing whisper." His head snapped up. "I wrote Madrigals because of the packages you left for me. Packages I never would have opened if not for Philippe de Chagny's blasted matchmaking. Of all things I can design, I wrote Madrigals. They are the foundations of opera. In the beginning there were no instruments, just voices. Voices, like the noise in my mind." His fingers rapped against his mask in tune to what he heard. "Voices which, in music, are manipulated to laugh, cry, scream, and sigh. Like my noise does. Like I wished to do in reality, but no one would listen. I wanted to write a new life and write out the old. Create a new beginning because of those packages."

Anna shook her head. "The Madrigals are gone. You can't keep starting over. The rest of the world needs to learn from their mistakes and so do you. We can't compose a different ending because we don't like the tune in our mind. Go. Leave me alone."

"No!" Erik pounded the floor until the planks split. He crawled closer to her. "Do not send me away. Do not take me from my baby." He leapt to his feet. "The only thought keeping me from plunging over the abyss of madness was returning and taking him from you, but I am not complete without you both."

Anna staggered backward. Her hands wrapped a shield around their child. "You were going to take the baby?"

"I did not want to be rejected again. My life has been spent in seclusion, shamed into the darkest places I could find. I was secure and in control at that theater. I am in control of nothing anymore." He punched the air with his fist. "This manhunt is. Every move I make is dictated by something I cannot control. I need to control!" He closed his eyes, allowing confusion to consume him. "You have had all the power and never has a woman had such rule over me. I wanted what I thought was solely mine, so I could return to the pathetic life I understood and do so without being alone." He reached for her and drew back sharply when she whimpered.

"Anna, it was a twisted moment between man and madman. I prepared to leave all of humanity behind again and there was no way I was going to leave my child to be rejected by anyone. Let alone leave him with a woman I thought was rejecting me."

"Who are you?" Anna's hands grabbed fists of her skirt. "Where did my Erik go? My Erik would not do that. He would not have returned to Christine. My Erik—"

"Erik is the Phantom of the Opera!" He approached, everything in his stance and attitude coming out in full menace. "He will never be only your Erik. Erik is not a normal man. Erik does not want you and Christine." He caged her between his arms against the door. A quiet shock rose behind the blue of her eyes turning his voice as gentle as a bleating lamb's. "I want you and my child. You must believe that." Erik slid his ring from his finger. He held it aloft. "I am a prisoner of my mind. There are things I will never escape. There are things I will never stop being, never stop questioning, and things I will never stop believing I am. I do not recognize your God, and we are not married in the eyes of normal man. But I will tell you one last time: I am not normal." He rolled the ring between his fingers. "I wore this so I could believe in the illusion I would have a companion in life." Anna stared intently at the ring. Erik stared beyond it to her watery eyes. The words fought around the lump in his throat. "You are my beginning, my end, my ability, and my love." He palmed the ring into his fist and held it against his heart. "You are my heartbeat—my Madrigal. You lift me out of darkness. Teach me to find the light."

He unfolded his hand and took her left in his. He slid his ring back onto her finger. Painting the room with a silken voice, he spoke the words he said to her the first time he sought her as his living bride. "Fate links thee to me forever and a day."

She responded by snatching his hand and pressing his palm across her belly. Erik's lips slipped open. He stepped into her and laid both hands across the movement in her womb.

"*Mon Dieu.*" Falling to his knees, his hands roamed across his child. A press here, a nudge there . . . he explored the life below his fingers, delighting as it reacted. His lips formed silent words of wonder. Erik almost didn't feel Anna remove his mask.

"This is our baby," she said. "He can feel you, and he can hear you. I want this child to grow knowing the man that created him. Not a Phantom, the man." Anna entwined a hand over his. "You've hurt me with a pain you will never understand, and that won't go away overnight. But Phantom or no Phantom—you're the only future I have ever known."

He knelt for a long while at her feet, like an obedient beast or a repentant priest, his eyes downcast and his forehead resting against the life that had long since settled. Erik slowly lifted his eyes to gaze into Anna's. She stayed rooted to her spot for as long as he needed her to remain. She cocked her head in that curious way of hers that questioned him without words.

Rising, he caved to the look on her face. He was not certain as to if her focus was with him or dwelling on the words they had let fly. He sought to find his answer upon her lips.

Nimble fingers raked aside the hair that hung in her face. "*Mon vie, mon couer.*" He covered her cheeks with his palms as he kissed her, artfully whispering her name over and over. "*Anna, mon amour . . .*" He controlled the resonance in his voice, making her buckle at the knees. She breathed deeply against his warmth and gave in, opening for him so he could kiss her deeper. Erik probed and explored her sweet recesses as if it was their first kiss all over again.

She shoved away, her hand flying to the blush on her cheeks. "Erik, no."

"Anna?"

"I can't. I'm sorry. I see you with her. I see you loving her and holding her and kissing her and I can't, not now. I love you, but right now I need—"

"What Anna?" That tone in her voice sent the music in his mind scrambling in unorganized notes. He panicked. Words were not enough? The idea he might still lose her tied a noose around his heart. "What do you need?" She didn't reply. The noose yanked tighter. Erik pawed at her shoulders, wrinkling the fabric of her dress. "Tell me." He fought for her lips again. She squirmed away. "Anna, what I am to do?"

Dread, heavy as an iron curtain, lowered upon him as Anna stared at the floor. He slid his hands over his exposed face, grabbing desperately at the mask of death he wore naturally. Fingers brushed his paper-thin face and ridges of exposed skull. He locked his hands behind his neck and pressed his elbows to his ears attempting to drown out her soft tears. He may never experience the glory of her kiss again.

What had he destroyed?

"Too many things in your life are interconnected," she lamented. "You need to cut the ties keeping you beholden to the past and let one of us go. I need your apology. I need you to find the man in madman."

Horror struck, he backed away. Mad and madman had been

intertwined for so long there was only one way to untangle them . . .

* * * *

The Phantom's Labyrinth

Erik cradled his violin like the child he would never have. He stared at the dying candlelight. His thoughts were washed away in a sweet and dizzying oblivion.

The rock dug into his back as he slid down the wall. A needle fell from his hand and rolled away. Collapsing to the floor, his eyes were heavy. He wanted to sleep. Every time he drifted off to give in to the drug, he was yanked back to consciousness until the cycle repeated. Eventually, he couldn't feel the rise and fall of his chest. He felt nothing, and nothing—was sweet.

He no longer felt the pull of his past. The jeers and the shouts of fear when men looked on him were a muffled memory. There were no battles between music and madness. To not see the horror in the eyes of man, to not be rejected or denied, but to finally be accepted in an oasis of peace—was sweet.

Most of all, he did not long for the scent of a woman. No desire for Christine.

Christine.

She had returned to bury that body the stranger laid out as him. Erik groped for the ring on his pinky finger. Dirt still caked around it. She buried the skeleton with the wedding band he had once given her. He had to retrieve it. Erik could not bear to see it rot for eternity with an anonymous corpse. The grave she dug was shallow—haphazard. She seemed more frightened than anything. His stranger was right—she did love the vicomte more than him.

No matter. His death was faked, and now, with nothing left in life, he could die as well.

Running his hands up and down the violin, he hugged the only things that loved him: music and solitude.

A trembling hand removed his mask. He wanted to greet Death without it. He closed his eyes and let it drop to the floor as the world slowed.

Death must be soon. Chills doused him one minute, heat the next. He could feel Death's grip lifting him and twirling him around like the mist on his lake. Death cried out his name

. . .

What a sweet sound.

* * * *

"Sorry son-of-a-bitch! You sorry, son-of-a-bitch!"

The stranger's voice nearly shattered his eardrum. Erik took an involuntary gasp of breath as he collapsed on the shoreline. Icy water ran over him in waves, the warmer air from the drawing room blasted him like a bellows to a furnace. Shouts pounded into his ears.

"I waste the better part of my time and—you blasted son-of-a-bitch!"

Erik's face violently slammed the water again, his head forced deeper. His eyes flew open underwater. He gargled and jerked. When yanked backward, his lungs filled sharply with air. Water poured off his body as he managed to roll away from whatever was putting him through hell. He scrambled away from the shores of his lake. Flat on his back, he shivered fiercely.

The stranger, equally drenched, took him angrily by the shirt collar. "How much of this did you take?" Erik tried to focus on the needle shoved in his face. A palm slapped against his chilled flesh. "Answer me, Maestro." His stranger poised to strike again, but Erik blocked the blow. "Good, fight me. Fight back. Get this poison out of your system."

"Release me."

"Pardon, Maestro? I did not hear you."

"Unhand me." All the hatred he could summon bled past Erik's waterlogged lips. A forearm pinned his throat to the ground, mangling his next protest.

"Make me." the stranger threatened.

Their faces were inches apart. A great roar tore out of Erik's core. He grabbed the throat before him, slamming the side of the stranger's head against the stone floor. He staggered to unsteady feet, his uninvited guest following suit. In a violent drug-induced rage, Erik attacked.

Furniture splintered into pieces as Erik tackled him into it. The collar in his stranger's shoulder snapped as their bodies hit the stone.

His stranger cried, but made limited attempts to fight back. He shoved Erik off with a great scream of agony. "That is it. Work it out of your body."

Erik silenced him with one forceful crack of a fist against the side of his perfect face. Blood colored the floor as the man hit it. He attempted to roll out of the way of Erik's oncoming kick, but it collided with his side. A second bone crushed, vibrating its crack up Erik's leg. He prepared to lunge again, but the house tilted. Both knees hit the ground simultaneously, that peaceful sensation rolled over him once more.

"No you do not," his stranger yelled. "Do not give in to that." He hauled Erik to his feet. "As long as this takes, Maestro. You can want to give into that bloody drug all you want. I might be a haughty, aristocratic, arrogant bastard myself, but I am not about to let you die."

Erik's face met water again as Death's grip faded away.

* * * *

He couldn't recall the music in his mind ever including timpani. The pounding in his head was remarkable. He hit the floor the instant he attempted to roll off the divan. Blinking at his empty coffin, the harsh reality of what happened hit him like a boulder. He lay on floor for several minutes, pressing his unmasked face against the cool stone. Eventually, he hauled himself to his feet and wove unsteady steps out of his chambers.

His stranger huddled in a corner, his immaculate evening dress wet and torn. His white shirt and vest soiled with blood, his jaw and eye swollen. Deep purples dressed his face. He favored one arm, which hung limp and useless. His other clutched his side.

"Ah. Mr. Mephistopheles is awake," he said through swollen lips. "Oh joy, oh rapture."

Erik collapsed onto his organ bench. "What happened?"

"I saved your sorry ass a second time. Suicide is a coward's way out. You disappoint me, Maestro."

Erik closed his eyes remembering that sweet oblivion. "I could have killed you. Why did you come here? Why did you do that?"

"I have been awake all night asking myself the same damn question. My virtues tend to get in my way. I really need to rid myself of them. Any life is too precious to throw away, even one as vile as yours."

"You should have let me die."

"I should have, but I did not. Now what are you going to

do?"

"What?"

"You heard me. Make your choice. Wallow and moan about life or pick yourself up. We fall for that reason." He struggled to his feet and unceremoniously brushed his damp hair back with an angry swipe. "You did this because of her did you not?" Erik turned away. "You are pathetic. I prove she loves another man, and you roll over and decide to actually die? When are you going to awake and realize she is not the be all and end all? Did you ever think perhaps your life could go on without her? Maybe there is something else out there worth living for? Dare I say someone else? Why do you think I offered to assist in faking your death and covering for you?" His hand sank to his side in defeat. "You really have no concept of how long I have been a part of this charade do you? How you went from Opera Ghost to madman is beyond me. You used to be quiet, reserved. Oh, granted this life is not exactly one worth mentioning. You are a wanted criminal now, not like years past, but maybe, just maybe there is a ray of light somewhere. When was the last time you tried to find that outside of Christine?"

Erik turned away again at the mention of her name.

"You are a genius, an unparalleled genius. Perhaps you should have some faith that men can look beyond the atrocities you have committed and see what good you could achieve if given the chance. Someday all this is going to be overlooked and the world will stand up and recognize you, but only if you let it."

His stranger gestured in disgust, wincing. Erik looked away.

"I give up. Do what you want. Be a coward, be a Phantom, be whatever you damn well want. I have done all the reaching out I can. I am sick and tired of roaming these damn cellars! Dragging unsuspecting people away from these vaults in that blasted, stupid costume and intimating to those I would rather not associate with that these bloody vaults were my way and lot in life! It has been too long for me, far too long. I have kept too many secrets. I have destroyed relationships in the process and driven myself insane because of you." He stopped before the organ pipes and studied himself in the polish. "Look at me. How am I going to explain this?" He scrutinized his purple jaw

line and his split lip. "I have not been bloodied since Heavens knows when." He surveyed his torn shirt, his filthy clothes. "I will have to go with some sort of mugging. That should keep them from questioning my whereabouts."

He gathered his coat, removed his pocket watch and billfold, and tossed them on the organ. He grumbled loudly and fumbled one-handed to remove his crucifix and religious medallions from his neck. He kissed the cross before laying it down. Erik watched the pile grow. The stranger paused; taking a ring from his hand, the motion of yanking it off must have caused a raging pain down his arm. He doubled over. Staring at the ring, endless seconds ticked by before he finally laid it on the organ as well.

"Just to add to the illusion of a mugging if you will." Sweat glistened on his brow as he limped toward the drawing room. He stopped and swung on Erik. "Random acts of kindness, Maestro, come in all shapes and sizes. I unfortunately was yours, so deal with it. But be forewarned." Erik watched with a scowl as he threw a candlestick through the open door to the drawing room. It contacted the lake with an echoing splash. The stranger pointed toward the result. "When you throw out one random act it tends to create ripples that reach outward until they hit the shores and come back to you. It is a frightening concept that so many good things in life are connected. But in order to bind them together, you have to unknot what is past. What are you going to do to make that happen? Ignore it or be a man?"

Fifteen

Once he pulled out of his black mood and allowed her time to rest in comfort for a change, Erik took Anna and left what extra coin he could for the young maid and departed. They fled the hotel via back alleys as soon as he was certain no one looked for them. He would worry about getting the horses later. The tension growing between him and Anna concerned him more. Even the sanctuary of the catacombs they walked through was in question now. Chagny inevitably knew his whereabouts in Lyon. If they were smart they would tear that opera house apart looking for him and then do the same to the underground, much as they had in Paris. A worried voice broke the growing anxiety.

"Anna? Are you out here?" The light from the torch came into view first, and then Pappy rounded a corner. "For the love of Christ woman! I have been looking all over the blasted place for you—" He stopped mid sentence, his eyes zooming in on Erik. "Well, our humming wonder makes an encore."

"Old man." The greeting rumbled into Anna's hair.

"What made you return?"

"My Anna and my child. What do you think?"

"*Your* Anna?" Pappy quipped with an aggravated puff of breath. "She's not property, Maestro."

"Pappy, enough," Anna warned.

"No, it's not enough. He runs off leaving you behind pregnant and upset and then waltzes back in again." The torch inched higher. "You've been crying." He eyed the small drops of red coloring her shirtsleeve. "I've had enough of this. This manhunt can't continue with you. You and that baby have suffered enough. You're going to come with me. I'll find a place to stay away from him and the jeopardy he imposes on you. I'll see to your every need and I'll raise that baby like my own."

Erik's anger flared. His hands sprung open before his face,

stripping his mask away. He stepped into the light of Pappy's torch. His voice cut through the darkness of the catacombs with more intensity than a thousand suns. "You will never be able to call him your own!"

The old man's breathing quickened. Pappy's eyes slid to and fro seemingly not able to focus. Erik smiled as every ounce of color drained from the craggy face. He took great pleasure in the way those wrinkles rearranged into shock. He smiled malevolently.

"Something wrong old man? It seems now you do not want to raise that baby. Not when he will look like this." He jabbed a long finger toward his face. Pappy's eyes rested on Anna's womb. Erik circled him and paused from behind, making certain the fool heard every word perched on his lips. "Oh yes, be it known I am made up of Death from head to toe. Death creates life . . . how macabre." Erik returned to the comfort found in wrapping his arms around Anna and his child. "You cannot rear what you do not understand."

Pappy rubbed his wrinkles, forcing a pink flush back to his face. "It makes me want to raise him all the more. More arms to hold him."

"Pity? Is that it? My child will be born dejected? My arms will hold him!"

"Get in line then. That baby isn't even born yet and it already has three people clambering to raise him."

"Who says you will have any part in raising my child?"

Pappy's arm lifted before slapping against his side. "I guess I won't be raising him with you around now. I'll have my hands full anyway, because before you can raise that baby someone has to raise you."

The words formed two arms and shoved Erik backward. He opened and closed his mouth in dumb stammers.

Pappy sniffed loudly and squared his shoulders. "You better tell me what is going on. Both of you look like you have seen ghosts and I tend to get ornery when women show up bloodied. If you're not used to my prying ways, boy, I suggest you get used to them." He nodded toward Anna. "She made her choice and asked me to make mine. You've finally met *your* Maestro, son."

* * * *

Anna held her hand in front of her eyes, shielding herself

from the glaring world of white. The dawn light shone on the snow with blinding intensity. She stayed half in half out of the shadow of the Church of St. Iréné scanning the hillside for Erik and Pappy's return with the horses. Erik had left with the old man, a look that combined murderous rage and awe behind his unearthly eyes. Never had Anna seen Erik rendered mute, but Pappy's stubborn fatherly streak had cracked a tiny hole in the tight wall Erik constructed around himself.

Anna was certain, if left alone in a sword-filled room, the two would do their best to kill each other, but a journey to get the horses moved in the right direction.

She sighed in relief when Pappy plodded up the path, the mare and stallion flanking either side of him. "Where's Erik?"

He nodded toward a decrepit cemetery. "He handed me the horses and told me to fetch you." Pappy tapped his temple with a crooked index finger. "That man is crazy. He is back in the cemetery talking to himself. He is sideshow freak, crazy."

Something knotted her shoulders. She had an unshakeable feeling of foreboding. Squinting in the sun, she headed toward the tombs. The stone markers were laughing, stopping Anna in her tracks. She heard Erik's voice but didn't see him. That foreboding grew as soon as the cemetery echoed with his voice.

"Problem, Monsieur?"

"Are you going to linger in the shadows of these vaults all morning, Erik?" The cold air nearly cracked her eyes in two when Anna pulled them open wide. That heavily accented voice was not Erik's. She dashed behind a stone angel as she heard him call again.

"What makes you so sure I linger, Monsieur?"

Anna darted her head in every direction following his laughter as it hopped like an invisible grasshopper from stone to stone.

"Damn you, Erik. Show yourself."

"If you insist."

Anna peered around the wing of the cherub as a swirl of a black cape brought him into view.

* * * *

Fanning his cloak aside, Erik propped one hip up on the lid of a stone crypt and regarded the Daroga. His old friend stared at him with numb disbelief.

"This is an unexpected surprise," the Persian said.

Erik lifted a shoulder in bored acknowledgement. "Erik is dead. Yes, it seems many believed those words. I am quite surprised you did not confirm that for yourself with your dealings with Philippe five years ago." Erik clapped his hands together like a gleeful child. "Oh—but Philippe—that would have been a shock to you as well since you were so certain I killed him back then." His sarcasm evaporated as he leapt to his feet.

"But he is dead now," the Persian said.

"Yes," Erik snapped, yanking his cloak aside so sharply it sent snow drifting back into the air. "Last I checked I was out here on the run, not in Paris killing a nobleman. Do you not have anything better to do with your time, Daroga? Leave me in peace."

"What happened to you, Erik? These rumors I have heard since your resurrection. A kidnapping? More murders? Monsieur le Comte de Chagny came to Lyon looking for me. He asked after you and a woman. First light today, he tracked me down again. His huntsman was bloodied and claimed that woman was seen with Christine Daaé. Who is she Erik? What have you gotten yourself into?"

With a calm indifference, Erik brushed the snow from his cloak. "What I am involved in has nothing to do with you, Daroga. When we parted in Persia, you went your way I went mine. Let us leave it at that, shall we?"

"I will not leave this alone if you are involved in any crimes."

The tension dressing Erik frayed like silk abandoned in the sun. "I have not seen or heard from you in five years. You have no right to interfere in my life."

"You killed Philippe de Chagny. You have no rights."

"Oh, always with the law riding perched on your shoulders, Daroga. So, I am a soulless being? A heartless beast permitted nothing other than a life wallowing in blood? Do you think my veins pulse such evil I feel no glory when my lips touch the woman I love?" Erik reeled toward the nearest stone angel. "Eavesdropping is most improper, Anna." His scold drowned out her yelp of surprise as he twirled her into view.

"Allah have mercy," the Persian said disbelievingly. "Let her go, Erik. Child, come to me."

Erik laughed as his old acquaintance gestured for Anna with

the wag of two dark hands. He painted the air with his pale ones. "Obey is not in her vocabulary. She is not Christine." The Persian's lips slipped open, struck stupid. Erik tipped his to Anna's ear. "Erik does not want a Christine."

"You don't know what you want," he replied. "Clearly you are as mad as the day we met. Let her go."

"I want a wife like everybody else," Erik said irritably, his hands springing open to release her. The Persian's face skewed in surprise when she made no move to run and displayed no fear of him. "A wife I can dote upon and that I can take for walks on a Sunday afternoon." Erik's voice rose with each and every sentence. "A wife who I can build a castle and compose music for. Whose feet I can lay before in worship because she is willing to accept all I am." Erik spread his arms and leaned into his words. "But I do not have Sunday afternoons or the ability to build castles. I have a horse blanket for my carpet and a campfire for lamplight. I do not have the wealth to shower her with finery or to travel with her to the wonders of the world." Erik gestured to Anna whose study of the exotic man had her circling the Persian. She looked him up and down, wonder painted on her face. It only made Erik angrier over what he could not give her. "Nor for that matter, do I have the world at my bidding. There is not a gift I can offer her. Not a charm I can give her in thanks. I have nothing but a damn muddy hair ribbon!"

Erik slapped the accursed piece of silk on top of the tomb. He watched shamefully as she picked up the silk and ran it through her fingers. She looked cautiously at the Persian.

"Who are you?" she bid.

"A disagreeable part of Erik's past. Come with me. I will take you wherever you desire to go."

"Why is it everyone assumes my desires lie elsewhere?" She leaned away from the Persian's extended hand and fixed him with an icy stare. "I truly suggest you be on your way, Monsieur, and speak of us to no one. For your own sake."

"You're a woman of sharp tongue." He lifted a single brow, pulling one green eye open wider. "You don't cave to Erik's whims?"

"I am not bound to him by sweet opiates of sound or fanciful illusions."

The Persian's brows flew up. "You've taken a scorpion to

your side."

A low rumble emitted from Erik's throat.

"I ask you pass no judgment against me or him," Anna snapped.

"I am a man of the law, Mademoiselle. If I passed judgment against him, the course of his life would have changed long ago. Dramatically so."

Erik clamped down on his teeth. For a moment, he worried Anna might question the Persian of his years he spent in Mazanderan entertaining the little sultana and participating in several important political maneuvers he would rather forget. There were elements of his life he preferred to keep buried, even from her.

"Erik's past is past, Monsieur," she said, her comment making Erik scowl at her blind acceptance. "It's not in my way, but you are. If you will excuse me?" She plowed past him.

"You would still desire to stay with me, Anna?" Erik asked sadly. She stopped. "The Daroga is a genuine man. Everything he does has noble reason. He is offering you a way out of this manhunt. Perhaps you should take it."

She turned, her hand clutched tightly against her chest. The frayed end of a muddy ribbon dangled out the bottom of her fist. "This is the first gift I have ever received."

Nothing else was added to that statement as she left. Erik tore his eyes away from her boot prints to stare into the question upon the Persian's face.

"North of Lyon is the village of Dijon," he said. "There you will find my old servant, Darius. He will speak of you to no one and see to it you are cared for. You have my word."

Erik laughed shortly. "How easily your scales are tipped, Daroga. What happened to me being a murderer with no rights?"

"You're distinguished. Even if it were hidden behind the tragic way you prostituted yourself through the years. You always had the potential to be a great man—if only, I believe, loved for . . . something. Whatever that something is in not up to me to uncover." The awkwardness of such a statement made Erik fold his arms. He presented the Daroga with his back. "There is something in that child's voice that is incapable of speaking lies. I told Chagny I wanted nothing more to do with you. I still don't, even if I had to see for myself if you were in

Lyon."

"You regret looking?"

"No. I am more at ease for it. For no woman looks on a man with that much love in her eyes if he were a cold-blooded killer and no man on her with such admiration who had not repented his past."

Back still turned to the Persian's confessions, Erik stepped out of the way in time to allow the Daroga by. He should follow, chase down this part of his dark existence and make certain it never surfaced in his life again, but Erik only felt a supreme gratitude for second chances. He watched the Daroga's back for a long time as the breeze swirled his snowy footprints away.

Time wasted.

He needed to get to Dijon before the winds changed.

Sixteen

The wind shifted direction, but Christine did not try to shield her face from its assault.

The trunks sped by, the trees acting as her jailer. Mud splattered as hooves thundered on the path. She knew she should not ride her old mare so hard or at all in her condition, nor take to the trails alone, but she needed the punishment. Since her return to Chagny, the circumstances that spun wildly out of control haunted her. Day in and day out as Loup readied his dogs, Raoul drilled her about Lyon. Was she certain Erik was not near? Was she positive all she saw was Anna? When Christine fought back accusing him of questioning the fidelity of her love, he responded with equal fervor, citing all the times he knew her to be alone with Erik . . . lured by Erik . . . seduced by Erik.

Dear God Christine, is André mine?

Christine snapped the reins and forced her mare forward, hoping the howl of the wind would drown the echo of her husband's ugly accusation.

Desperate to know why Loup started the lie she felt bound to keep, made her drive the horse faster down the trails. She needed to feel her body ache and the wind whip against her face. She wanted the air to sting the tears in her eyes. She needed invisible hands to slap her senseless and make certain the past never caught up to her.

The horse slowed its pace as soon as the kennels came into view. Mingled with the yowls of Chagny's foxhounds were the higher pitched yelps of the English dogs. Awkwardly, she slid off the saddle and gathered her riding skirt above her ankles.

"What is it you want?" she pleaded breathlessly as she hastened to him.

Loup turned. His deep-set eyes settled on the exposed flesh above her boots and traveled to her heaving breasts. He turned to his hounds.

"Anything you need. Name your price and it will be yours."

"Problem, Comtess?"

"Your price, Monsieur!"

Lifting a leg, he leaned back against the kennel and folded his arms. "Holy water." When Christine arranged her face into an assemblage of shock, he rephrased. "Absinthe—liquid green candy. You provide me with all the sinful delights your husband insists on keeping out of reach around here, and I will never tell him the truth of your rendezvous." His lips lifted to a menacing smile. "I don't like it when my candy is taken away."

Trepidation squeezed Christine's stomach. Thoughts raced in her head. Dare she do this? For the honor and sake of her son, she must make certain her husband never learned of her feelings for a hunted man. It would ruin him. She paced, wringing her riding crop. The veil on her hat tickled the back of her neck like the invisible legs of a spider in the midst of weaving a web.

"So, he suspects Erik was around, does he?" Loup nodded in the direction of the chateau. "Do you think he pictures you with him? I know I do—often." He grabbed the bulge between his legs.

"Stop, please." Christine turned away.

Loup walked toward her, his arousal straining obviously against his trousers. He stopped inches from her face. "I'm not stupid, Comtess."

Christine stood like statuary as he leaned to her. Tears stung the edges of her eyes when he slid her scarf aside and pressed his face against the nape of her neck. He sniffed her like a hound in search of meat.

"I know how scandalous this could be for your good name. Why do you think I crafted that little lie? What would happen if the Comte were to find out his wife wants to have that monstrous beast like a common whore? Care to shag me?" Teeth nipped the lobe of her ear. He sucked it between his lips.

The palm of her hand cut the air in front of her and left a nasty red welt upon Loup's cheek.

"Blasted bitch!"

With a throaty growl, he rounded and slammed her against the wall of the kennel. Air burst out her lungs. The momentum pitched her sideways, sending her rolling down several steep steps, before coming to a stop at the bottom of the dog pen. She lay still for several seconds, her body screaming from pain. Winded and frightened, Christine clutched her abdomen. Getting first to all fours, then inching her hands up the wall, she gradually made her way to her feet. It was a miracle he had not killed her! Loup's unfocused eyes set sights on her from the top of the flight of stairs. Christine gathered all her strength and attempted not to look meek. Making her way back up caused a sharp pain to race up her side.

"You pig," she cried. "You dare strike a pregnant woman? When I tell my husband—"

"When you tell your husband what? That I sent you tumbling down a few stairs?" Loup descended toward her. Boot by boot he stalked her, making Christine back down the steps. She clutched an iron railing with knuckle-whitening strength. "Do that and I mention what you did with Erik." Her breath caught in her mouth, the sound sending Loup's back arching in a fit of laughter. "That's right, Comtess! Be afraid! You can be certain the outcome would not be good for him or you."

Loup raced down the remaining steps. He came to a sudden halt where she stood and lunged. Christine yelped as her back slammed against the railing and wall. Tears of pain blurred her vision as Loup's hot breath coated her cheek.

"If you want my silence then you will do whatever I say when I say. Anything I want while I am at Chagny you will provide."

Christine, slightly doubled over, cried out in pain as he yanked her straight. Loup pulled her in close and ground his arousal into her hip.

"Alcohol, money, whores, property—whatever I desire you will deliver! Am I clear! If you so much as breathe a word against me, all deals are off and the world will know exactly what a whore you really are."

"Please," she whimpered. "Something hurts . . ."

He ground himself against her again, forcefully up and down so his intent was driven home through her petticoats. "Do we have an arrangement, Comtess de Chagny, or do I make you hurt in a way far more pleasurable for me than it will be for you?"

Christine bit her cheek until the tinny taste of metal flooded her mouth. She ignored the throb in her lower back. "You will not tell my husband of what transpired in Lyon? You will not tell him of Erik?"

Loup grabbed her chin. He crushed a foul tasting kiss to her lips and shoved her away. "I could care less about Erik. I only want Anna."

Christine stumbled and scrubbed her mouth with the back of her hand until her lips swelled. Tears streamed down her cheeks. "You shall have it."

"Excellent." He turned to his hounds. "Make certain my saddlebags are filled with the fairy and my pockets jingling with what I need to keep me content. I leave in the morning to find my toy and your lover."

Christine climbed the balance of the stairs relying on the railing for support. She hobbled to her mare certain her shoulder was bruised as well as her back. The lie would be simple. She would merely mention a tumble in the garden should anyone spy a bump or scrape upon her. The pain made it feel worse than it was.

Or so it seemed.

As she led her horse toward the trails of Chagny the wind gently swirled leaves around her feet. Behind her, Loup's tune of *Alouette* rose on the breeze and seeped immeasurably into her soul.

* * * *

Erik, Anna, and Pappy drifted through villages and towns for weeks never staying long in fear of reprisal or hostility.

The downed leaves made music of their own. Dry and withered, they cracked together as the hooves of the stallion swirled up pile after pile of them. Naked branches clacked together like wooden chimes, a tune Erik found oddly soothing. He allowed it to penetrate his soul.

It was all the music he had right now.

Decrees seemed to multiply in the weeks since Lyon. If it were his choice, Erik would have ridden day and night to the safe house mentioned by the Persian. But as the weeks increased, so did Anna's condition, forcing him to travel with steady caution.

The one person he thought he could talk to had locked him out of her thoughts. "Why have you been so quiet?" The reins fell against the stallion's neck. Erik trusted him to plod along at his own pace. He reached in front of Anna and worked her hair into a long plait.

"I'm not quiet." Her voice sounded tense.

He tied her braid off with a stray strand of her hair and smoothed it down. It was such a simple and intimate task, one he practiced countless times in his mind's eye as he explored and discovered her. She taught him well, in her own way, and he was still learning, but this time, no matter how he tried, Anna remained uncharacteristically introverted. Her fiery spirit had died away, and Erik didn't think the blame lay only with him. Something brewed inside of her to which he was not privy.

He reached around her and slowed the stallion. He dismounted and gave a quick survey of the small farmhouse and grounds before lifting her off the horse. Her knees buckled when she landed. He instantly tightened his grip. She waved off his concern and turned to grab the reins, a dark expression on her face. Erik grabbed her chin with one finger and gazed long at the emptiness behind her eyes. Her small lips were twisted into a tiny pout in such a way it brought an unintentional smile to his face.

Erik searched the depths of those eyes for some sign she was in there. He could savor that bottom lip for hours, but instead gently attempted to claim them as his. She turned her face at the last moment, bringing his lips in contact with her cheek. He noticed a glistening of tears in the corner of her eyes. He fought the urge to shake her like a frustrated child who could not understand the puzzle in front of him. Where was she? Where was the woman who made him a man?

With a final command toward Pappy to tether the horses, he headed up the path toward the house.

Hood up, he hammered a fist against the door. His acute senses took in everything at once. The farm was modest, not terribly well kept. Shutters hung at awkward angles, the sheep pen across the yard was in disrepair. A small outbuilding seemed solid—which was more than Erik could say about the barn. It annoyed the master architect in him to see any building left to rot.

The glow of a lantern caught his eyes, as a stream of light appeared first in the window then like a thin sliver beneath the door. Erik added more distance between him and the entry as it opened. Though the hood shielded his face and dressed him head to toe in the color of the shadows, the man recoiled as if smacked with broad daylight.

"You!" he gasped. "Erik."

They barely had any need to speak to each other during the years Darius served the Daroga. Beneath his mask, Erik rippled his brow. His name was fit for a king and Darius uttered it in true subservient fashion. A quick regard was all he needed to confirm nothing much had changed. The years in Persia were deeply etched into his stance. He was still a young man, having been nothing more than a boy when placed in servitude to the Daroga. A boy—born to serve a master. The idea of eunuchs perplexed Erik. Darius looked utterly ridiculous dressed in the simple garb of a French peasant instead of the rich robes of a servant of a member of the royal court. In an attempt not to look imposing, Erik fanned his cloak behind and bowed politely.

"*Asr be kheir*," he greeted.

"*Bonsoir*," Darius hesitantly replied. His hand twitched on the handle of the lantern.

"The Daroga sent me. He indicated you have a room to let."

"If he said that is so—then so shall it be."

"I will be staying through the winter, or for as long as I am able." When Darius nodded with staring eyes and a bent posture, Erik indicated his reasons. "I need time for my Anna." He gently waved her forward. Darius's face skewed with the same shocked expression the Daroga had upon seeing her. "The old man will be staying as well. I will pay what I can so long as you leave us in peace and make no mention we are here."

"Are you with child?" Darius asked of Anna.

"Yes, Monsieur."

The eunuch gestured wildly with the lantern, ushering them into his house. He indicated the fireside chair for Anna before flitting about his house like a moth against a windowpane. As he fell into a routine of serving them, Erik studied the small home: one large room served as kitchen and living space, a single room off to the side held a bed and a few recognizable Persian frivolities. The ladder to his side led to a loft and further living space if needed. Simple and oddly charming . . . Erik stood in a corner, watching Pappy warm his hands by the fire as Anna eyed the dark man doting upon her.

"How much longer do you have?" Darius asked eagerly.

Anna leaned away as he poured her an overflowing glass of

milk and shoved it in her hands. She stammered to the white liquid spilling over her wrist. "I . . . I really don't know. Five months? Four?"

"You're terribly thin." He gestured to the platter of crumbling cheese and bread he brought from the kitchen. "Have you had any medical attention?"

Erik stared out the window. He gnashed his teeth. Anna was tiring and frail and they had yet to find a region with a doctor or midwife that was not already aware of their descriptions. He thought many times to force himself upon one, but knew that would draw unwanted attention.

"Circumstance has not afforded us that. My first concern is for my child. I will pay whatever funds I can over your rent and do what I must to see she gets the attention she needs. I will mend your buildings and pens, reset the stones in your hearth—anything."

Darius tore his attention away from Anna. The boy looked strangely confused. Erik watched as he gestured to Anna as if indicating the obvious. "It was not the Daroga's intent to bring you here to serve me. It was his intent to bring the Mademoiselle here, so I may serve her."

Erik's hand sprung open and closed at his side as he struggled for composure. The Daroga's sly implications he was not man enough to care for the woman he loved rocked the foundation of his sanity. Silenced, numbed, and frustrated that Anna had barely uttered a word to him since she laid eyes on Christine, forced Erik toward the door with a chokehold about his neck. Perhaps the Daroga was right—Erik didn't know what he wanted. Perhaps Anna was right and he had to choose between the past and present. Or perhaps he was right and the world could go to hell.

Without a word, he yanked open the door and headed into the yard. They all couldn't stay in comfort in the small home anyway.

No one protested as he made his way to sleep with the sheep.

* * * *

The thin beasts roamed freely through the barn. Erik would complain as well if his home were left in disrepair. Flanked on either side by overgrown balls of wool, he crossed his arms and stared out the broken window of the barn. While he enjoyed sleeping on a sheepskin rug like any man, he preferred his not to be bleating.

"What did you do to her, Maestro?" Stale hay crunched beneath his boots as Erik turned to see Pappy leading the horses toward the stalls. "I can tell you did something to upset her, and she won't tell me."

Erik entwined his hands casually behind his back and bluntly answered. Not that he felt he needed to. "I betrayed her trust."

Pappy set the mare up in one stall, the stallion in the other. He hung the satchel on a hook and rummaged though his pockets. The pipe clicked as he popped it between his teeth. "Set her from your mind did you?"

"Set whom from my mind, old man?"

"Christine. Did you enjoy her?"

"You do not know when to keep silent do you?"

"No. Answer the question."

"Why would you want to know?" Erik leaned against the windowsill and struck a nonchalant pose. "Have you not enjoyed the company of a lady in a while?"

"Let's not begin the comparisons. When I was your age, and mind you," he pointed with his pipe, "you're not exactly a young man, I had many more ladies between the sheets than you. I'm going to say Anna was your first." Erik pivoted toward the window. "I'll take that as a yes."

"I have acquainted myself with women." Erik bit defensively. "I did not spend several years in exotic cultures not to have had pause to learn women are an inquisitive sort."

Sulfur filled the air as Pappy tipped a match to the bowl of his pipe. "Like I am going to believe that."

"Anna is the only woman I will ever want. Not that it is any business of yours."

"Then why betray her trust?"

"Leave me alone, old man."

Pappy groaned loudly as he lowered himself down on a bench. The sheep turned in restless circles. "From what I gather, Christine brings you power. She reminds you, you can control, when you think you cannot. She bends to your whims with a whisper of her name." He tapped his pipe stem against his teeth. "Anna's your poison, Christine your antidote. Tell me, does everything seem right when your mind retreats to her?"

Perhaps exhaustion made him too weary to care, but Erik felt compelled to reply. Despite the noise that rose behind his music when he thought of Christine, he muttered a quiet yes.

"You're a perfectionist, Maestro. To you Christine is perfection. She is beautiful, graceful, and she understands your music. All those can be found elsewhere, you know."

"I once was told that Christine was not the be all, and end all. When will I believe that?"

"You'll never find the perfect woman, Maestro. You'll need to take pieces of near perfection and be satisfied."

"I betrayed Anna because of my music. I cannot be without it. Christine always needed my music. She fulfills a part of my restless mind in a way Anna never could."

"Erik?"

The use of his name shot him right out of somber thoughts. It sounded so foreign coming from Pappy that it rendered him stupid.

"What packages did she deliver?" Pappy asked.

Erik moved around the barn with contemplative steps. He twirled a thin wrist in the air as he spoke in an attempt to track the old man's line of questioning. "Paper, ink, and figs." Wretched, disgusting fruits . . .

"Paper? What kind of paper?"

"Composition. Lined for a Maestro's notes."

"Anna doesn't understand music? You're certain of that? Let me tell you a secret and you decide whether or not Christine will be the only one to fulfill your needs. Anna couldn't always afford that paper—told me so herself. When she couldn't, she studied all that music she still can't understand, to figure out what a Maestro might need and lined plain paper herself, every last stanza, colon, clef, and treble. She didn't understand the music, but she wanted to hear it badly enough. Anna needed music too, except she didn't need it to help perfect some part of herself. She only needed it because it said what she could not." Pappy leaned toward Erik. "She heard your music, and she could not allow that to be silent. She had no idea at that time about the Phantom—or Christine. Anna had a lot to say. Except for her, it was not done through music; it was done through simple, random acts. You need to give that woman her voice. Child or no child, she deserves all of you and if you cannot give her that, then let her go. The first duty of love is to listen." Pappy tugged on his pipe. "Pity no one ever taught you how to do that."

"Someone did. I chose not to hear him."

"Who?"

"The man who sent Anna to me."

"Who sent me to you?" Anna grunted and tugged on the barn door to slide it shut.

"What are you doing out here?" Erik said anxiously. "You should be inside where it is warm."

"I don't need to be tended. I'm not a sheep." She waved toward the house like flicking aside a fly. "That dark man makes me uneasy."

Erik brought his fist down on the windowsill, splintering the rotten wood. "You defiant child! Why will you constantly not do as instructed?"

"Erik," Pappy cautioned, rising. He tugged on his ear. "Listen."

Reading between the lines on Anna's face brought Erik's anger down. Pappy scrubbed his stubble and nodded in her direction, cuing Erik to allow what Anna needed to say. He headed for the door.

"Pappy?" The old man stopped short at the sudden use of his name. Erik followed him to the door.

The old man shook his head and spoke so only he could hear. "You've nothing to say to me. Just promise you'll remember this turning point."

Snow blasted through the crack as Erik slid shut the door behind Pappy.

"Why were you speaking of me?" Anna insisted. "I was at that opera house for years. No one gifted me to you. I'm not property."

"You swallowed a serpent," Erik rumbled. "That is the most you have said to me in weeks." He folded his arms and matched her glower for glower. "What is it you need?"

"What is it I need?" Her voice jumped an octave. She pointed toward the house. "You did it again, Erik. You discarded me in a strange place only to wander off so you can lick your wounds in silence. You want to know what I need? I need the man for whom I left those packages. I need the reason back in my life as to why I lined all that paper and spent my last coin on ink and figs."

"I never asked you for any of that," he said dryly. "Especially the figs."

"Then give me back the reason as to why I became involved in this mess to begin with!" Anna shoved at the air between them with her hands. "No. Never mind. Forget it. Forget all of this. You will never understand what I am dealing with in this manhunt. Never! All I wanted was a simple hug, an apology for your mistakes, and maybe a little acknowledgement for all I have done—especially for giving you a second chance." She tugged the barn door and managed to slide it open enough to satisfy her freedom. Cold air blasted around them, punctuating her words. "Who else ever gave you that?"

"Philippe Georges Marie." The name cut through the air and stopped Anna in her tracks. "He gave me that chance by giving me you, and I never . . ." Erik turned his head to the side and rubbed his palms into his pants like a nervous schoolboy. "I never thanked him. I never thank anyone."

Wool swirled beneath his feet as he approached. Though she took a step out of his reach, he hooked her anyway. First by one arm and then the waist, he took her into his embrace and used all the care in the world to draw her into that hug she sought. It was like holding silent, cold marble. Enough had been done to end this chapter in their lives. The sins he committed drove away the woman whose emotions could usually be expressed in the touch of a hand or the blink of an eye. All feeling dripped out of his body until his chest shriveled and hollowed. Erik had finally found all he wanted in life—to be loved for himself—and he destroyed it. He tickled her ear with the tremble of her name, but Anna didn't respond.

If there is a God . . . please. . .

Erik thought he understood emptiness and loneliness. Sorrow had walked beside him all his life. But nothing penetrated his soul like this. He buried his lips in her hair and took a long pull of its earthy fragrance.

I will be good . . . I promise. . .

The tremolo of his voice pleaded for her to say something, but she replied with an unfeeling stance. Wrapping her tighter in his arms did nothing to encourage her out of her shell. If he could crush her into his heart he would.

Come back to me . . . please . . .

Silence.

His Anna was gone. They were over. With a dry mouth, Erik struggled for the words his lips had never formed. He projected his voice so the weight of his sadness joined them with unseen arms. He slid a hand to the swell of the baby. "Before you leave me, thank you. When this baby is born, tell him his father thanks him as well. Tell him I loved him before I ever knew how."

The barn fell silent as a tomb.

"I'm not leaving you, Erik."

"Philippe did."

"He died."

"Did I kill him? I killed a part of you. Did I kill him as well? Erik destroys all he is closest to."

"No. You couldn't have killed him and you didn't kill a part of me. You just—"

"I am sorry!" He crushed her in his arms, and apologized over and over again.

Anna rocked with the force of his embrace. He held her as if she were the last thing worth clinging to, the last piece of sanity and dignity to exist in his life. "I do not know how to do as you ask, Anna. I have been trying . . . for weeks I have been trying, but part of me still loves her. You knew I always would from the beginning. It was an infatuating love I almost died from. How do you relinquish something that powerful?"

"Wouldn't you have died alone?"

Erik jerked away. A Herculean truth reared before him and he was unprepared to face it. Backing away did nothing to change reality. The motion only bogged him down. Such truth was oppressively heavy. He stopped by the stallion and retrieved his violin. It would have been the only woman present when he did die—if not for Philippe. He spoke to the worn wood and ran his fingers over silent strings. "Erik is not alone anymore?" He looked up in time to see her mouth a silent no. "I love. Do you believe me when I say that?"

"I do, but this will take time. My sense of worth was stolen from me when Christine took a part of you. It will take however long it takes until she does not affect us. We're not a couple to be seen strolling boulevards or visiting salons. We have to face this pursuit and who we are together. Then raise this child. But don't expect my heart to heal overnight. Love is delicate.

Sometimes it frays."

The distance grew between them. As always, his violin remained faithfully at his side at times of his deepest solitude. He caressed it, wishing to retreat to the small scrap of himself he knew and comprehended. "Philippe wanted me to have a purpose for living. That purpose was and always will be music. That is why he gave you to me." The look on her face contorted. "You followed me through the opera house one night and discovered me, yes?" She nodded. "How did you know I existed?"

Anna lifted a shoulder. "A . . . a man . . . a patron . . ."

"Was he a kind man?"

"One of the few I have ever met. He had a box at the theater. But I only spoke to him once—when he shockingly addressed me. Men of his rank do not associate with women such as me. He asked if I was the one who tended the misfortunate. He told me if I waited in the theater I would find a man . . . he instructed me what to leave . . . told me to follow the man and I would understand why."

"He told you to leave paper, ink, and figs?" When she nodded, Erik sneered. "Philippe de Chagny and his need to have the final word. I hate figs. He was more than a patron of that opera house—much more."

When Anna moved toward him, for a moment he thought the divide between them would be bridged. Though it was not, his body still jolted with fire when she laid her hands across his on the violin. "Will you continue to tell me about him?"

He sat them on the barn bench. He had never spoken to anyone of the man and mystery that was Philippe de Chagny. "After all I have done to you, you still want to be a part of me in that way?"

"I am a part of you." A hand rested against their child.

Reaching out, he lightly touched the life he was anxious to meet and thought ruefully on the man who never would greet his child. "He was a man of irreproachable conscience and heart. Arrogant at times, except to the fairer sex—as I came to understand. He was a part of my life longer than I ever expected, and far beyond the years I knew. I suppose part of the reason I did not kill Raoul when he betrayed you to Barret was because of Philippe. I could never kill that damn boy no matter how much I despise him. Doing so would break Christine's heart and dishonor a loyal friend. Raoul and Philippe seemed similar, yet to me were so different."

"You say he was more than a patron. Who was he?"

A guillotine slammed down on his rare vulnerability. "Anna, I do not want to discuss this any longer." Turning her, certain she knew he meant no other intent, he invited her to lean against his chest. "I will let you in small amounts. All I understand is the darkness of those years. I do not know why, since his death, they haunt me so. Until Erik understands them—no one will." As he placed her hands across his violin and bow, he timidly asked, "You are really not leaving Erik?"

"There is more than one way you are able to love," she encouraged. Erik stared down in surprise to the top of her head. "Play for me?"

"No. My music cannot be known. It is too risky to allow that out. Even in a place like this where you feel secure. Someone may hear."

"Please, one last time, before we are forced to run again."

Running would be inevitable. Calculating how long they would be able to stay in this seemingly quiet part of France was impossible to do. Anna broke his thoughts.

"I'm not leaving. Love through that violin like you used to in the labyrinth, while you were teaching me the Madrigal." She moved to look up at him. "In a way that is what you were doing, was it not? I never knew your affection then, but I do now. We need a connection, and for now, it is the simplest thing we can do."

Power hit Erik with such a force of love, there was no other way to express it beyond music. Reaching around her with the bow like he did in her lessons, he chose a charmingly simple and serene tune.

Anna settled her head in the crook of his arm. A tear found its way down her cheek and into his heart. The title lilted its way into her ear. "Madrigal: *Abendlied.*"

* * * *

The Phantom's Labyrinth

He shoved the stale loaf and crumbling cheese aside. Staring at them made him feel more like a rat in a maze. Besides, he rarely ate when he composed anyway.

Note and stanzas blurred into one continuous line of black. Music was inside of him—somewhere. He needed to create a new beginning, but how? What began opera anyway? He had no idea at this particular junction. He was uninspired and bored.

"Do you ever intend to eat or are you trying to starve yourself to death this time?"

Erik lifted a brow and frowned at the few notes he jotted down. Any hope for peace this evening flushed away when he heard that voice.

"Seriously, you play the role of a skeleton rather well."

Erik clicked his tongue. The enemy had conquered, no sense trying to avoid it. He pivoted on his organ bench. "I do not recall inviting you here."

"I am fine, thank you kindly." The stranger replied removing the costuming Erik was accustomed to at this point. "I have a nagging cough that is tending to linger and a stiff shoulder thanks to you." He peeled off his gloves and shook them in Erik's direction. "You broke my collarbone, cracked two ribs, wreaked havoc with a kidney, and turned my flesh more colors than a rainbow. I should send you my medical bills. Learning to apologize would be a nice touch."

"Go away."

"Regrettably, not an option at this stage, Maestro. So tell me, have you made your choice about living up to the life we craft or ignoring it?"

"I am ignoring you.*"*

"What are you writing?"

"Your obituary! Wasn't faking my death supposed to allow me to live in peace? I was attempting to compose you damn fool, now go away!"

"Compose?" A bit too much color filled the stranger's voice. "That is refreshing. So perhaps we are up to living life, embracing change, being a man, finding a purpose for living . . ."

Erik buried his face in the pages to control his groan of frustration. "Leave. Leave. Leave."

"Why is that door open?"

Erik's face snapped out of his pages in time to see his uninvited guest point toward his Louis-Philippe inspired room. Christine's room . . .

"Did you go in there? That was Mademoiselle Daae's room was it not? You usually keep that locked."

Erik leapt to his feet. Crossing his home in a few strides, he slammed the door closed. The conversation turned back to his initial demand. "How did you get down here?"

"You are not still wallowing in pity over her are you?"

"Answer my question."

"I thought we knocked her out of your system when we knocked out all that poison."

"Answer my question."

"Answer mine."

"I had composed our nuptial mass and wanted to make sure I never laid eyes on it again." He jabbed a finger toward a charred pile of papers. "If you do not mind I would like to be left alone to compose something new. Get out!"

"Ah. Ridding yourself of such sentiments speaks to me of a man willing to move on." The stranger rubbed his chin. "We will need to foster this in you . . . yes . . . find a way to keep you looking toward a future, not the past and Christine . . . how . . . I will have to think on this." He smiled. "Interesting turning point the New Year has brought to you."

"I have no turning points," Erik said, his voice emotionless. "I only wish to be left alone, and I cannot do that with you here. Leave now. Leave forever."

The stranger winked and patted Erik's shoulder. He followed the intimate contact with outrage surging in his core.

"Life is like a key in a lock Maestro, with one twist you can have a turning point that can open more than simply doors." He bowed and gathered his hat, gloves, and the lantern he traveled with. "I will return in a few weeks time. Do not wait up."

Erik watched him disappear into the inky blackness listening to him hum a jaunty tune until the light from the lantern dimmed and his wet footsteps died off in a fading echo.

He stared remorsefully at his charred mass. If he had not burned it, he could have used the reverse side to compose something new. He was running low on paper. The pages would have been messy, but it would have saved him from going aboveground to purchase more. He would have to make do with what he had. Never again would he venture up there. The world could go on without him. He headed over to his organ, preferring to stare blankly at empty music in an attempt to find that blasted beginning. Attempted, for a faint smile turned up his lips . . .

"Someone should give him voice lessons."

Seventeen

Would her back ever stop throbbing?

Christine dug the tips of her fingers against the dull ache that lingered since her tumble down the stairs. She caressed the area in meticulous circles. Weeks went by and nothing helped. Yesterday's covert meeting with the physician told her all was well, despite the small amounts of blood she passed. The baby moved and the heartbeat was strong. Still—the terror of seeing that blood . . .

She shook her head clear of the thought. She dared not tell Raoul. The road they shared was rocky enough since Lyon and his stress was hitting mountainous levels. She could not bear a reprimand or the inevitable argument that would follow. They were familiar strangers in the halls of Chagny.

One thing she refused to do despite the doctor was stay in one spot and rest. There was no need to subject herself to another quarrel. Chagny was under siege as is. Out here, she knew she was safe—this was the one place that was not permeated by Loup.

She shoved the fabric samples aside, too weary to choose patterns for drapery. Redecorating the vicomte's room was called for since the nursery would be needed soon, but she lacked the temper for such frivolity. The winter sun grew soothing and hypnotic, enhanced by the floor to ceiling windows. Pulling in a deep breath of the flowers around her and giving in to the sun on her skin, Christine closed her eyes. Normally she enjoyed this wing of her estate. Right now, the conservatory caged her behind glass bars.

Her mood darkened when the doors opened at the far end of the glass house.

"Christine," Raoul jogged down the steps. His voice echoed along with his boots.

"Raoul, not now I am feeling poorly."

"Yes, now."

The chair skidded backward as she got to her feet. She wandered up and down the rows of plants pausing often to inspect a delicate bloom in her attempt to avoid him. She had been all month.

"I received a wire," Raoul declared. "Loup has found a trail. Mademoiselle Barret is in the area of Dijon."

Christine gazed steadily at the open mouth of a cymbidium. *Orchids represent flawless beauty*. "That is gracious news for Chagny." While she inspected blooms, he studied the fabrics.

"What have we here?" A smile lit the strain below his voice.

Christine buried her displeasure in the quivering stem of an oncidium. "I was selecting the decor for *your* vicomte's room." *Refinement and wealth.*

The slap of the fabrics hitting the table as Raoul slammed them down could have shattered the windows. "How many times am I going to have to apologize? Christine, what am I supposed to think? When it comes to the Phantom you become protective of your emotions. Half the time I don't know whether or not you want me to continue tracking him." Christine ignored his implied question and returned to inspect the orchid. "I would love to put this manhunt aside and move on with our lives, but I made a promise to protect you from him. Is it so odd such a thought of you being intimate with Erik would have crept into my mind?"

"I find it disagreeable that you don't trust me." She ignored the wrenching guilt that hugged her.

"I don't trust him. Even I can see how the man can seduce a maiden. It seems that is in Death's nature, after all."

Christine looked at him coolly, not appreciating the sarcasm to his tone. The look was well practiced and knocked down her husband's arrogance.

"My accusation was foolish, and cruel," he apologized. "I don't think it to be truth, but I do think you owe me credit for all I do to keep you safe from Erik."

The sun intensified making Christine shift from her spot. Their eyes briefly met as she slipped beyond him. Raoul portrayed a perfect gentleman this morning. Clothing pressed and brushed, the scent of his fine soap floated faintly on the air between them. Or was it the flowers? Either way he sharply contrasted the man of which they spoke. She plucked the large, buttery bloom of a cattleya and placed it gently in the palm of her hand. Raoul loved orchids. *Cattleyas are the symbol for many children.*

"You didn't need to protect me from Erik."

"Christine, your perspectives are clouded. That is not the point. I'm tired of competing against him. This hunt has begun in earnest and won't end until the Phantom is found. If he is captured, you will not be able to be with him. He'll go to prison and quite possibly be executed. The man can give you nothing, and here I am willing to give you everything and you won't let me."

Christine turned her attention back to the potted orchid. Doting on these plants was a passion of Raoul's—beyond her and horses. Before she could pluck another bloom, Raoul stormed toward her. He snatched the one from her grip and gestured at her with it.

"What do you want of me, Christine? Do you not want things around that remind you of me? I will end this now if you are not happy. If I cannot be all you need and desire, then I am not a man. My vows are my word and a man's word is what makes him! I promised you my life, heart, body, and soul. I vowed to live for you. But I am filled with dread you want Erik for reasons that are different from the path on which we started."

Christine caressed the dark green leaves in front of her. "Are you tracking Erik for me, or out of revenge for your brother?"

"That is not the discussion."

"You will never be able to understand the connection I have to him, so there is no discussion." If she were a bird in a glass cage, she would beat against the glass walls until free to fly away. Why was it suddenly so hard to love Raoul? His sad sigh twisted all the blood from her heart.

"Christine, I want to understand. If you will allow me that, I can love you even more."

He approached, and laid the orchid on the sill between them. Its broken petals reflected in the windows. *Even scarred, it's beautiful.*

"Please don't let this become a rift between us," he implored. Warm kisses traced the surface of her palm. It sent a shiver to her stomach. "I was wrong in my accusation of any infidelity, and I have died a thousand times because of those thoughts. Would you have me die a thousand more, knowing how much I have hurt you?"

Tell him . . . he is a forgiving man. He's his brother. Admit your indiscretions like Erik suggested. Then perhaps you could escape the past. Her gaze darted around the orchids. *Wealth, refinement, beauty, love, many children . . .*

The twitch in her side made her squint in pain. His words caressed her ear.

"I know there are things he is that I can never be. But I will change to what you want me to be, even if it means being a pauper. I am doing this all for you, Christine. You do want to see Erik locked away, do you not?"

"Yes." *No . . .*

He pulled away to gaze into her eyes. "Loup's correspondence confirmed sightings of a man traveling with Anna. From the descriptions, it can only be Erik." When Raoul caressed their unborn child, his eyes sparkled with excitement. "We have a beautiful new blessing on the way. Please—I want my baby girl to grow up free from the Phantom being tangled in our lives. I die a bit every day knowing André already is surrounded by this madness. Help me understand what you need in order to prevent this from destroying our family."

Christine studied the golden glow of the sunlight as it streamed through the window. Behind closed eyes, she tried to destroy the thought of a different glow that came from the eyes of the man of whom they spoke.

Freedom to love could not grow in a jealous heart. The past could not be put to rest so long as the love for two men took root in her soul—so long as another woman stood in the way of her redressing choices.

One who is jealous is surely in love . . . but was she jealous of Anna, or the freedom Christine thought she had?

* * * *

In the weeks that had passed, quiet afternoons faded away into the gentle slumber of evening with steadfast predictability.

Anna spooned close against him, having abandoned the bed Darius provided, much to Erik's chagrin. Instead of reprimanding her for not giving in to the comfort offered, he took Pappy's advice and listened to her. No words were exchanged, but he thought perhaps there was something to be said for why she visited his meager bed. Chest to her back gave him the most contact he'd had with her for a long while. Erik refused to move or breathe too hard lest he disturb the moment. Their relationship rocked heavily under the weight of all they had been through. Erik all but rebuilt Darius's house, mended the barn and reconstructed solid pens to contain the wandering bundles of wool.

Something had to be done with his pent up energy.

His long, thin arms caged the swell of his baby. The scent of Anna's hair intoxicated him. He longed to find her lips, even boldly explore the female body in full cry of womanhood, but knew that would bring a flash of sadness to Anna's face. Wondering when his child would arrive entertained him for hours, and chased away the remorse he had for all he did to damage Anna's trust. Tonight, for the first time in a long while, his mind calmed.

The screams from the yard jolted him back to reality as Darius's voice cut through the air.

On his feet faster than a bullet from a pistol, Erik raced to the door. It slid aside with a mighty crack. Horse and rider thundered up the road. Hooves broke through the crusty snow sending shards of hardened ice in every direction. Chickens scattered for their lives. Darius cried out again. Pulling on the reins, he didn't wait for the horse to stop before dismounting. A third cry sent Pappy bolting from the house.

"Gather the horses and your belongings," Darius commanded.

"What's going on?" Anna rubbed sleep from her eyes and took a spot by Erik's side.

"Marksmen. In the village."

"How many?" Erik propelled himself across the yard.

"Six. They were in the mercantile. Six men with twelve hounds."

"Hounds?" Anna gasped.

Darius nodded. "English bird dogs. Endurance trackers. It is a twenty-minute ride at full gallop between here and the village center. That's all you have."

"Loup." Erik's anger blazed like wildfire. The noise in his mind took firm control of his senses. He turned to Pappy. "Take the mare and the stallion and what provisions you can pack." The old man raced into the barn. He addressed Darius. "What is the best direction from here?"

"North. Follow the streambed to the river. Those dogs will still be able track in water, but it will at least slow them down."

Erik grabbed Anna's shoulders. "Do as he says. I will follow when I can."

Pappy reappeared and took her elbow, trying to drag her off, the reins of two horses in his other hand. Anna batted him away. "Erik, you can't stay here."

"Go, Anna."

"What are you going to do? I won't lose you again, Erik. I can't leave you!"

The odd beauty dripped out of his voice. Erik let all his murderous hatred and tension scratch out in metallic syllables. "I will do whatever is necessary to protect you and my baby." His fingers dug into his thighs as he controlled what surged through him.

Pappy grabbed her again, managing to get her a few paces toward the tree line before she yanked herself free. "I love you!"

Such fervor from her he had never experienced before. Erik gritted his teeth wanting to respond, but hatred swelled his veins. He prodded her toward Pappy.

"There is lamp oil in the barn. I'll burn the building," Darius decided. "The hounds will pick up their scent and yours quickly. The smoke will cover your trail and confuse them for a while."

"Why are you doing this?"

Darius stared at the tree line. "In the weeks you have been here, I have watched a man beneath that madman I secretly feared in Persia. Whatever anger you have in life disappears when you look at Anna. I do this for her and the unborn child I have grown to care for. I do this for the Daroga. He has always believed in you."

"You cannot do so," Erik said pointedly. "Destroy that building and you jeopardize your well being."

"Don't argue with me." Darius ran toward the barn.

Erik's darkened gaze slid to the trees that would act as either a prison or protector. Darius reappeared beside him with a lit lantern and bucket of oil.

"I couldn't hide her here. Not with armed men approaching. If I could keep her, I would. But I'm already an oddity. A woman with a eunuch . . . is . . . if perhaps I were a whole I . . ." he lowered his head in shame. "She holds the world in her heart. But I'm sorry . . ."

"You are more man than I could ever be."

The oppressive presence Erik fought day and night clawed its way to the surface. The victory he had over it for the short time he was here was hollow now. Anna couldn't outrun foxhounds, not even with time to her advantage. "You do what you must to protect your kind, but this I will not allow. I will not have you risk your future because of my sins."

"I won't have you kill for yours!"

Erik shot him a dangerous look. The ignorant fool would dare to challenge his authority?

Darius gestured toward the village center. "The authorities can do nothing to me. They have no proof I kept you here. You must leave."

"This farm is your life."

"The Mademoiselle is yours! If I could keep her here as a part of my own I would, but have mercy—will you let me help you?"

The presence of Samaritans, Erik constantly denied. Years had been spent crafting a need to do without men, but the pressure building in his chest as he thought of Anna he couldn't ignore. He stared at the lit lantern.

"I can never repay you," he replied humbly.

"Promise me one day you will put all others aside and do a great good and you will have repaid my sacrifice."

"You have my oath."

"Go, before it is too late."

Distant barks filled the night. Erik reached his hand across the expanse between him and the eunuch. "No. If the hounds will be confused, I stay. You will need my aide to extinguish the flame. I will not see that building burned to the ground." Erik's hand hovered in the empty space between them.

Darius nodded and slid his hand into Erik's. "I regret that time has placed this chapter in my life in such an awkward spot in yours. For I am certain in a different time and place, the Daroga would stand correct. Yours would have been a very noble life."

* * * *

Night was a welcomed friend, one that would cover and protect any who ventured out in it. However, the coming rays of dawn couldn't be avoided. They were the whips sending those who wished to hide deeper into unkind wilderness.

By a dying fire in the damp cold of a forest, Anna stared blankly into the embers. They couldn't afford the luxury of flame for fear of being seen. She quietly prayed her Samaritan, however odd he was, would be saved any injustice and Erik was safe—somewhere. Anna rolled the thin length of silk through her hands, her efforts at snaring a rabbit or polecat cut short first by her fear of being found, second by her growing inability to navigate her changing body. The gruff tones of Pappy's deep voice pulled her from her thoughts.

"What?" She realized he posed a question.

"You need to sleep." He pointed to the bedroll.

"I'm fine."

She was not tired, she was cold. Anna didn't want much in life, contented with the small things forgotten. But Darius's humble house, his ridiculous sheep, and the scrawny chickens made her want a home, a typical future.

Not a manhunt.

"I don't care," Pappy scolded, jolting her from her pity. He rummaged in the satchel and dug out the hunting knife. "You may not be tired, but the baby needs you to rest. I'll make sure no one finds this camp."

Anna refused to move. "I won't be able to rest until I know he is safe."

"Erik can take care of himself, the baby can't. You have to think beyond this pursuit."

"How am I to do that, Pappy?" Nothing but anger seemed to fill her now. "There is clearly no stopping Chagny. Not now, not with Loup. Tell me how I am to think beyond this when it devours every moment we have?"

Something snapped.

The camp fell eerily silent. Pappy held up his hand for her to be still. His eyes searched the dark trees behind her, while hers did the same behind him. Whatever it was, it was close. The hair on the back of her neck stood on end.

Something cracked.

Anna slammed shut her eyes. Was it her imagination or could she sense the sniffing hounds? *It's a red deer, just a deer in search of a drink . . .*

She imperceptibly moved her head. Nothing greeted her but darkness. A black and a foreboding sense they were not alone began its stranglehold. Threads of fear raked down her spine. *It's not the wolf. He's not here.*

Something splintered.

Anna rounded. The silk in her hand snaked through the air, hitting its mark. A sickening tautness raced up her wrist. She snapped backward and moved her other hand with lightning reflexes to grab the silk's remaining length in preparation for the final twist and yank. But the rope grew slack. A yellow glow moved from the cover of the trees, before a shadowy figure fell into view.

With deathly calm, Erik lowered his hand from the level of his eyes. He moved toward the center of the camp, untangling his arm from the silk and holding its tail up before his eyes. Utter astonishment painted his posture as he removed the Punjab from his neck. He coiled it neatly and tucked it out of sight.

"It is safe to say that has never happened before." Calm evaporated. His roar shook the branches of the trees. "Never throw with your dominant hand unless it is your intent to kill!"

As Anna fought to get air into her lungs, Pappy clutched his chest and sank against a tree. Erik's shoulders arched into his words.

"If I ever . . . ever . . . learn you have used that against a human being again, I will teach you a lesson you will never forget. I am never to discover or see that you have killed a man. Is that clear?"

Anna found her tongue. "Dear God, I am—"

His lips crushed her words. He kissed her with a savage intensity until she sobbed and fell lax in his arms. Erik was dirty, soot covered, and smelling of smoke, but his kiss had never tasted so sweet.

"I'm fine by the way," Pappy squeaked. "Just an old man having a heart attack. Pay me no mind."

Erik broke the kiss and pulled away. Anna searched the hopeful, yet sad hue to his golden eyes until he rolled his head to the old man. "You are a withered German goat. You are fine."

Pappy slid up the tree. "A mastermind such as you would be able to see into my chest right now?"

Anna followed a skeletal finger as Erik lifted it to her face. His mere touch pulled warm air into her lungs. He traced her lips, his eyes gleaming with golden seduction. "If you so like, old man, I will be more than happy to provide you with that heart attack so to be alone with my Anna."

"Are you all right?" Her chilled cheeks warmed with her blush.

"Your concern is never to lie with me. I heard what you said about this pursuit." Anna hung her head. He lifted her chin with one finger. "I am sorry—for everything. I will be the gentlest of creatures, you have my word, but I will not let anyone harm you."

"Erik, you didn't—"

"I shed no blood." He helped her to the bedroll and settled behind her. "The comte's new friend stands warned. Loup should watch where he treads."

The name marched down Anna's spine.

"Why do you shake, Anna? He is merely the lackey of an insolent boy, Raoul's pathetic excuse for a marksman."

"He is a ruthless hunter!" She withered in his arms and worked to conceal her tongue's betrayal. "I mean . . . shouldn't we be worried? He has hounds."

"You think I cannot handle a fool such as Loup? What do you know of him?" She shook her head and lifted a shoulder doing her best to hide what she knew. "I assure you, child, do not doubt who I can and cannot handle." His laughter trembled in the air, hovering before it fell around them. "He will meet my rope one day. He is of no concern to me."

No concern to you perhaps.

Erik couldn't see the color Anna felt trickling from her face. She mouthed to Pappy to keep his silence and did not unpin him with her eyes until he yielded with a reluctant nod. The fire left an afterglow in her vision as she lowered her lids and allowed that name to settle back into her soul.

Should she confess her sins to Erik? Tell him of her past? Let him know the real truth of what bothered her? There would be no outrunning this pursuit now, not with Loup.

One can only outrun the wolf for so long.

Anna pressed a thumb to her ear and took a cleansing breath. Nothing helped. It stuck in her mind and she could not chase it away. Once Loup's song for her invaded her soul, the tune of *Alouette Gentille Alouette* tended to stay.

"What now?" Pappy asked, poking at the fire. "We can't outrun tracking dogs."

"We can and we will." Erik's voice strained against what seemed a rehearsed confession. "Nonetheless, if you so want, I will end this now. If it will please my Anna and my baby, I will give myself to Chagny."

A single laugh erupted from Anna's lips before fury snaked off her tongue. "Hypocrite! You speak that no man can conquer you and yet you would allow Chagny to do just that? Your valor dresses you well, but I would rather you end such a masquerade. Turning yourself in would break my heart. You may think that would be the right thing to do, to sacrifice your sins for the sake of me and our child, but we are all sinners. When will Chagny realize their injustice in all this?" Erik's lips had tightened into a thin line. "Their stubborn inability to communicate is what keeps the truth of this hidden. You turn yourself in and you will never see this baby. I don't want him growing up with the stories I weave for him, or rumors he learns of a Phantom. I want him to grow up knowing his father: murderer, Maestro, magician, mastermind.

"You blindly accept I am all that?"

"I accepted it long ago. I am not one to judge you by your past. I didn't live it. But love is worth running for. Fighting for. It does not discriminate. If this will be our life, then so be it." She looked around the haphazard camp. "I found all I need right here. I dare Chagny to find the same."

Eighteen

The days tumbled into one another without much division as the months tumbled into spring—sun to moon and moon to sun. A warm rain fell, melting what snow was left. It caused a sticky mess that adhered to everything. Anna attempted to shake off what caked on her boot. Throughout the day, each step she took caused her back to tighten. Her impromptu jig only worsened the pain.

Their routine had become commonplace. They traveled by night mostly, unless comfortable they were not being tracked. Home included the camps of other roamers. Now that spring was upon them, Erik, Anna, and Pappy sought to move as much as possible instead of seeking out another Samaritan to take them in. The indiscretion in Lyon only spurred the manhunt forward. Since leaving Dijon two months prior, they had been forced to move at a steady pace. Marksmen met them at every village and byway.

For the moment, they were blissfully alone. The slower pace they traveled was a welcomed relief.

"Anna, we can stop if you need," Erik called back to her.

She snapped her head back and forth. The ability to form words disappeared an hour ago, the pain of it all having edged in on her like a dull ache. Pain had been commonplace for the last few weeks—aching feet, a throbbing back, all she figured from traveling rough ground. Whenever he could or when he became too fearful of having her sidesaddle upon the horse, Erik carried her in the cradle of his arms. When this new ache began she thought nothing of it. Now, pain crushed her lower back. Anna gnashed her teeth together and waited for it to subside.

"Anna?" Erik asked. "Is your back hurting again?"

She opened her mouth to reply, but the pain spiraled. She stopped moving and leaned against a tree, jamming her back against it as hard as she could. The pressure provided a relieving counterpoint.

"I think . . . I think . . ." her voice trailed away as the contraction wound around her.

"You are not due for another two months!"

Erik raced toward her and enveloped her face with his hands. A sharp curse soared off her lips. She flung her head side to side to knock his hands off her face. With thousands of invisible ants crawling across her skin making her sensitive to the slightest touch, she could do without his sudden panic.

"We have another two months!" Erik insisted. Anna opted not to reply. She was presently . . . engaged. Her lack of response ignited Erik's alarm. He shouted for Pappy's attention. Jerking his head, he indicated a decrepit barn on the rim of the property they skirted. "Help me get her inside."

Erik reached for her again prompting her to swat violently. Her body tingled with pinpricks of sensation. The vertebrae in her back seemed to shatter under the pressure of labor. Erik and Pappy's arguments buzzed dully in her ears as they settled her in the barn. Occasionally she tried to sputter out a sentence, but she wasn't in command of her body. The infant trying to claw its way out of her was. Her knees shook the instant they laid her down. Sweat and chills ran in equal passes across her brow despite the fire Pappy worked frantically to build.

"This is not happening," Erik cursed. "We can make it to a village that does not know us. We can do this there!"

Anna pawed at the air. She didn't stop her frantic pantomime until it was filled with Erik's hand. To her side, Pappy rummaged through the satchel. She jerked her head toward him, her eyes going wide when he tossed a rag over his shoulder and shoved the knife into the fire.

"Have you ever done this before?" Erik barked.

"I delivered my daughter. You?"

"Murder, Maestro, magician, mastermind . . . not midwife!"

"You're about to be one."

Anna grabbed at the air again, the contractions rolling over her in wild waves. An irresistible urge to push took control of her body.

"She needs to push with the contractions or the baby won't come," Pappy instructed.

A contraction took over the moment making her writhe

worse than a nest of angry snakes. She fought Pappy's efforts to remove her boots. A cuss tried to splutter out her lips as he hiked her dress and stripped her of her pantaloons. All she succeeded in doing was jamming her teeth into her tongue. Every move he made to help, made her body want to crack in two. Tossing the garments aside, he crawled behind her.

"Anna, hold behind your knees. Push when you feel the need."

She filled her lungs and bore down. Pushing relieved the urgent feeling consuming her until the new agony set in.

Burning. The pain. The burning pain.

Her lower body plunged into a pit of fire and she had no exit from the flames. A searing pain shot between her legs as flesh ripped. Crying, Anna fell back against Pappy, praying it was over. Only seconds passed before the cycle repeated. As she bore down she saw Erik's hands fly to his temple before she lost all sense of space and time.

* * * *

Nothing in his travels, accomplishments or sins had prepared Erik for what he witnessed. His arms and legs propelled him from what he saw faster than a crab could crawl.

"Good God, Maestro, grow a spine!" Pappy roared. "Is the head coming?" Every muscle in Erik's body shivered. He nodded. "Ease it out when you can, then turn it slightly and use your finger to guide out the shoulder. The baby should do the rest of the work."

Erik tried to get his shaking under control as the infant's head came into view. Pappy's commands and Anna's struggles were not nearly as loud as the whoosh of blood in his ears.

"I cannot. I cannot do this." Erik crawled farther away.

"I delivered my daughter only to watch her be taken from me years later by a murderer like you. You will deliver this baby!"

"What if he is . . . what if he is . . ." Erik couldn't finish the thought. Her face turned a sickly mix of ash white that colored to bright red with every push. Never had he seen such an expression. Terror gripped his senses.

"Maestro now is not the time. Whatever comes—" Pappy clung to Anna as she pushed again, "comes. Anna needs you!"

Pappy's yell forced his submission. Every inching moment drew him closer to meeting his child. His heart slowed with the seconds that ticked by. He did as Pappy instructed, feeling his way rather than looking, for he could not bear to see his own image brought into the world. He swallowed hard against the emotion ramming a rock down his throat and guided the infant's head. Erik turned it, aiding the shoulder out. With a great rush of fluid the infant slid into his arms.

Pappy slung the rag at him. "Smack it between the shoulders. Get it to cry, and clean out its mouth."

Warm, moist life pulsed in Erik's hand. He allowed a few seconds for the fear to take control, and then commanded himself to turn his head and tend to his child. He issued one firm slap and the barn filled with a loud wail. Erik rolled off his knees, the tiny life in his hands writhing against a cold, new world.

That world stopped. Nothing existed except for the fragile creature he held in his arms. His breath escaped the prison of his lungs. His shoulders slumped forward. Pasty yellow skin and small wrinkles gradually waned to bright pink, thriving flesh. Erik stared awestruck at the crying infant and watched in amazement as the life pulsed out of the cord that connected his son to the woman he loved.

His son.

Erik wiped the baby's face with an awesome reverence. Beneath his mask his eyes filled with warm tears. He stared in amazement at the life before him. The perfect, perfect little boy he held in his arms.

"Maestro?" Pappy craned to see.

Erik sobbed.

Pappy moved quickly, taking the knife from the fire and cutting the cord. Baby wailing in one arm, he crawled toward Anna. Wrapping their son in the blanket Pappy provided, he handed him to her and crushed Anna's head in an intense hug.

"Anna, you made him beautiful. *Merci . . . merci avec tout mon amour*."

Rocking Anna in his arms and laying his mask against her hair, Erik was certain he would forget to breathe.

His son had stolen his mind and heart.

* * * *

A gentle twilight arrived, not that Erik noticed. With Anna cradled protectively in his embrace while his other precious possession was wrapped in his opposite arm, Erik marveled at the infant, confounded by the entire thought this creation was his.

"How long are you going to look at him, Erik?" Anna asked. He smiled his reply at his son. "What are you pondering?"

"Christine," he replied with brutal honesty. "She will experience this moment soon."

Anna rolled her head away from his frank admission. "You speak as if you desire to be the one to have sired her child."

"I always imagined a moment such as this would be with her."

The baby's hand jerked out from under the multitude of rabbit pelts Anna had saved. He shook his head back and forth in his sleep.

"I disappoint?"

"No," Erik said, tracing her face with his thumb. "You have made everything perfect." A finger pressed into the center of her temple, making her cross-eyed. "It is silent. My mind is quiet and it has not been so since the moment I learned of Philippe's death. Only the sounds I control are there now, and you made it so. This blissful euphoria, this indescribable silence, this warmth . . . Anna . . . is this happiness? If it is, it frightens me."

She reached out to stroke her son's hand as Erik covered it with his. The contrasting images made him feel alive. He could not find a way in words or music to describe the sensation of holding them both.

"Instead of staring, might I suggest you name that mongrel?" Pappy said.

"There is only one name for my son. Philippe Georges Marie."

Anna moved uncomfortably. "No. I will not have my life forever associated with a Chagny."

"I am not associating our lives with a Chagny. I am acknowledging a life because of a Chagny." The sudden passion to his words filled the barn. "If there is one thing we have to seek in this affair, it is the good that came out of it. There was only one true Comte de Chagny and whether or not I want to admit it, I owe much to that man. The man who holds that title now is not even worth the word, man. I will never be able to repay Philippe, not only because of his death, but also because of the breadth of hatred I hold for his kin. Raoul is not a Chagny in my eyes. He never will be, and do not ever expect my hatred of him to wane. Because of him my opera house is gone, my music denied, my life hunted, and my face—my weaknesses—are known. But because of a man, who was a true Chagny I was given an ally, a choice, and a chance. I was given you. I was given my son. I do not want to owe anything to Chagny and I do not, but to Philippe, I do."

Their eyes locked in a battle of wills, before Anna conceded defeat. "Philippe Georges Marie."

"I took the name Erik at great risk. I never bothered with a surname."

"Then he will have none," Anna said sternly. "I will not have my child carry my surname and it's of no matter to me. You have one name and so do I now."

Erik tore his eyes from Philippe to stare intently at his companions. "My son will know nothing of my past, this manhunt, or the reasons behind it. That starts now."

"You can't be serious," Anna gasped. "How do you intend to keep this from him? We are wanted fugitives. Chagny has no intention of stopping this. You ask the impossible. Besides, he's a newborn. Why are we thinking of this?"

"Because the sooner it starts the sooner it will be second nature. My son will be raised strictly German. If we need to speak of anything we will speak French, but he will not."

"You're insane!"

"Enough! Do not defy me on this. My children will be raised German. My kin will be protected from all this."

Anna's mouth dropped open before her lips crept upward. "Your children?"

Erik inched an arm around her and laid her head against his chest, his sheepish grin speaking for him.

"What now?" she asked. Pappy and Erik looked at her in question. Anna gestured impatiently. "No one is going to take pity on us because there is an infant involved. We can't continue this pace with him. Chagny is not going to relent."

"*Österreich*," Pappy suggested. Anna agreed.

"No," Erik sternly said. "I said he will be raised German, but, Anna, I cannot head to Austria. Not yet. I cannot leave France."

"We are wanted throughout France. You can't tell me you expect to wander this country with an infant without ever having a destination in mind?"

"My destination is wherever they are not and you are. We will head to the border, but not yet. I need time. When I returned to France after bidding on the foundation for that opera house, I retreated to its bowels, trading that misery for the various stages of hell I found across Europe. Let me get my country back into my veins. We will find a way. We will continue on as we have as long as we are able. Eventually, the need will be there when we can no longer outrun what pursues us."

Anna's brow rippled. "Must his name be Philippe?"

"Yes, it must."

Erik stayed content with her against his chest for a long while staring into the glow of the fire, reflecting on the past and looking, as Philippe had wished, to the future.

* * * *

The rain settled, leaving thick drops of water hanging like jewels from the branches of still naked trees. They shimmered in the fading twilight. The warmer air hit the lingering snow creating low fogs against the saturated earth. Occasionally, a breeze kicked in, sending those jewels tumbling to the ground in a soothing, rhythmic pattern.

Shoulder against the open door, Erik glanced inside feeling his chest expand at everything around him. He reluctantly took his eyes off his son, pouring himself into a moment of creative glory. The rusty chain he'd broken apart turned his hands brown. He artfully wove two ends of his opera cloak in and out of a few links until the entire length of the elegant fabric draped in a delicate yet weighty circle. All the while, his head swayed back and forth to the music he composed, blissfully aware of the undisturbed silence behind it.

Pappy stopped poking at the fire and laid his stick aside. "What are you doing?"

Erik waved him over, telling him to bring Philippe. Pappy gently pried the child from Anna's grip, careful not to disturb her sleep.

"She is exhausted." Erik worried aloud.

"Rightfully so." Pappy rocked the still slumbering child.

Draping his cloak like a sash around the old man's shoulders, he gestured with his rusty hands toward his sleeping son. "Wrap Philippe."

Pappy shushed the coos of protest coming from the infant as he eased him into the cradle of fabric. Erik grinned proudly.

"Maestro, you're a genius."

"Women have been carrying infants this way for centuries. He will be warm, safe, and close to a heartbeat."

Erik was quick to smile but allowed it to fade once he surveyed their surroundings. "We will need to find better shelter if it continues to threaten rain." He nodded toward Anna. "Is she well?"

"She bleeds, but I think that's normal."

"She needs a decent meal, a warm bath, and rest." He rubbed his mask in frustration. "We find the next village and take those by force if we must. I will not bathe either of them in a cold stream."

"A father and a lover."

"I still do not like you, old man."

"Mutual, Maestro." Pappy winked.

Erik held up his hands. "There is a well outside. I am going to get fresh water and wash these."

Grabbing the bladders, he headed out of the barn. Warmth swelled inside of him, knowing when he returned in a few moments he'd be returning to his family.

That word brought him an indescribable feeling of purpose. Sitting on the side of the well's wall, such happiness seemed . . . misplaced. Happiness had no dissonance in it at all. It was music in its purest form and, for Erik, a sort of peace. The pull of darkness and the undercurrent of a Phantom dragging him toward Tartarus faded away. He smothered the trembling flames of Hades in his soul.

A twig snapped in the nearby brush interrupting the notes in his head. Twisting the cap off the bladder, Erik noted the metal on metal sound he heard came not from the soft leather he held.

"You're trespassing."

Erik lifted his eyes to meet the rifle's barrel and the quivering youth barely strong enough to hold it. Laying the bladders aside, he wove his hands neatly in his lap.

"Monsieur." Erik's eyes flitted toward the barn before returning to the rifle.

"This is my land," the youth replied. "You're trespassing."

"The land is not posted and is ill kept, the well almost dry, and your barn in deplorable shape. You are a terrible farmer." Erik reached for his bladders and began to twist the caps back on.

"Don't move, Monsieur!"

"I doubt you have enough spirit in you to pull that trigger. Allow me to see the night out here and I will be on my way."

"I already allowed you time. I saw you cross my border. I know who you are."

Erik's lips pursed as he placed the bladders aside, then rose. If this child were going to test his patience, he would need to be taught a lesson. Make-believe shows of bravado would not be tolerated. Cocking his head, Erik forced the butt of the rifle to the ground with one tap of his finger. "Who, exactly, might I be?"

"Turn. Slowly." The response did not come from the wide-eyed youth.

Erik pivoted as four rifles cocked simultaneously.

* * * *

Anna stirred. Her back had stopped aching as if nothing had happened, but a stinging pain occasionally ran up her legs. It dimmed as she looked at the bundle wrapped in her arms. Her brow lifted in surprise. Seeing Erik's opera cloak swaddling Philippe, she smiled and could not help but think of her son protected by the Phantom's embrace. The moment was marred by Pappy's low grumbling in the direction of the open door.

"Don't do anything stupid, Maestro." He frantically doused the fire. "Anna? Can you mount the mare or the stallion?"

"No. I'm a bit sore. Why?"

Pappy rushed around the barn and gathered their belongings. He threw them into the satchel.

"Come." He helped her up.

"What's going on?" Anna stumbled over to peer though the barn door. Her blood ran cold. "*Mein Gott*. Pappy, we have to help him!"

"We are, by leaving."

He pointed her toward the back of the barn. Moving as fast as Anna had ever seen him, he shoved old bales and rusty tools away from the barn wall. He worked frantically to pry enough rotting boards loose to free them and the horses.

"Pappy, we can't leave him!" she pleaded, keeping her voice low.

"He's keeping their attention away from us. With a newborn we are no match against five rifles." The mare and stallion in tow, he forced Anna toward the back of the barn.

"I'm not leaving him!"

Pappy lunged and covered her mouth. "You have to do this. We will move as far as we can and then rest." He lowered his hand.

"Pappy, I just had a baby. I can't run!"

"I know you can't, but you have to. You have no choice." Board after board split under his panic. "Erik will find us. Don't think for one minute that he'll allow anything to come between him and his son."

* * * *

Erik mindfully kept his hands in view. He turned his head toward an orange glow steadily approaching from the trees. Additional superbly outfitted marksmen traipsed ahead with torches, lighting the way for the mounted huntsmen. Erik's eyes tapered on the coat of arms adorning their vests.

Chagny.

"Excellent work, Monsieur." Loup dismounted.

The youth's head bobbed enthusiastically. "He's the one isn't he? The Phantom? You'll get my reward now?"

Loup perched one leg up on the well next to Erik and indicated for him to sit. He didn't move. The wolf sniffed loudly in reply and made a slight gesture to remind him that man and firepower outnumbered him. Barely containing his disgust, Erik whisked his cloak aside and sat.

"You'll get your money." Loup palmed the boy in the face and shoved him to the ground, all the while keeping his regard squarely on Erik. "You have been quite the little fox, Monsieur. We have not delighted in such a hunt in a long time."

"Your nose has healed. Pity, I aimed to break that."

"I like your humor, but I regret I'm in no mood. Where is she?"

"She? I travel alone. As you well know, I took my fill of women in Lyon."

Loup pursed his lips and nodded to his mounted companions. "In the barn perhaps?" The horses edged to the building. Loup addressed his men, never once taking his eyes from Erik. "Block the barn door, lock it from the outside."

"I am traveling alone." If not for the loaded rifles and the proximity to his family, he would kill Loup. “You wanted me before, now you have me.” His throat turned as dry as desert sand as he watched the marksmen slide the door shut and slam down the rotted bar that would keep it locked.

“Alone? Excellent.” Without warning Loup swung. The violent crack of his backhand sent Erik spiraling off the wall. Hitting the dirt, he scrambled to all fours, spitting blood from his mouth. A savage kick to his ribs laid him flat. He clenched his teeth and huffed through his nose keeping his instinct to kill in check.

“Bind him,” Loup commanded. “We will bring him to the village and keep him there until I make contact with Chagny.”

Like vultures to rotted meat, the men descended on him. Erik bit back a curse as a boot cracked his lower back. His arms were wrenched behind him. Writhing under their assault as ropes tied his hands, Erik swallowed an animal panic.

He hated being bound . . .

Loup waited until he was sufficiently restrained before he yanked him to his feet. “So you travel alone? Had your fill of women in Lyon? Then what is so interesting in the barn? You keep looking at it. Perhaps we should inspect it more closely?”

The acid tones of Erik’s hatred burned the air. “I travel alone.”

“Then you won’t mind too terribly?” He shoved Erik toward the trees and shouted to his men. “Burn it!”

The world moved in slow motion as Erik turned in time to see torches break what windows the barn had. Shattering glass echoed around him before the smoke rose. The barn went up like a tinderbox despite the previous rain. Blazing fire flashed before his eyes. Heat ripped through him. The roar of flame against wood was not loud enough to drown out his superhuman cry of rage and grief.

Erik saw nothing but the flames of Hades consume his life before his world was swallowed in darkness.

Nineteen

Raoul gathered the reins in his expert grip and nudged the horse into a trot, then a canter. The tight figure-eight formation they made helped to focus not only the stallion's attention, but his as well. Something about Legard's suggestion for a ride didn't sit well. Usually it was Raoul challenging Legard to a day on the trails. He signaled for the horse to change leads at the center of the eight, and looked toward the mounting block where Legard was swinging his leg over his chestnut. The stallion beneath him tensed, anticipating the next command as they crossed the formation again. Raoul didn't bother leaning to the left to issue the order. He broke off the exercise and urged the horse into a trot to follow Legard out of the stable yard. He didn't even warm his horse. Once on the carriage road leading away from Chagny and toward the miles of groomed trails, Raoul turned to his friend.

"Out with it."

"If you will forgive me for ruining the ride . . ." Legard fished in his jacket pocket and withdrew a note. Holding it between two fingers, he extended it to Raoul. "It seems Loup has found and subdued your Phantom. That drunk may be unorthodox, but I admit he is a better hunter then I ever could've been. They're transporting Erik to Chaumont."

Raoul's breath whistled out his teeth. An overwhelming urge to ride his horse at a breakneck pace through the wilder grounds of Chagny and on to Chaumont flashed through him. It seemed Legard read his mind.

"If the Phantom has indeed been captured, then there's no need for me to guard Chagny. To ease your concern, I can see to it one of your sisters and their kin reside on the premises. I won't have you traveling alone to meet the Phantom or that addict."

Raoul leaned forward and stroked the powerful arch of the

stallion's neck. "What now?"

"Upon our return, I suggest we contact the authorities in Paris. They'll take the Phantom off your hands and await your orders from there."

"I still want you here in service to Chagny," Raoul dictated. "Will you see to it only the brightest in Paris are assigned to my brother's case?"

Legard pulled sharply on the reins, so much so Raoul had to double back to ride at his side again. "Raoul, you've been told countless times. Philippe's death was accidental."

"My brother was murdered. The Phantom is under Chagny control now and I am not about to relinquish that. The one thing I will not do is allow the Phantom out of my grasp without him knowing how much he stole from me."

"Erik's suffering will not lessen the blow of Philippe's death."

Raoul snapped his head away from the steamed look on Legard's face. Instead, he stared down the perfectly manicured trails, remembering countless times he and Philippe tried to best one another in horsemanship. The hedge up ahead still bore the scar from the time Raoul plowed through it rather than artfully over it like his brother. Such memories still couldn't summon tears to his eyes.

Raoul knocked Legard's words aside and turned his horse abruptly back to Chagny. "The pregnancy has my wife's mobility compromised of late. I promised her a spring ride in the gig. Have my man contact my banker. Chagny just made one farmer very wealthy."

Before Legard could shout a protest, Raoul let the stallion take over the bit and shot down the trail. Horse and rider careened over fence and ditch at a pace that thrilled and feared—like he had years ago with his brother by his side. Raoul didn't think then such reckless riding could end badly, and he didn't think it now.

Nothing raced quite as fast as his careless thoughts.

* * * *

The notorious Chagny fog had burned away, finally providing Christine with a magnificent view of their holdings. They moved along at a lively pace, past century old oaks and patches of newly born flowers poking their heads out of the ground.

"Are you feeling well, Christine? This is not too much for you? The ground is still not firm. The horses feel unsteady."

"Stay at a slow pace and baby and I will be fine, Raoul. You fret too much."

Nonetheless, Raoul pulled his horse up and slowed the gig.

"Come, we walk from here." He jumped down first and settled the horse then helped her down. He led her down a grassy path to the shores of the Chagny pond, the thick blanket he retrieved from the floor of the gig tucked under his arm. The blanket billowed out as he tossed it in the air in front of him and let the wind gently spread it to the ground. He helped Christine to a seat. She smiled appreciatively. This baby made her rounder than when she'd carried André.

"The high seas of Chagny." Raoul gestured to the pond.

"It's good to see the ice gone." Christine took a deep breath of fresh air.

"Philippe used to bring me here for every reason under the sun, be it a lesson or a lecture."

Christine peeled off her gloves. She squinted in the light glinting off the pond as she straightened her hair. A light breeze prompted her to adjust the shawl around her shoulders. "Why is it the Comte de Chagny brings me here now? Lesson or lecture?"

"Neither." He took her hand. His lips tickled her palm. "Christine, I'll be leaving Chagny for a while on business."

She found a stone at her feet and tossed it into the pond. Newly emerged reeds bobbed and swayed on the ripples. "That's hardly a reason to bring me out here. You're called off frequently. How long will you be?"

"I cannot say. Legard will be coming with me. My sister, Paulette, will be here for you. Her husband will reside on Chagny ground in my stead. If you need anything, you are to tell them immediately."

Christine plunked her hands in her lap. "Raoul, you worry too much. The blood I pass has slowed." Though she'd wanted to, her heart was weak and she couldn't keep that detail from him. Raoul wanted the world for his baby. It still pained her to see the fear on his face. "The doctor says I'm fine."

"You are under far too much stress. The doctor said you should rest all you can, and here I am dragging you out for a ride. I should be run through." Christine giggled at the way his frown drooped one side of his moustache. "I blame Erik for this," he rumbled. Suddenly Christine was not laughing. "If not for him, you would not have undue anxiety jeopardizing your health."

"My health isn't in jeopardy. Erik has nothing to do with this." Even as she voiced it her back twitched. Tell Raoul about Loup's assault on her and he would reveal her sins with Erik. That would mar her husband's name, her son's title . . . She took another cleansing breath. The stress would have to be dealt with. She reached for Raoul's hands and laid them across her belly. "You should hear the heartbeat, Raoul. The doctor said this baby sounds like it is swimming upstream faster than André ever did. The baby will be fine. Fine and perfect."

"I cannot help myself. I want my daughter to be safe."

"There you go again. It could be a boy."

"A healthy and happy baby is all that matters." Raoul took her hands. "Christine, Erik is in custody in Chaumont. I leave tomorrow to bring this to a close."

The high seas of Chagny were calm, but the storm that churned in her belly was tempestuous. Folding her arms across her abdomen, she forced down the dizzying nausea. Her back tightened. The rock of uncertainty sat on her chest. "Raoul . . . what will happen to him?" Her hands tightened into her belly. "Where will they bring him? Will they bring him to Chagny?"

"No. I will arrange for him to go directly to Paris."

"Oh mercy." She struggled against her shape and got to her feet. She searched the comfort of her grand estate, her mind flipping though pages upon pages of her life. To think that one chapter may be ended and closed forever . . . "He will go to prison," she stated numbly.

Raoul rose. "Definitely. He will likely be executed." The look she gave him insisted he hold his tongue. "Rest assured you will be safe through this. He will not come near you, André, or our baby. I need to know if you will be all right. This ends a huge part of our life—of your life. But it will continue—blessed and better without his memory."

"What of . . . what of that woman?"

"I don't know if Mademoiselle Barret was with him or not. What weight do you carry that has you so pensive?"

Anna bore no fault in the abduction that started this manhunt—nor did Erik. They both fought to protect her from a ruthless man out for her husband's purse. But how could Christine bear the truth now?

"Is it Anna that burdens you?" Raoul asked. She meekly nodded. "She will not come near you. Her crimes go far beyond that opera house." Christine sucked in her breath as her heart lurched with fear. "Forgive me for trying to shelter you. You are stronger than I allow myself to believe. Anna Barret killed a nobleman's child."

Christine's finger sank possessively against her baby. "She what?"

"She murdered Duke de Molyneux's heir."

Before she could control it, she cried André's name. She feared, suddenly, for the life of her child. Raoul's confession did nothing to numb her disbelief.

"Loup has been looking for her for years."

"Keep that woman away from my son," she said through an angry tear filled throat. "Don't you dare keep such truths from me again."

"I didn't want to upset you."

"Upset me?" Any remorse Christine had for not admitting the truths of what launched this manhunt evaporated in the blink of an eye. "That woman hates our kind. She . . . that . . . lock her away! You promise to tell me the truth. Always!"

Raoul nodded as she wept on his shoulder until his jacket moistened with her tears.

How could she lose her Angel of Music to a woman such as her? How could she lose her Angel of Music?

"Raoul?" Although she had rehearsed this moment over and over again she still fought to form the words. "What . . . what if Erik did nothing to harm me a year ago? Would he still be sent away?" On tenterhooks, she waited for his reply.

"The past is the past. He has sinned for far too long with crimes he must pay for. Even if he were innocent, the truth is, he is aiding Mademoiselle Barret now. There is firm evidence of her crimes. That is enough to see him put away. You will never have to dwell on the 'what ifs' anymore, my love. This is over."

The 'what ifs'? What if she couldn't live without the connection she had for a dangerous man she didn't understand, and what if she could never grow beyond the truth that he was in love with a woman she would never forgive.

* * * *

"Why aren't they looking for us?" Something had to cut the stillness. The silence around them unsettled her to the point of madness.

Pappy bobbed Philippe slowly around the campfire, making sure he stayed swaddled in the warmth of the opera cloak. "Your lips are turning blue." He yanked a spare blanket from his saddlebag and held it open. "Come out now."

The pond rose to her chin as she sank lower into the water. Though frightfully cold, the buoyancy gave her respite from her aching muscles, and the chill numbed more than flesh.

"Anna, now." Pappy shook the open blanket as forcefully as her lips shook. She raised an eyebrow. "For heaven's sake woman, I'm an old man, lewd comes with the territory. I've stolen enough glimpses at you in all your bare glory to confirm that a certain part of my anatomy doesn't work. Now out!"

Rising from the water, the cool spring air instantly made her skin pebble. Crossing her arms in front of her breasts, she slunk toward Pappy and the blanket. "Bathe only to smell like a horse."

"You're a breath of fresh air compared to Maestro." Pappy chuckled, setting him and Philippe down in front of the fire.

Anna shrugged on a toasty dress, thankful for Pappy's foresight to warm it. She returned to the comfort of her fur-lined cloak. The days may have been warming, but the nights were still chilly. Her son cooed from the shelter of his cocoon when she relieved Pappy of his sling. He gave him a tiny pat with the tip of his finger.

"He has his father's nose."

"Pappy!"

The old man lifted his shoulders. "It's a jest, Anna. I'm trying to lift your spirits. You have lost all sense of hope."

"His father was arrested and the barn we were in burned to the ground. I have no way of knowing if Erik is alive and he, likewise, has no way of knowing the same. I've no idea why we're not being pursued and you expect me to find humor?"

"I expect you to have faith in him."

"They likely bound him," she muttered. "He hates being restrained. It takes away what control he thinks he has. Erik's mind is always balanced on the right side of danger, perched precariously between peace and the torment of madness. I have no doubt—total faith in an Erik you never want to meet is on the rise. If God is just, this child will have his mother's mind and his father's heart." Anna released her breath in a long sigh as she pondered the stars. "I look at Philippe and do you know what I see? I see Chagny. I envision an absolute castle surrounded by endless grounds of peaceful greens. I see a husband and wife comfortable in their riches and stubborn in their neglect of the truth."

"You sound jealous."

Anna silently named at least three constellations before continuing. "I see all that because that is what Erik would want. He would want to shower Philippe with all the riches of France and lay the world at his feet." Her hand absently touched the end of her braid. A drenched hair silk dripped water to the ground. "But instead of planning for that grand future in his stead, I need to decide how long I will wait by a campfire for him to make his way back to his son."

Pappy tossed a handful of grass onto the fire. It sizzled and withered before their eyes. "You doubt he will?"

"I doubt the limits to human endurance. The mind can handle only so much, even Erik's. I wonder who will return: father or Phantom."

* * * *

The fresh and earthy scent of hay mingled with the charred aroma of overcooked meat. The snort of a beast jolted him awake.

Tension was an unwelcome bedfellow as Erik lay prostrate on the floor of a dark and mobile prison. The magnificent throb of his head recalled the blow from a rifle butt. It matched the intense ache that spread across his chest. Erik twitched in his binds. A warm trickle of blood moved from his wrist to his thumb as the ropes split his thin flesh. It slid down his skin carving a tickling line so profound it jerked him to a sitting position. He struggled to his feet. The sudden motion made his head spin and he collapsed harshly to the floor. The carriage rocked side-to-side prompting a protest from the hitched team.

Raucous laughter circled the center of the camp. "Ah, it seems our nightingale is awake." Something solid contacted with the side of the carriage. A rock perhaps? He heard tankards clang together. "A drinking song, nightingale. Sing for us. Something lively. I am partial to *Alouette.*"

Erik leapt to his feet and rounded all his weight against the door. He shoved his mask against the barred window. "Where am I?"

Loup ripped into a wad of meat and spoke around it. "Neither here nor there. You are, however, going to Chaumont where a dear, old friend will meet you." He turned to his men. "What a reunion that will be! My money is on the sniveling little Comte."

Erik bucked against the door, desperate to rip the man's throat out with his bare hands. "Where is she? What did you do to her?"

Loup tossed his meal aside. He stood, brushed the dirt from his trousers and tugged on his vest. He grabbed a flaming branch from the fire. "She, Monsieur? Whomever do you mean? I thought you said you traveled alone?"

Erik followed the glowing line of the flaming branch and shook his head clear. A sickening dread rose from the pit of his stomach.

"You seem more coward to me than the cunning madman the Comte painted you. Pity. I was up for a challenge." Loup turned back to the camp.

"Where. Is. She." Erik's chest heaved.

Loup's arm cut the air in front of him. The makeshift torch struck the metal of the carriage. "She burned!"

Sparks flew into the sky and flame roared before Erik's eyes. He staggered backward. Heated points of light fell into his prison.

Loup tossed the stick aside. He leapt upon the carriage like an alley cat and clung to the iron bars. His cheek pressed close to the door, he looked at Erik with a wild glaze to his eyes. Erik recoiled again as soon as he began singing.

"*Alouette, gentille Alouette. Alouette je te plumerai . . .*"

Erik thrashed inside the carriage, screaming in a blind fit of rage as Loup dropped to the ground and rejoined the festivities. The entire camp was rowdy with the tune, making Erik writhe until he buckled on the floor, a battered heap.

The darkness behind his eyes gave no relief to the fire seared on his mind. The last cries of his family screamed behind the roar of flame. Were those flames stoked by Satan, or were they flared by his complete and utter failure? Tartarus called, and the current of Lake Avernus was too strong to navigate. At least the waters would extinguish the pain of losing his family. Lifelong madness was a bellows in the Devil's hand. Erik willingly handed a coin to Charon. An unusual calm washed over him. Crawling to the corner of his cage, he slumped against his knees, too numb to cry. Instead, a misplaced smile twitched across his lips. There was nothing left to do but follow where madness led.

Erik would travel to the underworld by any means he could and take with him all that tried to stop him.

Twenty

A mind tormented is searching for infinite possibilities—madness, a cancer endlessly looking for asylum. Erik tried to control his dementia, but the padlocks that covered his wrists also imprisoned his mind.

The carriage came to an abrupt halt, crashing him from one side to another. He'd lost track of the amount of times he transferred long ago. When the doors swung open, Erik crawled to the back of the cage.

"*Bon matin*, Monsieur!" Loup exclaimed. "Welcome to Chaumont. We'll rest here until we receive orders from your friend."

Erik thrashed and kicked the entire way to the cell, giving those who restrained him no small show of his fury. Loup yanked open the door, throwing him in with such force it pitched him against the far wall. The crack of his forehead against the stone he thought a fitting blow to match the berating in his mind. The cold floor rose to meet him as he sank first to one knee, then the other. Inching his way into a corner, he dragged pungent hay with him beneath his knees. He wanted to back away from the bars behind him, but the walls prevented his escape. A grim shadow of his life flashed before his eyes.

The bars and the cell were not what he hated—rather the idea of a prison not of his making. The idea of weakness and vulnerability. The illusion he was merely a beast with no feeling, no soul, and no control. A worthless child to be locked in dark basements, a worthless man to be jeered at, a skilled mastermind to be feared . . .

Memories roared to life. Erik spat incomprehensible words and fought violently for control as his hands were freed from the ropes that bound him, but his jailer was stronger. Rusty manacles replaced the ropes and with two ominous clicks, they encircled his flesh.

Loup untangled a well-worn chain at Erik's feet and reached around him to fasten one end to the manacles and clasp the other with a sickening click to a ring in the wall. He squatted and leaned in, inches from Erik's face. Loup jerked down on the chain.

The cell echoed Erik's pain.

"You tremble, Monsieur," Loup purred. "Tell me. Your quivering, is that out of fear of me, or do you miss her lips?"

Loup yanked the chain again. Laughter coursed the cell as metal ripped open flesh. Erik seethed, his breath puffing out between tightly clenched teeth. Deep inside he fostered an irrepressible urge to kill.

"You miss her, don't you, Monsieur? The scent of her flesh as she lingers close to you. Her taste as she offers you her lips . . ."

Loup traced a finger across Erik's mouth. The back of Erik's skull crashed into the wall as he wrestled his fury. His face blazed with heat. Shaking his head from side to side, he savagely tore his face away. He could break Loup's taunting his misery, but could do nothing to drown out his menacing laughter.

"Such cold lips you have. Cold . . . like the lips of the dead. Like her lips."

Erik lunged forward with a feral growl of rage. Loup skipped backward, tongue out, neck dangling at a mocking angle as he sang.

"*Je te plumerai le cou! Je te plumerai le cou . . .*"

Erik's murderous fury fell short, snapped back by his tether.

"Don't go far." Loup ran a finger across his mouth and slid it between his lips. He backed himself out of the cell and slammed its iron bars shut.

The silence would have been blissful save for the noise in his mind. Erik fought against the invisible arms that hauled him back into a world of his own horrors. The evil presence in his mind one minute had him laughing, the next cowering at ghastly thoughts. The arms were locked together like lovers in an untamed tango, dancing to a brutish rhythm.

He cursed as he struggled, giving one last yank on his chain before curling into a tight ball. As this malevolent dance twirled in his head, the memory of a dance of a different kind cut in.

Erik's eyes followed the vision. Sweat stung them, but he refused to blink. If he closed them again, she would be gone.

She laughed while he waltzed with her, her hair glimmering with highlights of copper. She was petite and full of spirit, so simple in a world so complex. Her smile intoxicated him. Her breast heaved with the anticipation of his touch. When she stood on her toes to reach for his lips, he eagerly leaned forward to greet her. The shimmering light in her tresses inched closer to his face until they erupted into a wall of flame and the vision of her was consumed by fire.

Erik slammed his eyes shut. His chained hands clawed at his mask, trying to tear his eyes free from the image. Jerking backward, he couldn't bear to watch her burn again. His blood raced, his strength failed him, fear took over, and he retreated into his memories—an unwilling partner.

His dance card it seemed—was full.

* * * *

The den was a palace of debauchery, not at all where Raoul desired to spend the end to a long and tedious journey. He and Legard wove their way through the establishment toward the back room. It held nothing to the luxury brothels of Paris, but still, even in a provincial town such as Chaumont it filled with respectable businessmen and was crowded with schoolboys—brothel tokens no doubt jingling in their pockets. They found their hunter lounging in a secluded room.

"You seem out of your element, Comte de Chagny," he immediately observed.

Raoul tossed the brief on the table. "Where is he?"

"Relax, Monsieur le Comte. Your Phantom is across town tucked safe and sound at the magistrate."

"Then why not meet me there?"

"Because I thought you might have the need to unwind. Celebrate this moment. Your Phantom is not going anywhere. You painted this man as dangerous. Pathetic more the word."

"What did you do to him?"

"Nothing, he simply does not like restraints." He turned to the whore to his right and tugged on her earlobe. "Or my fingers upon him."

Raoul's gut surged.

"What of Mademoiselle Barret?" Legard demanded.

Loup bolted upright, shoving the woman aside. "Or fire!"

He slapped his hands repeatedly against the table. “He does not like fire. Fire burns! I like fire . . . fire inspires.”

Raoul clenched his fist until nails bit into his palm. Looking to Legard, he followed his nod toward the empty bottle, water pitcher, and absinth spoon on the table.

“What of Anna? Did you find her?” Legard gestured to the note.

“I can’t confirm whether she was with him or not, but I suspect she was. My hounds were agitated. The Phantom was intrigued with the barn we found him in, so I burned it.” He studied the dirt under his nails. “I had fun. Your Phantom fellow was not happy at all.”

“You sick excuse for a man.” Raoul barely governed revulsion.

Loup leaned forward in his chair. “You really are far too admirable a man, Monsieur. You respect women too much. Anna is my candy, my toy, my whore. I will do with her what I want.”

A barmaid entered and placed a second bottle of Pernod Fils on the table. The sight of the absinthe sent Raoul’s anger soaring. He grabbed the bottle before Loup had a chance to reach for it. “I thought I told you no alcohol.”

“Who do you think you’re dealing with?” He indicated the bottle. “Deny me that all you want, this is not the ground of your hovel. You’ve no way of knowing where I am or what I do. That is the glory of being a hunter. You’ve no control over me.”

“Duke de Molyneux wanted Mademoiselle Barret brought in alive,” Raoul snapped. “Perhaps I will tell him exactly how you operate.”

How often could Raoul threaten him by using Molyneux’s name? Despite the hunter’s arrogance it seemed he did on some level fear the duke. Loup’s eyes tapered. Raoul kept his breath trapped in his lungs.

“Let us not match wits.” His voice contained a hint of defeat. “Have a seat and celebrate the capture of your Phantom. I paid a fine sum for this evening. The Madame has her best waiting for you upstairs. Just don’t think of deducting it from my pay.”

Raoul clutched the neck of the bottle to keep from exploding in fury. “I do not bed whores.”

“Really? Then what do you call your wife?”

Raoul dove forward, but Legard was the stronger man. He intercepted and forced him away. "He is drunk on the green fairy and has no command of mind or tongue."

"I have command of more than mind and tongue." Loup's hand reached under the table to between his legs. "Who I command is soft, naïve, and stupid."

"What does that mean?" Raoul fumed.

"Mention Molyneux all you want," Loup said with slow deliberation. "I can ruin you faster than you ever can me."

"How so?"

"Why not ask your wife whose lips she enjoyed in Lyon, and then attempt to threaten me again." A malicious smile opened Loup's mouth and exposed his pearly teeth. "*Au revoir*, Comte de Chagny. Go fetch your Phantom. My work with you is done. I will expect my payment in full when I am through here. Your coin will be nice to add to the lifetime of money your wife will be giving me to keep your good name intact."

"What are you talking about?" Raoul shouted, slamming the bottle down on the table with such rage it shattered.

"Enough!" Legard shoved him to the door.

Once outside, Raoul took several deep breaths. "Is this what it feels like? This disregard for everything? Is this what it feels like to want to kill?"

"Lower your voice." Legard urged him to walk.

Raoul pointed toward the brothel. "I could you know. I could kill them both. The Phantom and that wolf for his disgusting mouth."

"You never want to kill a man. Trust me. He spoke because of the drink, nothing more. We will transfer Erik to Paris and be done with Loup for good. I told you a hunter was not a wise idea."

"And Mademoiselle Barret?" Raoul crammed a fist against his lips.

"Loup only became involved with us because of her, and he wanted your purse. If you still desire to press charges, I will have to send someone to investigate the barn. See if her body—"

Raoul held up a hand for him to stop. The thought of searching through a charred barn to determine whether or not to continue with the hunt sickened him. "Christine fears her. Do what you must to make sure this manhunt is over." He watched the traffic grow on the street as the town woke for the evening. Their chosen establishment held far too much attention for comfort. He refused to be anywhere near it. "First we have a Phantom to see."

* * * *

"I do this alone." Raoul held out his hand to prevent Legard from following.

"No."

"He is chained and bound. I need this moment with him, do not defy me."

Raoul shot a contemptuous look at Loup's men. They snickered, apparently unconcerned and continued their card game. Legard swiped their table clear with an arch of his arm. Card and coin flew across the magistrate's office. He yanked each of them to their feet. Chairs fell over as curses filled the air.

"Fine. But we'll be on guard here," Legard enjoined. "One word and we'll be at your side."

Raoul nodded and insisted on the key. He took a moment to compose himself before taking the longest walk of his life. If he thought brothels to be despicable, this was no different. The massive iron bars were intimidating and the cell smelled of excrement and stale air. The bars moaned in protest at being opened. Stepping into the hold, he paused. A platter of bread, cheese, and flat ale sat untouched on the sticky floor. No means of comfort could be seen, not even a bench. It was not difficult to understand why. The stone surrounding a high barred window was riddled with scratches, testimony to one prisoner too many trying to pry their way out. Hay made a small section of the dark room slick, and it was on this hay a figure stirred.

What Raoul found didn't make any sense. This was a broken man, not the Phantom. Somehow he expected to see that oddly commanding presence, that unusually dignified and authoritative man who held Paris under his spell of intrigue and terror.

He swallowed whatever pity surfaced and stared at the ball in the corner. "It seems your travels are over, Erik. Quite foolish of you to call on Christine in Lyon. It led us right to you."

Erik leaned out of shadow enough for Raoul to reaffirm his hands were tightly bound and chained at an awkward angle. With the change of light, Erik's yellow eyes disappeared in the depths of his mask. Unnerved, Raoul looked away.

"So she had the backbone to tell you, did she?"

"She mentioned you called on her after a performance like a lovesick boy. How many times is she going to need to reject you before you understand she wants nothing to do with you?"

Erik licked cracked lips and slowly stirred. "You certainly are not that emotional young man anymore, but you are still foolishly overzealous. How long will it be before you realize there are different faces we all wear? She wears one for you and one for me. You are bedding a stranger, Monsieur. Pity you do not recognize who you choose to lie with. Life is but a masquerade to a Frenchman. Where is your domino?"

Erik slid up the length of the wall. Raoul had forgotten how intimidating he was at full height. "Make your jokes, Monsieur, there will be no humor where you are going."

"Where might that be—to hell? I have been there before, Monsieur le Comte de Chagny, and I use such formality loosely. You are not worthy of such noble respect."

Erik dismissed him with a flick of a slender finger and slumped back to the ground.

Raoul's voice scratched out his throat. "What did you do to him?"

"To whom, Monsieur?"

"Philippe."

"Philippe?"

A weighty darkness hung in Erik's voice. One that made Raoul take a cautious step backward. "You killed him."

Erik rolled his head back and forth against the wall. His voice was monotone. "I know no Philippe, Monsieur."

"You are a liar." Raoul had to lean in slightly to catch his next words.

"And a murderer, Maestro, magician, mastermind . . ."

"They found his body on the shores of *your* lake! Why did he go there? How did my brother die?"

Silence seeped through the walls around them. Erik lifted his head and stared blankly at Raoul's boots. Raoul looked to his feet, then behind him following Erik's eyes as they roamed the cell.

"Philippe . . ." Erik lamented. "So tiny. So perfect."

Raoul leaned away from the heart-wrenching sob that squeezed out Erik's chest. "You're mad! Why did you kill my brother?"

The cage rattled with an untamed groan. Bits of rusted chain shot toward Raoul causing him to duck as Erik, with one violent yank, severed the chain from the wall, shattering the manacle around his wrist. A fist cut the air between them as Erik cracked Raoul's jaw with one swing of his blood soaked hand. His punch knocked him against the wall, splitting the flesh of his scalp. Scrambling back on guard, Raoul grabbed the leaden tankard. When Erik lunged again, he swung at his head full force. The blow ripped the edge of his mask, knocking Erik off balance. Raoul set up to swing a second time, but Erik parried. The prison cell twirled as Raoul slammed against the wall. All of Erik's bodyweight crushed against him. Before he had a chance to shout for help, a metal chain wrapped like a noose around his neck. Erik dragged him into his embrace.

"Valiant effort, but you must feel to kill! It starts as a tiny flutter somewhere deep inside. A very low, monotonous pulse barely perceptible until it rises . . . yes . . . it is rising now. It rises until it matches the pitch in your mind. You have never heard what it is like to kill? The tones are different, you see. Killing for defense yields one tune, to be an assassin for the Sultana of Persia is music all its own. You stiffen, why? Oh, I have a colored past, Monsieur. It should not surprise you. But I have never killed for pleasure. Do I do that now or save that music for your wolf? A duet you say? No . . . I will not yield to it. I will not kill again." Raoul groaned against the chain. "Too many times you have stolen Erik's loves, Monsieur, in too many ways. For me to even use that word in plural form is pure irony. I know the pain of a heart that no longer beats, for I am finally complete. Erik is finally dead. I will not kill you, for I do not wish Christine to feel such agony or senseless loss." The chain bit into Raoul's throat making breathing difficult and swallowing the saliva flooding his mouth next to impossible. "I suggest, Monsieur, you strip her of her masks and burn them like she once did mine. Recognize her lies. I grow weary of this game. I do not know how your brother died and I would never dare kill the man responsible for giving me back my life. Do not make your brother's death into my burden. If you do not know who he truly was and why he would be at my lake, then that is your weakness to carry—not mine. I no longer care. When the almond tree ripens and the grasshopper is a burden—desire fails . . . Ecclesiastes, Chapter Twelve, verse five."

With a final bit of pressure applied to the right points, Raoul fell slack at Erik's feet. As soon as the tension was off his throat the room began to focus again, but Raoul was still stunned and weak. Prone on the floor and fighting for fresh breath, he watched Erik step out of the cell and toward the cloak of the night.

He dragged himself palm over palm upright against the wall, forcing great gulps of air into his lungs. His head throbbed magnificently. Despite it, he bent, picking up the broken manacle. Vertigo spun the room. He ignored it. Raoul grabbed the chain and slammed it into the far wall. It shattered to rusty pieces.

"Damn you to hell! Legard!" The sheer magnitude of his fury brought Legard and the balance of the marksmen skidding around the corridor in time to see him stumble from the cell.

Legard slid to a stop. "Raoul?"

"Whatever is the problem?" Loup called, appearing from the far end of the hall. He folded his arms and leaned against the wall. "Phantom issues?"

Legard steadied Raoul and helped him loosen his cravat. He rubbed the raised bits of flesh around his throat.

"That has to hurt," Loup mocked.

"Enough!" Raoul's vocal chords snapped. He managed a throaty whisper. "You may think you have something to lord over me, but while you are in France you operate under my authority."

Legard tightened his grip on his arm. "What are you doing? His association with us is over. Let this go."

Raoul jerked his arm free and took a few paces toward Loup. Nothing would satisfy him more than to wipe the smug look off his face. "You will bend to my every whim in this. Do I make myself clear?" Raoul ignored the curses rumbling out of Legard from behind him.

"My, my Comte de Chagny, such fire in your words. What exactly are you asking of me?"

Something singsong in the tone of Loup's voice sent an invisible sword running through him. "Find him. Find him until he is put away forever. I will pay double what Molyneux is if you put him first and worry about Mademoiselle Barret second." More curses sprung from Legard's mouth. Arms akimbo, he backed away from Raoul. "Dispatch some men to that barn and find out if she is alive or dead. In the meantime—find me the Phantom."

In response to his demand, Loup jerked his head in a well-practiced manner that sent several marksmen out the door. He pushed off the wall. "Return to Chagny, Monsieur le Comte. Inform your wife you are a failure and a disappointment. Tell her, her whimpers of being rid of me fall on deaf ears because of your stupidity in letting the Phantom go. It seems I will be clinging to Chagny like the ivy on the walls."

"Find him!"

Laughter tumbled around him as Loup turned down the hall. "Oh, and remind her not to forget our conversation."

The door slammed, leaving a heavy silence in the room. Legard turned his back to Raoul punctuating the strain of disapproval he heard to his voice. "Come. We need to get your head stitched and your bruising attended. I don't need you returning to Chagny looking like you lost a fight."

Raoul didn't look at him. Loup's last words were the only thing ringing in his ears.

* * * *

Though he tried to beat the memories out of his head by using the brick wall, nothing stopped the images of Philippe. They rose to the surface like a mushrooming cloud of ash, fogging everything in its path. Leaning against the wall of the alleyway, feeling his foundation shake from under him, Erik fought for calm. Unseen hands were all that held him back from plunging over a dark and familiar abyss. The ripped flesh around his wrists pooled blood into palms, coating them with red warmth.

"I did not kill him." Philippe de Chagny's face swam before his eyes. His face heated beneath the mask to an unbearable level causing him to roll his head to the side, seeking the cool relief of the brick. Erik pushed off the building, the momentum causing him to lose his balance and stagger toward an odd golden glow. Pad by pad, the hound's hackles rose as it bared its ghostly white fangs. Erik leveled his eyes on the figure that followed.

"You underestimate me." Loup's rifle leveled with Erik's chest. "I too have sought shadows in my day. You will have to learn to run longer, harder, faster, and smarter if you are going to win against me."

Erik dropped deeper into shadow. He had no weapons, and his throat was so parched, using his voice would do nothing but further his injuries. The dog moved forward. Loup lowered his rifle and tucked it carefully under one arm. The sound of his heavy footsteps echoed in the narrow alleyway, forcing Erik to slip back farther into a darkened corner. The alley erupted with a bright light, momentarily blinding even eyes as keen as his.

The match burned close to Loup's fingers before he flicked it forward. "Fire. You don't like it, do you? Why is that?" Match after match extinguished at Erik's feet, causing him to writhe like a charmed cobra. "Come. Kill me. You know you feel it." The next match lit a small pile of debris, flooding the alley with light. Erik's hands flew to the sides of his head. Loup laughed. "Kill me, or burn like she did."

Unable to contain the inferno of hatred within him, Erik's hands jerked forward aiming for Loup's neck. They never got close enough to satiate his taste for murder. The dog lunged. Man and beast tumbled back deep into the shadowy parts of the alley. Growls of rage, tearing fabric, and Loup's laughter rent the air.

Yet as abruptly as the night exploded with the fight, it ended. Despite the hustle of the streets beyond, the narrow space echoed with a throbbing silence. Erik, completely transformed, stepped from the shadows. In the crook of one arm he held the body of a dog, in his heart, no remorse. In the opposite hand, he clutched the emblem of his curse. Loup backed away, his eyes locked with a horror struck expression on the blood-draining image of Erik's face. The dog hit the ground at Loup's feet with a sickening, lifeless thud. Erik circled. He towered over the huntsman, locking his sunken eyes and inhuman ugliness on the dumb confusion on Loup's face.

A cry of pain filled the night. In a merciless mood, Erik grabbed Loup's throat and fiercely pinned him against the wall. Wild noise soared at a thrilling pace in his mind. Kill or not to kill? He leaned in harder, toying with his decision yet a flicker of light interrupted his pleasure.

The fire burned away and with it Anna's face. Exquisite grief edged him forward as arrows of pain drained his heart. His body came alive with the memory of her arms, but the translucent embrace was not strong enough to feel. Loved for a moment, alone for a lifetime. An overwhelming desire to join

Anna in death filled him. Why give Loup the satisfaction of such peaceful tranquility?

Guilt overpowered grief. Erik couldn't dishonor the memory of Philippe de Chagny by killing. After bringing life into the world, he could never prostitute his anger again. He stared at the flames until the embers faded, keeping his prisoner in check and in as much pain as he dared inflict. When the alley plunged into darkness, he leaned in close to Loup as if to study every pore on his face. They would meet again. Perhaps then, if his conscience faded, he would finish this deed. For now, the shroud of the night beckoned him.

Erik's fingers spread like bony spider's legs across Loup's face. He braced his head against the wall. He tipped his prey's head to the side and drew his lips into a tight smile. The tips of Erik's skeletal fingers raked down Loup's cheek as he lowered his palm. The fear and confusion on Loup's face he enjoyed. Erik tilted his head. Lips met lips in a feather light kiss.

Inches from Loup's face, he whispered: "The kiss of Death."

A quick adjustment to the pressure against Loup's throat made his knees buckle. He fell to the ground, unconscious. The edge of Erik's cloak brushed over him in one final caress as he headed toward the streets of Chaumont. Everything left his life. He no longer had the will to fight destiny. A light breeze stirred up the cloak, fanning it behind him like a black-winged messenger. Replacing his mask served only to hide his face—it could never cover the unspeakable crimes against humanity that made him who he was—a towering shadow of a man, glutted like a spider on the harsh breast of Death. Robbed forever of the gossamer wings of love, his life was a chrysalis of darkness.

When Anna died, new life was born.

The darkness welcomed the Phantom's return and though no one could hear the music, a symphony rose in Erik's mind and pasted its extraordinary melody on the night.

* * * *

The Phantom's Labyrinth

Life is like a key in a lock, Maestro, with one twist you can have a turning point that can open more than simply doors. *Those words pooled poison in his mind.*

Erik surveyed years of accumulated clutter. Every item in his house filled a void in his life. A part of that void seemed smaller, but he couldn't put his finger on what it was.

He reclined in a chair, one long leg slung over an arm, twirling a honey-colored glass of Tokay before his eyes. He stared through it so all the images before him were as distorted as his face. The nib in his opposite hand dripped ink onto the pages coating the floor. Another unfinished composition littered his home. He couldn't find his new beginning.

The wine turned in the opposite direction and he closed one eye. He was tired of writing symphonies and chamber music, operettas, and arias. He needed something different, but he could do no composing so long as the stranger's words about ripples and random acts kept plaguing him.

Who was this stranger of his? Pretty in visage, overly masculine in physique, elegant in clothing save for that damn cloak and hat. He had seen them before . . .

Erik bolted upright. Papers slid in every direction. How could he be so stupid? That blasted stranger is . . .

"What are you scrutinizing?"

Erik swung round, watching as his visitor removed his outerwear and laid them neatly aside. He spoke.

"You look better, less on the brink of death. You must be eating. I half expected to return and find you dead—finally." He roamed around the house as was customary at this point. Erik's eyes followed. "I actually do not know why I returned. Perhaps many things in life are connected—like a circle. I connected with you and now you are like a damn cancer—or addiction. I cannot seem to avoid coming here. Have you determined what you are going to do? Live like a man or ignore those connections?"

"Whatever choices I make are mine, stranger. They are in no way connected to you."

"Ah, but they are. You chose to let Christine go and Mademoiselle Daaé chose to marry a vicomte. You chose my assistance, and I chose to defy your wish for death." Erik's eyes dimmed as his stranger lifted a red pincushion artfully crafted in the shape of a skull. He scowled at the pins plunged into it before tossing it aside. "The next choice comes back to you. Those ripples make a circle you know."

"What I choose, Monsieur, is not to relive the past in any way. I have made important choices before, and had I elected

in the past to choose differently, the outcome of your precious ripples could have been very different."

His stranger folded his arms. "How is that?"

"I could have given in to my madness long ago and taken an ungodly number with me, killing for the sheer pleasure of it."

"But you did not. Why?"

"Because I love Christine."

"Because you have a conscience."

"Because I love Christine."

"Because you are not truly mad."

"Because I love Christine!"

"Because you love." Those words jolted Erik like they'd stung him. "Recognize your burdens, Maestro, and you can choose to change them." The stranger lifted a small brass sculpture of a grasshopper and examined it with interest. "You are a man getting on in years." He put the sculpture down. "Like the rest of us, you are trying to find your way in the world and realizing it is not as easy as one may think. You may indeed carry around the—pardon the alliteration, Maestro—mask of that Phantom persona you have woven for yourself and you may be comfortably shrouded behind it, but deep down you are simply a man searching for what all men need in life—a reason for living. Doing what we all do, carrying the weight of the world around on your shoulder, looking for the right match to help lessen the load." He smiled. "I am afraid, Maestro, that by the very fact that you have not attempted to kill yourself again, and have not made any attempts at killing me, proves you are finding that reason after all. Perhaps you realize they do not lie with Christine Daaé." He gathered his coat and hat. "Tell me, do you like figs?"

"No," Erik cautiously said. "Where are you going? To arrest someone?" He smiled at his carefully dropped allusion to his stranger's identity. Did he see a glint of anger in his eyes?

"I am going to leave you to unload your burdens for a while and to let you come to terms with the past," his stranger articulated. Erik detected a bit of malice in his voice. "I believe whatever you were looking for in that grasshopper was one of them." He gestured toward the sculpture. "I will leave you in

peace so you can ponder what you desire as a man, before, like the almond blossom, your blush turns from pink to white and you grow too old to care any longer. You should not be fearful of desire. They define you even if that desire is for love—not infatuation. Yet do not let them consume you. I will be back, rest assured." He waved with the back of his hand. "The grasshopper shall be a burden . . ."

"What?" Erik's eyes darted to the sculpture.

"Ecclesiastes, Chapter Twelve, verse five."

Erik toppled the chair into the far wall. It splintered into pieces. "You are my burden! Who are you?"

Twenty-one

Outside the window of the coach, Raoul watched elegant fingers of sunlight shine through the sentry of trees standing guard on either side of the road leading to the Chagny gate. Beyond their stoic and proud welcome, flashes of light danced above the reflecting pool, contorting the image of the stately chateau and its distant courtyard.

Raoul straightened his cravat and studied Legard's pensive stare out the carriage window. Not many words had been shared between them on the journey back from Chaumont to Chagny. The return had been long and difficult, but not due to the conditions of roads or the haphazard travel of carriages. While Raoul's bruises may be healing, his mental state had not. He wove an intricate web of deception to keep his true feelings safeguarded. Legard was, in many ways, his conscience. Although Raoul knew him to be the wiser man when it came to dealing with the hunter and hunted, the truth was not what he wanted to see.

Raoul had a feeling he had made a gross mistake with Loup, but any misgivings were crushed by the overwhelming confusion clouding his rational thought. A sickening feeling settled in his stomach. He cursed, knowing he not only had to continue to track the Phantom, but they still had yet to locate Mademoiselle Barret. The word, when they left Chaumont, was no remains were found in the charred barn. Though deeply relieved, Raoul's anger grew. The hunt became more complex as it wore on.

Once the brougham came to a stop, he took quick leave of Legard and made his servants aware he was not to be disturbed or waited upon. Time was needed to gather his senses back in order. There was only one spot on his mind, and Raoul retreated through the gardens toward the Chagny cemetery. He didn't stop until he reached the stone house on the hillside.

"You Judas!" Fists collided with the metal door of Philippe's crypt. "How did you know Erik so intimately? How?" Metal against stone created a thunderstorm of sound.

A voice shrieked across the gardens. "Raoul!"

He pivoted so sharply he stumbled. At the open iron gate that separated Philippe's hallowed ground from the rest of the souls, his sister covered her heart with her hands. Her eyes were glassy with horror.

"You have wept for Philippe," he implored her. "Why can I not?"

Arms outstretched, she walked toward her younger sibling. "You miss him. You've not had a chance to say goodbye. That's all."

Raoul rocked his head. "I can't say goodbye. I feel so much anger." Thrusting a leg forward he kicked the door and slapped his palm against Philippe's name. A cloud of rusty dust lingered in the air. Nothing he did, no pain he inflicted upon himself was enough to numb the sting of his failures and loss. With a roar of frustration, he beat out a year's worth of misery, but nothing would make the tears come. Nothing put his anger and newfound questions to rest. Metal echoed endlessly against the stone.

"Raoul, stop! Merciful Heaven, stop! That's my brother in there!"

He shoved off the crypt and stared into rust covered palms. "Leave me, please. I need to be alone."

His sister reached to him again. "Raoul, please, calm down. We tried to send word to you a week ago, but you were already underway. Christine has fallen ill. The doctor has stayed with her. There has been some additional blood—"

"Mercy no . . ."

"She's very weak. Raoul—"

"Mercy no!"

Raoul spun in horror toward the crypt. He grabbed his head at the sight of Philippe's name on those iron doors and prayed to God another one would not be added at its side. Pebbles scattered around his pounding feet as he ran to his wife's bedside.

* * * *

Exhaustion bent around her, but she couldn't sleep. Christine shifted to a more comfortable position. The cramping in her back intensified and the pain in her abdomen knotted her entire body. Her head pounded with images of Erik being imprisoned. She buried her cheek in a soft pillow and stared blankly into space. She should confess to Raoul all she knew regarding what happened in the bowels of that opera house. Make him listen to her this time. Shouldn't that be enough to save Erik despite his aiding Anna Barret? Frustrated tears pulled at the corners of her eyes. He would still have to answer for years of crimes she had no control over. If that were the case, he would still be taken from her. It was useless. Untangling a knot so wet was a futile endeavor. Unless . . .

Would Raoul have mercy on her if she confessed the stranglehold of blackmail Loup had wrapped around her? Could she tell him his threats were based on lies? But that would be lying. . . more cheats . . . more deceit. Could she tell him the truth of her affections for Erik, or would he dismiss her as a harlot for being in the arms of another man?

Pinching her eyes shut, she tried to ignore the pain in her heart and back. The more she thought of Erik, the tighter her body clenched.

"Christine?"

A cry of relief escaped her lips as Raoul hastened to her bedside.

"It's all right, love, I am home. I will tend you. I should never have been gone for so long."

"Raoul, don't leave me again. Don't ever leave. I've been so worried, so frightened."

"All is well, you should have no fear." He kissed her damp temple and laid a protective hand over their child.

"Where is Erik?"

"Quiet, Christine, not now. This has caused you far too much stress. We will speak of that later."

Chills ran across her forehead. "I need to know, Raoul."

"He is on the run again. But he will not harm you. We will find him, please, Christine, please, stop trembling."

She couldn't. An unnatural pain spread across her back. Nothing like the cramps she felt with André. Curling forward she grabbed her abdomen. Mouth gaping, she fought for breath and words.

"Christine?" Raoul cried.

A sudden rush of warmth spread down her lower body,

sticking the thin sheet to her legs with blood and fluid. The room dimmed to gray before fading into blackness. The pulse pounding in her ears joined Raoul's muffled cries.

"Christine? No, no, no, no . . . Christine? Christine, come back to me! It is too soon. Not the baby . . . not my baby . . . Christine!"

* * * *

Several long hours of emotion too heavy for even Chagny to bear had finally slipped away. A chateau—at last—slept. A spent doctor rested on a solitary chair outside the room where Christine slept, the dinner and a drink provided to him lay untouched on its silver tray. To his side a nurse and several servants stood banished to the hall by their master.

Through the door beyond him, Raoul could not tell the hour, other than the first rays of dawn had yet to color the sky. He walked the nursery, bobbing steadily as he comforted the tiny life in his arms. His face immersed in joy as he marveled at the child he carried. Raoul paused only long enough to reach into the crib as he walked by to check on his eldest. André slept, oblivious to anything that went on during a chaotic night at Chagny. Raoul tucked the blanket closer around him and then adjusted the soft wrap protecting his daughter.

He grinned at the contentment in her round face. How tiny could a child be? He could have placed her in the bassinet, but he was reluctant to let her go. Walking the nursery, keeping her close to his heart, Raoul lost himself in his thoughts for endless hours. He never wanted this introduction to end. He savored every second he had with the child he was so anxious to meet. The corners of his eyes pinched with exhaustion, but he refused to take his eyes off her face.

By the time dawn peeked into the room, he finally relinquished her to the comfort of the cradle. He adjusted the blankets so she was warm and content and placed a gentle kiss to the center of her tiny forehead. A tear fell from his eye. Using his knuckle, he stroked it from a soft cheek. Raoul finally had his little girl.

With one last look, he left her to sleep.

* * * *

An oppressive silence fell over Chagny during the hours that followed. Raoul could feel the throb of his heart keep cadence with Christine's tears. To tell the woman he loved their child was stillborn, were the most difficult and senseless words he ever had to find. Christine stared catatonically, her tears soaking Raoul's shirtsleeve before she found the presence to speak.

"Was she beautiful? I want to hold my baby."

Raoul bit his lip. "Let her go, Christine . . . and yes, she was the smallest of beauties."

The priest's voice broke their embrace. "Monsieur le Comte, I need to know her name, so I can send her to God."

Raoul's throat squeezed. He looked over his shoulder to glare at him. Such words hurt. He couldn't blame his wife, the doctor, or God for the death of his daughter. The doctor could not name the cause for Christine's faint bleeding or the stillbirth. But Raoul could. Erik was to blame. He was always to blame for Christine's heartache and stress. A woman carrying life is a fragile thing. The manhunt had been far too taxing.

"Eve," he finally replied. "We named her Eve."

"Evangeline," Christine blurted. "Her name is Evangeline." Shocked, Raoul studied the tears falling down Christine's face. They came faster and harder the more the reality of the moment seemed to set in. "I love her . . . I love Evangeline . . . I love . . ."—his heart ripped in two when he heard what no one else did—". . . my Angel of Music . . ."

How Raoul found the strength to breathe through those words he didn't know, for they suffocated all life from him. The priest looked for guidance. Numbed, Raoul rose from his wife's bedside. "Whatever she wishes."

Twenty-two

A mist hung above the ground, blanketing everything in an eerie fog. The dampness invaded everything, soaking through clothing to drench all it touched.

Erik lifted his head to watch the mist writhe before him. His eyes swam back and forth in his head as he followed its dance macabre. It reminded him of the bluish fog that would dance for him nightly above the lake beneath the Opera Garnier. Knees to chest, his cloak draped over him to protect his already cold frame from further assault, Erik laid his head back into the security of his arms. To any passerby, he was another tramp taking shelter beneath the train trestle.

Bracelets of blood caked around his wrists. They throbbed unrelentingly. His body ached from being thrown around in the back of that carriage. His mind bellowed with awful severity. Every time he closed his eyes, he saw the flames consume his life. Erik couldn't escape the sound of her screams or the vision of the fire-engulfed barn.

He didn't care about anything anymore. His life ended the moment he understood the profound power of grief.

Erik shifted to avoid the rain of mud as a carriage rumbled by. The offending matter splattered his already soiled cloak. He burrowed himself deeper into the sanctuary of his knees and tried to close out the world. He'd lived the life of the very wealthy and wasted away among the very poor. Now he existed in limbo.

Somewhere he heard a shout, a cry of pain and the groans of pleasure. The sounds were close and unrelenting. He lowered his face deeper into his knees and ignored it. Some pathetic human was seeking pleasure with another, far be it from him to interrupt.

He willed sleep to come. Inevitably, running would be a must again. It would only be a matter of time until they found him. Yet why run at all? He had nothing to run toward. The sounds got louder, peppered with an occasional sharp crack or sudden wail. Erik tried to drown them out by focusing on the only memory keeping his demons locked away.

Blinking, he remembered the snap of a log that sent orange sparks into the air. The evening had been warm as well. As the embers danced, he recalled waltzing with Anna, his voice providing the music and the woodland providing the hall. It was a happier time during a manhunt when he felt truly loved, before the memories set in and the past interrupted the present. The love that night was sweet and gentle. Its passion lingered long into the evening. It was all he ever dreamed for the first moment he would lay with a woman . . .

Erik's eyes snapped open. His head shot up. The cries increased and interrupted the sounds of ardor that had calmed his madness. He saw them on the other side of the trestle. Two men accosting a young woman. Reaching into the pocket of his cloak, he fingered the coil of silk. It was her cries he heard—cries of pain. Like the pain Anna must have endured when flame hit flesh. Like the pain she must have felt each time in her short life that a man used her.

Erik rose.

The man laughed and hit the woman again. Her head snapped to the side as she tried desperately to protect the purse they sought. She clutched it tightly against her chest. His laughter was echoed from the one who succeeded in pinning her from behind. She couldn't even struggle as her purse hit the ground, spilling one pitiful coin to the mud.

Moving like liquid darkness, Erik became possessed by the thought of a woman in despair. A need unfurled inside him, and he took no pity on who satisfied it. His nimble fingers fondled the length of silk. Murder was a companion one could never quite dismiss. The need would continually come back—uninvited—during the darkest moments. He watched the disgusting dance as they taunted her, his soul smoldering with repulsion. It awoke every perverse need in his body.

Laughter coated everything before the devil rose. Approaching them from behind, he projected his amusement around the trestle. Neither man had time to react. A thin lasso snaked around one, neatly garroting him, and with a savage jerk he was yanked from his prize. Mud spattered as he hit the ground. The girl whimpered and struggled against the grip of her second tormentor. Controlling the man with the awesome power of his larynx, Erik's voice cut through the tunnel. "Leave her for me. Now."

The man froze in trancelike stupor.

Erik paused long enough to release his length of rope from the other man's neck. He discreetly pressed two fingers to his pulse long enough to be certain blood still flowed. Garroting was a fine art. Had he wanted, he had only need to apply slightly more pressure to the rope to kill. He coiled and tucked it out of sight. It only took a lift of his inhuman eyes and the glimpse of a mask to send the man's still shocked companion running. Erik watched him trip and slide down the road before looking at the man at his feet. He stepped over his body and turned toward the woman at his side.

His gaze slid from her feet to her mousy hair. Somewhere beneath her muddy face hid an elegant young woman, if permitted a chance to shine. She leaned against the wall of the tunnel, trembling as she cringed. Her face was a mess of bloody bruises. She wiped at her lip with a filthy sleeve and nodded in the direction of the fleeing man. Bravery tried to color her voice, but her youth defied her.

"They were paying customers." She licked blood. Pulling herself up straighter and smoothing out her bunched up skirts, she pushed a strand of hair from her eyes. "You cost me my meal. I . . . I would have done anything for a meal. Tried anything . . ." Erik stared at her. Her voice shook. "Are you going to hurt me?"

He cocked his head. The girl had pressed herself flat against the wall of the tunnel, yet he could still see she trembled. He watched her bosom heave.

The back of her hand shook as she wiped her upper lip again. "What do you want from me?" Sniffling loudly, she shoved off of the wall. "I'll do anything you ask, so long as you have the coin. I'm hungry."

Erik stood motionless. All emotion left him at the moment. The thought of the woman he loved and lost was willed from his mind. She was too young—young, bold, defiant, and desirable. A woman willing to fight to survive the round life dealt her by doing anything—even sullying her honor.

Erik dipped his skeletal fingers into his pocket. He

withdrew the only remaining coin he had. He lifted them before her eyes before pressing them into her eager palm. The girl smiled and tucked them into the pocket of her dress.

"What do you fancy, Monsieur?"

"Find a room in town."

"A room? Do . . . do these things happen in . . . rooms?"

Erik shot his head to the side and clamped down on his teeth. So blasted innocent! She would ruin herself before life gave her a chance to live. His hands pulsed.

"What . . . I know what I am to do as . . . a . . . just don't hurt me . . ."

Erik stepped out of reach. "Locate a physician to tend to your wounds then take a meal and hot bath." The girl's face twisted. "Spring is damp. Spend the night in comfort." Erik pulled his cloak closer around him and backed himself into the shadows. "Come morning locate a loaf and enough food to last you through the day."

He left the girl dumbstruck and started down the road.

"Monsieur?"

Erik heard her footsteps pound against the muddy ground. He stopped.

"God bless you," she said.

"Where is the closest camp?"

The girl swallowed hard and pointed. "Tramps find safe haven west, down the tracks."

Erik turned in the direction she indicated. Feet met mud again as she ran to catch up to him. She grabbed a corner of his cloak.

"Please, Monsieur, let me repay you. Share the meal perhaps?"

Erik spun. "Leave, damn you! Leave now before I change my mind!" The girl stumbled backward; she opened her mouth to reply. "Damn you child, leave while you still have your life and your last shred of innocence, because I can and will destroy them both! Speak of me to know one, do you hear? No one! I was not here." He took two strides into her and raised a gnarled finger to her face. "If I find I am followed or betrayed, I will know why and I assure you, the result I will befall on you will not bring as much pleasure for you as it will me." When she trembled, Erik pointed back toward the town. He lowered his voice to the coo of a dove. "Go, you bleed, tend to your needs."

He ignored the throb of his own wounds and left her standing in the darkness. He heard her cry as she fled.

"You're my angel!"

Was he angel, Phantom, lover, or father? Erik no longer knew. The only distinctions he understood were that of life versus death, joy versus sorrow, lust versus love, and of man battling madman.

Retreating once more to the only memory slowing the rising noise in his mind, Erik pushed on into the night, one foot in front of the other, a dance he performed alone.

* * * *

Numbness stiffened his fingers as he traced the horizontal lines carved in the trunk of the tree. The universal sign throughout France that an area was friendly to tramps had become a sought after emblem. Erik spotted a camp in the distance. Hood up, he headed toward the promise of shelter, in need of rest and freedom and from bars closing in around him.

The old mine was filled with roamers. Erik kept his head down and scanned the space. There were no signs of gendarmes or hounds. Loup was cunning. On more then one occasion Erik found himself slipping away from a waiting ambush.

Crackling fires herded people from all walks of life. Somewhere, a melancholy tune played on a mouth organ. Erik wove his way through the masses, ignoring the salutations extended to him. They cared not about his appearance or current state; vagabonds rarely made mention of his mask.

The desolate pay no mind to difference Erik, only indifference.

He shredded Anna's voice until it no longer existed. Recalling it was too painful. Two young boys dodged in front of him in an enthusiastic game of tag, bringing Erik up short. He fought off the images that chased him—the Philippe he gave life to and the one he killed.

Though didn't he kill them both?

Erik found a secluded spot. Completely sacked by exhaustion he slumped to the ground. His fingers pounded with pain the instant he attempted to flex warmth into them. Infection was imminent. The motions he made to assure his fingers still obeyed him cracked the dried blood on his wrists and caused fresh to pool into his palms. Crimson filled his hands, and he rubbed his palms frantically against his cloak. He couldn't have blood on his hands if his hands had not killed.

The tune on the mouth organ shifted to an overly upbeat one and the camp exploded in a loud whoop of jubilation. Erik tore his eyes from the litter-strewn ground. Wanderers of all ages and sizes took to their feet, dancing merry reels and clapping enthusiastically to the tune. They eventually blurred before him. He blinked back the tears and carried on a silent argument with the demons in his mind. *I am not mad. I am a man.*

"You're bleeding."

Erik turned. The young man smiled and laid a bundle at his feet. "I'm not much for dancing myself. It's cornbread. We have plenty." He indicated Erik's hands. "You should tend your wounds. You need to take care if you're hurt, infection could set in and you can't wander if you're ill." The youth knelt. A kerchief appeared from a pocket as he reached for Erik's wrists.

He yanked his hands out of reach. "Stay away from me! I am a madman."

The man was not deterred. "You're not mad. You're a wanderer and hurt. We all reach a point of thinking this life is madness."

With an incoherent cry, Erik knocked him off balance, sprawling him onto his back. His hand clamped tightly around the man's throat as he pinned his tormentor to the ground. Erik's voice tightened. "I am a madman you see, and my hands do not even have to touch to kill any longer."

He dug his fingers into his neck only to feel the sensation that he still had a grip on something. A bubbling cry gargled out the man's lips. Sick terror dawned in his eyes. His struggles were just loud enough to screech the music to a halt and send numerous wanderers racing across the mine.

"Stay away from me!" Erik wailed to the approaching mob. Inadvertently, enough slack came off the boy's neck to permit him to speak.

"I'm all right," he hoarsely declared. His voice shook toward Erik. "She said you would be unstable. She said to stay calm if you seemed frightening because you truly don't intend to harm."

"Who said I do not intend harm?"

"The little Austrian." A voice cried from the crowd.

"What Austrian?"

"We don't know her name, Monsieur. We have met her on these trails before—she and the old man."

Erik blinked. An Austrian and an old man knew of him? It could not be. They burned!

"She said you would come for them," the man below him lisped.

Erik leaned down inches from his face. "She? A baby? Did she have a baby?"

"She had an infant, Monsieur," added a man in the crowd.

Erik leapt to his feet. He twirled in a frantic circle and sought the man who spoke. "You mention an infant? My son! Did you see my son?"

The man nodded rapidly. "He was fine. She and the infant were fine."

Erik grabbed him by the back of his neck and yanked him close. "You lie." He shoved the man backward and crouched low into his pain. "You all lie! You all deny. Why should such exquisite words be applied to my life?" He straightened and puffed his chest. "Death does walk! Death does talk, and I am the only man built of death to do so." Erik backed himself away from the camp. "You lie."

"She said to tell you they were heading to Dieppe," a voice informed.

The words kicked him in the chest.

"They left two days ago," another echoed.

The power knocked him aside. Before he thought he could be beaten any worse by the words, a third person replied.

"She said they tried to wait, many times."

Blood pounded loudly in his ears. A low moan vibrated the air. "No. I watched them burn. I killed them." The circle of misfits around him nodded, trying to convince him of the truth. He shook his head speaking with a grim but regal authority. They were the fools in this. "As long as I live, I live in vain. There is nothing in the foolish, glad words of man that can penetrate a mind existing on infinite darkness. I am not played the nave. My reign is in a kingdom that no woman or child can ever comprehend. Even I believed for a moment your folly."

He pushed his way through the crowd, but stopped. He took a few quick strides toward the man he assaulted. Fear played openly on the youth's face. Erik's voice poured out with an unearthly quality. "In darkness I was born. In darkness I live.

In darkness I die. All hope for light extinguished when she left me." He extended a hand to him surprised when the man hesitantly accepted it. Once on his feet he looked at the blood that transferred to his palm. Erik backed away. "I am not mad. I am a man . . ."

His sadness floated into the night like a gust of wind.

* * * *

Raoul needed to leave Chagny.

The air around him pebbled his skin and the entire room stood stoic and dark. Not even the dim light from the glowing stained glass windows provided any sort of comfort or warmth. Raoul stared across the tiny box in front of him to the doors leading to the chapel. It would be good to leave Chagny for a time. His return to his ancestral home had been laced with too much emotion over the last year. A small gathering of those near and dear to his heart stood waiting in the pews to share in Chagny's sorrow where they had expected to celebrate.

Raoul reached out and laid a hand on the coffin in front of him. His fingers traced the ridges of the Chagny coat carved in its surface. The colors stood out against the stark whiteness of the box. Never had the coat ever been carved so small. He thought it should be a sin for such boxes to be made so tiny. Raoul blinked back tears.

He knew. The moment Christine called their daughter her Angel of Music, he knew he was second in her heart. The image Loup planted of his wife's lips around another man made sense now. Christine's unsteady passion for finding Erik one moment and locking him away the next seemed so logical.

She didn't know who she loved, and Raoul feared he did.

His palm spread across the cold wood. Every day since he'd known of this child he'd awoken with joy and anticipation of her life. He wanted to be angry and vengeful over the idea of his wife's intimacies with the Phantom. He wanted to scream out his rage for Christine's betrayal of their sacred vows. But he could not, not so long as this tiny victim lay before him.

The box blurred and warped as a tear fell over the brim of his eye. Try as he might, Raoul couldn't understand the connection between mother and child. The physical and emotional link as two hearts beat as one for month after month. How was he to understand the grief, guilt, and failure that must come when that life is taken too soon? But he understood *his* pain, and he understood how much it hurt to be touching cold unfeeling wood and not the warm laughter-blushed cheek of his little girl.

Raoul tried to turn away from the box numerous times, but he was drawn to it, as if touching its surface would somehow bring back the sweet life inside. But every time he turned his eyes away, the tears stung and whipped him worse than forty lashes. His mind bellowed over and over: *I want her back!* But he could never get her back and he'd never have the chance to know her. He clenched his teeth to maintain his composure, but he could not resist. As if heavenly arms were forcing him down, his forehead fell against the cold wood and his hands draped across it in a final embrace. What he would not pay to understand the injustice of it all.

Breath dragged into his lungs in a staggering cry. Perhaps he should have allowed Christine to hold her? No. Fingers rubbed the side of the box as if caressing the golden curls that might have been. The dimmed light in her eyes devastated the image of her angelic face. He could not have allowed his wife to see that vacant stare. It would plague him enough as it was. Numbness washed over him as the door behind clicked open.

"Is she here?" Raoul turned to Legard who solemnly shook his head.

So Christine would not attend? He didn't blame her. She was weak and in pain in more ways than one. The hours she spent staring catatonically out into space locked her in a prison no worse than his. It was probably best they handle this separately.

"Jules," Raoul bravely smiled through the tears he dared to show. "She was to have petticoats and frilly things. I would have put flowers in her room every day. I would have given her silks for her hair. One for every day, of every week, of every year she was mine. Anything she wanted, she would have had. I would have wiped her tears and laughed with her and danced at her wedding." Raoul stroked the coffin. "Christine . . . called her the Angel of Music. She is in love with Erik." The confession dropped his friend's jaw. "No one is to know. Is that understood?"

"Loup's statement in Chaumont?" Legard muttered. Raoul nodded. "Raoul, what are you going to do?"

"I am true to my vows, Jules. I will find my way to deal with the pain this had brought me. I love Christine and she needs me. I cannot face this infidelity right now." He abruptly jabbed a finger in Legard's face, shocked at his sudden passion in the wake of his grief. "But you can! You find him. No matter how long this takes, another year another ten—you tell Loup to find him. Erik has broken my family. He took my brother. He took my wife." He grabbed in desperation at his daughter. "He took this little girl! I blame him for her death. Erik has broken my heart for the last time." Raoul scrubbed his face trying to twist away the pain of his next confession. "The doctor says Christine cannot bear any more children. The damage during delivery was too severe." He gestured desperately around the chapel. "My dreams of having Chagny filled with pieces of me and my wife are gone! Erik took that from me!"

"Raoul, you don't know—"

"Erik took that from me! Children are not supposed to be hurt by all this. They are supposed to show us the way in life, not lead the way to our Father."

Music poured through the chapel doors. Somberly turning from Legard, he swiped his eye with the sleeve of his waistcoat and knelt before the tiny box on its stand. Raoul positioned it in his arms. Legard rushed to help, but Raoul sternly shook his head. He stood, his daughter at long last perched on his shoulder.

"I am her father. Christine carried her for seven months. Let me carry her now."

"You are a stronger and more forgiving man than I could ever be, Raoul."

Raoul kept his gaze on the doors, but was unable to keep the crack out of his voice. "Suffer the little children to come unto me and forbid them not: for such is the Kingdom of God."

Twenty-three

Larks chattered in the trees like arguing lovers. She did her best to ignore them. The secluded spot in one of Chagny's more remote gardens provided a needed respite from the hustle of her Chateau. The moss on the bench where she sat was cool to the touch. One hand absently stroked it, while the other clutched her prayer book to her chest. She stared at the distant walls of her home. The revered Chagny ivy, mere tiny specks of green on the stone from this distance, spread like gaunt fingers across the walls. She wondered if they were attempting to claw their way into her heart.

Christine hated those vines.

She sat beneath the canopy of a chestnut having shooed away her lady-maid and the handmaids dutifully attending her. Her body mended, but she could not speak for her heart. After weeks of being doted upon, the blissful solitude was welcomed.

"My heartfelt condolences on your loss."

The shadows the massive tree cast could have come to life, and she would not have feared it as much as she did that voice. The hound bounded into view first. Instinctively, Christine pressed *The Imitation of Christ* closer to her breast. "What are you doing here?"

Loup leaned on the tree. "I follow where my hounds lead. Did you miss me?"

Those vine-like fingers tightened their grip upon her. Her eyes studied the expanse of grass. *Loup follows where the hounds lead . . .*

Were Erik and that woman here?

Loup moved close, seeming to read her mind. "If the hounds are here, then she is near. If she is near, then is he?" He swept his arm in front of her, and unwillingly she followed his gesture across Chagny. "What shall I do when I find him? Bring him to you? Tell him your womb is free for his child? Oh . . .

pity . . . you can never bear his child now, can you?"

"My daughter was born of the man I love. As was my son. She was a beautiful little girl. You are never to speak of her—never!"

He plucked the stem of a nearby rose and began to shred its petals. One by one blood red bits landed at her feet. "Would Erik's children be beautiful do you think? Is it possible he might seed someone? Do you think that he might elect someone else to be the object of his—tutelage?" Bit by bit the pile of petals grew. Loup tossed them in her lap instead. Their scarlet hue contrasted the deep black of her dress. "What do you think of another woman carrying the Angel of Music's child? I'm sure he will have children someday. He is, after all, merely a man."

Christine bit her tongue and watched the wind carry the torn petals from her lap.

"If it were you bearing his seed, would the child be born looking like Death or with your beauty?" Loup chuckled. "Forgive me. You're in love with a noble. You would never ponder such inappropriate things, now would you?" He blew in her ear. "Care to lie with me? I don't mind you are worthless as a woman now that your womb is ruined. What is one more man to desire between your legs?"

"I desire only my husband." Tears stung her eyes.

A shrill whistle cut through the air as Loup called for his hound. "You are practiced in the art of deception, Comtess. Try as you may, you cannot deceive yourself." He fingered the black lace on her mourning dress. "A fitting color for you. The color of one mourning the loss of her baby, her point as a woman, and the man she loves—Erik."

"I love my husband." The wind carried away her sigh.

"Lucky for you our arrangement still stands. I won't tell the Comte you sit here wondering what, if any, children will be brought to your Angel of Music by that scandalous harlot. She is—scandalous. Why the way that woman can please a man—forgive me, where are my manners? I won't tell your husband you weep over the fact it will never be you in Erik's bed. If you will excuse me, my hounds need to rest before we take to the hunt again. Your lover awaits my attentions, my pocket your payment, and my lips a bit of refreshment." He sauntered down the grassy path toward Chagny. "The offer for my bed stands."

The faint strains of *Alouette* twanged in her ears as he

disappeared. Christine's fingers turned white against the book of prayers. Would she never be rid of her deceptions and that man? The book bent in her hand as she clung to it. Loup was right. Her point as a woman was destroyed. She could never give her husband a daughter. She could never fulfill the dreams of the man she loved.

The image of Anna giving Erik all the love she could not give Raoul rose in her mind. Christine swallowed the heated rock in her throat and regarded the ivy of Chagny. Though she could not see it from the distance, she knew the ancient vines arched over the entry to the chateau and encircled the Chagny coat of arms. It crept up the sword that signified their noble right to bear arms. The crown it was thrust through showed loyalty to France and a hand, palm open, rested behind the sword, not grasping the hilt, but at the ready. Chagny was most proud of that hand—of their philanthropy. Above the coat of arms the ivy rambled around the motto chiseled six hundred years prior.

Fidelity and compassion: the sacred endowments of our mind.

Through green leaves and grass, and toward those distant vines, jealousy and envy stared at her like laughing enemies.

* * * *

The vines clung desperately to every ridge and crack winding their way up and down the stone crypt. They stretched across its surface like a network of nourishing veins, budding out in effort to bring a bit of life to the stone's dead surface.

Raoul loved the Chagny ivy.

He stared at the plants thinking of how they will develop, reflecting on how he would watch them change in the coming weeks and realizing, with a heavy heart, that he would never be able to do the same for his daughter.

His head hung between his hands, his forearms pressing into his legs. His hands, folded in prayer, stroked against silent lips as he watched the sunlight gleam against the religious medallions woven through his fingers. Saint Joseph and Thaddeus swung gently against the newly added Saint Nicholas. They swayed in a slight breeze and chimed in a high-pitched, angelic way. When old enough, he would give Saint Nicholas to his son.

He could never give the red scarf in his lap to his daughter.

He fingered it as he looked over the fresh name added on the Chagny crypt. There were too many names on that door.

"Monsieur le Comte?"

Raoul barely lifted his head. He let his breath seep from his mouth. Stoically he returned the chain to his neck and remained silent in the several moments it took to tuck them back into place and reassemble and tighten his cravat. His hands returned to their previous position. "Please, Jules, do not call me that. I do not want to be a nobleman at present. I just want to be a father."

"Are you well?"

"I am empty."

Legard took a seat on the bench. He indicated the scarf. "A bit feminine for you."

Raoul smiled sadly at his humor. He studied a torn end. "It was Christine's. It flew into the sea when we were children. I met her after I rescued it. Dove in clothing and all to fetch it." He laughed softly. "She gave it to me in thanks for my gallantry and promised it would bind us together some day." He tore his eyes from it to read his daughter's name. "As a young boy I dreamed if I had a girl with Christine, I would give it to her. I would drape it around her neck as a gift from the first man to ever love her, and a reminder no matter what man might come between us, she would be bound to me and my heart forever." His eyes misted and he cleared his throat. "I cannot bring myself to place it in a crypt." Legard grabbed his neck and gave it a quick squeeze. "I am drained," Raoul said. "Drained and tired. I cannot figure out why I can come up here and be moved to tears at the sight of her name on that door and not over the name of my brother." Raoul leaned off his knees and winced at a sharp twinge in his back. He had not moved in quite some time. "How is my wife?"

"Sleeping. Something upset her. I suspect she is still not healed. The doctor has her mildly sedated."

Raoul rubbed his eyes. "No more drugs. She needs to deal with this. I will not have her compromised any longer."

"I'll let him know your wishes. What are you going to do? Regarding what you mentioned in the chapel?"

He lifted his face heavenward, and watched a puffy cloud bob across the sky. "If Christine did make a mistake, if she does love Erik, what can I do? I follow the law of my faith and church. I will not divorce. I can move on from this."

"I think you're too forgiving. Your peers take mistresses to their side all the time. You have never even thought of another woman. If your beliefs and judgment are correct, this is a betrayal a man such as you does not deserve—especially given your situation. I believe the church would understand. You love her so deeply. Don't you deserve someone who loves you the same?"

"The church does not need to understand. Only I need to. She bares no blame. I blame him."

Legard kicked at a sun bleached stone. "She doesn't act like a woman who was forced upon, Raoul. I have seen women who were. Your wife chose this. She has some blame." Raoul's face fell into his frown. Legard gestured toward the child's tomb. "Perhaps it is not so? Christine was distressed when she called Eve her Angel of Music. Maybe she doesn't love Erik at all."

"Whether she loves Erik or me doesn't matter." He pointed at the doors to the crypt. "What matters is that I will never hold her. I will never spoil her, dote on her, or break up a quarrel with her brother. I will never wrap her in this scarf." Raoul's voice cracked. It changed as he shifted his finger and pointed to the other name. "I will never understand my brother, or who he was, or why he left me. I will never understand why I cannot defeat the man who took them both from me."

Legard rose and patted him gently on the shoulder, turning to leave him to his prayers.

"Jules, don't leave." He extended his hand. "You are the only one who has not lied or betrayed me."

Legard clasped his forearm. The simple gesture from friend to friend allowed Raoul the comfort he needed. Legard remained silent as Raoul wept for his daughter until he could weep no more and the sun faded away.

* * * *

The creature sighed its last remnants of steam. Vagabonds scanned the area before jumping out the boxcar and racing for cover. While the last illegal passenger dodged to safety, Erik attempted to calm the pain in his head.

From Dijon and the counties of Burgundy with its endless expanses of vineyards and quaint provincial towns, to the dairy lands in-between, Erik made his way across the countryside of France. For months he followed a trail of Anna's existence, but it was to no avail. He did nothing now but wander aimlessly. There was no point in trying to make it to Dieppe. She was gone. The stories he heard of her were nothing more than well-crafted lies.

Erik did his best to disassociate himself with the world he despised. Alone, he tuned out the glad tidings of men. Optimism died upon the last empty camp. Foolish expectation faded, and a curtain of silent despair drew across his mind, blinding him to anything other than desperate misery. Without the hands that always drew that veil aside, he lived in vain, he hoped in vain, he loved in vain.

Never knowing if he would see the ethereal rays of joy again, Erik embraced his destiny and shrouded himself in the chilling echoes of madness.

Sitting on the cold wood floor of the boxcar, he listened to the sound in his mind. Music had disappeared long ago. It no longer existed in his life. It no longer chased away the whispers that screamed like a constant banshee in his mind. Outside the slumbering train, a couple argued. Their heated conversation only added to Erik's discomfort. The old man insisted upon the quick way to travel, the woman begged they cover the distance they needed to slowly. Erik shifted and tried to ignore their ranting. His eyes dipped shut. All he desired was darkness. The argument switched from French to German.

Erik bolted upright.

Did he hear his name? They argued about leaving a horse behind.

Could it be? Erik squeezed his eyes and slammed his head against the metal wall. The sound ricocheted like gunfire. Anna was dead. He watched her burn.

The piercing sound of an infant's wail filled the air. Erik's heart flipped. He jerked off the wall. The argument became impassioned. The older voice insisted about comfort for a child, the woman demanded more time and feared the authorities.

They mentioned Chagny.

Erik leapt to his feet. He strained to listen.

Silence.

Balling his hands into fists, he pressed them against the throb in his temple. Madness was playing tricks on him. This whole situation was a joke, a brutal string of lies meant to swing him on a violent pendulum before plunging him into an endless abyss of loneliness.

His family couldn't have lived.

The sharp cry of an infant cracked its way into his mind and stirred what small ember of consciousness he had left. The boxcar door slid open further. From his shadow, he watched an old man clamber onto the train. Then, he grabbed for an infant, lifting him in the air before cradling him in his embrace. Erik's chest constricted. The old man extended his hand. A smaller one filled it.

His throat clamped the instant he saw her, his voice filling the boxcar with immeasurable grief. "I watched you burn."

She shrieked. The old man jolted. Stepping from the shadow, Erik lifted a finger. "You are dead."

"Erik!" Anna cried.

This was not possible . . . "You burned."

He huffed through his nose. The mask bit into his flesh when he covered his face. A flood of music churned the noise, making his head sting like he wore a thousand thorns. Two arms clamped around his waist like armor as she buried her head in the center of his chest. He rocked backward from the force of her embrace. Anna cried his name over and over.

She could not be crying for him—she was dead.

Erik shook violently. Her touch seared his skin like a hot iron. Lowering his hands, he shoved her aside. "You are no Phoenix . . ."

Without warning, he leapt out the door and into the night, fleeing through the train yard like a man possessed. He ran in disoriented circles until he spotted the stallion abandoned next to crates of cargo in a distant corner of the yard.

This was not happening . . .

"Erik, wait!" Anna cried, jumping from the train.

Whirling toward her, his eyes zoomed in on the satchel over her shoulder. Anna reached for him. With razor sharp reflexes, Erik's hand encircled her wrist. He grabbed for her opposite shoulder and yanked the satchel with such force he spilled them and it to the ground.

The old man caught up to them in time to drag Anna out of the way. Ignoring his yells, Erik sprawled on the ground grabbing at the contents of the satchel as if searching for the one small scrap of sanity he thought he had left.

"Erik, you're scaring me," Anna shouted, dropping to the

ground before him. "What has you so desperate?" The contents flew in every direction. "What has happened to you? What are you looking for?"

"Little bag, little bag of life and death. Where is my bag! Give me my bag!"

Her hands trembling, Anna rummaged through the debris. He cried out when he found the small leather pouch and greedily lunged on it. Its contents dumped to the ground when he tore it open. Frantically, he scattered the articles before him: two small brass keys, a gold chain adorned with two medallions, a pocket watch, a heavy gold ring, and a small piece of newsprint. With an unusual calm, he reached for the article and stood, staring intently at the words. Erik's shoulders hunched as disbelief ran into his veins. The article he had long ago ripped from the Époque made no mention of where Philippe de Chagny died.

Raoul lied . . . he had to have lied . . . he could not have been down in my labyrinth again . . . I did not kill him . . .

Anna rose, clutching the pouch and its former contents to her chest. He watched her dumb expression and her hands shake as she tried to refill it.

"It does not say. It does not say." Erik crumpled the page in his fist and thrust it aside.

"Erik, please speak to me."

"I killed him." Shooting his hands out in front of him, he grabbed her shoulder and yanked her inches from his mask. "My hands no longer have to touch a man to kill." He laughed deliriously as she stiffened in his arms. He spied the pouch she desperately clung to. "Give me back my bag."

"Erik, you're scaring me."

"Be very afraid child! Rightful you should!" He flung her aside with such absent-minded force she landed with enough violence to splinter a board on a crate. Anna cried out. Erik's heart drained from remorse. Horror struck, he backed away from her wide-eyed, cowering form.

Dear God, will my madness hurt her further?

Pappy rushed toward her careful to keep the baby tucked safely out of the reach of Erik's dementia. The child wailed.

She took him from Pappy's arms and huddled on the ground, shushing the baby silent. Erik swung toward his son. Philippe cried. Anna trembled . . .

Will my madness frighten them all?

He reached for the baby as if trying to touch an apparition. "Philippe Georges Marie . . ."

"Erik, stop," Anna begged.

"I killed him."

"Erik, no."

"Why did he go down there?"

"Go away!"

Erik reached for his son, but Anna yanked him away. She tried in vain to calm Philippe's discomfort.

"You cannot calm the cries of a Siren, you fool!" Erik hollered. "They will drive you mad!"

Anna buried Philippe's cries against her shoulder. "Who is the Siren? Who did you kill?"

"Philippe Georges Marie. I killed Philippe."

Anna's shook her head. "The Comte de Chagny? Damn you, Erik, you were nowhere near Paris when he died!"

The red faced look of combined anger and frustration on her face inflamed Erik's disbelief. "Not me . . . Erik's Siren."

"I don't understand!"

"Try to!"

"Then help me!"

Their cries volleyed back and forth. Erik took a sharp step and loomed over her. He leaned down as far as he dared. "How did he die, Anna?"

"He drowned at the shores of a lake. But that is not your concern!"

"Not any lake, *my* lake under the opera house!" When Anna stammered senseless words, he thrashed his head from side to side. "Philippe went down there because of me. If not for me, he would never have returned to that lake and he would never have drowned and he would be alive . . . alive!"

"That doesn't mean you killed him." Anna yelled over their baby's cries and his nonsensical shouts. "You did nothing wrong."

"No," Erik moaned, too overcome with dementia to see her point. "If not for me, he would not have gone down there again. My fault . . . my fault . . ." Clutching his mask, he rocked. "Music . . . music . . . to drown out the Siren you must hear the music . . . you have to follow the music . . . there is no point in fighting it anymore. I killed again." Arms across his breast, he tossed his head back in ecstasy. He swayed as if madness was a euphoric drug that had pushed its final load into his veins. "Orpheus cannot play to cover the Siren's song without music . . ."

"You have given in to your madness," Anna gasped. "The Siren is your madness; music is what calms it. Pappy! Give him the violin."

The old man complied without question. Erik's eyes darted back and forth as Pappy lifted it from the scattered contents of the satchel and unwrapped the cloth that swaddled it. Erik looked at him, his face twisting grotesquely beneath his mask. He snatched it and the bow from the old man's hands. Anna held Philippe close to her breast while Erik hugged his violin tightly against his chest. In his desperation to feel it against him, he nearly snapped it in two.

"Play, Erik," she pleaded.

Erik stared at her as if she were a sick hallucination and hugged the instrument tighter.

"Whatever you have to do to stop this madness, do it!" she screamed.

Reeling his back to her, he assaulted the violin. His music screamed what his heart could not and wrapped his family in indecipherable tones of anguish and beauty.

Twenty-four

"Anna?"

Erik rubbed his upper arm and flexed his hand, trying to get feeling back into his fingertips. How long had he played? The eve that had surrounded him in an isolated area of the train yard long ago waned into dawn. Rusty old cars, piles of ties, and track lay in stacks around him. In the distance, the train he recalled traveling on geared up for a new day's travel. Far down the tracks the day's first passengers milled around. Did he dream? Or was he awake? There were no signs of flame or fire and yet, he remembered her. Was she a ghost? He stared at his violin. *How did he get it?*

"Anna?" Erik begged for an answer, but only a lone rat scurried out from a boxcar in reply.

He sagged into his sorrow and turned toward the tracks, resolved that he would navigate this uncharted sea of grief alone. It had all been a dream, an illusion lit by the fires of Saint Elmo. The sounds of footsteps crushing rock made him stop. Pappy and Anna moved from the crate they had huddled behind.

Erik stared at the child sleeping in her arms. He reached for him with a murmur of his name, but Anna backed away.

"Anna?" He moaned in one long breath. "My Anna?"

"What do you remember?" The restrained tremolo in her voice slapped him across the face.

"What?"

"You don't remember the Siren?"

Blinding pain pierced him behind the eyes. "I played the Siren away. I calmed my madness. Oh Anna . . ." Hugging the violin, he dropped to his knees as if a cloak of iron had been thrown across his shoulders. Everything rolled over him in lucid waves. He laid the instrument aside. He begged her with open arms to come to his level, but she didn't move.

The agony! The denial!

"Please let me hold my son."

She crouched before him, but refused his request. "No." A nonsensical wail clawed out his throat. "Not until I know it is *you* who will be holding him."

"Then I will never feel his arms," Erik bemoaned, taking the violin and clutching it to his breast again. "Because I never know who I am. I never expected Philippe to return to me when we parted ways years ago, but he said he would. I once intended to kill that man—blaming it on my madness . . . the Siren. Now, when I grew to be thankful he lived, my madness ended up killing him anyway. For if not for the need for an innocent man to check on a monster, to make sure I had not sinned again, he would still be alive. I am responsible for this. I killed the man who gave me my life. What am I that this madness lies so close to the surface? I am not worthy of this child, Anna. Take him away. My mind will assuredly destroy him and you—like it did Philippe. It will harm all I have ever held dear to my heart. I cannot make him go away. I cannot make the Phantom go away."

Anna reached for him and turned him to face her. He lashed out at her contact.

"You foolish child. Did you not hear me? Take him away!" Erik threw his body into his pain. "Take that child from me before I destroy him, lest you want me to ruin his innocence. Go with him! The Phantom is here. The Phantom will never leave me."

A leather pouch pressed into his hand. "He shouldn't. He's part of you."

Beneath his mask, Erik's eyes widened and his face tightened in disbelief. He sighed at her touch and the gentleness to her voice. Laying the violin aside, he poured the contents into his lap, trembling as he lifted the gold ring and stared at its ornately carved signet. "I did not mean to kill him. He was my friend."

"His death was an accident, Erik. You may feel responsible because you once intended harm years ago, but it is merely coincidence that he drowned in your lake. If he went down there he did on his own accord. Something you had no control over."

He sheepishly looked to Anna and held out his hands. "Do not take my child from me. I did not mean it. Let me hold my son."

Carefully, Anna laid Philippe in his arms. Erik melted against his embrace. How much he had grown! He smelled like a fresh breeze after new rain. He was warm and soft. Erik's breath came in great gulps as he fought to control the emotions surging within him. Philippe was still perfect. He picked up the gold chain and medallions and laid it over his son's head.

"This belongs to him," he said decisively. "They were Philippe de Chagny's and now they are his namesake's. He will be watched over by Joseph and Gertrude—one a patron saint of fathers the other a patron saint of sinners." He nodded as he stood. "Come. We leave now."

Anna took his violin and bow and clutched them to her chest. She hesitantly looked to Pappy.

"You hesitate. Why?" Erik regretted his tone when she scowled. "I will always be unstable, Anna. No one needs to understand that. I cannot be understood and I no longer aspire to be." He lowered his gaze and spoke to the trusting look in his son's eyes. "I have no equal, save you." Those words only deepened the ripple across her brow. "You are not an equal through madness or genius, but in knowing the limits of a heart. My heart. I know I have frightened you, hurt, deceived and betrayed you but please—stay by my side."

Erik held her gaze. It reminded him of a moment not so long ago when he forced her to make a critical decision in an opera house and demanded she choose between the man he wanted to be and the man she knew he was.

"We leave, now." The words were as timid as a child uncertain as to right or wrong. No reply came. His cheeks moistened. "I cannot find the man in madman, Anna. I have tried for too long. It is my burden to carry to the end of my years. Philippe opened my heart to show me a way to carry that burden, by letting people in. It is my fate to do so, but in your eyes . . . fate was never more divine." He gestured around the train yard as the dawn light grew. "I want to take you as far away from my nightmare as I can, but I do not know where that road is. Please,"—the hand he extended to her shook—"lead me home."

Time was a cruel master of the moment, standing perfectly still. The sensations of her fingers as they laced in his made his body come alive with hope. She drew his hand toward her heart and clung to him and his violin. In Erik's other arm, Philippe dipped closer to sleep.

"All I can do is love you," she replied.

Her tiny frame dwarfed against his, but for the first time in his life it was Erik who felt small. The unlikely woman who leaned against him completed a void he'd been trying to fill for many years.

Christine may have been his voice, but Anna was his music.

"I must make a stop first." Erik brushed his lips against her hair. "There is something I must do."

Turning from her, he helped Pappy gather the remaining items into the satchel. A shrill voice made him spin round.

"You there! Girl!"

A conductor hastened down the tracks, his attitude not pleasant.

"Erik, hide!" Anna harshly commanded.

Erik rose to his full height, Philippe close against his chest. He didn't move, instead stared down the tracks like a matador does a bull. Pappy grabbed him and swung him and the baby out of sight. Heart pounding blood into his ears, Erik gripped his son in an effort not to charge the man in all his masked glory.

"I see you, girl. Don't think I will let you get away with jumping this car." The conductor pointed back toward the train and slowed as he approached. "You damn Bohemians. This is a train station, not a concert hall."

Anna hugged the violin to her chest. "I was doing no harm, Monsieur."

"You won't any longer. I don't tolerate vagabonds on my boxcars. You're coming with me. We will see how the magistrate handles you."

He grabbed her arm. As Erik leaned out of his spot to rip the man's hands off her, Pappy yanked him back.

"Let her go, Monsieur," a voice called. "She is merely a child."

The conductor opened his mouth, a protest perched on his lips when a man approached and pressed several bills into his hand. Erik's eyes narrowed first on the man's dark skin then on his jade eyes.

The Daroga. Tension of a different sort twitched its way up Erik's spine.

"I will pay for her ticket. She won't jump any more trains on your route as a result. Isn't that right, Mademoiselle?"

"Yes," Anna stammered.

With a mumble of thanks to the stranger and a sharp reprimand to Anna, the conductor left.

"You are that Persian man," Anna said.

"The Daroga of Mazanderan, yes. Why are you not with Darius, my servant?"

"That's not your concern."

"Then answer to where your child is. When I last saw you, you were well underway."

"Child?" Anna shifted from one foot to the next. "I won't answer that either."

"Then where is Erik? You cannot convince me you traded your baby for a violin and have taken up the life of a wandering minstrel. No person can play music like that, but Erik. I heard you across the train yard. You are damn lucky half the town isn't over here."

"Lower your voice, Daroga. That is no way to address a lady."

Stepping from the shadow and into the early light, Erik leveled his eyes on his old friend. The Daroga stiffened, as he always did when Erik snuck up on him. He stared for a moment at the infant in his arms, and then lifted his piercing green eyes to Erik's face.

"I have only ever heard music that angry during the Rosy days of Mazanderan," the Daroga said. "When your madness was so consuming all the sands of Persia shook with your music."

Erik moved further from his spot. He instructed Pappy to reclaim the stallion he'd tethered. "Worry not over my madness, Daroga. I thought you wanted nothing to do with me."

"When the entire town is practically woken by such music, Erik, I am duty bound as an investigator to put aside my travels and discover why. You can be sure that conductor will still bring the authorities. Vagabonds are not welcome on trains."

"What will you do when they come?" Erik asked. "Turn us in to Chagny?" He laughed. "I have not been followed by any marksmen for many months. I fear they have given up." His smile faded upon seeing the blank stare on Anna's face.

"Anna?"

"Loup's hounds found us a fortnight ago," she replied.

The Daroga huffed, causing Erik to whirl toward him. He looked over the Daroga's clothing from his polished boots to the Ashakran hat upon his head. "Betray us if you must, Daroga. But you do not seem like the man who is in need of a bounty."

"Leave," he replied sharply. "Go where you need to go, and I'll not say a word you were here."

Erik's eyes tapered. "Why do this for me? It only tangles you in my life and we both know how unwise that is."

"I do this for the child."

The Daroga stepped forward. Instinctively, Erik stepped back and pulled Philippe closer to his chest. "May I?" the Daroga asked.

Erik sought confidence in Anna's eyes. She subtly nodded. It mattered not to him what strangers looked on his infant. Strangers had no knowledge of what lay beneath his mask. But to have such an intimate man as the Persian see his child filled Erik with awkward unease. He peeled back the cloth of his opera cloak and stared at Philippe's pink and flawless face.

Familiar wrinkles inched into the corner of the Daroga's eyes. He smiled with paralyzed wonder etched on his face. Shame heated Erik's cheeks. He had forgotten the years of strained friendship that lay awkwardly beneath their bitter disdain for each other.

"Your . . .?"

"Son," Erik replied.

"His name?"

"Leave, Daroga. It is best we stay away from one another." He pushed beyond him only to be hooked by the arm.

"Christine Daaé has asked I instruct her if our paths ever cross. Why?"

"That is a question to ask her. Not me." Erik broke free and took two paces away only to be snared again.

"You are not a stable man, Erik. What do you intend to do with the girl?" The Daroga nodded toward Anna and the old man. They were slowly making their way down the tracks. She occasionally looked toward them. Tearing his eyes from her, Erik addressed the years of mistrust that leeched into that statement. He pressed his sleeping son to his heart.

"Every madman has a part of himself screaming about

being mad, Daroga. Mine screams 'you can love.' Pity that frightens you so."

Without a further word Erik hastened down the tracks, leaving this particular part of his life standing dumbstruck in his wake. Exhausted, Erik simply wanted to wander as far as he could with his future in his arms and the rest of his existence buried somewhere behind him. He watched his child sleep and swirled his name around him so it blanketed the train yard as it had done years ago in his labyrinth.

Philippe Georges Marie . . .

Whether or not the Daroga heard he didn't know. Erik didn't turn to find out.

* * * *

The Phantom's Labyrinth

They roamed the dank vaults as if they were the natural and commonplace. These nightly walks had become a tradition through the years. There was no fighting his stranger's visits and once Erik stopped trying, he found his perpetually uninvited guest quite charming. Their regular rituals turned away from one lecturing the other on morale or madness, and more into casual conversation.

Erik briefly looked at the communard road leading from the cellars to the opera house. He kept on walking. "What are they planning on performing for the winter season?" he asked. Erik began to understand that this stranger was a much needed lifeline to the world above.

"As if you do not know. Come now, I am fully aware you never once heeded my demand to stay away from that theater. You still haunt the place."

Erik clasped his hand behind his back and replied frankly. "Rarely. I barely find any reason worth going up there anymore."

His companion's eyebrow cocked. "Fine then. The new managers, Laroque and Wischard have selected a series of works by Händel."

The words stopped him in his tracks. "Why not allow the good citizens of Paris to destroy this theater on their own then? Are they insane? They would be better off digging their grave than perform work by a German composer." He pointed to his stranger. "That country is not exactly high in French regard."

"This theater is failing. It has been since . . . well you are aware. The new managers seem to think risk is worth the chance. Sounds like scandal to me."

"Even I despise scandal, but still, Händel? I will admit, however stupid on the managers' behalf, Händel is a brilliant choice."

"Stay away from that theater," his stranger shouted before caving to defeat. "At the very least, you best not be seen."

"I assure you, I want nothing to do with your precious world."

"We have been taking these strolls for a while now and you still have not shunned or killed me, so that cannot be entirely true."

"Momentary sanity."

"Tell me, Maestro, why have you not inquired about her? It has been quite some time since I even heard you whisper Christine's name."

Erik's hands remained behind his back, his focus in front of him as if all that mattered to him was what was ahead. He sighed deeply toward the ceiling. "There is no past that we can bring back by longing for it. There is only an eternally new now that builds and creates itself out of the best as the past withdraws."

The words brought his stranger up short. "That was poetic."

"That was Göethe."

"Powerful words. Since when did you take an interest in German philosophy? I thought you despised all things German."

"I do. I am simply running out of ways to entertain myself." He sized up his stranger. "Three feet is all that is necessary to kill with a Punjab. Target practice would entertain me."

"I have no doubt it would."

They fell into a comfortable silence, their tandem strides echoing together through the wet halls and passages. The stranger broke the silence.

"I am taking my leave of Paris for a while, Maestro."

Erik looked at him but didn't slow his pace. "If you missed it, that was my sob of sorrow."

"Ah. Sarcasm, I have come to like that on you."

"Where are you going?"

"I have some affairs to attend to in Bayonne, and then I figured a little respite in Pamplona might be nice. It has been awhile since I have seen Spain."

Erik grumbled under his breath. "Must be nice to be afforded the freedom like a normal man."

"You could have freedom, Maestro, if you were willing to accept the changes and consequences it would bring."

"I want nothing to do with mankind. I told you that."

"No one is used to solitude. Man was not designed to live alone. If you so wanted that, why are you walking with me?"

Erik couldn't answer. Did he feel indebted to his stranger for saving his life, even though at the time he truly wished he had not? He didn't know why he hadn't attempted to end his existence a second time. The life he led now was worse than before. Forced into shadows deep underground as a wanted man, only surfacing in the dark of night if he had to, relentlessly pursued by the memories of days long gone. Perhaps he lived for his music?

"I will call on you again when I return from my travels," the stranger assured. "I do not know when that will be, but I will return."

"Again, if you missed that, such was my skip of excitement."

Erik's sarcasm fell by the wayside as he stumbled, tripping over a bundle on the ground. Scowling, he picked up the parcel—a simple brown package with no markings, tied neatly with twine. He turned it over, perplexed.

"What is that?" the stranger asked.

"How should I know?" Erik noticed the sewer archway above his head. "It must have fallen from a carriage."

"Open it."

"I am not going to open it. It is clearly not meant to be here." He reached overhead to shove it back through the archway when his stranger stopped him.

"I would wager a guess that it was. Random acts my friend, are found in all sorts of bizarre places. Open it. I may be a virtuous old fool, but I am not stupid. Free is free."

Erik waved a gloved hand over the parcel and eventually tore into it. "Is this some sort of joke?"

His stranger shrugged. "Interesting contents. Perhaps it is not so random . . . proves my point do you not think? How things tend to tumble into one another?"

Erik wasn't listening. He rifled through the contents as curious as a child on Christmas, music screaming to be released in his mind.

"Au revoir, *Maestro, till we meet again." His stranger turned to leave.*

"Erik. My name. It is Erik."

The stranger nodded and smiled. "I know. Au revoir, *Erik." He continued on his way.*

"Are you not going to afford me the same courtesy, stranger? Or am I still to go through the years not knowing your rightful name?" He paused in his exploration to issue a stern glare through the halls of his labyrinth. His stranger gave him an equally challenging look. Erik spread his arms wide. "Should I not know the identity of The Shade?"

His stranger stiffened. "The Shade?" he echoed

Erik laughed. "So noble you act—so innocent. For all the years I have been a presence in this opera house, a mysterious man wandered about my labyrinth dressed in a cloak and felt hat arresting those lost in the cellars and returning them above ground. So easy for all to assume that was I, but the clues were there that it was not. Erik is everywhere, but even I cannot be in two places at once. Come—how long have you been doing so? How long have you known of me?"

"How long have you known of me?" he asked cautiously.

"Long enough. Do you make it a habit to be so philanthropic with your time, or do you enjoy dressing up and wandering around dark cellars?"

The man's eyes tapered. "I am a wealthy man. I have spent many years making sure the less fortunate are safe and cared for."

"I need to be cared for?"

"No. You need to be understood, and it is time someone beyond me starts to do that. You are ready to move on." He pointed to the ceiling. "I would rather you leave that old box keeper you used to annoy alone. Her heart is not exactly strong. Don't go looking to her for outside help while I am away." He gestured to the package. "I made other arrangements. Someone knows you are down here."

Erik's eyes flew open in anger. "You liar! I thought you

faked my death to keep me anonymous."

"No," he snapped. "I faked your death to prove men can be forgiven for all transgressions—even attempted murder."

"You are still a persistent little fart. I told you, I had nothing to do with the death of that sniveling nobleman. He fell simply and naturally into the lake." Smiling he gestured to the dark water. The man before him found no humor in his lie. "Who knows of me?" Erik demanded sternly, not liking his sudden brusque posture.

"Just a good Samaritan. I made certain your new caretaker knows of your needs. Leave it alone and accept the packages with an open mind. Perhaps in this you will find your new beginning." He gestured to the parcel. "Do what you want with the figs. You did say you liked them, no?" He waved his hand and turned away "God speed, Erik."

Erik watched his stranger walk deeper into the shadows of the sewers. Confusion tumbled in his mind. He did not expect his emotions over this kindness to be so disorganized. "Your name, Monsieur!"

"I truly do not think you want to know."

"Think otherwise."

"Philippe."

Erik tucked the package under his arm. "Till we meet again, Philippe."

The man stopped. He turned. "Philippe Georges Marie. I am the Comte de Chagny."

Paris never heard such awesome silence.

Twenty-five

Days shouldn't be sunny, and the first moments of twilight not serene when a heart was heavy with sorrow. The sun beat around her, but Christine barely acknowledged its touch. She hugged her shawl to her shoulders and approached the crypt, her unseeing eyes ignored the shadows of hundreds of flowering plants as they waved in the wind. Chagny had long since returned to its usual pace and its serene beauty. How could the world still move when a child was taken from her?

She made her way through the gardens and up the stone terrace pausing when she reached the top step and first saw the doors. A powerful heart-shredding wind churned around her, spinning Christine's back to those metal doors. Grief nearly doubled her over. She forced a few deep breaths of courage into her lungs and faced her daughter's resting spot.

Evangeline Christine Marie de Chagny.

The sun cast a shadow of her trembling hand as Christine traced the outline of the letters. Surrounded by the deep aroma of the bouquets scattered on the ground, she noted they too were fading away in death. How many bouquets did Raoul bring here over the weeks?

She wanted to hate the world, but instead was numb. An empty womb and an empty heart were one and the same. Trembling outside and within, Christine removed a neatly folded piece of parchment from her sleeve. She held it to her breast before she slid the paper under the door.

"A gift for you, my Angel." Droplets of tears watered the lilies below. "Don't ask me to speak of its composer. Sleep, and know you are my Angel of Music as well. I'll not tell you of him—ever. I'll let you rest in the peace I have not had since the day I met him." She caressed the noble indicator before the Chagny name. "I couldn't bear to think what would happen if I spoke of my true love for him—even to you, my Angel. I'll not shame my husband's name. Please forgive me for keeping secrets. I've lost so much already."

"Christine?"

Her breath hitched. How glad she was that he could not see the nerves popping inside her belly. If Raoul heard her, he didn't let on. She took his extended hand and accepted the guidance into his arms.

"I have you and André, Christine. Even if we are never further blessed by children, I have you, him, and the memory of Evangeline."

Did he know her secrets? Did it matter? Could she love as she loved without harm to him? She cried for a long while on his shoulder, tears of loss, love, and confusion. All the while Christine prayed she would have the strength to bury Erik like she should have years ago.

* * * *

Raoul allowed her the time she needed to rest in his arms while he stared at the name on the doors. He wrestled the hatred inside of him. Christine moved to lay a hand against the door of their daughter's tomb. Her tears tore him apart. As much as he hated hearing her call Eve an Angel of Music, as much as he despised her trying to reconnect with Erik via their innocent child, and as ardently as he wanted to thrust open the doors and remove whatever note she placed beneath them, he couldn't deny Christine her grief. He couldn't bring back what was past, nor could he offer anything that would serve to cushion a mother's pain. His eyes wandered to the older door sharing the ivy-covered house.

Below the massive gate, lying reverently at the foot of Philippe's tomb was a fresh lily, its mouth wide open and singing toward the heavens in an everlasting gesture of music. How kind of Christine to leave it.

Bending to retrieve the flower, a glint of light flashed before Raoul's eyes. The gold ring spilled from the lily's mouth to join the pebbles of the garden path. Confused, Raoul picked it up. The crown and sword of his family crest were as worn as they always were, yet the open palm signifying the Chagny outreach and philanthropy was unmistakable.

The original Chagny signet gleamed before his eyes. His chest constricted. Panic edged upon him like a marching army. Raoul frantically searched the tree line edging the garden.

Was Erik out there, lurking in the shadows of Chagny like he lurked in an opera house? Like he lurked in their lives and their souls? The lily still wept at the stem where it had been severed from the plant. The bloom had yet to wilt. *He is near.* Raoul's stomach fell to his boots.

He heard Philippe's voice cry out his name as sure and loud as a thunderclap. Raoul slammed his eyes shut. The memory of his brother stumbling through the doors of their Paris flat—mugged and beaten within an inch of his life rose before his eyes. Blue and purple, swollen and broken, he remembered Philippe's hand filling his, his finger empty of the signet he so loved. Even his beloved religious medallions that never left his neck had been torn from his body. Raoul remembered . . . remembered his brother begging for help . . . crying in pain . . .

He opened his eyes and stared at the lily. Who else could have left the ring, but the man who killed him?

A shaking breath seeped out Raoul's mouth as he fought for control. *Slip away, Erik, just this once. Slip away*. Christine needed him now. She was his exclusive responsibility in life. He would find Erik some other time.

With a final look around the cover of the trees, he followed Christine down the hillside and toward Chagny. Her gaze wandered back to their daughter's tomb.

"Raoul, do you know what an *Abendlied* is?"

Raoul kept his focus in front of him, burying the agony those words caused and answered to the trees. "I believe it is a lullaby, my love, among many things." He folded the signet into his palm and clutched it to his chest.

"A lullaby? How perfect."

He paused on the steps as he watched her walk toward Chagny. The black of her mourning dress contrasted sharply with the colorful flowers abounding around her. He swore the trees watched him, and the air they stirred was the breath of an Angel, Phantom, and fugitive. A soft swish of fabric drew his attention back to his wife. Raoul's heart slowed as she approached him, a curious look shining behind her eyes.

"Raoul?" She paused at the base of the stairs and held his gaze before ascending them. She stopped before him, her voice lowering as she curled into his chest. "I love you. Someday . . . someday I will give you all of me."

He gently drew her off his chest and lifted her chin so to

stare into the deep blue of her eyes. "What makes you think you do not?" She didn't reply and he didn't expect her to. Her eyes had moved from his face to the crypts beyond.

"I will never forget how your love for me created her," she said. "But I . . . we must move on for the sake of our son."

"Merely never forget my love and we will always move forward, Little Lotte."

Her kiss held all the compassion in the world and the grief that was a jailer in his mind was rattled by her lips, begging to be set free. He locked his heart down tighter, refusing to let it out. He broke the kiss and brushed his thumb across her cheeks, coaxing her back to Chagny. He watched her again knowing without fail it was he who would one day give her all of him for somewhere the trees still watched with golden eyes. Their power over him, however, was weakened through the strength of Christine's kiss. Love could end grief and someday his love would end this hunt. Raoul rolled the signet in his hands and jogged down the stairs.

A deep and wrenching pain filled his chest. The ring, combined with her kiss, flung open the doors to his inner prison.

Grief pierced the armor around his heart. His body gave up its strength and he sank to the steps below. One hand reached to a rock wall, his fingers digging in deep to a mossy cover as he braced himself from complete collapse. The gardens blurred until he could no longer distinguish the colors of the blooms. He pressed a knuckle to his lips and with it the signet in his palm while he searched for a way to control the torment in his heart.

Alone, he took one final look toward the crypt.

His eyes barely finished reading Philippe's name when the long lost tears for his brother finally came.

Twenty-six

Dieppe, France

The waves crashed in the distance and the air was heavy with salt. The sea seemed to calm the gypsy life, for once a gypsy reached the sea where else could he wander? Months had passed without pursuit. France was large, but the time would come when they would have to move again. For now, they rested and Erik watched Anna marvel at the sea she had never seen before. Erik pondered her distance. Somehow he would find a way to repay her and the kindness and sacrifices of strangers along the way.

Philippe mirrored the waves as he rolled on the small bed. Something in the air held his interest. Pappy was off taking care of their needs, working for the family that owned this property in trade for shelter. They had all fallen into roles and routines that became commonplace. Philippe gasped. Erik turned his attention toward the bed.

Confounded, he followed his infant's eyes and tried to trace whatever spirit had caught his attention this time. Philippe batted the air frantically.

"What?" Erik asked in clipped German.

His son turned his eyes toward the sound of his voice. Erik folded his arms against his chest and scowled, expecting a response.

"Well?" he insisted, pushing off the wall. Philippe let out a string of nonsense and continued to chase his ghost. Erik drilled a disapproving look into Anna's back. She seemed oblivious to his fuss.

"Are you hungry? Tired?" With a weary glace to Anna's lack of current interest, he lifted Philippe and perched his wobbly legs on his thighs. He winced as Philippe's tiny palms pounded into his unmasked face. A string of silly babble drooled out his mouth. "Yes, I am quite aware. Your father has no face." He volleyed his head to block Philippe's unrelenting pounding. "You at least have the beauty of your mother."

Anna turned her head. "You find me beautiful?"

An insecure disbelief hid behind her tone. Erik frowned as she rolled her attention back out the door. He turned from his son to let his eyes roam over the small hovel currently called shelter and pondered the vacant look to her eye. Philippe bounced unsteadily on his lap as he challenged his tiny legs for walking. He could give his son and Anna a life of privilege if circumstances were different. They didn't deserve this.

"Can we stay here, Erik? Right here, in this tiny shack by the sea?"

Erik's brows rushed up in surprise given his current thought. He laid Philippe back on the bed where he instantly found something of interest in the salty air around him. "We can stay as long as we are able, Anna. I only wish I could give you more."

"What more could I want? I have you, Philippe, and Pappy. I don't need more."

"Perhaps." He shared the door. He slipped his hand behind her braid, enjoying how her highlights shown in the sun and how soft she felt against his knuckles. "I will give you a home someday. This will not last forever. Chagny will give up. I will provide you with all the riches in the world. I will take you out on Sundays, entertain you during the week, and I will fill our house with music." He caressed the faded, stained ribbon wound around her braid. "You have my word."

"You would give me your music?"

"It has always been yours."

"The music was Christine's."

Erik stopped stroking her braid at the mention of that name. It had not been spoken for quite some time. "The music stopped being Christine's the moment my son was born. You have given me a gift Christine never did—compassion and a beautiful, perfect child. How could I not love the woman who did that with all my heart and soul?" This time he contemplated the surf. "Erik can exist without Christine."

"So you have truly let her go?"

Glancing at her sideways, he understood for the first time what her distance regarded. "I let her go during a barn fire. I let her go in a prison cell. I let her go in Lyon. Nothing in that moment felt right. Nothing has felt right since I hurt my Anna."

Anna leaned her head against the doorframe. She wondered aloud, "Why do you call me that? My Anna?"

"When a woman has seen my face as you have, she belongs to me."

"Christine saw your face. Years ago."

"Not as you have." He turned her chin up to look at him. "Christine took what she wanted from me when she took my first mask and burned it." He nodded toward the leather that had replaced silk. "Do you think in all my life I ever asked anyone to remove my mask?" Anna shook her head. "But I asked *you*. The only person in my life I ever asked or wanted to look upon my face was you. You became a part of me that night, my missing link, my little song, my freedom, and simply—my Anna." He turned from her. "I miss my Anna."

She leaned off the doorframe, choosing instead to lean against his chest and draw his arms around her. Erik sighed. She was warm . . . always so warm.

Anna coiled her hands around his waist and stared into his eyes. "I've missed you."

Baffled, Erik looked at her. Could those words mean what he wanted? That he would be allowed back in to love her in the ways he so deeply wanted and needed? He'd respected her in the months since Lyon, giving her the time and the space she needed to heal from the deep and raw wounds he'd caused her. They both had needed time to sort through madness and misunderstood feelings. He brushed the windswept strands of hair away from her face.

"Pardon?"

"Teach me to love without fear."

Erik lost himself in the complexity he found in her eyes. "Me, teach you to love?"

"I always thought it would be simple to love, but it's not. You've never been frightened. You've always been a man to fear—by the very nature of this face alone."

A jolt of desire raced through his body when Anna caressed his flesh.

"But you have never feared so much as the most basic of emotions," she marveled. "I always have. I always knew I would find love, but was terrified of what would happen when I did.

You never feared love."

"You foolish child. How can you, of all people, be so naïve and innocent? The one thing in life I feared the most was love. Anna, I have done nothing in these last few months that has shown you any ounce of respect. How can you tell me you need me to teach you about love when it is I that have learned from you?"

"What could you possibly have learned from me?"

"That Erik need not fear his madness. He need not silence a disoriented mind. That this face can be looked upon in something other than horror. I can live with the consequences of my choices like a normal man, and be bound by the rules of a world I shunned. I can . . ."—he looked to his son—"create beauty. That Erik . . ."—he squeezed his eyes shut, willing that part of his persona away—"that I . . . am a man, Anna. A normal man."

Erik's hands kneaded her shoulders as he stared into her watery eyes. For the first time, he didn't view himself as above the human race. He only viewed himself as a man who wanted the simplest of things: a warm hand in his, a companion at night, and a child to raise. "I will repay you, Anna. Someday I will repay all the Samaritans in my life. That is my promise to you. If you will have me more imperfect than ever."

Erik tipped her chin until she met his gaze. His lips brushed against hers. She smiled. The way her lips parted wrung his heart, and Erik's body surged with a painful need.

God, he loved her. But he dared not put his heart first. He bowed his head in shame. He looked on her with apprehension, fearful that memories would surface for both of them and chase away what time had so carefully begun to heal. Anna turned back inside and sat at the edge of the second bed.

Erik hesitated. The screaming tyranny of his body wanted to lunge on her, but instead he took a few hesitant steps toward her. He reached out and traced her face from the tip of her forehead down to her chin. He lowered himself next to her.

Gently, as if he didn't want to shatter the most fragile gift, he laid her backward and spent every last minute of the waning daylight spooning her close against him. They listened to the waves and smelled the salt air, and they watched their son squirm and chase invisible ghosts. Eventually, there was music in Erik's mind—an achingly slow and sensual tune, one he would never share and one he swore he would never put on paper.

His head moved slowly to the sounds of the notes that rolled within him. His thin and nimble fingers moved back and forth, undoing the length of Anna's braid. He placed her name into her ear, his voice a husky tremor.

He forced her shoulder down, turning her to face him. Slanting his mouth over hers, his cold lips heated from her salty taste. The music rose. He often wished she could hear this music, but for now he just wanted it to be his. He may be the one to hear it, but his Anna would always be the one to feel it.

"Anna?"

When she replied by opening her mouth and deepening their kiss, his moan was swallowed by her passion for the moment. He teased her lower lip with his tongue as a thrill of anticipation uncurled in his core.

In time there was nothing between them but Anna's auburn locks and the music in Erik's mind. He hovered above her, covering her in his kisses, not wanted to rush the moment. Anna wrapped herself around him. Taking the invitation, Erik joined their bodies completely. He buried himself deeply in her heat, relishing the way she shuddered as his body responded to the decadent way she felt around him. Tight. Complete. Lush.

Erik moaned.

The music in his mind demanded he move. He rocked into her in time to the sounds conducting her with care and adoration. Not a note was to be missed, not a beat or a stroke were to be passed by or rushed. His body bowed and swayed against her, the tempo in his mind and the pace in which he loved remaining steady and constant in his thrusts for the longest time.

Erik only heard music like this with her: primed in its harmony, balanced in its counterpoint. He slowed his conducting, not wanting the music to end. He stared into her flushed face. Her eyes were closed, her lips parted in a tiny 'o'.

The image was to be savored, the contrast of her supple body below his monstrous form, enjoyed.

There was no other way to share music like this. Anna's breathing quickened as the flush on her face colored her chest. He followed with his lips, never permitting them to leave her flesh. Her back lifted from the bed, offering him more and he took all she presented, moving his needs into her deeply with the arch of her hips. Erik was the conductor for the moment, but she was the Maestro. Anna taught him every last note and chord and created the stanzas he so adored. Eye closed, he lifted his head to the ceiling. There were deep tones to the music rumbling low inside him and high melodious tones drifting above. His head moved back and forth as he stared down at her. Anna's eyes were filling with anticipation. Her breast heaved.

Erik smiled.

Slowly, he lifted her hands above her head and pinned her lightly against the bed. His mind filled with gentle sounds. Those notes were hers. He listened and followed the music letting it dictate his every move. Each hand pinned her down so she could not protest; Erik lifted the bulk of his weight from atop her. He continued to slide into her like a bow would across the finest of violins, gently leaning in and out of the notes, sometimes caressing other times pressing harder. Whatever his Maestro commanded he created. Anna's back arched. Her breasts tightened. She called his name breathlessly. Her passage convulse around him as she gasped in pleasure.

He smiled and tilted his head as the music heightened with her cries. It was stronger now, more daring and a bit faster. He shifted his conducting to match what he was hearing and feeling, moving in such a way as to be a part of what he was discovering all over again. If he did ever put this symphony it on paper, it would be unmatched. The music he composed swelled to a fevered pace. He did not hold back any longer.

What was adagissmo for Anna slid aside and the music insisted on an affrettando. Wild notes drove Erik's beat, curving the woman beneath him to additional planes of pleasure while unrelentingly driving wave after wave of desire through him. A tremolo was ordered and he moved with great rapidity, repeating the same beat. Like a bow hammering—accenting the martelé against the stings—Erik did not stop until the crescendo came, and he cried out with its great surge of sound. He sought Anna's lips when it did, wanting nothing more than to be connected to her in every way possible. He shuddered, crushing her tiny frame in his embrace until he was empty within her. They laid together in exhausted silence. For a long while neither spoke.

"Erik?" Anna murmured. Erik rolled lazily toward her and the quiet coos of their son. "I think we have learned a lot from Philippe."

Erik buried his face in her hair before rolling atop her. That music began again as Anna smiled at him. He clenched his teeth to tether the wave of emotion surging from the recess of his heart, mind, and soul. Erik's lips trembled as he sought hers. He kissed her with all the love and passion he could muster. He memorized every last sensation she caused. His voice cracked as he rested his forehead against hers locking their gaze, and entwining their bodies as close as he could get them. He mumbled best he could through his tears.

"Anna, which Philippe?"

Twenty-six

Breisgau-hochschwarzwald, Germany

The wind streaming from the mountaintops tossed the scent of fir through the air, a far cry from the shoreline they had traveled along for years. The spring of 1895 was cold, but oddly Erik didn't feel chilled. The years they'd spent attempting to stay in France were not content, and by the time they chose to flee to the German border, the manhunt for them was a second shadow. Surely the foolishness of this hunt to bring him to justice for the death of Philippe de Chagny would be at an end all these years? Such simmered like hot oil in Erik's soul. No, so long as the comte was devoted to his passion for his brother and angry over ties that bound him to Christine, Erik was certain Chagny and Loup would continue to hunt them until their death. The German countryside was no kinder than France until a poor village nestled in the Black Forest presented opportunity for respite.

Silence and solitude is what these months here had given him. Before the sanctuary of the Black Forest, they'd fled another assault of greedy farmers, the unlikely army of Chagny. Anger filled him at the thought of Loup and the house he served, and he willed the name of de Chagny away.

Erik scowled at the chattering that disturbed his train of thought. The village doctor gestured excitedly around the courtyard like a bee on a sugar high while the Brother nodded and listened patiently to the doctor's case. Erik scanned the grounds. No doubt the spot would be appropriate for a garden for Anna. With the combination of sun and shade, any number of herbs could be grown. Such a gift would be well received and far less complex than the other that came attached with it—indefinite asylum with the promise his identity would remain safeguarded. It had been a month since the sickness waned.

Having stumbled upon the village in the dead of night, a weak and poor soul warning passersby away with a lantern and a rifle, Erik elected to stay. His skills saved a poverty stricken village and humble monastery from ruin and quite possibly saved a part of his jaded soul as well. Here he chose to repay his Samaritans. Here, it seemed, his past was forgiven.

They couldn't stay. No matter how much he wanted to give the boy skipping stones across the pond a home and solid life, Erik would not risk putting villagers and simple men of the cloth at risk because of his sins. Nor would he permit those men to risk censure. Somberly, he turned to Anna.

"There have been too many times you have told me that," he finally sighed. "Too many times of filling our dreams only to watch you bleed throughout them, until you finally bleed them away." He shook his head and shoved at the air between them. He could not bear her to lose another one of their children. Not a single time had she carried successfully since the birth of Philippe. "Please, Anna, this is another false hope that will end with my hands digging a grave." Agony seeped into his voice. He stared down at his long fingers meant once to compose and create, recalling time and again the dirt and tears chafing them. "Do not make me dig another."

Anna stepped into his sagging posture. "Erik, the doctor says I'm fine. He feels for certain the reason we lost all the others was because of the constant stress of running from Loup and this manhunt. But we are here now. He will care for me—as will the Brothers. They desire to do this. They see the good in you as I. Please, we need a home."

"Do not make me risk an entire village because of my sins too! The deaths of my children are more than enough!"

The penetrating gaze of her blue eyes was too much to take. He wandered away from their assault and stared toward the two men in the distance.

Brother Lukas smiled and calmly endured the doctor's animated gestures. Erik overheard talk of various herbs useful in medicine. The Brother occasionally glanced toward him, his peaceful expression matching the mentality of his simple, poor flock. Why this man of God forgave him his transgressions he knew not. Erik would always be murderer, Maestro, magician, mastermind.

But he paced as he watched them, realizing for the first time his ankles were not brushed by the length of a wool cloak and his shoulders not weighted down by a cowl. Erik waved his hand absently over his mask, recalling several days when he hadn't worn it at all.

Anna had wrapped her arms around herself in a hug and was watching Philippe enjoy being a boy. The fading sun played in her hair and her face was lit up with a hope just as bright. His lips parted. A gentle sigh escaped.

"What day is it?" he walked toward her.

"Sunday."

Erik circled her, watching as the sun hit parts of her hair. He lightly dragged his hand around her shoulders. "Sunday?"

He blinked the disbelief out of his eyes. It was Sunday and this woman, though not named by the church, the one he would call in his heart, his wife. They were out, amongst villagers like normal people. Erik's eyes swam in emotion. His first opera was finished long ago, at a time when he wanted to live like everybody else. That was denied him until he finished a much simpler opera, one he lost by a camp the first time Anna told him he created life.

A *Madrigal* Opera.

He never thought his dreams of taking his wife out on Sundays would include the results of her love. Erik stopped circling and raked his long fingers down the length of her hair. "Are you truly?"

Anna's smile reached her ears. Erik tore off his mask to swipe at his eyes. He pressed his palms to them and tipped his head back. The warm rays of sun beat through his fingers and even though his palms blocked out the light, what he saw was blinding. Erik grabbed her and caged her in a protective embrace he swore she would always have. For the first time in a long while a pursuit faded away and all that mattered was a lifetime of Sundays. Gently, he lifted her until her feet no longer touched the ground and the eyes he always lost himself in were level with his. He purled his thanks into her ear over and over again and sought her lips to affirm that all this was real. After so many years his other blessing was finally on its way. If it skipped any more, Erik's heart would dance from his chest.

This . . . was happiness.

He smiled against Anna's lips as he kissed her, not caring that his mask slipped from his grasp to the ground at his feet.

When he broke it and pressed his forehead to hers, all the joy in the world wrapped around them with his words.

"We are home, Anna. We have a home."

Epilogue

One would liken you to a lark or nightingale perhaps? No, you are my blackbird. For in all your life, you will not lean your breast against a thorn as I have, but tempt as the blackbird does. Man will look upon you as a dark omen because of the nature of your plumage, but you will have a song of such intense beauty you will entice men in ways unknown. They will love you so deeply they will throw themselves upon the nearest thorn bush in order to save their souls. Indeed you are a blackbird, yet. . . perhaps a raven? Sacred to the God of Music? Yes, petit corbeau, your song will be played upon Apollo's Lyre.—Erik

* * * *

The screams.

Erik sat at the far end of the table, hand balled into tight fists in front of him. Not even the pain of his nails biting into his palms could block out the screams. Philippe cowered in a corner cradled in Pappy's arms. The old man comforted the boy, explaining that the sounds were natural. They were a part of the process; no one was purposely harming his mother. The screams had to come in anticipation of the joy.

Erik found nothing natural in the sound of those screams. He leapt up and kicked the chair across the room with such force it splintered into pieces. Philippe yelped and Erik's hand shot up in silent apology. Anna did not scream this painfully with Philippe. Every sound coming from the far room stabbed into him. He couldn't take it any longer, he had to go in. Swinging on the door, Erik pounded it with desperation.

They ignored him.

Something was wrong. He could feel it. Philippe's cries intensified as the sounds got worse. That was the last straw. He had had enough. Erik rounded all his fury against the door causing it to crack inward. No one was going to separate him from his Anna, not while she was in pain. He tumbled into the room.

"Anna!" The blood rushed down his spine at the sight of her.

Anna clung desperately at the bedpost. Erik heard the pain in her whimpers. He started toward her.

"Brother Lukas, get him out of here," the doctor shouted, moving enough for Erik to see the amount of blood.

"Erik, come, leave them be." The Brother left his spot by Anna's side and gently took his arm. Erik violently threw him off. His eyes narrowed on that blood. She arched into a wave of pain and let out a cry.

"Anna!" He scrambled for her.

"Brother Lukas, now!"

The Brother was not so gentle this time. He forced all his bodyweight against Erik's protest and shoved him from the room. He grabbed Erik's arm and dragged him away, pushing him toward the door and yard. "Outside, now."

Erik paced, gesturing wildly toward Anna. "Why? Why? Why is she screaming like that? Why the blood?" He grabbed the monk, his eyes blaring in fear. "What is happening to my Anna?"

"The baby is wedged Erik, it will not come." Erik swerved, forcing the Brother to shove him to the ground. "The doctor knows what he's doing, but it will take time. You need to stay calm. There will be blood. We are all praying at this moment. Have faith in our Lord that she is in good hands."

Erik looked up, horrified. That didn't sound good. He could do nothing to stop Anna's pain. For the first time in his life his genius was paralyzed. He tried to drown out the sounds again when the screaming stopped. Erik froze.

Brother Lukas looked toward the house. "Stay here."

The doctor's wife intercepted him at the door. "You need to come," she said. Pale and shaking, she added in Erik's direction, "Stay away."

Leaping to his feet, Erik was through the front door, pushing them out of the way in his haste to reach her side.

"Anna?" He stopped dead. She was ash gray, but turned her head when he called.

"Erik?" she whispered. "My baby?"

He commanded his legs to move and bent to kiss her salty

lips. He searched the room, his eyes falling on where the doctor huddled over a silent infant. The monk looked at the doctor and began his prayers. They made attempts at blocking the infant from his view.

Anna reached up with a shaking hand. “Why can’t I hear my baby?”

Erik brushed the mat of sweat-drenched hair from her face. He looked over to the table where the doctor was moving his hands at a frantic pace. There were no sounds in the room besides Anna’s labored breathing and the doctor’s silent cursing.

“Breathe damn it, breathe,” the doctor whimpered.

A chill coated Erik’s cheeks as he stared at Anna. She closed her weary eyes, oblivious through her exhaustion to the horror in the room.

The sounds of the monk’s prayers floated on the air. Erik counted the length of time his infant had been without taking its first breath and without the life-giving connection to its mother.

They were losing their baby.

His eyes closed to the unbelievable grief. He cradled Anna’s head in his arms, not wanting her to hear the prayers or the desperate pleas of the doctor. The minutes ticked by and Erik knew.

He knew his baby was gone.

Anna tried to mumble questions through her exhaustion, but Erik shushed her silent. Too many minutes had gone by. He knew what the damage would be. He whispered in her ear and kissed her temple, his lips trembling through the hollow space in his heart. The doctor continued to curse through his own apparent tears and the Brother pleaded softly with him to stop. He begged him to let the child go to God. The doctor backed away from the table clutching his hands behind his neck, his deep breaths causing his shoulders to heave.

Erik knew.

His baby was gone.

His eyes locked with the doctor’s for a moment, his cold face beneath leather meeting the doctor’s pale face beneath a mask of failure and pain.

“Erik?” Anna muttered.

He swallowed hard against the lump in his throat and tore

his eyes from the doctor to read the question forming over and over on her weak lips. *Why can't I hear my baby*?

Laying a trembling hand against her lips, he attempted to stop those words from forming. He gathered her closely in his arms, his body shaking with the effort not to cry. He stroked her hair, following its tangled length to the empty womb that had once given his child life and security. A low moan caught in his chest as he fought to maintain control. He couldn't tell her. They had waited so many years for this second blessing. He couldn't tell his Anna their baby was gone.

The doctor shook his head at the sight of mother and father and swung back toward the infant. He leaned his elbows on the table and buried his head in his hands. Could he not bear to see a parent's grief? Was the horror of such death too much?

Anna's lips formed the question. He turned to her. How? How does he tell her their baby was dead? His eyes closed and he tasted the salt of tears as they found their way down his hidden cheeks to his quivering lips.

"*Dies irae, dies illa* . . ." Grief softly sang into her ear. "*Solvet saeclum in favilla* . . ."

Anna rolled her head to the side and pressed her cheek against the leather of his mask. She mouthed 'no' over and over again as Erik sang a private requiem through his sorrow.

The Brother laid a hand on the tension between his shoulders. Erik rocked Anna's head in his arms as he forced the music from his soul. He clung to her as desperately as those notes clung to the room, trying to crush her heart into his heart to numb his pain.

"*. . . teste David cum Sibylla* . . ."

A wrenching pain filled his chest as he leaned over her, and he finally wept openly in her arms. His tears soaked her neck. Deeper and deeper he drowned in the current of his sobs until a loud wail filled the room. Erik's head shot up in time to see the doctor collapse against his forearms. He frantically searched Anna's eyes to make certain she heard that sound. Relief flooded her face.

The pain in his heart released its stranglehold and his chest filled with joy. He rushed across the room to greet his child, his arms aching as they never had before.

The world came to a screeching halt for a second time.

Everything faded to black. He slowly turned and met Anna's

eyes before stumbling out the door. He collided with Pappy.

"Erik? What is it? What's been going on?"

Erik shoved him aside and fell through the door, collapsing in a heap in the courtyard. The yard became a whorl of blurry images. Acids inched up his throat as agony kicked him in the stomach. Tighter and tighter the shackles of sin wound around his body. What had he done? He tried to fight it down, but the nausea overcame him and he retched in violent convulsions. Erik knelt, staring at the ground. His palms pressed into the earth, bracing him from complete undoing.

How could he have done this to that woman? Give her a child that tore her body apart and give an infant a life that was cursed. How could he be so selfish? Erik barely even saw, but what he saw was enough. Boy or Girl? He didn't even know. He saw enough! Erik kept staring at the ground, remorse shaking his body so violently his arms threatened to give up their strength. He dug and clawed at the dirt until his fingers bled, trying to grasp hold of something that would stop his world from spinning out of control.

He clutched his head. God Almighty why did the doctor fight? If he saw that, why did he fight? The infant was born dead and it should have remained dead! His stomached emptied again.

He started when a hand came across his shoulder. Brother Lukas sat beside him and extended a pocket square. Erik took it with a trembling hand and wiped the bitter taste from his lips. His voice soothed as if he'd spoken of such things a thousand times over.

"Anna is fine. Hurting, but fine. She is resting now, cradling the miracle of a very lucky and tired little girl."

"Girl?"

"Girl."

"I saw . . . I saw . . ." Erik swiped at the dirt in nervous circles. "How severe?"

The monk took a deep breath. Could it be nothing in his ordainment prepared him for this?

"Three quarters of her face. It extends from her jawline to her ear which is not . . . entirely there." Erik's world went black again. Unseen arms of remorse pressed him down until his forehead met the ground. He clamped his arms over his head trying to shield himself from the words. "The deformity includes her forehead as well, her nose is—"

Erik's face yanked up. "What?" He could not have heard that! That could not be true! Erik groped desperately at his mask. "What?" He thrust the monk backward and rolled to his feet.

How could that be? How could a child he loved so much be cursed with his face? He swung toward the man of the cloth as he watched him stand. "Her eyes!"

"All infants are born with blue eyes, Erik."

"Her eyes."

"Very pale yellow. Though it is dim in the room and they seem to intensify—" He stopped when Erik cut him off with a frantic wave of his hands. "She is a blessed baby, Erik, in every way. The Lord smiled upon her delivery, and will continue to smile on her recovery."

"The Lord?" Disbelief bound Erik. "You believe in a Lord? What Lord punishes a child? What Lord takes pleasure in creating demons? The Lord clearly wanted her! What Lord thinks the life I have led is better than death? What is he trying to perfect in my baby girl? You preach a Lord to me?" Erik ripped his mask from his face. "Look at me you bumbling fool! You told me she is cursed with this?" He grabbed the monk by the robe and yanked him close. "Baby girls should not look like Death. I suppose now I should count my blessing that here is one who is cursed as I."

"Then I suppose Frau Anna is cursed as well? Let me know now if she is, because I left a woman in there crying tears of joy over her child. A child she created. That has a part of her soul and spirit. As a man of the cloth if she is cursed as well then let me know." With an uncharacteristic strength, Brother Lukas shoved Erik backward. "She is in pain, but you would never know it by how she is gazing at that little girl. She sees nothing in her but the man who gave her a life and whose life she is now holding thanks to the efforts of one who did not see Death, but an innocent little Lamb of God! I am going to step outside my bounds and assume there were no arms to hold you when you were born that way. No one willing to fight to give you life and if you so claim this child to be cursed then I will pray that all children who are born are so cursed because I have never stood in a room filled with such love in my life."

The monk turned on his heel and headed inside, but not

before snatching Erik's mask from the ground and shoving it in his hands.

Erik stared at the fog of dirt left lingering on the air and then at soft leather in his hands, a lasting reminder of the first present from his mother. He brushed the dirt from it and placed it on his face, imprisoning himself like his parents did years ago. With a downcast and empty gaze, he returned to Anna's side.

The doctor and his wife had replaced the spot by the fire as they warmed themselves. The doctor was clearly exhausted. His shirtsleeves were rolled to the elbows, his face still buried in his hands. He looked up when Erik entered and nodded him wearily toward the room.

Erik paused before pushing the door open. "When will we know?"

The doctor looked to the Brother before turning to Erik. Stiff shouldered, Erik stared at the door and spoke again. "Anna does not know? She does not understand yet?" The doctor sadly nodded. "When will we know?"

"She didn't breathe for some time, Herr Erik. We will not know for several months if any damage has been done. It will be obvious when she is strong enough to show development. Then we will know how her mind works."

Erik closed his eyes and forced himself to remain calm. He had destroyed that little girl's mind—and her face. He cocked his head toward the doctor. "You fought for her. Her face . . . no one tried to . . ." Erik had to clench his jaw to control his voice. "No one fought for me like that. No one tried to fix me. You are a doctor. You brought her back. You can fix her now."

Hopeful anticipation hung in the air.

"No, I cannot fix her."

The soft moan of agony made its way down Erik's throat as he opened the door to the room. His family was there, Pappy's arms wrapped around Philippe as they gazed from Anna to him. Philippe smiled broadly at the tiny bundle his mother cradled. He began to speak, but Anna laid a hand on his arm. She called to Erik.

"Are you frightened?"

Erik looked at Pappy and his son then to Anna. He nodded. Anna smiled and waved him over with a weak flick of her hand. "She's not."

He apprehensively approached and sank next to her. His daughter was bundled in a blanket, warm and content.

"When you are ready," Anna said.

Erik reached out and cautiously stroked one tiny hand. His baby slept peacefully; totally oblivious to the way she'd entered the world. He took a deep breath and moved part of the blanket aside. His heart bled. Erik stared at his mirror image save for a line of perfection extending from the corner of one eye down a pink and unblemished cheek to, ruby lips that jutted out in a tiny pout. Erik's eyes swelled with tears.

All he could mouth was *I am sorry*. Erik leaned into Anna's caress as his tears moistened his ravaged cheeks. Anna moved the blanket aside a bit more. The blast of cold air hitting the infant's face made her wail in protest. Erik jumped at the sheer pitch behind her cries. He had never heard a voice so determined to be heard.

It frightened him.

"Erik?" Anna asked, wrapping the baby once again.

"Listen," he said. There were such powerful sounds coming from that tiny, marred face, such intense, youthful energy. He turned to Anna and gently took his daughter in his arms. The baby's face puckered with her cries coloring her thin-yellowed flesh to vibrant red. Dizzied by the desire he heard in her cries, Erik's eyes drew wide. Certainly no man could resist such a lure. "Is this what a man hears when he looks on beauty? Can it have a voice?"

"What are we naming her?" Philippe asked, clambering up on the bed behind his father. He threw his arms around Erik's neck and reached to touch his sister's hand. She continued to cry and coo in tones that could not be described.

"Listen." Erik leaned his head back against the warmth of his son. He cupped Philippe's perfect face with his hand. "Do you hear her? One who hears—also listens."

He closed his eyes to the tones hitting his heart. The world would hear her voice. It would force men to listen. She would hear their praise. The praise he was denied as a boy. He turned to Anna. "One who hears also listens. Simone . . . that is what it means."

The monk appeared in the doorway and waved the room clear. "Doctor's orders, let them rest. Out, everyone." Pappy and Philippe reluctantly headed off as Brother Lukas came and laid a hand on Erik's shoulder. Erik never took his eyes from his baby.

His Simone.

"She is quite the package, Herr Erik," he congratulated.

Erik reached for Anna's hand, tears raining down his cheeks. "One of Anna's packages."

* * * *

The Phantom's Labyrinth—Spring 1885

Erik trudged through the darkness anticipating what he would find when he reached the spot. It was there again. He glowered at it, though in reality, he was relieved to see the blasted thing.

The package was there, like it was every month, waiting in the dark and dampness for its intended recipient. The consistency was flawless, the care taken to wrap it involved and deliberate. He found what he'd always found: no markings, no card, no indications whatsoever of where it came from or who'd left it. He stalked circles around it. If Erik could scream at the damn things he would, but talking to inanimate objects would only prove he was going insane. Instead he scowled at it.

Deeply.

He glared at the archway but saw no one, as usual. Erik rumbled in frustration. Greedily swiping the package up, he tucked it under his cloak to protect it from any further dampness. He hastened his way through the blackness, cradling his bundle like a helpless infant. The notes of his new Madrigal already formed in his head. He thought to tear into the package right then and there, but there was no real need. He knew its contents.

Paper. Ink. Figs.

AUTHOR'S NOTE

"... he was a great nobleman and a handsome man. He was a little taller than average, with agreeable feature, despite a somewhat forbidding forehead and slightly cold look in his eyes. He manifested a certain polite refinement toward women and a disdain toward men who were not always willing to forgive him his worldly success. He had an excellent heart and an irreproachable conscience."

—Gaston Leroux on Philippe, Comte de Chagny, The Phantom of the Opera.

If ever a passage caught my attention it was the above. Leroux's original novel is an extraordinary work of captivating characters that constantly leaves a reader questioning. Erik, the Phantom, is described as a murderously vengeful madman. Leroux pens him as a monster and alludes to images of Death and fear throughout his book, yet he contradicts everything with Erik's genius and subtle compassion, leaving the reader to choose for himself to love or hate him. Was he a man of beauty capable of being a gentle lamb if only he were loved for himself, or was he the ultimate representation of sin?

What of Philippe, Comte de Chagny? He was a central figure in the original book, highly influential in the life of his younger brother, Raoul, but barely rounded out by his author. Each time I read Leroux's Phantom, I kept pondering Philippe's life and his untimely death. Knowing Leroux and his background in law, I was confounded by much of what I read. I found myself drawn to a part of the book in the final few chapters, and it was here a single remark by Leroux sparked my imagination and The Madrigals were born. Why not craft in Philippe what he did in Erik, and make him a contradiction to the plot? Create in him something so unsuspected you stare at the pages and question like I did. Perhaps even re-read something with fresh eyes and new possibilities. . .

In a speech Leroux gave in Nice, he claimed his works had no pretences except to distract the reader without overstepping the boundaries of propriety. This is what I aimed to do with Philippe de Chagny, his role in the Opera Garnier, and ultimately in the lives of the characters involved. Naturally, I adhered to Leroux's plot as close as possible, but certain elements were changed to assist the flow of The Madrigals. The glory of fiction and the pleasure in writing it is the reactions that linger with us long after the last word is read.

I sincerely hope Philippe de Chagny, my favorite figure of classic literature, will captivate readers as he did me. I never enjoyed experiencing and crafting a character more.

Jennifer Linforth

ABOUT THE AUTHOR

If one is going to query a publisher, Jennifer suggests not doing so in pink ink. Her first, written when she was twelve, was nothing if not colorful. She is a member of the Historical Novel Society and the Romance Writers of America in addition to being a writing mentor. Writing historical fiction and historical romance with unusual themes and locations, such as autism and the social mores of the mentally ill in the 19th century, she has a passion for Austrian culture and is often found searching for stories in long forgotten histories.

It was her love of research and classic literature that brought her to expanding Leroux's The Phantom of the Opera. Writing from a tiny loft office, Jennifer admits to being country mouse with city mouse tastes and is constantly fighting to keep the little critters in line. She can't pronounce pistachio, hates lollipops with gooey centers, and dearly loves to laugh.

She enjoys hearing from her readers. E-mail her at author@jenniferlinforth.com

She can be found on the web at www.jenniferlinforth.com

Praise for Highland Press Books!

Holiday Op - "Get ready for special operations men the way you've never seen them before. For holiday adventures you'll never forget, be sure to treat yourself to this wonderful collection by Avocato, Nina, Elizabeth, DeVane and DeAngelo."

~Christina Skye

* * * *

The Mosquito Tapes - Nobody tells a bio-terror story better than Chris Holmes. Just nobody. And like all of Holmes' books, this one begins well—when San Diego County Chief Medical Examiner Jack Youngblood discovers a strange mosquito in the pocket of a murder victim. Taut, tingly, and downright scary, *The Mosquito Tapes* will keep you reading well into the night. But best be wary: Spray yourself with Deet and have a fly swatter nearby.

~ Ben F. Small, author of The Olive Horseshoe,
Preditors & Editors Top Ten Pick

* * * *

Cynthia Breeding's ***Prelude to Camelot*** is a lovely and fascinating read, a book worthy of being shelved with my Arthurania fiction and non-fiction.

~ Brenda Thatcher, Mystique Books

* * * *

Romance on Route 66 by Judith Leigh and Cheryl Norman – Norman and Leigh break the romance speed limit on America's historic roadway.

~ Anne Krist, Ecataromance
Reviewers' Choice Award Winner

* * * *

Ah, the memories that ***Operation: L.O.V.E.*** brings to mind. As an Air Force nurse who married an Air Force fighter pilot, I relived the days of glory through each and every story. While covering all the military branches, each story holds a special spark of its own that readers will love!

~ Lori Avocato, Best Selling Author

* * * *

Filled with the perfect blend of intrigue and plot twists, ***Luck of the Draw*** by Teryl Oswald is a stunning debut by a fresh new voice in Women's Fiction. A no miss!

~ Renee Ryan, Award Winning Author of Inspirational Fiction

* * * *

In ***Fate of Camelot***, Cynthia Breeding develops the Arthur-Lancelot-Gwenhwyfar relationship. Cynthia Breeding gives Gwenhwyfar a depth of character as the reader sees her love for Lancelot and her devotion to the realm as its queen. The reader feels the pull she experiences between both men. In addition, the reader feels more of the deep friendship between Arthur and Lancelot seen in Malory's Arthurian tales. Breeding does not gloss over the difficulties of Gwenhwyfar's role as queen and as woman, but rather develops them to give the reader a vision of a woman who lives her role as queen and lover with all that she is.

~ Merri, Merrimon Books

* * * *

Rape of the Soul - Ms. Thompson's characters are unforgettable. Deep, promising and suspenseful this story was. I couldn't put it down. Around every corner was something that you didn't know was going to happen. If you love a sense of history in a book, then I suggest reading this book!

~ Ruth Schaller, Paranormal Romance Reviews

* * * *

Static Resistance and Rose – An enticing, fresh voice. Lee Roland knows how to capture your heart.

~ Kelley St. John, National Readers Choice Award Winner

* * * *

Southern Fried Trouble - Katherine Deauxville is at the top of her form with mayhem, sizzle and murder.

~ Nan Ryan, NY Times Best-Selling Author

* * * *

Madrigal: A Novel of Gaston Leroux's Phantom of the Opera takes place four years after the events of the original novel. The classic novel aside, this book is a wonderful historical tale of life, love, and choices. However, the most impressive aspect that stands out to me is the writing. Ms. Linforth's prose is phenomenally beautiful and hauntingly breathtaking.

~ Bonnie-Lass, Coffee Time Romance

* * * *

Cave of Terror by Amber Dawn Bell - Highly entertaining and fun, ***Cave of Terror*** was impossible to put down. Though at times dark and evil, Ms. Bell never failed to inject some light-hearted humor into the story. Delightfully funny with a true sense of teenagers, Cheyenne is believable and her emotional struggles are on par with most teens. The author gave just enough background to understand the workings of her vampires. Ryan was adorable and a teenager's dream. Constantine was deliciously dark. Ms. Bell has done an admirable job of telling a story suitable for young adults.

~ Dawnie, Fallen Angel Reviews

* * * *

The Sense of Honor - Ashley Kath-Bilsky has written a historical romance of the highest caliber. This reviewer fell in love with the hero and was cheering for the heroine all the way through. The plot is exciting, characters are multi-dimensional, and the secondary characters bring life to the story. Sexual tension rages through this story and Ms. Kath-Bilsky gives her readers a breathtaking romance. The love scenes are sensual and very romantic. This reviewer was very pleased with how the author handled all the secrets and both characters reacted very maturely when the secrets finally came to light.

~ *Valerie, Love Romances and More*

* * * *

Highland Wishes by Leanne Burroughs. The storyline, set in a time when tension was high between England and Scotland, is a fast-paced tale. The reader can feel this author's love for Scotland and its many wonderful heroes. This reviewer was easily captivated by the story and was enthralled by it until the end. The reader will laugh and cry as you read this wonderful story. The reader feels all the pain, torment and disillusionment felt by both main characters, but also the joy and love they felt. Ms. Burroughs has crafted a well-researched story that gives a glimpse into Scotland during a time when there was upheaval and war for independence. This reviewer commends her for a wonderful job done.

~*Dawn Roberto, Love Romances*

* * * *

I adore this Scottish historical romance! ***Blood on the Tartan*** has more history than some historical romances—but never dry history! Readers will find themselves completely immersed in the scene, the history and the characters. Chris Holmes creates a multi-dimensional theme of justice in his depiction of all the nuances and forces at work from the laird down to the land tenants. This intricate historical detail emanates from the story itself, heightening the suspense and the reader's understanding of the history in a vivid manner as if it were current and present. The extra historical detail just makes their life stories more memorable and lasting because the emotions were grounded in events. ***Blood On The Tartan*** is a must read for romance and historical fiction lovers of Scottish heritage.

~Merri, *Merrimon Reviews*

* * * *

Chasing Byron by Molly Zenk is a page turner of a book not only because of the engaging characters, but also by the lovely prose. Reading this book was a jolly fun time all through the eyes of Miss Woodhouse, yet also one that touches the heart. It was an experience I would definitely repeat. Ms. Zenk must have had a glorious time penning this story.

~*Orange Blossom, Long and Short Reviews*

* * * *

Moon of the Falling Leaves is an incredible read. The characters are not only believable, but the blending in of how Swift Eagle shows Jessica and her children the acts of survival is remarkably done. Diane Davis White pens a poignant tale that really grabbed this reader. She tells a descriptive story of discipline, trust and love in a time where hatred and prejudice abounded among many. This rich tale offers vivid imagery of the beautiful scenery and landscape, and brings in the tribal customs of each person, as Jessica and Swift Eagle search their heart.

~Cherokee, Coffee Time Romance

* * * *

Jean Harrington's ***The Barefoot Queen*** is a superb historical with a lushly painted setting. I adored Grace for her courage and the cleverness with which she sets out to make Owen see her love for him. The bond between Grace and Owen is tenderly portrayed and their love had me rooting for them right up until the last page. Ms. Harrington's ***The Barefoot Queen*** is a treasure in the historical romance genre you'll want to read for yourself!

Five Star Pick of the Week!!!

~ Crave More Romance

* * * *

Almost Taken by Isabel Mere takes the reader on an exciting adventure. The compelling characters of Deran Morissey, the Earl of Atherton, and Ava Fychon, a young woman from Wales, find themselves drawn together as they search for her missing siblings.

This is a sensual romance, and a creative and fast moving storyline that will enthrall readers. Ava will win the respect of the readers for her courage and determination. Deran will prove how wrong people's perceptions can be. ***Almost Taken*** is an emotionally moving historical romance that I highly recommend.

~ Anita, The Romance Studio

* * * *

Leanne Burroughs easily will captivate the reader with intricate details, a mystery that ensnares the reader and characters that will touch their hearts. By the end of the first chapter, this reviewer was enthralled with ***Her Highland Rogue*** and was rooting for Duncan and Catherine to admit their love. Laughter, tears and love shine through this wonderful novel. This reviewer was amazed at Ms. Burroughs' depth and perception in this storyline. Her wonderful way with words plays itself through each page like a lyrical note and will captivate the reader till the very end.

Read ***Her Highland Rogue*** and be transported to a time full of mystery and promise of a future. This reviewer is highly recommending this book for those who enjoy an engrossing Scottish tale full of humor, love and laughter.

~Dawn Roberto, Love Romances

* * * *

Bride of Blackbeard by Brynn Chapman is a compelling tale of sorrow, pain, love, and hate. From the moment I started reading about Constanza and her upbringing, I was torn. Each of the people she encounters on her journey has an experience to share, drawing in the reader more. Ms. Chapman sketches a story that tugs at the heartstrings. I believe many will be touched in some way by this extraordinary book that leaves much thought.

~ Cherokee, Coffee Time Romance

* * * *

Isabel Mere's skill with words and the turn of a phrase makes ***Almost Guilty*** a joy to read. Her characters reach out and pull the reader into the trials, tribulations, simple pleasures, and sensual joy that they enjoy. Ms. Mere unravels the tangled web of murder, smuggling, kidnapping, hatred and faithless friends, while weaving a web of caring, sensual love that leaves a special joy and hope in the reader's heart.

~ Camellia, Long and Short Reviews

* * * *

Beats A Wild Heart - In the ancient, Celtic land of Cornwall, Emma Hayward searched for a myth and found truth. The legend of the black cat of Bodmin Moor is a well known Cornish legend. Jean Adams has merged the essence of myth and romance into a fascinating story which catches the imagination. At first the story appears to be straightforward, but as it evolves mystery, love and intrigue intervene to make a vibrant story with hidden depths. ***Beats a Wild Heart*** is well written and a pleasure to read. Once you start reading you won't be able to put this book down.

~ Orchid, Long and Short Reviews

* * * *

Down Home Ever Lovin' Mule* Blues** by Jacquie Rogers - How can true love fail when everyone and their mule, cat, and skunk know that Brody and Rita belong together, even if Rita is engaged to another man? Needless to say, this is a fabulous roll on the floor while laughing out loud story. I am so thrilled to discover this book, and the author who wrote it. Rarely do I locate a story with as much humor, joy, and downright lust spread so thickly on the pages that I am surprised I could turn the pages. ***Down Home Ever Lovin' Mule Blues is a treasure not to be missed.

~Suziq2, Single Titles.com

* * * *

Saving Tampa - What if you knew something horrible was going to happen but you could prevent it? Would you tell someone? What if you saw it in a vision and had no proof? Would you risk your credibility to come forward? These are the questions at the heart of ***Saving Tampa***, an on-the-edge-of-your-seat thriller from Jo Webnar, who has written a wonderful suspense that is as timely as it is entertaining.

~ Mairead Walpole, Reviews by Crystal

* * * *

When the Vow Breaks by Judith Leigh - This book is about a woman who fights breast cancer. I assumed it would be extremely emotional and hard to read, but it was not. The storyline dealt more with the commitment between a man and a woman, with a true belief of God.

The intrigue was that of finding a rock to lean upon through faith in God. Not only did she learn to lean on her relationship with Him, but she also learned how to forgive her husband. This is a great look at not only a breast cancer survivor, but also a couple whose commitment to each other through their faith grew stronger. It is an easy read and one I highly recommend.

~ Brenda Talley, The Romance Studio

* * * *

A Heated Romance by Candace Gold - A fascinating romantic suspense tells the story of Marcie O'Dwyer, a female firefighter who has had to struggle to prove herself. While the first part of the book focuses on the romance and Marcie's daily life, the second part transitions into a suspense novel as Marcie witnesses something suspicious at one of the fires. Her life is endangered by what she possibly knows and I found myself anticipating the outcome almost as much as Marcie.

~ Lilac, Long and Short Reviews

* * * *

Into the Woods by R.R. Smythe - This Young Adult Fantasy will send chills down your spine. I, as the reader, followed Callum and witnessed everything he and his friends went through as they attempted to decipher the messages. At the same time, I watched Callum's mother, Ellsbeth, as she walked through the Netherwood. Each time Callum deciphered one of the four messages, some villagers awakened. Through the eyes of Ellsbeth, I saw the other sleepers wander, make mistakes, and be released from the Netherwood, leaving Ellsbeth alone. Excellent reading for any age of fantasy fans!

~ Detra Fitch, Huntress Reviews

* * * *

Like the Lion, the Witch, and the Wardrobe, ***Dark Well of Decision*** is a grand adventure with a likable girl who is a little like all of us. Zoe's insecurities are realistically drawn and her struggle with both her faith and the new direction her life will take is poignant. The references to the Bible and the teachings presented are appropriately captured. Author Anne Kimberly is an author to watch; her gift for penning a grand childhood adventure is a great one. This one is well worth the time and money spent.

~Lettetia, Coffee Time Romance

* * * *

The Crystal Heart by Katherine Deauxville brims with ribald humor and authentic historical detail. Enjoy!

~ Virginia Henley, NY Times bestselling author

* * * *

In Sunshine or In Shadow - If you adore the stormy heroes of 'Wuthering Heights' and 'Jane Eyre' (and who doesn't?) you'll be entranced by Cynthia Owens' passionate story of Ireland after the Great Famine, and David Burke - a man from America with a hidden past and a secret name. Only one woman, the fiery, luscious Siobhan, can unlock the bonds that imprison him. Highly recommended for those who love classic romance and an action-packed story.

~ Best Selling Author, Maggie Davis,
AKA Katherine Deauxville

* * * *

Rebel Heart - Jannine Corti Petska used a myriad of emotions to tell this story and the reader quickly becomes entranced in the ways Courtney's stubborn attitude works to her advantage in surviving this disastrous beginning to her new life. This is a welcome addition to the historical romance genre.

~ Brenda Talley, The Romance Studio

* * * *

Pretend I'm Yours by Phyllis Campbell is an exceptional masterpiece. This lovely story is so rich in detail and personalities that it just leaps out and grabs hold of the reader. Ms. Campbell carries the reader into a mirage of mystery with deceit, betrayal of the worst kind, and a passionate love that makes this a whirlwind page-turner. This extraordinary read had me mesmerized with its ambiance, its characters and its remarkable twists and turns, making it one recommended read in my book.

~ Linda L., Fallen Angel Reviews

* * * *

Cat O' Nine Tales by Deborah MacGillivray. Enchanting tales from the most wicked, award-winning author today. Spellbinding! A treat for all.

~ Detra Fitch, The Huntress Reviews

* * * *

Brides of the West by Michèle Ann Young, Kimberly Ivey, and Billie Warren Chai - All three of the stories in this wonderful anthology are based on women who gambled their future in blindly accepting complete strangers for husbands. It was a different era when a woman must have a husband to survive and all three of these phenomenal authors wrote exceptional stories featuring fascinating and gutsy heroines and the men who loved them. For an engrossing read with splendid original stories I highly encourage readers to pick up a copy of this marvelous anthology.

~ Marilyn Rondeau, Reviewers International Organization

* * * *

Faery Special Romances - Brilliantly magical! Jacquie Rogers' special brand of humor and imagination will have you believing in faeries from page one. Absolutely enchanting!

~ Dawn Thompson, Award Winning Author

* * * *

Flames of Gold *(Anthology)* - Within every heart lies a flame of hope, a dream of true love, a glimmering thought that the goodness of life is far, far larger than the challenges and adversities arriving in every life. In ***Flames of Gold*** lie five short stories wrapping credible characters into that mysterious, poignant mixture of pain and pleasure, sorrow and joy, stony apathy and resurrected hope.

Deftly plotted, paced precisely to hold interest and delightfully unfolding, ***Flames of Gold*** deserves to be enjoyed in any season, guaranteeing that real holiday spirit endures within the gifts of faith, hope and love personified in these engaging, spirited stories!

~ Viviane Crystal, Reviews by Crystal

* * * *

Romance Upon A Midnight Clear *(Anthology)* - Each of these stories is well-written; when grouped together, they pack a powerful punch. Each author shares exceptional characters and a multitude of emotions ranging from grief to elation. You cannot help being able to relate to these stories that touch your heart and will entertain you at any time of year, not just the holidays. I feel honored to have been able to sample the works of such talented authors.

~Matilda, Coffee Time Romance

* * * *

Christmas is a magical time and twelve talented authors answer the question of what happens when ***Christmas Wishes*** come true in this incredible anthology. Each of these highly skilled authors brings a slightly different perspective to the Christmas theme to create a book that is sure to leave readers satisfied. What a joy to read such splendid stories! This reviewer looks forward to more anthologies by Highland Press as the quality is simply astonishing.

~ Debbie, CK2S Kwips and Kritiques

* * * *

Recipe for Love *(Anthology)* - I don't think the reader will find a better compilation of mouth watering short romantic love stories than in ***Recipe for Love***! This is a highly recommended volume–perfect for beaches, doctor's offices, or anywhere you've a few minutes to read.

~ Marilyn Rondeau, Reviewers International Organization

* * * *

Holiday in the Heart *(Anthology)* - Twelve stories that would put even Scrooge into the Christmas spirit. It does not matter what *type* of romance genre you prefer. This book has a little bit of everything. The stories are set in the U.S.A. and Europe. Some take place in the past, some in the present, and one story takes place in both! I strongly suggest you put on something comfortable, brew up something hot (tea, coffee or cocoa will do), light up a fire, settle down somewhere quiet and begin reading this anthology.

~ Detra Fitch, Huntress Reviews

* * * *

Blue Moon Magic is an enchanting collection of short stories. ***Blue Moon Magic*** offers historicals, contemporaries, time travel, paranormal, and futuristic narratives to tempt your heart.

Blue Moon Magic is a perfect read for late at night or even during your commute to work. The short yet sweet stories are a wonderful way to spend a few minutes. If you do not have the time to finish a full-length novel, and hate stopping in the middle of a loving tale, I highly recommend grabbing this book.

~ Kim Swiderski, Writers Unlimited

* * * *

Legend has it that a blue moon is enchanted. What happens when fifteen talented authors utilize this theme to create enthralling stories of love? Readers will find a wide variety of time periods and styles showcased in this superb anthology. ***Blue Moon Enchantment*** is sure to offer a little bit of something for everyone!

~ Debbie, CK²S Kwips and Kritiques

* * * *

Love Under the Mistletoe is a fun anthology that infuses the beauty of the season with fun characters and unforgettable situations. This is one of those books you can read year round and still derive great pleasure from each of the charming stories. A wonderful compilation of holiday stories.

~ Chrissy Dionne, Romance Junkies

* * * *

Love and Silver Bells - I really enjoyed this heart-warming anthology. The characters are heart-wrenchingly human and hurting and simply looking for a little bit of peace on earth. Luckily they all eventually find it, although not without some strife. But we always appreciate the gifts we receive when we have to work a little harder to keep them. I recommend these warm holiday tales be read by the light of a well-lit tree, with a lovely fire in the fireplace and a nice cup of hot cocoa. All will warm you through and through.

~ Angi, Night Owl Romance

* * * *

Love on a Harley is an amazing romantic anthology featuring six amazing stories. Each story was heartwarming, tear jerking, and so perfect. I got tied to each one wanting them to continue on forever. Lost love, rekindling love, and learning to love are all expressed within these pages beautifully. I couldn't ask for a better romance anthology; each author brings that sensual, longing sort of love that every woman dreams of. Great job ladies!

~ Crystal, Crystal Book Reviews

* * * *

No Law Against Love *(Anthology)* - If you have ever found yourself rolling your eyes at some of the more stupid laws, then you are going to adore this novel. Twenty-four stories fill this anthology, each dealing with at least one stupid or outdated law. Let me give you an example: In Florida, USA, there is a law that states 'If an elephant is left tied to a parking meter, the parking fee has to be paid just as it would for a vehicle.' Yes, you read that correctly. No matter how many times you go back and reread them, the words will remain the same. The tales take place in the present, in the past, in the USA, in

England . . . in other words, there is something for everyone! Best yet, profits from the sales of this novel will go to breast cancer prevention.
A stellar anthology that had me laughing, sighing in pleasure, believing in magic, and left me begging for more! This is one novel that will go directly to my 'Keeper' shelf, to be read over and over again. Very highly recommended!

~ *Detra Fitch, Huntress Reviews*

* * * *

No Law Against Love 2 - I'm sure you've heard about some of those silly laws, right? Well, this anthology shows us that sometimes those silly laws can bring just the right people together.

I highly recommend this anthology. Each story is a gem and each author has certainly given their readers value for money.

~ *Valerie, Love Romances and More*

Now Available from Highland Press Publishing:

Non-Fiction/
Writer's Resource:
Rebecca Andrews
The Millennium Phrase Book
Historicals:
Jean Adams
Eternal Hearts
Isabel Mere
Almost Silenced
Jean Harrington
In the Lion's Mouth
Cynthia Breeding
Prelude to Camelot
Cynthia Breeding
Fate of Camelot
Isabel Mere
Almost Taken
Isabel Mere
Almost Guilty
Leanne Burroughs
Highland Wishes
Leanne Burroughs
Her Highland Rogue
Chris Holmes
Blood on the Tartan
Jean Harrington
The Barefoot Queen
Ashley Kath-Bilsky
The Sense of Honor
Judith Leigh
When the Vow Breaks
Jennifer Linforth
Madrigal
Brynn Chapman
Bride of Blackbeard
Linda Bilodeau
The Wine Seekers
Diane Davis White
Moon of the Falling Leaves
Molly Zenk
Chasing Byron
Katherine Deauxville
The Crystal Heart
Cynthia Owens
In Sunshine or In Shadow

Jannine Corti Petska
Rebel Heart
Jeanmarie Hamilton
Seduction
Phyllis Campbell
Pretend I'm Yours
Historical/Horror:
Dawn Thompson
Rape of the Soul
Mystery/Comedic:
Katherine Deauxville
Southern Fried Trouble
Action/Suspense:
Chris Holmes
The Mosquito Tapes
Eric Fullilove
The Zero Day Event
Romantic Suspense:
Candace Gold
A Heated Romance
Jo Webnar
Saving Tampa
Lee Roland
Static Resistance and Rose
Contemporary:
Jean Adams
Beats a Wild Heart
Jacquie Rogers
Down Home Ever Lovin' Mule Blues
Teryl Oswald
Luck of the Draw
Young Adult:
Amber Dawn Bell
Cave of Terror
R.R. Smythe
Into the Woods
Anne Kimberly
Dark Well of Decision
Anthologies:
Leanne Burroughs/Amy Blizzard/Susan Barclay/
Patty Howell/Judith Leigh
On A Cold Winter's Night
Polly McCrillis/Rebecca Andrews/
Amber Dawn Bell/Erin E.M. Hatton/
Billie Warren Chai
All That Glitters
Lori Avocato/Anne Elizabeth/DC DeVane/
Tara Nina/Lia DeAngelo
Holiday Op

Gerri Bowen
On the Wild Side
Cynthia Breeding/Kristen Scott/Karen Michelle Nutt/Gerri Bowen/
Erin E.M. Hatton/Kimberly Ivey
Second Time Around
Judith Leigh/Cheryl Norman
Romance on Route 66
Anne Elizabeth/C.H. Admirand/DC DeVane/
Tara Nina/Lindsay Downs
Operation: L.O.V.E.
Cynthia Breeding/Kristi Ahlers/Gerri Bowen/
Susan Flanders/ Erin E.M. Hatton
A Dance of Manners
Deborah MacGillivray
Cat O'Nine Tales
Deborah MacGillivray/Rebecca Andrews/
Billie Warren-Chai/Debi Farr/Patricia Frank/
Diane Davis-White
Love on a Harley
Zoe Archer/Amber Dawn Bell/Gerri Bowen/
Candace Gold/Patty Howell/
Kimberly Ivey/Lee Roland
No Law Against Love 2
Michèle Ann Young/Kimberly Ivey/
Billie Warren Chai
Brides of the West
Jacquie Rogers
Faery Special Romances
Holiday Romance Anthology
Christmas Wishes
Holiday Romance Anthology
Holiday in the Heart
Romance Anthology
No Law Against Love
Romance Anthology
Blue Moon Magic
Romance Anthology
Blue Moon Enchantment
Romance Anthology
Recipe for Love
Deborah MacGillivray/Leanne Burroughs/
Amy Blizzard/Gerri Bowen/Judith Leigh
Love Under the Mistletoe
Deborah MacGillivray/Leanne Burroughs/
Rebecca Andrews/Amber Dawn Bell/Erin E.M. Hatton/
Patty Howell/Isabel Mere
Romance Upon A Midnight Clear
Leanne Burroughs/Amber Dawn Bell/Amy Blizzard/
Patty Howell/Judith Leigh
Flames of Gold

Polly McCrillis/Rebecca Andrews/
Billie Warren Chai/Diane Davis White
Love and Silver Bells
***Children's Illustrated*:**
Lance Martin
The Little Hermit

Check our website frequently for future releases.

www.highlandpress.org

CPSIA information can be obtained at www.ICGtesting.com
Printed in the USA
BVOW022353230412

288442BV00001B/10/P